VERBA MUNDI is a new series that offers the best
in modern literature—whether by such established masters as José Donoso, Leonardo Sciascia,
Fernando Pessoa, and Cesare Pavese, or by some of
the world's most notable younger writers, many of
them making their first appearance in English.
Over time, the titles published in VERBA MUNDI
will constitute a library of present and future classics from a wide variety of countries and languages.
By offering these superbly translated, attractively
designed volumes, we mean to invite adventurous
readers to partake in a diversity of cultures. These
books are not intended to be familiar products for
the American mind, but rather works that—combining international perspective with universal
significance—complement and enhance our ap-
preciation of the world in which we live.

First published in 1995 by
DAVID R. GODINE, PUBLISHER, INC.
Box 9103, Lincoln, Massachusetts 01773

This compilation originally published in 1964 by
Farrar, Straus and Company, New York. Reprinted
by arrangement with Farrar, Straus & Giroux, Inc.

LIBRARY OF CONGRESS CATALOGING-IN-PUBLICATION DATA
Babel', I. (Isaak), 1894-1941.
[Selections. English. 1994]
Isaac Babel : the lonely years, 1925-1939 : unpublished stories
and private correspondence / translated from the Russian by
Andrew R. MacAndrew and Max Hayward : edited and with
an introduction by Nathalie Babel.
p. cm.
(Verba Mundi)
Originally published: New York : Farrar, Straus, 1964.
ISBN 0-87923-978-6 (pbk)
1. Babel', I. (Isaak), 1894-1941—Translations into English.
I. MacAndrew, Andrew Robert, 1911- . II. Hayward, Max.
III. Babel, Nathalie. IV. Title. V. Title: Lonely years, 1925-1939.
VI. Series.
PG3476.B2A25   1994
891.73'42—dc20   93-35936 CIP

First Verba Mundi edition
Printed and bound in the United States of America

Isaac Babel
The Lonely Years 1 9 2 5 - 1 9 3 9

UNPUBLISHED STORIES AND
PRIVATE CORRESPONDENCE

Translated from the Russian by
Andrew R. MacAndrew and Max Hayward

Edited and with a new Introduction by
NATHALIE BABEL

Verba Mundi
DAVID R. GODINE, PUBLISHER
Boston

Acknowledgments

The production of this book has been a difficult task. The writing of the introduction alone was a traumatic experience. After coping more or less successfully with it, I was faced with problems in editing the remainder of this book, problems which certainly lay outside the realm of my professional competence. It was at this point that I had to lean on the knowledge of my friends. I hereby express my gratitude to all of them.

I wish to thank my aunt, Mrs. Shaposhnikov, and an old friend of the family, Mr. A. Fraenkel, for their indispensable aid in filling in the gaps in my knowledge of biographical detail.

Two of my friends have special rights to my gratitude. I wish to thank Patricia Blake for her friendship, encouragement, and readiness to share her special knowledge of Babel's life and work. I also want to thank Patricia J. Carden of Cornell University for putting her scholarly skill at my disposal. Her assistance in the writing of the notes for some of the stories and her editorial help have proved invaluable.

From among the Columbia University faculty I have been aided by Professors Robert L. Belknap, John N. Hazard, and Leon Stilman, but especially by Prof. Robert A. Maguire, whose knowledge of Soviet literature was of help to me on more than one occasion.

Two Russian literature specialists, R. N. Grynberg (the editor of the

Russian-language magazine, *Aerial Ways*) and George Reavey made many valuable bibliographical suggestions.

Several students at Columbia have helped in various ways, and from among these I want to single out Ramon H. Hulsey for special thanks.

The bulk of this book is translated material. The difficult task of handling such a complex body of material, including both stories and letters has, of course, been successfully and vividly achieved by Andrew MacAndrew. However, I wish to extend my thanks to Max Hayward, who, as a personal favor to me, made excellent translations of four of the stories.

All of the above-named people have saved me from errors, but, of course, I alone am responsible for those that remain.

NATHALIE BABEL

Contents

APPENDIX ‡ 381

PHOTOGRAPHS appear in the text following page 196

INTRODUCTION

BY *Nathalie Babel*

My mother, Evgenia Borissovna Babel, née Gronfein, was arrested
in France a few months before my twelfth birthday. It was the spring
of 1941, after the collapse of the German-Soviet Pact. Stalin and
Hitler were no longer allies, and all people of Russian origin
residing in occupied France were now thought to be politically
dangerous. The French provincial town where the 1939 exodus
from Paris had deposited us had little experience of political prisoners. The police just rounded up the dozen or so Russian women
of the town and took them to the local jail. There were no men.
Children were left at home, alone or with whoever was handy.

As I remember them, these Russian prisoners were middle-aged
or elderly women of the old Russian Orthodox intelligentsia, the old
bourgeoisie, and even a tall, impressive lady with a white mane of
hair who had been in attendance at the court of Empress Alexan-
dra—altogether a gentle and distinguished group of émigrés. They
shared a few cells of the prison: the warden had decided, for their
protection, I surmise, to separate them from the ordinary criminals.
They did not partake in the routine activities of prison life but ate
in their cells, were allowed into the courtyard at odd intervals, and
had different visiting hours from the rest of the inmates.

Clearly these women were not dangerous, and eventually they
were released—all except my mother. For weeks I petitioned to
have her freed, first to the French authorities, then to the German

Kommandatur. I told them that my mother was innocent of any crime, that I had no one else, and that they had to let her go. Finally, on the day before my birthday, my mother walked back into the tiny cottage where we lived. The Kommandant had made her promise to sign in at the registry every day, a promise she faithfully kept until the German army fled France three years later.

Why wasn't my mother released with the other Russian women? Because the other prisoners were émigré White Russians, whereas she was Red. She was the wife of Isaac Emmanuilovich Babel, a well-known Soviet writer and a Jew. By the time these events took place, my mother had lived in Paris for some fifteen years, but had kept her Soviet passport, perhaps out of fidelity, or out of a desire not to harm her husband, or out of nostalgia for a homeland to which she would not return—all of these reasons, I would say.

When my father came to France in 1932 and met me for the first time, when I was three years old, he took me to the Soviet Embassy and made me a Soviet citizen, too. Why? For many years, Babel had hoped that his wife and child would join him in Moscow: perhaps that is the answer. Or perhaps it was patriotism. One thing I do know is that being the daughter of Isaac Babel has not been a simple or placid position in life.

In the introduction that I wrote for the original edition of *The Lonely Years* (1964), I said:

> I grew up wishing that someday, somewhere, a door would open and my father would come in. We would recognize each other immediately and without seeming surprised, without letting him catch his breath, I would say: "Well, here you are at last. We've been puzzled about you for so long. You left behind much love and devotion, but very few facts. It's so good to have you here. Do sit down and tell us everything."

> I have imagined this reunion many times, but most vividly in 1961, when I first visited the city in which my father chose to live—Moscow—where one can still meet people who loved him and continue to speak of him with nostalgia. There, thousands of miles from my own home in Paris, sitting in his living room, in his own chair, drinking from his glass, I felt utterly baffled. Though in a sense I had

tracked him down, he still eluded me. The void remained; I knew so little about him.

Even today, when we know all about the end of his life, the creation of a documented biography of Isaac Babel is no easy task. A jovial person whose humor is still remembered, who is recalled with undying loyalty, Babel was also a man of bewildering contradictions who enjoyed mystifying others and sometimes deluded himself. Whether as a conscious strategy or not, Babel wrapped himself in enigmatic ambiguities, which has led to confusion, errors, and gross discrepancies even in the records and studies that attempt to be factual. Babel has been successful at eluding definition or categorization and becoming a sort of mythical figure, world famous yet still unknown. Was he a good Jew or a bad Jew? Was he a Communist at heart or simply a radical democrat? Did he have some personal sympathy for Stalin as a kind of fascinating monster, or was he overcome by an ultimately fatal artistic curiosity? Are his writings autobiographical or not? Was he a good husband, father, lover?

In 1924, a series of autobiographical sketches by writers of the period was published in Moscow. Babel's contribution, about his youth and the beginning of his literary career, is characteristic of the artist who so memorably wove fact into fiction and fiction into fact:

> I was born in 1894 in Odessa in the Moldavanka district, the son of a Jewish shopkeeper. My father insisted that I study Hebrew, the Bible, and the Talmud until I was sixteen. My life at home was hard because from morning to night they forced me to study a great many subjects. I rested in school. The school was called the Nicholas I Commercial School of Odessa. The school was gay, rowdy, noisy and multilingual. There the sons of foreign merchants, the children of Jewish brokers, Poles from noble families, Old Believers, and many billiard-players of advanced years were taught. Between classes we used to go off to the jetty at the port, to Greek coffee houses to play billiards, or to the Moldavanka to drink cheap Bessarabian wine in the taverns. This school also remains unforgettable for me because of the French teacher there, a Monsieur Vadon. He was a Breton and, like all Frenchmen, possessed a literary gift. He taught

me his language. From him I learned the French classics by heart and came to know the French colony in Odessa very well. At the age of fifteen I began to write stories in French. I gave this up after two years; my peasant characters and my various reflections as an author turned out to be colorless. I was successful only with dialogue.

Later, after graduation, I found myself in Kiev and then in 1915 in Petersburg. I didn't have a residence permit, and had to avoid the police, living on Pushkin Street in a cellar rented from a bedraggled, drunken waiter. Also in 1915 I began to take my writing around to editorial offices, but I was always thrown out. All the editors (the late Ismailov, Posse and others) tried to persuade me to get a job in a store, but I didn't listen to them. Then at the end of 1916 I happened to meet Gorky. I owe everything to this meeting, and to this day I speak the name of Alexei Maximovich with love and reverence. He published my first stories in the November 1916 issue of *Letopis*. (For these stories I was charged under Article 1001 of the criminal code.) Alexei Maximovich taught me extremely important things and sent me into the world at a time when it was clear that my two or three tolerable attempts as a young man were, at best, successful by accident, that I would not get anywhere with literature, and that I wrote amazingly badly.

For seven years—from 1917 to 1924—I was out in the world. During this time I was a soldier on the Rumanian front; then I served in the Cheka, in Narkompros, in the 1918 expeditions for provisions, in the Northern Army against Yudenich, in the First Cavalry, in the Odessa Gubkom [Provincial Party committee]. I was production supervisor in the 7th Soviet Publishing House in Odessa, a reporter in Petersburg and Tiflis, etc. Only in 1923 did I learn how to express my thoughts clearly and concisely. Then I set about writing once again.

Therefore I consider that my literary career started at the beginning of 1924 when my stories "Salt," "A Letter," "The Death of Dolgushov," "The King," and others appeared in volume four of the Magazine *Lef*.

Though he had been exempted from military service in 1914, he volunteered for the army in October 1917. He was thus able to start in on that apprenticeship to life that Gorky had exhorted him to seek. Babel served on the Rumanian front until 1918, when, having contracted malaria, he was evacuated back to Odessa.

In this "autobiography"—one not unworthy of his own characters Froim Grach and Benya Krik—Babel recounts the period of his life from 1917 to 1924, providing some extremely picturesque details; but except for the emphasis that he places on his meeting with Gorky, he does not differentiate between important and trivial details, or, more precisely, such distinctions are poetically figured. Babel also imaginatively distorted autobiographical facts, partly because he needed to depict a past appropriate for a young Soviet writer who was not a member of the Communist Party. (For example, my mother told me that his service with the Cheka was pure fabrication.) The problem is compounded by Babel's usual delight in playfully mixing fact and fiction, as though the power of poetic language was more than sufficient to make things real.

* * *

At the beginning of 1905, Babel entered the Commercial School of Odessa, an institution open to the sons of Jewish merchants who were members of the first or second guild. His parents, who lived outside of town, sent him to stay with his two aunts and his maternal grandmother on Tiraspolskaya Street. One of his aunts was a midwife, and the other, Katya, a dentist. More than once these poor women were in danger of being burned alive while they slept, for their nephew Isaac, instead of being in bed, sat hidden by the tablecloth under the dining room table reading by a kerosene lamp. Later that year, Isaac's father, Emmanuel Babel, decided to return to Odessa proper. The Babels rented an apartment at 17 Reschelevskaya Street, a street considered one of the prettiest in the city, and would live there until Emmanuel's death in 1923.

Dandyish, elegant, and good-looking, Emmanuel Babel was a man of imposing physique and impetuous nature. One of his ambitions was to educate his children as well as possible—especially his son, for whom he had a scarcely concealed preference. Nothing was too good for the boy. For Emmanuel, education meant that his son must speak a number of foreign languages, study music and Hebrew. My father had an unusual gift for languages but none whatsoever for music. Despite his obvious lack of interest in the violin, his lessons continued under the supervision of his paternal grandmother, a rather formidable old lady with a great passion for her grandson. When it was time to practice, Isaac would saw away at his fiddle with a book, instead of a score, open before him on the music stand. The more agonizing the sound that issued from the instrument, the happier the old woman became. One day Mr. Solyarsky, my father's violin teacher, stopped by at the house to inquire about the health of his pupil, who had not shown up for his lesson, ostensibly because of illness. But the "patient" was down at the harbor, a favorite hangout, which he found more fascinating than Mozart. Thus ended Babel's career as a virtuoso.

Because of the *numerus clausus*, or Jewish quota, Babel was unable to attend the University of Odessa. His father therefore decided to send him to Kiev to continue his studies in the Institute of Financial and Business Studies. Babel entered the Institute in 1911.

While in Kiev, Babel was introduced to Boris Venyaminovich Gronfein, a manufacturer and importer of agricultural machinery who had been dealing with Emmanuel Babel for years. Naturally, Gronfein was happy to entertain his friend's son. Babel was then sixteen years old, a graceless, blushing, puffy-cheeked young provincial. The atmosphere at the Gronfeins' was relaxed and elegant. Boris Gronfein was a cultured, indulgent, generous man. His opinions and style of living were thoroughly westernized. His wife was a handsome but somewhat melancholy woman who devoted much of her time to reading and playing chess. The couple had a son and two daughters.

Evgenia (Zhenya), the younger daughter, who was to marry Babel, was then fifteen, a shy, romantic girl already planning a career as an artist. Great Russian literature, the Italian Renaissance, Sir Walter Scott, Goethe, Strindberg, and Balzac were more familiar and less disturbing to her than the outside world. Even years later, after many sorrows, she could still find serenity and renewed courage by absorbing herself in a book or a beautiful object. My mother and father, from adolescence on, shared a commitment to art and a belief that one ought to sacrifice everything for it.

This was an era of social unrest and intellectual exaltation; my parents were determined to live heroically. My mother refused to wear the furs and pretty dresses her parents gave her. My father, to harden himself, would walk bareheaded in the dead of winter without an overcoat, dressed only in a jacket. These Spartan efforts ended abruptly one day when my parents were walking, lightly clothed as usual, and a woman stopped and, apparently dumbstruck by what she saw, pointed at my father and shouted, "A madman!" Thirty years later, my mother was still mortified when she remembered this incident! Nor had she forgotten her astonishment when her fiancé took her out for tea for the first time and she watched him gobble down cake after cake with dizzying speed. At the Gronfeins, he refused everything but tea. His explanation was simple: "When I start eating cake, I can't stop. So it's better for me not to start at all."

Babel went to St. Petersburg in 1915, ostensibly as a student, but it is unlikely that he did much studying. My guess is that in his autobiography he somewhat dramatized that stay in the capital. His father still sent him money. Moreover, although Jewish students were allowed to remain in Petersburg only for a limited period of time, this period could be extended. Then, with the Revolution of 1917, the residence permit for Jews was abolished.

He was still in St. Petersburg in 1919. His school friend Alexander Fraenkel remembers that in the spring of that year Babel spent his days sleeping in his unpretentious room on the Nevsky Prospect and his nights losing himself in the city. He also seems to have found time to work for the People's Commissariat of Education. And on August 9, my parents were married in Odessa.

Then in 1920, during the Civil War, my father rejoined the army and was assigned to the cavalry, where he served as correspondent in the army for ROSTA, the predecessor of TASS. On his first day of duty, and very likely his first time on horseback, he had to ride for about fifty miles. He not only managed to survive the ordeal; he also fell in love with horses. At the end of that year he was reported dead, but ultimately returned, completely exhausted, covered with vermin, and suffering from acute asthma.

After Babel returned to his bride from the war, for a while he worked in a government publishing house, but he was still very ill. To facilitate his recovery, my parents took a house in the Caucasus in the neighborhood of Batum, where on the side of a mountain my mother was initiated into the mysteries of housekeeping. To go marketing, one had to walk several miles in country that was far from safe, and my father's asthma was still so bad that he was unable to make the trips himself. He taught my mother how to do the laundry without bruising her hands. Once she served him soup so thick that he took his knife and pretended to cut it. Finally, he introduced her to an old Tartar who taught her the arts of steaming rice and roasting pieces of lamb over an open fire. They found themselves penniless, and for a very strange reason: Boris Gronfein had given them a thousand-ruble note, but no one in the district was rich enough to break the bill.

It was in 1923, during his stay in the mountains, that my father began to work on the stories which eventually appeared as *Red Cavalry*. Achieving the form that he wanted was an endless torture. He would read my mother version after version; thirty years later, she still knew the stories by heart.

My parents moved to Moscow in 1924. My father's first stories were being published at the time, and he became famous almost overnight. His letters give an idea of what this glory brought him and how much it cost. In them, Babel is at times jubilant and enthusiastic, at others tired and discouraged. He begs, he implores, he loses his temper.

These letters began in 1925, after many members of Babel's family—his sister, his wife, his mother—had left Russia for various parts of Europe. Starting with the earliest ones, a constant concern is health, Babel's as well as that of his family. (For years Babel, almost an invalid because of his asthma, tried to avoid big cities and to travel in warm climates.) Later, the irregularity of the mail, compounded by Babel's natural tendency to dramatize and worry, added a shrill note to his preoccupation with the health of those from whom he was separated.

Keeping the papers of the various family members in order is another major concern in these letters. It was bad enough to have had to contend with the inefficient Soviet bureaucracy, but Babel's task was further complicated by the fact that at the time there was no Soviet embassy in Brussels, where his mother and sister lived.

There was an embassy in Paris, but his wife dreaded each visit there, and often let her papers expire. Babel himself was able to go to France for some fifteen months, from July 1928 to October 1929, but he had to wait until 1932 before he was allowed to take another trip, the one during which I saw him for the first time.

Money matters also tormented him. To make more money, he had to work more under increasingly difficult conditions. Moreover, the impractical Babel would let his generosity run away with him. Whether he was in Moscow or Paris, distant relatives, friends, and friends of friends were constantly imploring him for financial help. A few weeks after his return to the Soviet Union from a trip abroad, he would find himself totally impoverished, his Russian friends having finished the job begun in Paris. Babel's only fear for himself was that his economic position would affect the quality of his work. His life centered on writing, and it can be said without exaggeration that he sacrificed everything to his art, including his personal relationships, his family, his liberty, even his life.

Finally, and somewhat paradoxically, Babel's desire to be reunited with his family is another of the leitmotifs that runs through his correspondence. In 1925, shortly after having sent his wife abroad and even while planning his mother's departure, Babel wrote to his sister of his longing for a family reunion:

> December 25, 1925: What do you think of my suggestion about coming to live in Russia. . . . It is my ardent wish that, of all our family, you at least should have a permanent place to rest. . . . If you had a place where we could all meet, that would make my life much easier.

Nine years later, he would angrily repeat:

> December 23, 1934: The only thing the matter with me is my separation from Mama and the rest of you. So, instead of moaning about me, help me, come and live with me.

As for his wife, it was more than ten years before Babel admitted that the trip she took to Paris in 1925—a trip that he had a hand in arranging, while her own desire to travel was at first quite nebulous—had led to the disintegration of his marriage. Initially, he was to accompany her (see his letter of February 23), but then there was a change of plans. In any case, whether he had really meant to go abroad or planned from the start to send her alone, I do not think he ever imagined that hers would be a one-way journey. But Evgenia Borissovna never went back.

Babel never gave up on his desire to bring her back to Russia; his letters from 1935 still show a hope of her return:

> March 30, 1935: I've received a letter from Zhenya in which she informs me of her plans. She is now taking a course in ethnography, is very much involved with it and will come to Moscow when she has completed her lectures. That's when the weight will roll off my heart.

When in June of that year he left for Paris as a delegate to the Congress of Writers for the Defense of Culture, he started off on his journey determined to put an end to his separation from his family. We know of this resolution from a close friend with whom he discussed the matter the evening before his departure. Babel said that he felt the years creeping up on him and that he must now have a home; if his wife refused to return, he would start afresh and create another family. His wife did refuse, but he was not one to abandon hope easily. On his return to Moscow, he tried again:

> January 28, 1936: It is very hard for me to watch over Natasha's destiny at a distance and so the only thing is for her and her mother to come and live here with me.

The government, meanwhile, told him that he could see his family again "when he had some output to show." But then even these hopes came to an end: with the death of Gorky in June 1936, Babel lost not only a friend but a powerful protector as well. There was no further possibility of traveling abroad and the promise of a coming reunion that Babel kept extending to his family became a complete illusion.

* * *

My mother made no secret of her reasons for staying in France: she despised and feared the Soviet regime; on top of which, as an artist, she wanted to study and paint abroad, and what more obvious choice at the time than Paris? But only much later, when she was dying of a generalized cancer, did she reveal to me her main reason for not returning to Moscow and her husband. "You should know," she told me, "that you have a half-brother. I left Russia mostly because of an affair your father was having with an actress, a very beautiful woman. She pursued him relentlessly, and didn't care that he was married. She wanted him and his fame and she had a son by him. Perhaps one day you might meet this man, and you should know that he is your brother and not someone you could fall in love with. Later this woman married another writer, and I am told that she is still alive. That is all I have to tell you."

By 1925, the year of her departure, Babel had become a celebrity, and all doors were open to him. "Babel is the rage of Moscow," Konstantin Fedin wrote to Gorky on July 16, 1925. "Everyone is mad about him." The city was at his feet, including many of its women. Perhaps the newfound celebrity was beginning to take its toll, for Babel wrote to his mother on November 29, 1926:

> In a few days I am leaving for Kiev where I will stay for quite a while because I would like to work in a quiet, secure atmosphere. Then I'll leave for abroad for quite a long time. I am liquidating the horrible "Moscow period" of my life that has been so painful to me. Don't let's ever talk about it again.

"Don't let's ever talk about it again." I, too, tried to follow this injunction some thirty years ago, when I first wrote about the "horrible Moscow period" for the original edition of this book. I was also very concerned at the time about being fair and objective. Here is how I described the episode which was so crucial to my parents' lives, as well as to my own emotional journey: "This time Babel had a love affair with an actress which lasted for about three years, though the woman's ardor seems to have been greater than his." My restraint amazes me today. Not a word about the circumstances in which I learned of these events. Not a word about the impact it had on me. Not a word about seeing my mother's sorrow and bitterness, the sources of which were concealed from me and others all her life, and only came to the surface in her final moments. Now I am older than my mother was when she died, and do not care too much about being objective.

Four years after my mother's death, in 1961, I traveled to the USSR for the first time. There I learned that my mother's deepest secret was common knowledge. Everybody knew that Michail V. Ivanov was in fact Babel's natural son. He was still a small child when his mother, Tamara Vladimirovna, married Vsevolod Ivanov, who adopted, raised, and loved Michail as his own.

Tamara V. Ivanovna is not what Americans would call a shrinking violet. She is now ninety-four years old, and from all reports is doing fine. In 1992, she decided to publish the 171 letters that Babel wrote to her between April 1925 and December 1928, adding her own reminiscences by way of commentary. I should note that it was extremely dangerous for her to keep Babel's letters for so many years, even while in hiding. Few people took such risks: the friend to whom Babel entrusted *her* letters to him, for example, burned these and other papers in 1937.

At the time of their meeting, Tamara Ivanovna was, by her own account, twenty-five years old, with a nice husband and child, leading a busy professional and social life. But she was "bored, oh so bored." Babel, "the incomparable raconteur," appeared in all his irresistible splendor and her boredom vanished. He stole her heart; the future belonged to them. Things were not simple, of course. The enamored Babel had many conflicting commitments: he had to travel, to face a lot of family complications and obligations, and also to find time to reflect and write and make money, since he felt responsible for everyone, Tamara included.

About a year and a half into their liaison, Tamara would have been well advised to send her lover packing. As she later wrote:

By July 1926, I thought he was through with his all-absorbing family problems: his wife was abroad, and everything was ready for his mother's departure. . . . According to me, time had come at last to take care of us. Such was my fateful mistake: since for him "us" did not exist. He existed and I existed, but separately.

By then a fairly banal scenario was unfolding: he intending to be with her on his own terms and in his own time, she wanting more of him than he would give. He would dissimulate, not only with her but with everyone, rearranging reality to fit his needs, organizing his conflicting feelings and obligations into some credible pattern. But in spite of such a frustrating and confusing situation, Tamara decided to have a child.

Babel was now facing a new situation: his lover had become the mother of his son. The relatively carefree romance was over. Was he going to build a family with Tamara and Mischa, as she desired, and make a real break from his wife?

Thank goodness for Vsevolod Ivanov! Little by little, Tamara recognized in him "the man of her life" and by the end of 1928 she had had enough of Babel's "insincere" and "condescending" letters. Her last message to him was, "Leave me alone and never write to me again."

Tamara was not my mother's only revelation to me that day. As it turned out, I had not only an older brother, but also a younger sister. In 1956, Ilya Ehrenburg, on a visit to Paris, communicated to my mother for the first time both the official date of Babel's death and the totally unexpected news that, in the years before his arrest, Babel had made a home with another woman, Antonina, by whom he had had a daughter named Lydia (born in 1937). Both of them had survived the purges and the war.

I first met my half-sister in 1961, during that same trip to Russia. We spent that first day walking around the streets of Moscow, testing the ground for emotional landmines. Despite the circumstances, we quickly formed a deep emotional attachment to each other. Then Lydia said, "My mother is expecting us for tea."

One remembers forever these moments of decision, which in retrospect seem freighted with fate. We went to what had been my father's last home, where Lydia and her mother still shared two rooms and access to a communal bath and kitchen. As we entered the dark foyer and climbed the stairs, I saw a woman on the landing. I looked at her and what came out of my mouth has never failed to astonish me. "How you resemble my mother!" I blurted out—and then we both cried in each others' arms. I was amazed. Here was another woman who, like my mother, had never stopped loving my father, who had never wavered in her devotion to him. For close to forty years now, Antonina Nicolaeva Pirozhkova has led the crusade for Babel's revival in Russia, to have his works republished and to bring the man and his legacy back from the dead. As for Lydia, since that first visit she and I have remained part of each others' lives, despite many obstacles. She and her mother are my father's greatest gifts to me.*

* * *

Babel did not seek to hide or elude his contradictions and doubts; he almost seemed to rejoice in them. On the 13th of June, 1935, he writes as follows:

> My nice Mama, if I write seldom it is not because my life is hard—compared with millions of people's, my life is easy, happy and privileged—but because it is uncertain and this uncertainty derives from nothing else but changes and doubts connected with my work. In a country as united as ours, it is quite inevitable that a certain amount of thinking in clichés should appear and I want to overcome this standardized way of thinking and introduce into our literature new ideas, new feelings and rhythms. This is what interests me and nothing else. And so I work and think with great intensity, but I haven't any results to show yet. And, inasmuch as I myself do not see clearly how and by what methods I will reach these results (I do see my inner paths clearly, though), I am not sure myself where and in what kind of environment I ought to live if I am to achieve my goal, and this is what causes my reluctance to drag anyone along behind me and makes me an insecure and wavering man who causes you so much trouble.

---

*An English translation of Pirozhkova's memoir of Babel (1989) is included in *Canadian Slavonic Papers/Revue canadienne des slavistes*, XXXVI:1-2 (May-June 1994).

I do not know whether one should consider Babel hero or victim or perhaps, in his private life, a bit of a rake. In any event, life scarcely rewarded him for the sacrifices that he imposed upon himself and those he most loved. Babel was convinced that a writer mutilates himself and his work by leaving his native country. He always refused to emigrate; on top of which, his sense of honor and love of the limelight demanded that he stay among his own people. We know that Babel was well aware of the cruelty of the Stalinist regime, for he talked about it with intimate friends on the trips that he did take abroad. Nothing, however, could shatter his feelings that he belonged to Russia and that he had to share the fate of his countrymen. What in so many people would have produced only fear and terror awakened in him a sense of duty and a kind of heroic fatalism.

* * *

From 1936 to 1939, Babel's letters gradually drain of substance; they resemble more and more the reports an employee makes to his superiors about his work and health. One has the impression that Babel led an uneventful life in a country devoid of problems. He did not even mention things to his sister that the censor would very likely have passed, such as the birth of his daughter Lydia.

He lived in silence and secrecy. Only a few people knew of his terrible anxiety, of his certainty that he would eventually be destroyed like the others. To the very last day he presented a bright, optimistic face to the members of his family and continued to assert that he had never been so happy. And indeed, on the surface, Babel still occupied a privileged position in the Soviet Union. He could even more about freely—so long as he did not leave the country. He had a house and servants in Moscow, a car with a chauffeur. He liked to dine out and could spend the equivalent of a worker's monthly pay for a meal. Access to the artists' cooperative permitted him to eat much better than most of his countrymen. Moreover, a villa had been built for him at Peredelkino, the writers' village thirty-five miles from Moscow.

But although Babel availed himself of these advantages and used them to help his friends, in all other respects he did not conform or play the game. He refused to write according to the directives of the

Party and retreated into silence despite the large rewards promised him on the condition that he publish again. Babel's answer was, "Creativity does not dwell in palaces" [V dvortse tvorchestvo ne tvoritsya]. When arrested, he said only, "I was not given time to finish" [Ne dali konchit]. That was the last that was seen or heard of Babel until 1954, when the official date of his death was given as March 17, 1941. His death certificate reads as follows:

Name: Isaac Emmanuilovich Babel
Date of Birth: 13 July 1894
Date of Death: 17 March 1941
Place of Death: _____
Cause of Death: _____

* * *

During the quarter century he ruled the Soviet Union, Joseph Stalin never underestimated the power of the written word. Sometimes he even "corrected" the manuscripts of novels that had been cleared for publication, making his changes in red or green pencil. Not everybody had the privilege of being edited by Stalin: more often, he simply made poets and novelists disappear. Now we know that about 1,500 such men and women were executed or died in the Gulag, along with millions of others. When writers were arrested, mostly when the terror was at its peak in the late 1930s, their manuscripts, notebooks, and letters were arrested with them. All this material sat locked in the vaults of the secret police for half a century. Only after glasnost was well underway did the KGB admit that—oh yes, we forgot—they did have some papers. Courageous writers and intellectuals pressured the government for about two years until finally, with the discreet help of a top Gorbachev aide, Alexandr Yakolev, the first documents began to emerge from the secret archives.

The administrators of Stalin's terror, it turned out, had kept detailed records about all their victims: when they were arrested, what questions they were asked, what crimes they confessed to, what sentences were inflicted upon them, and when and how these sentences were carried out. Minutes of interrogations, manuscripts, notes, unanswered inquiries, intercepted letters from friends and family, denunciations, confessions, retractions of confessions, final pleas—everything was reduced to a bureaucratic timelessness, filed in dossiers marked "to keep for eternity." Kilometers of such files were kept by the KGB, which the writer Vitaly Shentalinsky is now helping to rescue and bring to light.

Some of the materials discovered in the literary archives of the KGB are also appearing in the West. In one volume, published in France in 1993, a sixty-five-page chapter documents Isaac Babel's file and fate. One of the trademarks of Stalinism was to compel all prisoners to discover or invent or admit their "guilt." The methods designed to extract such confessions has by now been well documented, and are familiar to students of medieval witchcraft, or of fascism. During Stalin's Great Purge of the late 1930s, one of the most common of these methods was called the "conveyor belt": prisoners were beaten and deprived of sleep for days on end until the desired confession was extracted.

One of the prisoners subjected to these methods was Isaac Babel. In his KGB file, he is quoted as stating: "For a long time now . . . I wrote contrary to the interests of the masses of the Party, I fell into slanderous generalizations. . . ." Apparently searching for something that would satisfy his tormentors, he confessed to giving state secrets to the French writer André Malraux. This was recorded by the interrogator as: "Babel testified that . . . he had passed on information to Malraux on a number of subjects. These were: the state of the Air Force; the equipment and command structure of the Red Army; the Soviet economy; the current arrests; and the mood of the intelligentsia." Evidence of Babel's torture is found in his last photograph, which forms part of his dossier. The face is swollen, large dark bruises circle the eyes. Most devastating of all is that the man, who since early childhood had to wear eyeglasses in order to see, has no glasses in this photo. Everything had been taken from him, including his sight.

Babel's end began in the dawn of May 16, 1939, when, on the orders of People's Commissar Lavrenti Beria, he was arrested. The police went first to his Moscow apartment, then to the writers' village, Peredelkino, where they found him in bed. Both lodgings were searched and all papers seized, as was the custom.*

Babel spent ten months in jail—a long time indeed if spent mostly under interrogation and torture. The logic followed by the investigating officers was pure Kafka: "You have been arrested, therefore you are guilty. You confess, expose your crimes, and so of course we were right to suspect you! You resist? Proclaim your innocence? Only a thoroughly corrupt individual could do such a thing!" This theater of cruelty was played out endlessly with an endless number of victims. Its touchstones included spying, sabotage, Trotskyism, terrorism, consorting with enemies of the State, and whatever else the prisoner and the helpful investigator could come up with.

On September 11, no doubt with his interrogators' encouragement, Babel addressed a "confession," as both an individual and a creative artist, to Beria himself:

> The Revolution opened the path of creation for me, the path of useful and happy labor. My individualism, false literary opinions, and the Trotskyist influences I fell under from the earliest days of my work turned me away from this path. With every passing year my writings became a bit more useless and hostile to Soviet readers. But I thought I was right, and they were wrong. This lethal separation dried up the very source of my creativity. My attempts to free myself from the hold of that blind and egotistical narrowmindedness proved pitiful and vain. My liberation came while I was in prison. During these months of incarceration, I have perhaps understood more things than in my entire previous life. I've seen with horrible clarity the mistakes and crimes I've committed. . . .
>
> Citizen People's Commissar, at my hearing, without sparing myself and possessed only by a desire for purification, I detailed my crimes. I would now like to discuss another aspect of my existence:

---

*None of these papers and manuscripts has resurfaced; the KGB claims it cannot find anything. Personally, I would tend to believe them in this instance. Since the 1960s there has been an official willingness to locate Babel's missing papers, without success. Most likely everything was burned, together with tons of other materials held by the secret police, as the German armies were threatening to enter Moscow.

the literary work that I did unbeknownst to the outside world, painstakingly and in fits and starts, but continually. I beg you, Citizen People's Commissar, to allow me to put some order in the manuscripts that have been confiscated from me. They contain drafts of essays on collectivization and the kolkhozes in the Ukraine, notes for a book on Gorky, the drafts of several dozen stories, a half-written play and a finished screenplay. These manuscripts are the fruit of eight years' work and I was hoping to prepare some of them for publication this year. I also beg you for authorization to sketch out the plan of a novel describing the path—which in many ways is typical—that led me to my downfall and to crimes against the Socialist state. This book shines in my head with a painful and merciless light. I feel the ache of inspiration and of my returning strength. I am burning with a desire to work, to atone, to denounce this life which I have spent in such an incorrect and criminal fashion.

Still, Babel could not long hold to the fiction of his "crimes." Apparently resigned to his own death but fearing for others, he twice sent word (on November 5 and 21) to the Public Prosecutor's office, begging them to let him rectify his testimony: "My confession contains incorrect and invented statements imputing anti-Soviet activities to individuals who are working honestly and selflessly for the good of the USSR. The thought that my words could prove directly harmful to my country is causing me immeasurable pain. I consider it my primary duty to lift this horrible burden from my conscience."

Neither these nor a third plea on January 2 had the desired effect. Instead, on the 25th, Babel was handed his indictment. That same day, he sent one final letter to the president of the Supreme Court—the last words he ever wrote:

On November 5 and November 21, 1939, and again on January 2, 1940, I wrote to the Public Prosecutor of the USSR to explain that I had some extremely important declarations to make about my case. In them, I state that I slandered innocent people in my confessions. I ask to be heard by the prosecutor of the Supreme Court before my trial begins.

I also ask for authorization to bring in a lawyer on my behalf and to summon, as witnesses, A. Voronski [who, unbeknownst to Babel, had been executed in 1937], I. Ehrenburg, the writer Seyfullina, the director S. Eisenstein, the artist S. Mikhoyels, and the editor of the magazine *The USSR Under Construction*, R. Ostrovskaya.

I also ask to be allowed to see my file, since I read it more than four months ago, very quickly and late at night, and have retained almost no memory of it.

Isaac Babel's trial took place on January 26, 1940, in one of Lavrenti Beria's private chambers. It lasted about twenty minutes. The sentence had been prepared in advance and without ambiguity: death by firing squad, to be carried out immediately. Babel had been accused and convicted of "active participation in [an] anti-Soviet Trotskyite organization" and of "being a member of a terrorist conspiracy, as well as spying for the French and Austrian governments." The next morning he was shot.

Babel's last recorded words in the proceedings were: "I am innocent. I have never been a spy. I never allowed any action against the Soviet Union. I accused myself falsely. I was forced to make false accusations against myself and others. . . . I am asking for only one thing—let me finish my work. . . ."

It has taken fifty years for this truth to come to light, the hideous truth of the fate of Babel and of many of his generation, a fate meted out to men and women of obdurate good will by those who captured and betrayed their utopian hopes.

—WASHINGTON, D.C., 1995

STORIES

Three stories in this volume "Kolyvushka," "Froim Grach" and "My First Fee" have never been published before—either in the Soviet Union or abroad—in book form. They were published in Russian in the literary magazine *Aerial Ways*, no. 3, New York, 1963, and appear here for the first time in English. "Answer to an Inquiry" was published in English as "A Reply to an Inquiry" (the translator was not named) in *International Literature*, Moscow, 1937. Subsequently the same translation appeared in *The Noble Savage*, no. 3, New York, 1961. The story has never been published in Russian, but the present translation of "Answer to an Inquiry" was done from the original Russian text.

"Mama, Rimma and Alla," "Ilya Isaakovich and Margarita Prokofievna," and "The Tale of a Woman," and "Gapa Guzhva" appear here in English translation for the first time. Babel made his literary debut with the publication of "Mama, Rimma and Alla" and "Ilya Isaakovich and Margarita Provofievna" in Gorky's magazine *Letopis* in 1916. He did not include these "tolerable attempts," as he called them, in later editions of his works.

None of the stories published in *The Lonely Years: 1925-1939* was included in the Soviet edition of Babel's *Selected Works* published in 1957.

N.B.

Kolyvushka*

FROM A NOVEL *Velikaya Staritsa*

Four men came into the yard of Ivan Kolyvushka's farm: Ivashko, the representative of the District Executive Committee, Yevdokim Nazarenko, the head of the Village Council, Zhitnyak, the chairman of the newly formed *kolkhoz*, and Adrian Morinets. Adrian walked around just like a clocktower on the move. Pressing his folding cloth briefcase to his hip, Ivashko ran past the barns and the sheds and marched straight into the house. Ivan's wife and his two daughters were spinning yarn by the window on a blackened spinning wheel. With their kerchiefs and long gowns, with their bare feet, tiny and clean, they looked like nuns. On the walls, hanging between the embroidered cloths and cheap mirrors, there were photographs of ensigns in Tsarist uniform, schoolmistresses, and townspeople on vacation in the country. Ivan followed the visitors into the house, and took off his cap.

* "Kolyvushka," dated Spring, 1930. Subtitled "From a novel *Velikaya Staritsa*." The head of the District Executive Committee (*selrad*), Ivashko, appears as a character both in this story and in the story "Gapa Guzhva." From these two stories which are available to us, it appears that Babel had in mind a loosely connected series of stories, each complete in itself, all dealing with the theme of collectivization in one village. No doubt he thought of producing a second book comparable to *Red Cavalry*, his earlier series of sketches dealing with the theme of the 1920-1921 Red Army campaign in Poland.

"How much tax does he pay?" Ivashko asked, twisting around.

Yevdokim, the head of the Village Council, stood there with his hands in his pockets and watched the spinning wheel fly around. When he heard that Kolyvushka paid 216 rubles Ivashko snorted:

"Can't he manage any more?"

"He can't, by the looks of it."

Zhitnyak spread his dry lips and Yevdokim just went on staring at the spinning wheel. From where he was standing in the doorway, Kolyvushka winked at his wife, and she took a receipt from behind the icons and gave it to the representative of the District Executive Committee.

"And what about his seed fund?" Ivashko asked his questions brusquely, tapping his foot impatiently and digging it into the floorboards.

Yevdokim raised his eyes and looked around the room.

"In this farm," he said, "everything's been handed over, comrade chairman. There couldn't be anything here that hasn't been handed over."

The whitewashed walls converged over the heads of the guests to form a low, cozy dome. The flowers in the glass lamps, the plain cupboards, the polished benches, all reflected painstaking cleanliness. Ivashko made a move and hurried to the door with his dangling briefcase.

"Comrade chairman," Kolyvushka said, following him out, "Will I be hearing from you, or what?"

"You'll get a notification," Ivashko shouted, his arms swinging, and he hurried off.

Adrian Morinets, larger than life, went after him. Timish, the cheerful bailiff of the Village Council, appeared fleetingly in the gateway at Ivashko's heels. He was churning up the mud of the village street with his long legs.

"What's it all about, Timish?" Ivan beckoned him and grabbed him by the sleeve. Timish bent down like a grinning beanstalk and opened his huge mouth crammed with a purple tongue and set with rows of pearls.

"They're taking your house away."

"And what about me?"

"You're being expelled."

Then Timish ran off with his long strides to catch up with his superiors.

There was a harnessed horse standing in Ivan's yard. The red reins were thrown over some sacks of wheat. In the middle of the yard near a crooked lime tree, there was a stump with an axe stuck in it. Ivan touched his cap with his hand, pushed it back and sat down. The mare came up to him dragging a sledge behind her. She put out her tongue and curled it up. She was with foal and her belly was very distended. Playfully she caught her master by the shoulder of his padded coat and nuzzled at it. Ivan was looking down at his feet. The trampled snow around the stump dazzled him. With hunched shoulders he jerked out the axe, held it up in the air for a moment and struck the horse on the head. One of its ears jerked back, the other twitched and then lay flat. The mare groaned and bolted. The sledge turned over and wheat scattered in curved lines over the snow. The horse reared up with its forelegs in the air and its head thrown back. Beside one of the sheds it got caught up in the teeth of a harrow. Its eyes appeared from under a veil of pouring blood and it whinnied plaintively. The foal stirred inside it and a vein swelled up on its belly.

"I didn't mean it," Ivan said, stretching out his hand towards her, "I didn't mean it, little one."

The palm of his hand was open. The horses's ear was limp, its eyes were rolling and there were bloody rings around them. Its neck formed a straight line with its head. Its upper lip was curled up in despair. It pulled on the harness and moved forward again, dragging the harrow behind it. Ivan drew back his hand with the axe behind his back. He hit the mare right between the eyes. The foal stirred once again as the mare lay on the ground. Ivan wandered round the yard, went up to a shed and dragged out a seeding machine. He smashed it with long slow blows and twisted the axe in the delicate mesh of wheels and in the drum. His wife appeared on the steps of the house in her long gown.

"Mother," Ivan heard his wife's voice in the distance, "Mother, he's wrecking everything."

The door opened and an old woman in canvas breeches came out of the house leaning on a stick. Her yellow hair hung down over the hollows of her cheeks, her shift hung loosely on her thin body like a shroud. She stepped down into the snow in her rough stockings.

"Murderer," she said to her son, taking the axe out of his hand. "Have you forgotten your father? Have you forgotten your brothers who worked like slaves?"

Neighbors crowded into the yard. The men stood in a half-circle and looked to one side. One of the women started forward and began to wail.

"Shut up, you bitch," her husband said to her.

Ivan stood leaning against a wall. His stertorous breathing could be heard all over the yard. It was as though he were doing a job of heavy work, gasping and panting.

His uncle Terenti was fussing near the gate and trying to close it.

"I'm a man," Ivan said all at once to the people standing round him, "I'm a man, a peasant——haven't you ever seen one before?"

Terenti hustled everybody out of the yard. The gates creaked and shut. They opened again only in the evening. A sledge piled high with belongings came out. The women were sitting on bundles like frozen birds. A cow was hitched to the sledge by the horns. It went round the edge of the village and disappeared in the flat wastes of snow. The wind blew close to the ground, moaning in this wasteland and stirring up blue waves. The sky beyond them was leaden. The sky was covered by a glittering diamond mesh.

Kolyvushka, looking straight ahead, went down the street to the Village Council. A meeting of the new *kolkhoz*, "Rebirth," was going on there. The hunchbacked Zhitnyak was lolling behind a table.

"Now, this change in our life: what's it all about, this change?" The hunchback pressed his hands to his body and held them out again. "We are going over to dairy farming and market-gardening. This is of the greatest importance. Our fathers and grandfathers walked roughshod on a treasure and we are now digging it up. Isn't it a disgrace, isn't it a scandal that living about forty miles from the town, we haven't started farming on scientific lines? Our eyes were closed, we've been running away from ourselves. What is forty miles, does anybody know? In this country it means about an hour in time, but that short hour belongs to us, it's worth something."

The door of the Village Council was flung open. Kolyvushka came in and stood by the wall in his fur-coat which looked as though it had been cast in a mold. Ivashko's fingers twitched and stabbed at the papers in front of him.

"I must ask people deprived of the vote," he said, looking down at his papers, "to leave our meeting."

Outside, beyond the dirty window-panes, the sun was setting in a flood of emerald rays. In the half-light of the village hut sparks gleamed faintly in the thick smoke of home-grown tobacco. Ivan took off his hat and his mop of hair tumbled down.

He went up to the table at which the committee was sitting: Ivga Movchan, a woman who had worked as a farm hand, the chairman Yevdokim and the tight-lipped Adrian Morinets.

"People," Kolyvushka said, and he put a bunch of keys on the table, "I'm leaving you."

The steel fell on the blackened boards with a clank. Adrian's twisted face peered out of the darkness.

"Where will you go, Ivan?"

"People won't have me—maybe the ground will." Ivan went out on tiptoe, his head bobbing up and down.

"He's up to something," Ivashko screeched, as soon as the door shut behind him, "it's all a provocation. He's gone for his shotgun, he's gone for his shot-gun, that's what!"

Ivashko banged his fist on the table. Words about panic and the need to keep calm rushed to his lips. Adrian's face went back into its dark corner.

"No," he said out of the darkness, "maybe he hasn't gone for his gun, chairman."

"I have a proposal!" Ivashko shouted. His proposal was that a guard should be posted outside Kolyvushka's house.

They appointed Timish, the bailiff, as guard.

Making faces, he brought a bent-wood chair out of the house onto the porch and slumped into it. He placed his shot-gun and truncheon at his feet. From the top of the steps, from the height of his village throne, Timish shouted to the girls, whistling and hollering and rattling his gun. The night was mauve and heavy like a precious stone. It was streaked with the veins of frozen streams. A star fell down a well of black clouds.

In the morning Timish reported that there had been no incidents.

Ivan had spent the night with Abraham, an old man covered with proud-flesh. Abraham had gone out to the well in the evening.

"What for, Abraham?" Ivan asked.

"For the samovar," the old man said.

They stayed in bed late. There was already smoke over the other houses in the village, but their door was still shut.

"He's bolted," Ivashko said at the kolkhoz meeting. "We shan't shed any tears. What do you think, friends?"

Zhitnyak, his bony, tremulous elbows spread wide apart on the table, was writing down in a ledger the descriptions of confiscated horses. His hump threw a moving shadow.

"We can never have enough now," Zhitnyak prated, whenever he had a free moment, "we need everything there is: water-sprinklers, hoeing machines, tractors, pumps. That's gluttony for you, friends. The whole of our country is gluttonous."

The horses he was writing down were either bay or piebald; they were called either "Lad" or "Lass." Zhitnyak made each owner sign against his name.

He was disturbed by a noise like a distant, muffled thudding of hooves. A tidal wave was rolling nearer and breaking over the village. A crowd surged along the broken street. Legless cripples scuttled along in front. An unseen banner fluttered above them. When they reached the Village Council, the crowd changed step and drew up in formation. A circle opened up in their midst, a circle of ruffled snow, an empty space like the one made for priests during a church procession. Kolyvushka was standing there with his shirt hanging out from under his waistcoat, and his head all white. The night had silvered his mop of gypsy hair; not a black hair was left. Snow flakes, tired birds carried by the wind, drifted past under a sky which had grown warmer. An old man with broken legs pushed forward and looked eagerly at Kolyvushka's white hair.

"Tell us, Ivan," the old man said, raising his hands, "tell us what you have on your mind."

"Where are you sending me?" Kolyvushka said, looking round. "Where can I go? I was born among you."

The crowd began to mutter. Morinets elbowed his way up to the front.

"Let him stay and work." The cry could scarcely leave his body, and his low voice shook. "Let him work. Will he take food out of anybody's mouth?"

"Yes, out of mine," Zhitnyak said with a laugh. He shuffled up to Kolyvushka and winked at him.

"I slept with a wench last night," the hunchback said. "When we got up, she made a lot of pancakes. We ate so much, we were farting all over the place."

The hunchback broke off and stopped laughing; the blood drained from his face.

"You've come to put us up against the wall," he said in a quieter voice, "you've come to torment us with that white head of yours. Only we won't be tormented, Ivan. We're fed up with being tormented nowadays."

The hunchback came nearer on his thin, bandy legs. Something inside him whistled like a bird.

"You should be killed," he whispered, as the idea came to him, "I shall fetch the gun and destroy you."

His face lit up. He touched Kolyvushka's hand gleefully and dashed off to the house for Timish's shot-gun. Kolyvushka gave a lurch and walked away. The silver fleece of his head receded into the distance between two rows of houses. His legs were unsteady, but then his step got firmer. He turned off on the road to Ksenyevka. He was never seen again in Velikaya Staritsa.

Translated by Max Hayward

Froim Grach*

In 1919 Benya Krik's men ambushed the rear guard of the White
Army, killed all the officers and captured some of the supplies. As
a reward for this, they demanded three days of "Peaceful Insurrec-
tion," but permission was not forthcoming, so they looted the

* "Froim Grach"—not dated. This story belongs to the series of Odessa stories
which include "How It Was Done in Odessa," "The King," "The Father,"
(in which Froim Grach appears as a leading character), and "Lyubka the Cossack." All of these stories are available in English translation in *Collected
Stories* of Isaac Babel, edited and translated by Walter Morrison, Criterion
Books, 1955 and in *Lyubka the Cossack and Other Stories*, translated by Andrew R. MacAndrew. Signet, 1963.

Although the story has not yet been published in the Soviet Union, the
thematic and stylistic relationship of the story to the other Odessa stories has
been discussed by a Soviet scholar. (Smirin, "Odesskiye rasskazy I. E. Babelya," in *Trudy kafedry russkoi i zarubezhnoi literatury*, Kazakhsky Univer-
sitet, Alma-Ata, 1961.)

The story can be considered as a conclusion to the Odessa series. The new
Soviet power represented by the Cheka puts an end to the heroic but illegal
activities of Froim Grach and his gang. In the pre-Revolutionary world these
activities were expressions of proletarian justice, but in the new Soviet society
they are regarded as dangerous survivals of the past. The unmistakable nostalgia with which the author views the passing of his colorful heroes probably
accounts for the fact that the story has still not been published in the Soviet
Union.

goods in all the shops on Alexandrovski Avenue. After that they turned their attention to the Mutual Credit Society. Letting the customers enter ahead of them, they went into the bank and requested that the clerks put bales of money and valuables into a car waiting on the street. A whole month went by before the new authorities started shooting them. Then people began to say that Aron Peskin, who ran a sort of work-shop, had something to do with the arrests. Nobody quite knew what went on in this work-shop. In Peskin's apartment there was a large machine with a bent bar made of lead and the floor was strewn with shavings and cardboard for binding books.

One morning in the spring Peskin's friend, Misha Yablochko, knocked on the door of the work-shop.

"Aron," Misha said to Peskin, "it's wonderful weather outside. You have before you a man who thinks of getting hold of half a bottle of Vodka and some snacks and going up to Arkadia for a ride in the fresh air. You might laugh at me but I just like to take my mind off things once in a while."

Peskin put on his coat, went off with Misha and took the street car to Arkadia. They rode around in a hansom until evening. At dusk Misha came into the room where Madame Peskin was washing her fourteen-year-old daughter in a tub.

"Good evening to you," Misha said, and he raised his hat, "We really had a great time. The fresh air was something out of this world; the only trouble was, it's not easy to talk to your husband. He's an awkward customer, your husband."

"You can say that again," Madame Peskin said and she grabbed her daughter by the hair and yanked her back and forth. "Where is he, that adventurer?"

Misha replied, "He's resting in the back garden."

Misha Yablochko raised his hat again, said good-bye and went off on a street car. Not waiting for her husband, Madame Peskin went into the garden to look for him. He was sitting, his straw hat on, slumped against the rustic table, showing all his teeth.

"You adventurer," Madame Peskin said to him. "It's all very well, your grinning all over your face, but that daughter of yours is having fits, she won't let me wash her head. Come and have a word with that daughter of yours."

Peskin didn't say a word and just kept on showing his teeth.

"No good son-of-a-bitch," Madame Peskin said. She looked under her husband's straw hat and screamed. The neighbors came running.

"He isn't alive," Madame Peskin said to them. "He is dead."

But she was wrong. Peskin had been shot through the chest in two places and his skull was broken, but he was still alive. They took him to the Jewish hospital. Doctor Zilberberg himself, no other, did an operation on him but Peskin had no luck and died under the knife. That same night the Cheka arrested a man nicknamed The Georgian and his friend Kolya Lapidus. One of them was the fellow who had driven Peskin and Misha Yablochko around in the hansom and the other was the one who had been waiting for them in Arkadia, on the seashore next to the turning that leads out into the open country. They were shot after a very brief questioning.

Only Misha Yablochko got away. They lost track of him and it was a few days before an old woman selling sun-flower seeds came to the yard of Froim Grach's house. She was carrying a basket full of the stuff. One of her eye-brows rose up like a shaggy black bush and the other, only faintly outlined, ran in a curve over the eye. Froim Grach was sitting with his legs wide apart near the stable, playing with his grandson, Arkadi. Three years ago the child had fallen out of the mighty womb of his daughter, Baska. Froim stuck his finger out and the child grabbed hold of it, hung onto it and began to swing back and forth as if it were a cross-bar.

"You little devil," Froim said to his grandson, looking at him with his only eye.

The old woman with the bushy eye-brow and man's shoes tied with string, came up to them and sat down.

"Froim," said the old woman, "these people have no human feelings, I'm telling you. They are like wild animals. They are slaughtering us in the cellars like dogs. They don't give us a chance to talk before we die. We ought to go for them with our teeth and tear their hearts out. . . . Why don't you say something, Froim?" asked Misha Yablochko, "the boys are waiting for you to say something."

Misha got up, put the basket in his other hand and went away arching that black eye-brow. Three girls with their hair done in braids met him by the church on Alexeyev Square. They were walking arm in arm.

"Young ladies," Misha said to them, "I can't treat you to tea and honey-cake."

He tipped some sun-flower seeds out of the glass into the pockets of their dresses and made off around the church.

Froim Grach was alone in his yard. He was sitting there without moving, staring into space with his one eye. Mules captured from the White Army munched hay in the stable and over-fed mares with their foals were grazing in the paddock. Coachmen played cards in the shade of a chestnut tree, sipping wine out of broken cups. Hot gusts of wind swept the limestone walls, and the sunlight, blue and relentless poured down over the yard.

Froim got up and went onto the street. He crossed over Prokhorovskaya which was blackening the sky with the poverty-stricken smoke of its kitchen, went through the rag market where people draped in curtains were trying to sell them to each other. When he got to Yekateriminskaya Street he turned off by the statue of the Empress and went into the Cheka building.

"I am Froim," he said to the duty officer, "I want to see the boss."

The head of the Cheka at that time was Vladislav Simen who had come from Moscow. When he heard about the arrival of Froim, he called in one of his interrogators, Borovoi, to find out about the visitor.

"He's a fantastic fellow," Borovoi told him, "you will see the whole of Odessa in this man."

The duty officer led the old man into the room. He was in a long canvas coat. He had red hair and was as huge as a house with one eye closed and a badly scarred cheek.

"Boss," Froim said, "who do you think you're killing? You're killing the best. You'll be left with nothing but riff-raff, boss."

Simen made a movement and opened the drawer of his desk.

"I've got nothing on me," Froim said, "I've got nothing in my hands or in my boots, and I've got nobody waiting on the street outside. Let my boys go, boss, just name your price."

They put the old man in an arm chair and brought him some

brandy. Borovoi left, went to his own room and called in all the interrogators and commissars who were in Moscow.

"I want you to see this fellow here," he said. "He's a legend, there's nobody like him."

Borovoi told them that it was the one-eyed Froim not Benya Krik who was the real boss of Odessa's 40,000 thieves. He kept very much in the background but it was the old man who had masterminded everything—the looting of the factories and the municipal treasury in Odessa, the attacks on the White and Allied troops. Borovoi waited for the old man to come out so they could have a talk with him, but there was no sign of him. He went through the whole building and finally went out into the yard at the back. Froim Grach was lying there sprawled under a tarpaulin by an ivy-covered wall. Two Red Army men had rolled themselves cigarettes and were standing smoking over his body.

"He was strong as an ox," the older of the two said when he saw Borovoi, "never seen anything like it. An old man like that'd live forever if you didn't kill him. There were ten bullets in him but he was still kicking." The Red Army man was all flushed, his eyes were shining and his cap askew.

"You're talking out of the top of your head," said the other soldier. "He just died like they all do, they're all the same."

"They're not the same," the other one shouted, "some of them go down on their knees and scream and others don't make a sound. How can you say they're all the same?"

"They're all the same to me," the younger one went on stubbornly. "They all look alike, I can't tell them apart."

Borovoi bent down and pulled back the tarpaulin. The old man's face was still contorted in its last grimace.

Borovoi went back to his room. It was a circular room and the walls were covered with damask. There a meeting was going on about new rules of work. Simen was reporting on the irregularities which he had found on taking over—the illiterate way in which sentences were written out and the nonsensical fashion in which the records of interrogations were made. He was insisting that the interrogators should form themselves into groups for study with legal experts, and that they should conduct their business in accordance with the rules and regulations laid down by the Chief Directorate in Moscow.

Borovoi listened from his corner of the room. He was sitting by himself, a long way from the others. Simen went up to him after the meeting and took him by the arm.

"I know you're angry with me," he said, "but we are in power, Sasha, we are the power of the State, you've got to remember that."

"I'm not angry," Borovoi replied, "you're not from Odessa and you couldn't know how it was about that old man here." They sat down side by side, the head of the Cheka who was just 22, and his subordinate. Simen pressed Borovoi's hand.

"Tell me as a Chekist," he said after a pause, "tell me as a revolutionary: what good was this man for the society of the future?"

"I don't know." Borovoi sat motionless and stared in front of him, "I suppose he wasn't . . ."

He pulled himself together and drove away his memories.

Then Borovoi livened up and began to tell the Chekists from Moscow about the life of Froim Grach, about his cunning and elusiveness, and about his contempt for his fellow men—all these extraordinary stories that are now a thing of the past.

Translated by Max Hayward

Answer to an Inquiry*

For your information and in answer to your inquiry, I started out on my literary career rather early in life—at the age of twenty or so. I was drawn to it by natural bent and by my love for a woman called Vera. She was a prostitute, lived in Tiflis and was well known among the other girls for her business sense. She did a bit of pawnbroking, took newcomers under her wing and made an occasional deal with the Persians in the bazaar. Every evening, she went out on Golovin Avenue and, big, tall and white-faced, sailed along in front of the crowd like the Virgin Mary on the prow of a fishing boat. I used to follow her all the time and never said a word, but I saved up my money and at last I plucked up my courage. Vera asked for ten rubles, pressed her large, soft shoulder against me and then never gave me another thought. In the bar where we ate a *lyule-kebab*, she got all excited trying to persuade the owner to launch out and set up his business on Milhailovsky Avenue. From the bar we went on to a shoemaker's where Vera had to pick up a pair of shoes, and then she left me to go to a girlfriend who was having a baby christened. It was about twelve o'clock at

* "Answer to an Inquiry [*Spravka*]," not dated. This story, it can be surmised, is an earlier variant of Babel's "My First Fee." In its condensation, it is close to the stories of the early twenties, the *Red Cavalry* period.

night when we got to her hotel, but she still had some things to do there. There was an old woman who was getting ready to go and see her son in Armavir. Vera knelt on her suitcases to help fasten them and wrapped her pies in grease-proof paper for her. The old woman, with a reddish handbag dangling at her hip and a light gauze hat on her head, ran from one room to another, saying goodbye. She shuffled along the corridor in her galoshes. She was crying, but she was still smiling, showing all her wrinkles.

I waited for Vera in the room. It was cluttered with three-legged chairs. There was an earthenware stove, and there were patches of damp in the corners. In a small glass bowl filled with a milky liquid flies were dying—each in its own way. There was another life outside in the corridor with people shuffling their feet and laughing loudly. It was ages before Vera returned.

"Now, let's get down to it," she said, closing the door behind her.

She prepared for it very much like a surgeon preparing for an operation. She lit a kerosene stove, placed a saucepan of water on it, poured the water into a jar which had a white rubber tube coming out of it. She threw a crystal into the jar and started pulling off her dress.

"So we've seen our Sofya Mavrikyevna off," Vera said. "Believe it or not, she was like one of the family to us. The poor thing is going all by herself, she has nobody to go with her."

In the bed, her flabby nipples staring at me blindly, lay a large woman with sloping shoulders.

"What's the matter with you? —scared to part with your money or something?" Vera asked me, pulling me toward her.

"I am not worried about money."

"What d'you mean not worried? You're a thief, maybe?"

"I'm not a thief, I'm a boy."

"I can see you're not a cow," Vera said with a yawn and her eyes closed.

"I'm a boy," I repeated, "I'm a boy . . . with the Armenians." and I went cold all over at this tale I had made up on the spur of the moment.

It was too late to go back on it now and I told my chance companion my story as a boy with the Armenians.

"We used to live in Alyoshki, in Kherson Province," I invented for a start. "My father was a draftsman and wanted to give us children a good education; but we took after our mother, she was interested only in gambling and having a good time. At the age of ten, I started stealing money from my father, and when I grew up, I ran away from home to Baku where my mother had some relatives. They introduced me to an Armenian called Stepan Ivanych, and I lived with him for four years."

"But how old were you then?"

"Fifteen."

Vera thought I was going to tell her about the wickedness of the Armenian who had perverted me. But what I said was:

"We lived together for four years. Stepan Ivanych was a very trusting man and took everybody at his word. I wish I'd spent the time learning some trade, but the only thing I cared about was billiards. Stepan's friends ruined him. He kept handing out bogus bills of change to them and they sued him for payment on them."

Lord knows how I thought of these bogus bills of change, but I did quite right to mention them. After that she believed everything. She wrapped herself in a red shawl and it quivered on her shoulders.

". . . Stepan was finished. They kicked him out of his apartment and sold all of his furniture. He got himself a job as a commercial traveller. There was no sense my staying on with him now he was penniless, so I moved in with a rich old man, a church warden."

A church warden! I filched that out of some book or other, and it was the invention of a lazy mind. To make up for this mistake I gave the old man asthma in his yellow chest and horrible fits of choking and coughing. The old man jumped out of his bed at night and wheezed into the Baku air with its stench of oil. Before long he died. His relatives kicked me out. So here I was in Tiflis with twenty rubles in my pocket. The waiter in my hotel had promised to send rich customers up to my room but so far he had brought only Armenian innkeepers.

And I started spinning tales about these innkeepers, about their crudeness and stinginess—a lot of stuff and nonsense I'd heard some time or other. I was beginning to feel so sorry for myself it nearly broke my heart, and I seemed bound to come to a very bad end. I fell silent. That was the end of my story. The kerosene stove had gone out. The water had boiled and gone cold again. The woman crossed the room silently over to the window. I could see the movement of her sad, fleshy back.

"The things that go on," she whispered, opening the shutters. "God, the things people do."

In the square of the window, a narrow, twisting Turkish street climbed up a steep, stony slope. The flagstones seemed to hiss as they grew cold. A smell of water and dust came from the pavement.

"Well, have you ever been with a woman?" Vera said, turning around to me.

"How could I? They wouldn't let me."

"Ah, the things that go on. . . . God, the things people do," Vera said.

I must break off my story at this point, Comrade, to ask if you have ever seen how thick and fast and gaily the shavings fly from the plank he is planing when a village carpenter builds a house for a fellow carpenter?

That night, this thirty-year-old woman taught me her simple art. I experienced that night a love full of forbearance and heard the words that one woman speaks to another.

We fell asleep at dawn. We were wakened by the heat of our own bodies. We went out and drank tea at the bazaar in the old town. A placid Turk served us tea out of a samovar wrapped in a towel; the tea was brick red and steamed like newly shed blood. A caravan of dust was floating toward Tiflis—the town of roses and mutton fat. The dust was blotting out the purple bonfire of the sun. The long, drawn-out braying of donkeys blended with the hammering of tinsmiths. The Turk kept on pouring us more tea and kept count of the bread rolls we ate on his abacus.

When I was all covered in beads of sweat, I turned my glass upside down and pushed two five-ruble gold coins over to Vera. Her plump leg lay over mine. She pushed the money away.

"Do you want us to quarrel, sister?"

No, I did not want us to quarrel. We arranged to meet in the evening and I put the two gold coins back into my purse. This was my first author's fee.

Translated by Max Hayward

My First Fee*

To live in Tiflis in the springtime, to be twenty years old and not to be loved is a terrible thing. It happened to me. I had a job as a proof-reader in the printing plant of the Caucasus Military District. The river Kura seethed under the windows of my garret. As it rose behind the mountains, the sun lit up its muddy whirlpools in the mornings. I rented the garret from a Georgian couple who had just been married. The man had a butcher's shop in the Eastern Market. On the other side of the wall he and his wife, crazed with love, turned and twisted like two large fish in a small tank. The tails of these two frantic fish thrashed against the wall. They made the whole attic shake—it was burnt black by the sun—tore it from its foundations and bore it off into infinity. Their teeth were clenched tight in the relentless fury of their passion. In the mornings the wife, Miliet, went downstairs for bread. She was so weak she had to hold on to the banister in order not to fall. Groping for the steps with her small feet, she had the faint, vacant smile of someone recovering from an illness. With her hand on her small

* "My First Fee [*Moi Pervy Gonorar*]," dated 1922-1928. This story, apparently a later reworking of "Answer to an Inquiry," indicates by its more developed narrative method that it belongs together with stories of Babel's later period, such as "Guy de Maupassant" and "First Love."

breasts, she bowed to everybody she met on the way—to the old Assyrian, who was green with age, to the man who came round selling kerosene, and to the old hags, deeply seared with wrinkles, who sold skeins of wool. At nighttime the heaving and moaning of my neighbors was followed by a silence as penetrating as the whine of a cannon ball.

To live in Tiflis, to be twenty years old, and to listen at night to the storms of other people's silence is a terrible thing. To get away from it, I raced out of the house down to the Kura, where I was overwhelmed by the steam-bath heat of the Tiflis spring. It hit you for all it was worth and knocked you out. I wandered along the hump-backed streets with a parched throat. The haze of spring heat drove me back to my attic, to that forest of blackened stumps lit by the moon. There was nothing to do but to look for love. Of course, I found it. For better or for worse, the woman I chose was a prostitute. Her name was Vera. I prowled after her every night along Golovin Avenue, not daring to speak to her. I had neither the money for her, nor the words—those tireless, trite and nagging words of love. From childhood all the strength of my being had been devoted to the invention of tales, plays and stories—thousands of them. They lay on my heart like toads on a stone. I was possessed by devilish pride and did not want to write them down prematurely. I thought it was a waste of time not to write as well as Leo Tolstoi. My stories were intended to survive oblivion. Fearless thoughts and consuming passions are worth the effort spent on them only when they are dressed in beautiful clothes. How can you make these clothes?

It is difficult for a man who has been captured by an idea and tamed by its snake-like gaze to expend himself in the froth of meaningless and nagging words of love. A man like that is ashamed to cry in sorrow; he hasn't got the sense to laugh in joy. Being a dreamer, I hadn't mastered the absurd art of happiness. I would be forced, therefore, to give Vera ten rubles out of my meagre earnings.

When I had made up my mind, I started to wait one evening outside the "Sympathy" restaurant. Tartars in blue Circassian tunics and soft leather boots sauntered past me. Picking their teeth with silver tooth-picks, they eyed the crimson-painted women—

Georgians, with large feet and slender thighs. There was a touch of turquoise in the fading light. The flowering acacias along the streets began to moan in a low, faltering voice. A crowd of officials in white coats surged along the boulevard, and wafts of balmy air from Mount Kazbek came down towards them.

Vera came later, when it was dark. Tall and white-faced, she sailed ahead of the ape-like throng as the Virgin Mary rides the prow of a fishing boat. She drew level with the door of the "Sympathy" restaurant. I lurched after her:

"Going somewhere?"

Her broad, pink back moved in front of me. She turned around: "What's that you say?" She frowned, but her eyes were laughing.

"Where are you going?"

The words cracked in my mouth like dried sticks. Vera changed her step and walked by my side.

"Ten rubles, is that all right?"

I agreed so quickly she got suspicious.

"But do you have ten rubles?"

We went into a doorway and I handed her my purse. She counted the twenty-one rubles in it; her grey eyes were screwed up and her lips moved. She sorted out the gold coins from the silver.

"Give me ten," she said, handing back the purse, "we'll spend another five and you keep the rest to live on. When do you get your next pay?"

I said: in four days' time. We came out of the doorway. Vera took me by the hand and pressed her shoulder against me. We went up the street, which was growing cooler. The pavement was littered with withered vegetables.

"It'd be nice to go to Borzhom and get away from the heat," she said.

Vera's hair was held by a ribbon which caught and refracted flashes of light from the street-lamps.

"Well, clear off to Borzhom."

That's what I said: clear off. That's the expression I used, for some reason.

"I haven't got the dough," Vera said with a yawn and forgot all about me. She forgot all about me because her day was made and because I was easy money. She knew I wouldn't turn her in to the police, or rob her of her money and her earrings during the night.

We reached the foot of St. David's Mount. There, in a bar, I ordered *kebab* for us. Without waiting for it to come, Vera went over and sat with some old Persians who were discussing business. Leaning on their polished sticks and nodding their olive-coloured skulls, they were telling the owner it was time he expanded his trade. Vera butted into their conversation. She took the side of the old men. She was for transferring the business to Mikhailovsky Boulevard. The owner, blinded by flabbiness and caution, just wheezed. I ate my *kebab* alone. Vera's bare arms flowed from the silk of her sleeves; she banged her fist on the table, her earrings flitted to and fro among the long, faded backs, yellow beards and painted finger-nails. The *kebab* was cold by the time she came back to the table. She had become so worked up that her face was flushed.

"You can't shift him, the mule . . . You can really do business, you know, on Mikhailovsky with Eastern cooking."

One after another, Vera's acquaintances came past the table— Tartars in Circassian tunics, middle-aged officers, shopkeepers in alpaca jackets and potbellied old men with tanned faces and greenish blackheads on their cheeks. It was midnight by the time we got to the hotel, but Vera had a hundred and one things to do here as well. There was an old woman who was getting ready to go and see her son in Armavir. Vera left me and went to help her pack— knelt on her suitcase, strapped pillows together, and wrapped pies in grease-proof paper. The broad-shouldered old woman in a gauze hat with a handbag at her side went around to all the rooms saying goodbye. She shuffled along the corridor in her elastic shoes, sobbing and smiling with all her wrinkles. It took a whole hour to see her off. I waited for Vera in a musty room with three-legged chairs, an earthenware stove and patches of damp in the corners.

I had been tormented and dragged round the town for so long, that this love I wanted now seemed like an enemy, an inescapable enemy.

Outside there was another, alien life shuffling in the corridor or suddenly bursting into laughter. Flies were dying in a phial filled with a milky liquid. Each died in its own way. The death throes of some were violent and lasted a long time. Others died quietly, with a slight quiver. Next to the phial on the worn table-cloth was a book: a novel by Golovin about the life of the boyars. I opened it at random. The letters lined up in a single row and then got all jumbled together. In front of me, in the square frame of the window was a steep, stony hill-side with a winding Turkish street going up it. Vera came into the room.

"We've just said goodbye to Feodosya Mavrikeyevna," she said. "She was just like a mother to us, you know. She's traveling all alone, the old woman, she's got nobody to go with her."

Vera sat down on the bed with her knees apart. Her eyes were far away, roaming in the pure realms of her care and friendship for the old woman. Then she saw me in my double-breasted jacket. She clasped her hands and stretched herself.

"You're tired of waiting, I bet. . . . Never mind, we'll get down to it in a moment.

But I just couldn't make out what Vera was going to do. Her preparations were like those of a surgeon getting ready for an operation. She lit a kerosene stove and put a saucepan with water on it. She threw a clean towel over the headboard of the bed, and above it hung an enema bag with a douche; the white tube dangled down from the wall. When the water got hot, she poured it into the bag, threw a red crystal into it and started taking off her dress, pulling it over her head. A large woman with drooping shoulders and a crumpled stomach stood before me. Her flabby nipples pointed blindly sideways.

"Come over here, boy," my loved one said, "—while the water's getting ready."

I didn't move. I was numb with despair. Why had I exchanged my loneliness for the misery of this sordid den, for these dying flies and three-legged chairs?

O Gods of my youth! How different it was, this dreary business, from the love of my neighbors on the other side of the wall, their long, drawn-out squeals.

Vera put her hands under her breasts and wobbled them.

"What are you so miserable about? Come here." I didn't move. She pulled her petticoat up to her belly and sat down on the bed again.

"Are you sorry about your money?"

"I don't worry about my money," I said in a cracked voice.

"How come you don't worry about your money? Are you a thief or something?"

"I'm not a thief."

"Do you work for thieves?"

"I'm a boy."

"I can see you're not a cow," Vera muttered. She could hardly keep her eyes open. She lay down, pulled me towards her and started running her hands over me.

"I'm a boy," I shouted, "a boy with the Armenians, don't you understand?"

O Gods of my youth!—Five of my twenty years had been spent in making up stories, thousands of stories which gorged themselves on my brain. They lay on my mind like toads on a stone. Dislodged by the force of loneliness, one of them fell to the ground. It was evidently a matter of fate that a Tiflis prostitute was to be my first 'reader.' I went cold all over at the suddenness of my invention and I told her my story as a "boy with the Armenians." If I had given less time and thought to my craft, I should have made up a hackneyed tale about being the son of a rich official who had driven me from home, a tale about a domineering father and a downtrodden mother. But I didn't make this mistake. A well-devised story needn't try to be like real life. Real life is only too eager to resemble a well-devised story. For this reason—and because this was how my listener liked it—I was born in the small town of Alyoshki in Kherson province. My father worked as a draftsman with a steam-boat company. He sweated over his drawing board day and night to give us, his children, a good education, but we all took after our mother who was interested only in having a good time. At the age of ten I started stealing from my father. When I was grown up I ran away to Baku, to some relatives of my mothers. They introduced me to an Armenian called Stepan Ivanovich. I moved in with him and we lived together for four years.

"But how old were you then?"

"Fifteen."

Vera was expecting me to tell her about the misdeeds of the Armenian who had corrupted me, but I went on:

"We lived together for four years. Stepan Ivanovich was the most decent and trusting person I've ever met. He believed every word his friends said to him. I ought to have learned a trade during those four years, but I didn't do a thing. All I cared about was playing billiards. Stepan Ivanovich's friends ruined him. He gave them bogus bills of change, and his friends presented them for payments."

'Bogus bills of change'—I don't know how they came into my mind, but I did right to bring them in. Vera believed everything after that. She wrapped herself in her shawl which quivered on her shoulders.

"Stepan Ivanovich was ruined. He was thrown out of his apartment and his furniture was sold by auction. He became a traveling salesman. I wasn't going to live with him now that he had no money, so I moved in with a rich old church warden."

The 'church warden' was filched from some writer: he was the invention of a lazy mind which can't be bothered to produce a real live character.

I said "a church warden" and Vera's eyes flickered and went out of my control. Then, in order to restore the situation, I installed asthma in the old man's yellow chest. Attacks of asthma made him wheeze hoarsely. He jumped out of bed at nights and panted into the kerosene-laden air of Baku. He soon died. The asthma finished him off. My relatives wouldn't have anything to do with me. So here I was in Tiflis with twenty rubles in my pocket—the very same rubles which Vera had counted in the doorway on Golovin Avenue. A waiter in the hotel where I was staying had promised to get me rich customers, but so far he had sent me only Armenian inn-keepers with great fat bellies. These people liked their own country, their songs and their wine, but they trampled on other people, men or women, as a thief tramples on his neighbor's garden.

And I started talking a lot of rubbish I had picked up about inn-keepers. My heart was breaking from self-pity. It looked as though I was utterly doomed. I was trembling with sorrow and inspiration. Trickles of ice-cold sweat started down my face like snakes moving over grass warmed by the sun. I stopped talking, began to cry and turned away. The kerosene stove had gone out a long time ago. The water had boiled and gone cold again. The rubber tube was hanging from the wall. Vera went silently up to the window. Her back, dazzling white and sad, heaved before me. In the window, it was getting light around the mountain tops.

"The things people do," Vera whispered, without turning around. "God, the things people do."

She stretched out her bare arms and threw the shutters wide open. The paving stones on the street hissed slightly as they grew cooler. There was a smell of dust and water. Vera's head was shaking.

"So you're a whore—like us bitches."

I bowed my head.

"A whore like you."

Vera turned round to me. Her petticoat hung sideways on her body like a rag.

"The things people do," she said again, in a louder voice. "God, the things people do. Have you ever been with a woman?"

I pressed my cold lips to her hand.

"No, how could I? They wouldn't let me."

My head shook against her breasts which welled freely above me. The taut nipples thrust against my cheeks. They were moist and wide-eyed like baby calves. Vera looked down at me from above.

"Sister," she whispered and sat down on the floor at my side. "My little sister."

Now tell me, I should like to ask you: have you ever seen a village carpenter helping his mate to build a house? Have you seen how thick and fast and gaily the shavings fly as they plane a beam together? That night this thirty-year-old woman taught me all the tricks of her trade. That night I learned secrets you will never learn, I experienced a love which you will never experience, I heard the words that one woman says to another. I have forgotten them: we are not supposed to remember them.

We fell asleep at dawn. We were awakened by the heat of our bodies, a heat which lay in the bed like a dead weight. When we woke up, we laughed to each other. I didn't go to the printing plant that day. We drank tea in the bazaar of the Old Town. A placid Turk poured us tea from a samovar wrapped in a towel. It was brick red and steamed like newly shed blood. The hazy fire of the sun blazed on the sides of our glasses. The long-drawn-out braying of donkeys blended with the hammering of tinsmiths.

Copper jugs were set up in rows on faded carpets under tents. Dogs nuzzled at the entrails of oxen. A caravan of dust was flying towards Tiflis, the town of roses and mutton fat. The dust was blotting out the crimson fire of the sun. The Turk poured out more tea for us and kept count of the rolls we ate on an abacus. The world was beautiful just to give us pleasure. When I was covered all over with fine beads of sweat, I turned my glass upside down. After I'd paid the Turk, I pushed two five-ruble pieces over to Vera. Her plump leg was lying across mine. She pushed the money away and removed her leg.

"Do you want us to quarrel, sister?"

No, I didn't want to quarrel. We agreed to meet in the evening and I put the two gold pieces, my first literary fee, back into my purse.

All this was a long time ago, and since then I have often received money from publishers, from learned men and from Jews trading in books. For victories that were defeats, for defeats that turned into victories, for life and for death they paid me trifling sums—much smaller than the one I received in my youth from my first 'reader.' But I am not bitter. I am not bitter because I know I shall not die until I have snatched one more gold piece—and this will be my last—from the hands of love.

Translated by Max Hayward

Gapa Guzhva*

THE FIRST CHAPTER OF *Velikaya Krinitsa*

Six weddings were celebrated in Velikaya Krinitsa on Shrove Tuesday of 1930. They were celebrated with a zest such as had not been witnessed for a long time. The ways of the old were reborn. A drunken matchmaker insisted on trying a bride— a custom that had been discarded in Velikaya Krinitsa for a good twenty years. The matchmaker had already removed his belt and tossed it on the ground. The bride, weak with laughter, was pulling at the old man's beard. He advanced on her, guffawed and stamped his big boots. Actually though, there was nothing much for the old man to be excited about: of the six sheets raised over the cottages, only two were reddened by nuptial blood. The other brides, it turned out, hadn't escaped intact from some earlier gay party. One of the sheets fell to a Red Army man on leave and Gapa Guzhva climbed for the other. Whacking at the men's heads to push them out of her way, she clambered onto the roof and started shinning up the pole. The pole bent and swayed under her weight. Gapa tore down the reddened rag and let herself slide down. On the flat

* "Gapa Guzhva," dated Spring, 1930, and subtitled "The First Chapter of *Velikaya Krinitsa.*" This story was published in *Novy Mir*, 1931, no. 10, pp. 17-20. Several of the characters also appear in "Kolyvushka," (see footnote).

part of the roof there stood a stool and a table with half a liter of vodka on it and some sliced cold meat. Gapa drank from the bottle, waving the sheet in her free hand. At her feet the crowd roared and danced. The chair under Gapa was slipping, cracking, breaking apart. Berezanka drovers, driving their oxen to Kiev, stared at the woman drinking vodka up there under the very sky.

"She's no woman," the matchmakers explained to them, "she's a hell cat, that widow."

Gapa was hurling bread, twigs, and plates down from the roof. When she'd drunk up all the vodka, she smashed the bottle against the corner of the chimney. The men crowding down below roared. The widow jumped down to the ground, untied her hairy-bellied mare who was dozing by the fence and galloped off to get liquor. She returned bristling with liquor as a Caucasus hillsman bristles with ammunition. The mare was foaming and throwing back her head; her enlarged belly contracted and swelled and she rolled her eyes in madness.

At the weddings they danced with handkerchiefs in their hands, their eyes lowered, stamping on the same spot. Only Gapa let herself go as they do in the big cities. She danced opposite her lover, Grishka Savchenko. They grappled as in combat; with stubborn fury they tore at each other's shoulders, beating out tattoos with their boots, falling to the ground as if knocked over.

The third day of the wedding celebrations was beginning. The friends of the newly-weds, covered with soot, their sheepskin coats turned inside out, banged on stove-lids as they ran all through the village. Fires were lit in the streets. People with horns drawn on their foreheads leapt over them. Horses were harnessed to troughs. The troughs banged against the uneven ground and flew over the fires. Men fell, knocked down by sleep. Housewives tossed out broken crockery. The newly-weds washed their feet and climbed onto their high beds, and only Gapa was still dancing in an empty shed. Bareheaded, she spun round and round holding a cudgel in her hands. The tar-covered club pounded against the walls. Her blows shook the structure and left black, sticky wounds behind them.

"We're deadly," Gapa whispered, waving her cudgel around.

Straw and boards were raining on her, the partitions were collapsing. Bareheaded, she danced amidst the ruins, amidst the din, amidst the dust of the splintering partitions, of the flying, rotten wood and breaking boards. Her red-rimmed boots, beating out their tattoo, turned in the midst of the debris.

Night was coming down. The fires were going out in the holes they had melted in the snow. The shed lay at the top of a slope in a bristling heap. In the Village Council across the road, a little, ragged-edged fire appeared. Gapa threw away the cudgel and ran across the street.

"Ivashko," she shouted, rushing into the Village Council, "come and have some fun with us. Come and let's drink away our lives."

Ivashko was the representative of the District Executive Committee for collectivization. For two months he had been discussing the matter of collectivization with Velikaya Krinitsa. Ivashko sat in front of a crumpled, tattered pile of papers, his hands resting on the table. The skin at his temples was rippled and a sick cat's pupils hung inside his eye-slits. Over the slits were stuck two bald pink arches.

"Don't you turn up your nose at our peasants," Gapa shouted, stamping her foot.

"I'm not turning my nose up at anyone," Ivashko said gloomily, "only it's not proper for me to be seen drinking with you."

Waving her arms and stamping, Gapa danced past him.

"Come and have a good time with us and you'll have us eating out of your hand," the woman said. "You'll speak for the authorities tomorrow, not today."

Ivashko shook his head.

"It's not proper for me to have a good time with you," he said. "You think you're people. You're like a snarly pack of dogs and I've lost twenty pounds since I've started trying to talk to you."

He made a chewing motion with his lips and lowered his lids. He stretched out his hands, groping for a canvas briefcase. He got up, slumped forward and, dragging his feet as if walking in his sleep, went toward the door.

"That citizen is worth his weight in gold," Kharchenko, the secretary of the Village Council, said when Ivashko had left. "There's a great feeling of responsibility in him. But Velikaya Krinitsa has really given him too rough a time."

Above his button nose and the pimples on his forehead, Khar-chenko had an ash blond tuft of hair. He was reading a newspaper, his feet resting on a bench.

"If the Voronkov judge comes over here," Kharchenko said, turning over the page of his newspaper, "they'll remember and be sorry."

Gapa took a bag of sun-flower seeds from under her skirt.

"How come you keep thinking of your duties, secretary," she said, "and how come you're so scared of death? Who ever heard of a man refusing to die?"

Out in the street a black, swollen sky was seething around the church belfry; the damp huts bent over and crawled away; above them the stars stood out faintly; the wind flattened itself out on the ground.

Through the entrance door of her hut, Gapa heard the monotonous murmuring of a hoarse, unfamiliar voice. A woman pilgrim, who had come to spend the night, sat on the shelf above the stove, her feet tucked under her. The filaments of flame from the icon lamps formed a raspberry-colored mesh in the holy corner. Quiet hung over the neat hut and the fragrance of apple alcohol came from the walls and partitions. Gapa's big-lipped daughters, their noses in the air, were staring at the pilgrim woman. The girls were covered with short, equine hair, their lips were turned inside out, their narrow foreheads had a greasy and lusterless shine.

"Keep lying, Grandma Rakhivna," Gapa said, leaning against the wall. "I like lies."

Sitting high up under the ceiling Rakhivna had plaited herself a whole row of braids around her small head. Her washed, deformed feet rested on the top of the stove.

"There are three patriarchs in the world," the old woman said, lowering her crumpled face, "the Moscow Patriarch has been locked up by our government and the Jerusalem Patriarch lives among the Turks, so it is the Antioch Patriarch who's the master of all Christians . . . And so he sent forty Greek priests to the Ukraine to lay a curse upon the churches from which our government had had the bells removed. The Greek priests passed by Kholodny Yar and they were seen around Ostrogradsk. By Palm Sunday they'll be here, in Velikaya Krinitsa."

Rakhivna lowered her lids and lapsed into silence. The light from the icon lamps reached into the hollows of her feet.

"The Voronkov judge," the woman said, coming out of her torpor, "carried out collectivization there in one single day. He had nine landlords jailed and the next morning they were to be packed off to Sakhalin. Everywhere there are people; everywhere they worship Christ. The landlords were left in jail for the night and when the guards came in the morning to take them away, what did they find but the nine landlords swaying under the rafters on their belts."

Rakhivna fussed around for a long time before she lay down. As she arranged her rags, she kept talking to her God in whispers, as she would have whispered to her old man, stretched out near her above the stone. Then, suddenly, she began to breathe lightly and regularly. Grishka Savchenko, another woman's husband, was sleeping on a bench next to the stove. He lay there folded up on the very edge, like a man run over on the road, his back arched, his waistcoat sticking out on it, his head sunk in the pillows.

"That's man's love," Gapa said shaking him. "I know what man's love is. A man turns his snout away from his wife. But you aren't in your own place here. You're not with your Odarka now."

For half the night they rolled about on the bench in the darkness, tight-lipped, their arms outstretched. Gapa's braid kept flying over the pillow. At dawn, Grishka sat up, moaned and fell asleep, his mouth twisted in a snarl. From where she was Gapa could see the brown shoulders of her daughters, their low foreheads, thick lips and black nipples.

"Such camels," Gapa thought, "how can they be mine?"

The darkness moved away outside the oak window frame; dawn opened up a violet strip among the clouds. Gapa walked out into the yard. The wind gripped her like cold water in a river. She harnessed the sled and loaded some bags of wheat onto it—for during the celebrations flour had been pre-empted from everyone. The road crept by through the fog and vapor of dawn.

At the mill, it took them till the next morning to finish. All day long it snowed. By the very entrance to the village, short-legged Yushko Trofim, wearing a soaked cap with ear-flaps, emerged from under a dripping wall. His shoulders, covered by a snowy ocean, were enlarged and sagging.

"So they woke up in the end," he muttered, approaching the sledge and raising his dark, bony face to Gapa.

"What are you talking about?" Gapa said, pulling at the reins.

"The high-ups came over during the night," Trofim said, "and that settled your old woman. The head of the District Executive Committee and the secretary of the District Party Committee have come. They kicked Ivashko out of the way and put that judge from Voronkov in his place."

Trofim's mustache rose like a walrus's, making the snowflakes which were caught in it move. Gapa started the horse off, then pulled at the reins again.

"Why did they grab the old woman, Trofim? What for?"

Yushko stopped and trumpeted at her through the driving snow.

"They say she was making propaganda about the end of the world."

Favoring one foot, he walked off and in no time his broad back was hidden by the sky which merged with the earth.

Gapa drove up to her hut and knocked on the window with her whip. Her daughters were standing by the table wearing shoes and shawls as if they were at a party.

"Ma," said the elder daughter, taking the bags from the sled, "while you were away, Odarka came and took Grishka home."

The daughters set the table and lit the samovar. Gapa ate her supper and left for the Village Council. There, the old men of Velikaya Krinitsa sat in silence on the benches which lined the walls. The window, broken during earlier arguments, was covered with a sheet of plywood, the glass covers of the kerosene lamps had been rubbed thin, a sign on the pockmarked wall read, "No Smoking."

The Voronkov judge, his shoulders hunched, was reading at the table. He was reading the official records of the Velikaya Krinitsa Village Council. The collar of his thin woolen overcoat was turned up. Next to him, Secretary Kharchenko was writing out an indictment against his village. He was entering on columned sheets all the crimes and failures to deliver, and the ensuing fines: all the wounds—those that were hidden as well as those that were obvious.

When Osmolovsky, the Voronkov judge, had arrived, he had refused to call a general meeting of the citizens as other representatives of the higher authorities had done. Nor had he made any speeches. He had simply ordered that a list be drawn up of those who had failed to meet their delivery quotas, another list of the former shopkeepers, and inventories of the people's belongings, of the land sown and of the number of farmsteads.

The people of Velikaya Krinitsa sat on the benches saying nothing. In the silence, Kharchenko's pen scratched and whistled. But there was a general stir when Gapa walked in. Yevdokim Nazarenko, the head of the Executive, came to life when he saw her.

"Here is our main asset, Comrade Judge," Yevdokim guffawed, rubbing his hands, "our widow who has led astray all our young men."

Gapa, screwing up her eyes, stood by the door. Osmolovsky's lips gave a barely perceptible twist, wrinkles appeared on his thin nose. He lowered his head and said, "Good day."

"She was the first to apply for collectivization," Yevdokim said, trying to discharge the threatening atmosphere in a flow of words. "But then kind people told her differently and she changed her mind and had her name taken off."

Gapa stood immobile. A brick-colored blush covered her face.

"Some nice people say," she boomed in her loud, resounding voice, "that in farming collectives everyone's to sleep under the same blanket."

One of the eyes was laughing in her immobile face.

"Well, I'm against that kind of sleeping. We like to sleep two by two around here and we love our vodka too, a hell of a lot."

The peasants began to laugh but then stopped abruptly. Gapa's eyes were narrowed. The judge lifted his red, puffy eyes to her and nodded. He shrank even further, took his head in his narrow hands covered with reddish hairs and plunged back into the Velikaya Krinitsa records. Gapa turned, and her majestic back flashed before those who stayed behind.

Outside, Grandpa Abram, all covered with scar tissue, sat on the wet boards, his knees spread wide apart. Yellowish tangles of hair fell onto his shoulders.

"How's things, Grandpa?"

"Bad."

At home, Gapa's daughters had turned in. Late at night a light hung like a drop of mercury in the small hut of Nestor Tyagai, the member of the Young Communist League. Osmolovsky arrived at the quarters assigned to him. A sheepskin coat had been thrown on a bench. Supper was waiting for the judge: a bowl of sour milk, a hunk of bread and an onion. The judge, who had been nicknamed in the district "Two-Hundred-and-Sixteen-Per-Cent," removed his glasses and covered his sore eyes with the palms of his hands. He had earned the nickname when he had managed to obtain that figure in grain deliveries throughout the reluctant town of Voronkov. Secrets, songs, popular legends had evolved around Osmolovsky's percentage.

Chewing his bread and onion, he spread out in front of him a copy of *Pravda*, the instructions of the District Committee and the directives on collectivization from the People's Commissariat for Agriculture. It was late, after one o'clock, when his door opened and a woman in a shawl tied crosswise in front appeared in his doorway.

"Judge," Gapa said, "what'll happen to the whores?"

Osmolovsky lifted his face, covered by patches of light.

"They'll gradually disappear."

"Will they be left in peace, the whores, or not?"

"They will," the judge said, "but they'll find that some other way of life pays better."

The woman stared into a corner with unseeing eyes. She touched the string of beads on her breast and said:

"Thanks for what you said."

The beads made a clinking sound. Gapa walked out, closing the door behind her.

The raging, piercing night hurled itself upon her, tossing about the bushes of clouds and the hunchbacked masses of ice with their black reflections. The low-flying clouds swept by, growing lighter as they passed. Silence spread over Velikaya Krinitsa, over the flat, grave-like, icy desert of the village night.

Translated by Andrew R. MacAndrew

Mama, Rimma and Alla*

From morning on, the day had been a busy one.

The maid had become difficult and quit the evening before, and Varvara Stepanovna had to do everything herself. Secondly—the electricity bill came first thing in the morning. Thirdly—the two student lodgers, the Rastokhin brothers, made a quite unexpected claim. They said they had received a telegram from Kaluga in the middle of the night informing them that their father was ill and summoning them to his bedside. Therefore, they were giving notice that they were vacating the room and wanted Varvara Stepanovna to return them the sixty rubles she had borrowed from them.

To this, Varvara Stepanovna replied that it was unusual to vacate the room in April when no one was likely to rent it, and that she found it difficult to refund them the sixty rubles because she hadn't really received that sum as a loan but as rent, although, it is true, it had been paid in advance.

The Rastokhins didn't go along with Varvara Stepanovna's arguments. The conversation took on a protracted, unfriendly character. The students were a couple of stubborn blockheads in neat, long-skirted coats. They felt they might as well kiss their money

* Published in *Letopis*, 1916, no. 11, pp. 37-44.

good-bye. The older brother then suggested that Varvara Stepanovna should give them her dining room sideboard and pierglass as security.

Varvara Stepanovna turned scarlet and declared that she wouldn't tolerate being spoken to in that tone, that the Rastokhins' suggestion was absolutely outrageous, that she was quite familiar with the law and that her husband was a member of the circuit court at Kamchatka. The younger Rastokhin exploded and said that they didn't give a lousy goddamn whether her husband was a circuit judge in Kamchatka or not, that when Varvara Stepanovna once got hold of a kopek, no one could ever claw it out of her hand and that the brothers would never forget their stay at Varvara Stepanovna's, with all the mess, filth and fuss, and that, although the Kamchatka circuit court was far away, the Moscow justice of the peace was nearby.

And that's how the conversation ended. The Rastokhins left, pouting in dumb spite, and Varvara Stepanovna went to the kitchen to make some coffee for her other lodger, a student called Stanislaw Marchotski. Sharp rings had been coming from his room for quite a while.

Varvara Stepanovna stood in the kitchen in front of the kerosene stove. On her thick nose sat an old nickel-plated set of pince-nez which had grown loose with age, her graying hair was dishevelled, the pink cardigan she wore in the mornings was covered with stains. She was making coffee and thinking to herself that those nasty brats would never have dared to speak to her in that tone if it hadn't been for the eternal shortage of money that unfortunately drove her to grab whatever she could lay her hands on, to maneuver and pretend.

When Marchotski's coffee and omelet were ready, she took his breakfast to his room.

Marchotski was a tall, blond, bony Pole with polished fingernails and long legs. That morning he was wearing an elegant housecoat with frog fastenings.

He looked at Varvara Stepanovna with displeasure.

"I've had enough of this," he said. "The maid never answers. I have to keep ringing for her for a whole hour and then I'm late for my lectures . . ."

It was true that often the maid wasn't there and that Marchotski had to ring for a long time. But this time his displeasure was caused by something else.

The previous evening, he and Rimma, Varvara Stepanovna's older daughter, had sat on the sofa in the living room. Varvara Stepanovna saw them exchange perhaps three kisses and then put their arms around each other in the darkness. They sat there until eleven, until midnight, then Stanislaw put his head on Rimma's bosom and went to sleep. But who, in his youth, hasn't dozed in the corner of a sofa on the bosom of a pretty schoolgirl met on the path of life? There's nothing so wicked about that, and it has no sad consequences. But still, one ought to have consideration for others and remember, for instance, that the girl might have to be at school the following morning.

It was only at one-thirty that Varvara Stepanovna declared rather sourly that some people ought to know when to stop. Marchotski, full of Polish susceptibility, pressed his lips together and left the room. And Rimma darted a furious look at her mother.

And that's how the matter had ended. But Stanislaw apparently was still thinking of it the next morning. Varvara Stepanovna brought in his breakfast, put some salt on his omelet and left.

*

At eleven, Varvara Stepanovna pulled back the curtains in her daughters' room. The gleaming beams of the still cool sun lay on the rather dirty floor, on the clothes scattered all over the room, on the dusty bookshelf.

The girls awoke. The elder, Rimma, was small, slight, quick-eyed, black-haired. Alla, a year younger than her sister—only seventeen—was white and slow-moving, with tender, soft skin and languorous, dreamy blue eyes.

When their mother had left, she spoke. Her full, bare arm lay on the blanket, her pretty white fingers moving perceptibly.

"Rimma," she said, "let me tell you what I dreamed. Imagine a small town, very small, a strange Russian town . . . A low, light-gray sky and the line of the horizon very close. And in the narrow streets, the dust is gray, smooth and undisturbed. The whole place is dead, Rimma. No sound, no one around. And then I'm walking along those unknown narrow streets, past the quiet little wooden houses. I keep getting into dead ends, then finding my way out again onto the main street where I can only see ten steps or so ahead of me, but I keep walking on and on, indefinitely. Somewhere ahead of me there's a twisting column of light dust. I come closer to it and see wedding carriages there. In one of the carriages sits Mikhail with his fiancée. She is wearing a long bridal veil and looks very happy. I walk alongside the carriages and it seems to me that I am taller than anyone there, and that there is a slight pain in my heart. Then they all notice me. The carriages come to a stop. Mikhail comes over to me, takes me by the arm, and slowly leads me away into a sidestreet. 'My dear Alla,' he says in a flat voice, 'I know how sad all this is. But it can't be helped because I don't love you.' And so I walk by his side, my heart fluttering, and new gray paths keep opening up in front of us."

Alla fell silent.

"A bad dream," she added then, "but who knows, perhaps just because it was bad, everything will change for the better and that letter will come."

"The hell it will," Rimma said. "You should have used your head before, instead of running to see him . . . I, by the way," she said unexpectedly, "am going to have it out with Mama today."

Rimma got up and went over to the window.

Spring had come to Moscow. Warm dampness glistened on the long, bleak fence opposite their window. It ran almost all the way to the end of the narrow sidestreet.

In the churchyard the grass was damp and green. The sun softly gilded the tarnished settings, rippling over the dark figure of the icon set on a leaning post by the entrance to the yard.

The girls went into the dining room. There, Varvara Stepaanovna was seated at the table, eating with great concentration, attentively examining through her glasses the toast, the coffee and the ham. She drank her coffee in short, resounding gulps and ate the small piece of toast quickly, avidly, almost stealthily.

"Mama," Rimma said sternly, lifting her fine little face proudly,

"I must have a talk with you, Mama. Don't flare up now. Everything can be settled quietly, once and for all. I cannot live with you any longer. Let me go. I want to be free."

"Please suit yourself," Varvara Stepanovna said, quietly raising her colorless eyes to Rimma's. "Is this because of what happened yesterday?"

"Not because of yesterday, but because of him. I'm suffocating here."

"So what do you intend to do?"

"I'll take a shorthand course. There's great demand now for. . . ."

"They're using shorthand-typists to bait fish, there're so many of them around. But perhaps they're just waiting for you."

"I won't come running back to you, Mama," Rimma said stridently. "I won't come running back to ask you for help. Let me go."

"Please go ahead," Varvara Stepanovna said again. "I'm not stopping you."

"Give me my passport."

"No, I won't give you your passport."

The conversation had been an unexpectedly quiet one, but now Rimma felt that the passport gave her a good reason to get angry.

"Well, I like that," she said with a sarcastic burst of laughter. "Who'll ever rent me a room without my passport?"

"I won't give you your passport."

"Then I'll find a man to keep me," Rimma shouted hysterically. "I'll sell myself to a policeman."

"Who'll take you?" Varvara Stepanovna said, looking up and down the slight, trembling figure and flushed face of her daughter. "So you think a policeman can't find anything better than you?"

"I'll go out on Tverskaya Street," Rimma raged. "I'll go and live with some old man. I can't go on living with you any more, you stupid, stupid, stupid fool."

"Ah, so that's the way you talk to your mother," Varvara Stepanovna said in a dignified tone as she got up, "and at a time when we're so hard up, just when everything is collapsing in the house, when we're having such a tough time. I'm trying to take my mind off it all for a second, but you . . . Papa will have to know about this."

"I'll write to Kamchatka myself," Rimma shouted hysterically. "I'll get my passport from Papa."

Varvara Stepanovna walked out of the room. Little Rimma paced up and down in agitation. Individual irate phrases from her future letter to her father flashed through her head.

"Dear Papa," she'd write, "I'm well aware that you have your own worries but I must tell you . . . I leave to Mama's conscience her accusation that Stannie slept on my bosom. He slept on an embroidered cushion, but the center of gravity was somewhere else again. Mama is your wife and you're bound to be partial but still, I can't live at home any more. She's a difficult person to get along with. If you wish, I'll come and join you in Kamchatka, but anyway, I need my passport, Papa."

Rimma walked up and down. Alla sat on the sofa, looking at her sister. Quiet, sad thoughts came down on her heart.

"Rimma is worrying," Alla thought, "but I'm just miserable. Everything's so painful, so complicated."

She went to her room and lay on the bed. Varvara Stepanovna passed by in her corset, thickly and naively powdered, flushed, worried and pitiful.

"I just remembered," Varvara Stepanovna said, "the Rastokhins are leaving today. I have to pay them back sixty rubles. They threatened to sue me. The eggs are on the shelf— make some for yourself. I'm off to the pawn shop."

When Marchotski returned from his lecture at around six, he saw packed suitcases in the entrance hall. Noise was coming from the Rastokhins' room. They must have been having an argument. He was still in the hall when Varvara Stepanovna came to him and, with the determination of despair, borrowed ten rubles from him. It was only when he was back in his room that Marchotski realized his blunder.

Before Stanislaw had even had time to change into his house jacket, Rimma walked quietly into the room. She was received quite coolly.

"Are you angry with me, Stannie?" the girl asked.

"I'm not angry," the Pole said, "but I'd have greatly appreciated it if I could have been spared being a witness to your mother's excesses."

"Soon it'll all be over," Rimma said. "Soon I'll be free, Stannie."

She sat down next to him on the little divan and put her arm round him.

"I am a man," Stanislaw began then, "and this Platonic stuff is not for me. I have my career to think of."

And irritatedly he went through all the phrases that, in the end, at one time or another, men address to certain women, to whom they have nothing to say, whose tenderness bores them, who are reluctant to get down to business.

Stannie said that desire was oppressing him, preventing him from studying, making him anxious; it must be settled one way or the other—he hardly cared which way, so long as it was settled.

"Why are you saying all this now?" Rimma said thoughtfully. "Why should you come out with this 'I'm a man' and 'it must be settled?' Why is your face so cold and angry? Do we really have nothing else to talk about? Oh, this is all so painful, Stannie. It's spring outside; everything's so beautiful while we're so irritated."

Stannie didn't answer. They fell silent.

A fiery sunset was going out, flooding the far-off sky with its blood-red gleam. From the other side of the sky a flimsy, slowly thickening darkness was descending. The room was lit by the last reddish light. On the divan, Rimma was leaning more and more tenderly toward the student. What was happening was the same thing that went on almost daily between the two of them at that beautiful hour.

Stanislaw kissed the girl. She put her head on the pillow and closed her eyes. Both caught fire. A few minutes later, Stanislaw was kissing her constantly and in a fit of angry and unquenchable passion was tossing her slight, hot body around. He tore her blouse and her brassiere. Rimma, her lips dry and with circles under her eyes, offered her mouth for his kisses while defending her virginity with a twisted, sorrowful grin. In the middle of it, someone knocked on the door and Rimma started helplessly rushing about the room, pressing the rags of her blouse to her bosom.

They took their time opening the door. Then it turned out that it was a friend of Stanislaw's from the university. The man followed Rimma with a sarcastic look as she slipped past him out of the door.

Rimma darted into her own room and went over to the window to cool off.

*

In the pawnshop, they gave Varvara Stepanovna only forty rubles for the family silver. But then she had the ten rubles from Marchotski. To get the rest of the money, she went to the Tikhonovs, walking all the way from Strastnoi Avenue to Pokrovka Street. In her agitation, it never even occurred to her that she might have taken the streetcar.

At home, besides the raging Rastokhins, Mirlits, a lawyer's clerk, was waiting for her. He'd come on business. He was a tall young man with rotten stumps for teeth and gray, liquid, rather stupid eyes.

Some time ago, hard pressed for money, Varvara Stepanovna had decided to mortgage a small house her husband owned in Kolomna. Mirlits had brought the draft of the deed. Varvara Stepanovna had the impression that something was wrong and that she ought to ask someone for advice before going ahead with the transaction. But she had, she said to herself, more than her share of troubles, and so to hell with everything, with her lodgers, with her daughter, with all the disobliging things she had to listen to.

After talking about business, Mirlits uncorked a bottle of Crimean muscatel. He knew this was Varvara Stepanovna's weakness. They emptied a glass each and were ready for another. Their voices rang louder. Varvara Stepanovna's fleshy nose turned red, the whalebones of her corset bulged out till they could be counted. Mirlits was telling a very funny story and roaring with laughter. Rimma, who had changed her torn blouse, sat quietly in a corner.

When they had emptied the bottle of muscatel, Varvara Stepanovna and Mirlits went out for a walk. Varvara Stepanovna felt slightly drunk and was rather ashamed, but at the same time she didn't really care because she had too much trouble in life as it was —so, to hell with everything.

Varvara Stepanovna got back earlier than she had planned because the Boikos, whom she had gone to visit, hadn't been home. She was struck by the silence reigning in the place. Usually at this hour her daughters were fooling around with the students, giggling and dashing about. The only sound came from the bathroom. Varvara Stepanovna went to the kitchen where she peered through a small, high, inside window from which she could see what was going on in the bathroom.

Her eyes met an extraordinary scene.

The hot water boiler was red hot. The bathtub was half-filled with boiling water. Rimma was kneeling by the boiler. She was holding a pair of curling tongs in the fire. Alla, completely naked, stood by the bath. Her long plaits were undone. Tears were rolling from her eyes.

"Come here," Alla said. "Listen, can you hear its heart beating?"

Rimma put her ear against the silky, slightly swollen belly.

"I can't hear it," Rimma said, "but that makes no difference. There's no possible doubt."

"I'll die," Alla said. "I'll be scalded in that water. I won't be able to stand it. We don't need the tongs and, anyway, you don't know how it's done."

"Everybody's doing it this way," Rimma said. "Stop whimpering, Alla. Why, you don't really want to have the baby, do you?"

Just as Alla was about to get into the boiling bath, they heard the quiet, inimitable, slightly hoarse voice of their mother:

"What are you up to, children?"

A couple of hours later, Alla, tucked in, caressed and cried over, lay on Varvara Stepanovna's wide bed. She had told everything. She felt relieved. She thought of herself now as a small girl who had gone through a silly, childish sorrow.

Rimma was moving about the room wordlessly and noiselessly. She tidied up, made some tea for her mother, forced her to eat something and made the place look clean and comfortable. Then she lit the icon lamp which, for two weeks or so, they had kept forgetting to fill with oil, undressed and lay down on the bed next to her sister.

Varvara Stepanovna sat at the table. She could see the little lamp. Its dark red flame threw a dim light on the Virgin Mary. The alcohol vapors were still turning strangely and lightly inside her head. Soon the girls were asleep. Alla's face was large, white and calm. Rimma was leaning against her, sighing and shivering in her sleep.

At around one in the morning, Varvara Stepanovna lit a candle, placed a sheet of paper before her and wrote a letter to her husband:

Dear Nikolai,

Mirlits came to see me today. He is a very decent Jew. Tomorrow I am expecting the gentleman who is bringing me the money for the house. I think I am doing the right thing but I keep worrying because I'm never sure of myself.

I know that you have your own worries and your work and perhaps I shouldn't bother you with this, but our life here does not seem to be going too well. The children are almost grown up and, nowadays, life is very demanding on young people—they have to take courses, learn shorthand and all that sort of thing. So the girls want to be more independent. They need a father. Perhaps I should shout at them but it is useless to rely on me for that. I can't help thinking that your departure for Kamchatka was a mistake. If you had been here now we could have moved to Starokolenny Street where they have a nice, light little apartment for rent.

Rimma has grown very thin and doesn't look too well. For a whole month I ordered cream from the dairy and the girls picked up some weight, but I have stopped taking it now. My liver makes itself felt at times and at others it leaves me in peace. Write more often. After your letters I am more careful; I don't eat salt herring and then my liver doesn't bother me. I wish you'd come back, Koliya, and we could all have a good rest. The girls send you their love. Many kisses,

your Varvara.

Translated by Andrew R. MacAndrew

Ilya Isaakovich and Margarita Prokofievna*

Ilya Isaakovich Gershkovich left the police inspector with a heavy heart. He had been told that if he were not on board the first train out of Orel he'd be sent out forcibly with an escort. And leaving now meant losing business for him.

Lean and unhurried, his briefcase in his hand, he walked down the street. A tall female shape on the street corner called out to him:

"Won't you drop in on me, dearie?"

Gershkovich raised his eyebrows, glanced at the woman through his flashing glasses, thought for a second and answered with composure:

"All right, I'll drop in."

The woman took his arm and they turned the corner.

"Where are we off to? To the hotel?"

"I must spend the whole night at your place," Gershkovich said.

"That'll cost you three rubles."

"How about two?"

"It don't pay."

They settled on two-fifty. They went on.

* Published in *Letopis*, 1916, no. 11, pp. 32-37.

The whore's room was small and clean, with torn curtains and a pink lantern.

When they walked in, she took off her coat, unbuttoned her blouse . . . and winked.

"Ah," Gershkovich said, screwing up his face, "how idiotic."

"You're in an angry mood."

She sat on his knee.

"I bet," Gershkovich said, "you weigh around a hundred and ninety?"

"Hundred and seventy-five."

She kissed his graying temple violently.

*

"Ah," Gershkovich said, screwing up his face again, "I feel so tired."

The whore stood up. Her face became spiteful.

"Are you a Jew?"

He looked at her through his glasses and said:

"No."

"Listen," she said, speaking with deliberate slowness, "that'll be ten rubles."

He rose and crossed toward the door.

"A fiver," the woman said.

Gershkovich came back.

"Make my bed then," the Jew said in a tired voice. He took off his jacket and looked for a place to hang it. "What's your name?"

"Margarita."

"Change the sheets, Margarita."

It was a wide bed with a soft eiderdown.

Gershkovich started to undress slowly, pulled off his light socks, fanned out his sweaty toes, locked the door with the key, put the key under his pillow and lay down. Margarita, yawning, unhurriedly removed her dress, watching Gershkovich out of the corner of her eye, squeezed a pimple on her shoulder and started braiding her thin hair for the night.

"What's your name?"

"Ilya Isaakovich."

"You a shopkeeper? What d'you sell?"

"What we sell . . ." Gershkovich answered ambiguously.

Margarita blew out the candle and got into bed.

"You eat well," Gershkovich said, "I can feel that."

Soon after that they were both asleep.

*

The following morning, bright sunbeams filled the room. Gershkovich awoke, dressed and went over to the window.

"We have the sea—you have the countryside," he said. "It's lovely."

"Where're you from?"

"Odessa," Gershkovich said, "the country's first city, the nicest." He smiled slyly.

"You," Margarita said, "I can see you feel nice wherever you are."

"That's right," Gershkovich agreed. "It's nice wherever there are people around."

"You're a damn fool," she said, sitting up in her bed, "people are mean."

"No," Gershkovich said, "they're nice. They were led to believe they're mean and they believed it."

Margarita thought for a while and then smiled.

"You're funny," she said slowly and looked him up and down. "Look the other way while I dress."

After that they had tea and rolls for breakfast. Gershkovich showed Margarita how he buttered his roll and put a slice of salami on top in a special way.

"Try it some time," he said. "But come to think of it, I must be on my way."

As he was leaving, Gershkovich said:

"Take three rubles, Margarita. Believe me, there's nowhere I can make a kopek around here."

Margarita smiled.

"You miserable skinflint. All right, let's have the three rubles. Will you come back in the evening?"

"I will."

In the evening Gershkovich turned up with supper: a herring, a bottle of beer, a salami, some apples. Margarita wore a dark dress, long-sleeved and closed at the neck. As they ate, they talked.

"Fifty a month don't go round in this trade," Margarita explained to him. "If I don't dress right, I don't get enough for a plateful of soup in the evening. And you must remember, I pay fifteen for the room."

Gershkovich thought for a moment, then declared, as he concentrated on cutting the herring into two even pieces:

"In Odessa, where I come from," he said, "you can have a palatial room for ten rubles in the Moldavanka district."

"You have to take into account too," Margarita said, "the fact that I come across all sorts and can't always avoid drunks."

"Everyone has his worries," Gershkovich said, and he told her about his family troubles, about his shaky business situation, about his son who had been drafted into the army.

Margarita listened to him; she rested her head on the table and there was a quiet, attentive, dreamy expression on her face.

After supper Gershkovich took off his jacket, wiped his glasses thoroughly with a piece of cloth, pulled the kerosene lamp toward him, sat at the table and wrote business letters. Margarita went to wash her hair.

Gershkovich wrote slowly, raising his eyebrows in concentration and now and then stopping to think. After he had dipped his pen in the ink, he always remembered to shake off the excess drops.

When he was through with his writing, he sat Margarita on his ledger.

"I say you're a real weighty lady. Please sit here, Ma'am—do me the honor."

Gershkovich smiled, his glasses gleamed and his eyes became tiny, shiny cracks.

The next day he left. As he walked up and down the platform waiting for his train, he caught sight of Margarita. She was coming toward him, walking in little steps. She was carrying a small package. The package contained little meat pies and, in spots, the fat had soaked through the wrapping paper.

Margarita's face was red and miserable, her bosom was heaving from walking fast.

"Give my love to Odessa," she said, "give it my love."

"Thanks," Gershkovich said. He took the pies, raised his eyebrows, thought of something and shrank into himself.

The final bell sounded. They shook hands.

"Good-bye, Margarita Prokofievna."

"Good-bye, Ilya Isaakovich."

Gershkovich got into the carriage and the train moved off.

Translated by Andrew R. MacAndrew

The Tale of a Woman*

Once upon a time there lived a woman called Ksenya. Big bosom, heavy shoulders, blue eyes. That's the kind of woman she was. Couldn't wish for a better one for you or me!

Her husband was killed in the war. For three years the woman lived without a husband, working for a rich family. Three times a day those people had to have a hot meal. They never burned wood in the stove; nothing but coal. The heat from coals is unbearable; fiery roses glow in them.

For three years the woman cooked for those people and behaved uprightly with men. But what are you going to do if you have a forty-pound bosom? What can you expect?

Her fourth year there, she went to see a doctor and said to him:

* "The Tale of a Woman [Skazka pro babu]," published in Siluety, 1923, no. 8-9, pp. 5, 6, and in Krasnaya Nov, 1924, no. 4.

Although this story was published at the same time as Red Cavalry, it reminds one more of the Letopis stories (1916). This calls attention to the difficulty of assigning a specific date to any one story, whether the author chooses to date it or not. "The Tale of a Woman" may well have been written during an earlier period and later reworked for publication. Konstantin Paustovsky has pointed out that this process of rewriting was characteristic of Babel's method of work. (See Dissonant Voices in Soviet Literature, edited by Patricia Blake and Max Hayward, Pantheon Books, 1962, pp. 46-47.)

"My head feels something terrible. Either it's like fire in there, or else I go weak all over."

And the doctor came out with:

"What's the matter? Aren't there any fellows around your yard, or what? Ah, woman—"

"I wouldn't dare," Ksenya whined. "I'm sensitive."

And it's true that she was sensitive. There was a rather bitter tear in her blue eyes. So the old Morozikha woman took things in hand.

The old Morozikha woman was midwife and quack for the whole street. The likes of her are pitiless with a woman's insides. They'll steam them out and after that even grass won't grow there.

"I," she said, "can guarantee results, Ksenya. It's just like the earth getting dry and splitting into cracks. All it needs is for God to send a little rain, see. A woman must always have that mushroom stuff coming up in her, damp and stinky, you know."

And she brought someone. Valentin Ivanovich he was called. Not much to look at, but good fun—knew how to put a song together. Nobody to speak of, long hair and a whole rainbow of pimples. But what did Ksenya need? He made up songs, he was a man —what more could she ask for? So the woman cooked maybe a hundred pancakes and a plum cake, and put three featherbeds and six pillows on the bed, all of them soft and downy. Now come and roll yourself on it, Valentin!

In the evening, company packed the tiny room off the kitchen. Everyone emptied a glass of vodka. Morozikha wore her silk kerchief and looked terribly respectable. And Valentin made a marvelous speech:

"Ah, Ksenya, my dear, dear friend, I'm a man who's been abandoned in this world, an underfed youth. I don't want you to be somehow thinking lightly of me. When night comes down with its stars and black fans, a poem isn't enough to express one's feelings. Ah, I'm awful timid . . ."

One word followed another and, of course, they killed two bottles of vodka and three of wine on top of that. Without exaggerating, easily five rubles went on the refreshments—and that's nothing to spit at.

Valentin turned from pink to positively brown, and his voice sounded like a trumpet when he started reciting poetry.

Then Morozikha got up from the table.

"The way I see it, Ksenya dearie," she said, "God bless me, you two, you'll love each other. So," she said, "when you lie down, make him pull off his boots, otherwise you'll never stop laundering with a man."

But the vodka was doing its work and Valentin clutched his head, then pulled his hair and started twisting it.

"I," he said, "have visions. I always have visions after I've had a few drinks. And now I see you, Ksenya, and you're dead and your face is a disgusting sight, and I'm a priest and I'm walking behind your coffin and waving a censer."

And at this point, naturally, he raised his voice.

Well, she was just a woman after all and it goes without saying she had already unbuttoned her blouse, as it were by coincidence.

"Don't shout, Valentin Ivanovich," Ksenya whispered, "don't holler like that. The mistress will hear."

But what chance did she have of stopping a fellow once he felt so bitter?

"You've really offended me," Valentin declared, weeping and rocking back and forth. "Ah, you sneaky people! What did you want to do? Buy my soul? Ah no, I may be illegitimate, but I'm still a nobleman's son, d'you hear, you cook?"

"I'll be nice to you, Valentin Ivanovich."

"Let me go."

He got up and threw open the door.

"Let me go out into the world."

But how could he go, the poor thing, in his drunken condition? So that servant of God fell onto the bed, gave a good belch, spewed over the sheets, if you'll pardon the expression, and fell asleep.

But Morozikha was already busy.

"There's no sense leaving him here," she said. "We'll carry him out."

So the women carried Valentin out to the street and laid him down by the gate. They went back and there was Ksenya's mistress waiting for them in her housecap and the kind of pants rich women wear, and she reprimanded her cook!

"So, you receive men at night and have orgies in your room. I'm giving you notice, here and now, and I want you out of my house tomorrow morning. This is a respectable family," Ksenya's mistress said, "and moreover, I have an unmarried daughter in the house."

Until the blue dawn, Ksenya cried desperately and kept repeating:

"Grandma Morozikha, ah, Grandma Morozikha, what have you done to me, me a young woman? I'm ashamed of myself. How can I raise my eyes and look at God's world, and what can I expect from it now?"

The woman wept and complained, sitting amid the plum cakes, amid the snow-white featherbeds, the holy icon lamps and the grape wine. And her warm shoulders shook.

"It was a mistake," Morozikha answered. "What we needed was someone simpler. We should have taken Mitya."

And the day had come round again. The milkgirls were going from house to house. It was a pale blue morning, a frosty one.

Translated by Andrew R. MacAndrew

LETTERS

In February, 1925, Babel's sister left Russia for Belgium, where she was joined by her mother in July of the following year. The letters in this volume from February 1925, until July 1926, some of which bear no salutation, are therefore addressed to Babel's sister alone; after July, 1926, Babel's letters are addressed to his sister and mother, who were living together in Brussels.

Babel's sister, Meri Emmanuelovna Babel, was born in 1899. She is referred to in the letters by various names and diminutives: Mera, Merochka, Mendel, Mendele, Mendelovich, Pupik, Kisya, etc. Her husband, Dr. Grigori Shaposhnikov, is sometimes called Grisha or Esculapius. Dr. and Mrs. Shaposhnikov still reside in Brussels.

Fanya Aronovna Shvevel, Babel's mother, was born in Odessa in 1868, and died in Brussels in 1942. Babel refers to her variously as Fenya, Fedoseyushka, Fenka, etc.

N.B.

1 9 2 5

This is to let you know the result of our latest family council: in a few days I will probably leave for the Caucasus, to undergo a course of treatment there. I'll be away for a month and a half to two months (the treatment takes a month and a half). When I return to Moscow, I will do my best to get permission for us all to go abroad—that is, for me (and Zhenya,* of course) to go to the south of France or to Italy, to rid myself once and for all if possible of all my ailments. And it would be very nice if Mama could spend the summer with you while I am taking this cure, and then we could all meet in Paris in the fall. I am writing all this tentatively only, since I don't know what your plans for the summer are, but I imagine we will be able to adjust to each other anyway. If you have no objection to this arrangement, I would ask you to start *right away* making the necessary efforts to get a visa for Mama, because it's always a long business. We, of course, will not need Belgian visas as we are planning to accompany Mama only as far as Berlin where we will hand her over to you, and then go on from there to whatever spa they tell us to. Let us know *at once and urgently* about anything that may come up concerning this matter, because we will be handing in our applications for passports for travel abroad in a couple of days, so that they can prepare the passports while I'm in the Caucasus. You can write to our Moscow address, because Mama and Zhenya will mostly be there from now on. I consider it essential to carry out this plan—it is time to take drastic steps to restore my health and I think such steps will be possible. Pass my request about the visa on to Shapi and tell him that he would oblige our entire "famille" by being helpful. Write to me in Moscow immediately. I'll let you know my address in the Caucasus later.

Your Is

P.S. I have given you such a terse account of this matter, because I decided to leave Mama the chance to write you sixteen pages of dampened text, which you will receive tomorrow. As you will see, we have not only taken care of down-to-earth matters—caviar, halvah†—we are also guarding your spiritual interests and providing you with an entertaining account of life in Odessa.

I.B.

* Evgenia Borisovna Gronfein (Zhenya) was born on November 9, 1897, in Pereyaslav (Ukraine), was married to Isaac Babel in 1919 in Odessa. She lived in France from 1925 until her death on May 17, 1957.

Beginning with the 1930's, Zhenya is referred to occasionally as "Enta" for reasons of censorship.

† Words like halvah, caviar, mushrooms, and books are used more often than not as code words to signify the dispatch of money.

Moscow, May 12, 1925

Dearest Pupik,

Three days ago I returned from a trip to Kiev and Kharkov. Have a lot of work to do. I propose to move to Sergievo tomorrow so that I can get it down. I have to write several scenarios. I may have to sit in Sergievo* for a month or more. I've sent for Zhenya to come here too. B.D.† is a little better, but she is still an invalid and a very troublesome one. Zhenya will bring her to the summerhouse, where she will arrange for a nurse to come, and then she will come to Moscow to take the final steps about the passport and visa. It's quite likely that Zhenya will go abroad by herself in the summer, because I have a multitude of things which I cannot possibly get out of doing. Mama's trip to visit you also looks impracticable to us for the moment. Mama could only come if you were firmly settled somewhere (Paris, for instance). She would not be able to travel around abroad in search of a place to settle. So Mama and I will wait till we hear from you on this subject. If Sh.‡ finishes this year and settles down somewhere toward autumn, then we could talk about Mama's coming over. As far as I could gather from our conversation in Kiev, Zhenya is planning to go to France or Italy, but it's very hard to obtain a French visa in Moscow. You have to go through Italy or find some other means. Perhaps you could give us some advice in this matter or be of actual assistance? I suppose Mama has written to you that my health has improved. I had a pretty bad winter, but now I feel fine. Apparently the northern winter has a ruinous effect on me. But my mental state leaves much to be desired. Like everyone else in my profession, I am oppressed by the prevailing conditions of our work in Moscow; that is, we are seething in a sickening professional environment devoid of art or creative freedom. And now that I am swaggering among the generals, I feel it more strongly than before. My earnings are satisfactory and in a few days we'll send you a small sum. We received the pictures. I think they came out very well. Can you find out whether my book has come out in Russian in Paris? Is it possible to get it? Are you busy with languages as before? How do you plan to spend the summer? You should go for walks, go out to the countryside. In the West, that's easily arranged. Above all—don't laze around. And on that note, good-bye.

Regards to Shaposhnikov,

With love,
I. Babel

---

* Sergievo, now renamed Zagorsk, is a small city about forty-five miles from Moscow. Babel lived there with his family in 1924.

† B.D. is Berta Davydovna ("Blyuma") Gronfein, Babel's mother-in-law.

‡ "Sh." is Shaposhnikov.

Moscow, June 5, 1925

Dear Mera,

I haven't yet been to Sergievo and so haven't read your letters. I expect Mama will bring them to Moscow tomorrow. I am awfully glad you have moved to Brussels. Don't try to save a hundred francs or so, but get a better apartment—you must keep in mind that one day Mama may come and stay with you. They're not issuing Belgian transit visas here; in four days or so, Zhenya is leaving for Paris. In a few days, I'll send the story to be translated from Sergievo. Next week we'll send you fifty dollars. But where, to Brussels or to Liége? I enclose a letter to Shaposhnikov, Surgeon and Obstetrician.

Yours, I.

Moscow, July 15, 1925

Tomorrow, July 16, I'll send you seventy-five rubles which I trust you will receive in good time and spend to good purpose. The day after tomorrow, I am leaving for Voronezh Province to spend a couple of weeks at the Khrenovaya stud farm and then I'll come back to Moscow to see Zhenya off. The whole question is whether Sylvia will get her visa or not. We are going through difficult times now. I still intend to take a cure in Kislovodsk* toward the end of the summer. I would have very much liked to simplify my family life, that is, not to be divided among three or four households. I'm waiting impatiently for you to settle somewhere, for only then will we be able to speak about Mama's and my trip. What are your plans and prospects in this respect? Zhenya promises to send you medical journals. Please send me any translations and any articles mentioning me *you may come across*. In August, Mama and I intend to go to Odessa for the unveiling of the monument.† By the fall, I'll be out of Sergievo, for I *must* spend the winter in the south. Have completed a scenario for the movies. According to competent authorities, I did a good job. Generally speaking, I have suddenly manifested some talent where movies are concerned and so am sort of a success in that field. From the money point of view, it is better than pure literature. Now that I have completed the scenario, I'll go back to my usual work and in the fall will write another scenario. You *must* go to the seashore for a while. Ostend is, I think, too expensive a spa and something you don't really need, but I think you would immensely enjoy living for a while in a fishing village. We'll wire you the money you'll need. Give me a quick answer. Tomorrow is your birthday. Congratulations, the best of health to you and, above all, be cheerful. Write and tell me whether you have grown cleverer abroad and whether you have become accustomed to the life there. Kolya is now in Moscow. Thanks to his character, he has already lost a job, I believe. But there is hope that he will find another one.

My heartfelt greetings to Shaposhnikov,

Good-bye, my dearly beloved Pupik,

Your loving I. Babel

* Kislovodsk is a health resort in the Caucasus, famous for the mineral water "Narzan."
† Babel is referring to the tombstone for the grave of his father, who died in 1923.

Sergievo, August 21, 1925

Dear Mera,

We got your letter. Zhenya left for Kiev on the eighteenth. On the twenty-fifth, Mama is leaving for Odessa. In forthcoming weeks, I'll be here alone. I am still working for the movies. It is quite possible that I may have to make a trip abroad in connection with my cinematographic activities. On what dates exactly will be decided between the fifth and the tenth of September. Do you think we could possibly get a Belgian visa? I wish you would see to it, but only if it is a *very* easy matter. A letter has arrived from Mme. Rollin; she writes that the wheels are greased. M. Rollin is trying to get things going, but according to their regulations, it is necessary to make *une demande* here to the French Embassy. But unfortunately, they are not accepting any *demandes* here, which makes entry into France very difficult indeed. This unexpected obstacle does delay the matter but I hope to overcome it somehow.

It is quite possible and even probable that, during the trip, I will be able to detach myself from the expedition for a few days and go and spend time in Liége. If you don't succeed in moving to France, what will you do then? I think you ought to be prepared for the eventuality that they won't let you in that soon, and have an alternative plan in reserve. This concerns me very much because if you don't have anything definite, Mama will have to spend the winter in Moscow alone. Write what you think about all the questions raised here. I sent you a picture. Did you receive it? When you write to Mama now, write to Odessa; and when you write to me, write to Sergievo. Of course, Mama will let you know before she leaves. We hope you received the money.

I have nothing special more to report. Ledsky came to see us and said he had a friend whose aunt had met Shaposhnikov once last year in the cloakroom of a movie house, although the aunt is not quite certain whether it was really Shaposhnikov or some other man resembling him. But the movie was a good one, I believe; it was *The Mask of Zorro* with Douglas Fairbanks. The theater was very crowded and some fellows tried to cut out the aunt's pocket. As to her nephew, that superb young man with his statesmanlike wisdom . . . well, in brief, we received the message through Ledsky and so we wish good health both to you and to your husband.

Babel

Moscow, November 16, 1925

Dear Mera,

Here is the situation: Today Zhenya received all the transit visas and tomorrow we're buying her a train ticket. I suppose she will leave in about three days. As to me, business will hold me in Moscow for another six weeks or so. Only then will I be able to make any sort of plans for Mama and myself. During that time, you'll probably get acclimatized in Brussels. Shaposhnikov's job situation will be settled, and so on. Mama's trip is a serious matter for her and so it cannot be arranged in a hurry. Remember that you will have to make sure to get her a more or less permanent place to live.

I have ordered a few issues of *Meditsinskoye obozrenie* [*Medical Review*] and Sh. will soon receive them. I am holding things up with *Red Cavalry*** because I refuse to accept certain deletions. All this time I have been busy with the movies but in ten days or so will get back to purely literary work. I hope that by now you have received the money (seventy-five dollars). I was late sending it because Zhenya's trip led to unexpectedly large expenses. After I have handed in the scenario, I hope to receive quite a tidy sum of money and then I'll be able to supply you with a continuous flow of fuel. Tell Shap. that his article will be placed immediately and that the money for it has been sent.

My health has been quite satisfactory all this time.

With comradely greeting,
Yours respectfully,
I.B.

P.S. The money was sent to the Liége address. Have you seen to it that it will be forwarded to you? Mama has been in Moscow all this time preparing Zhenya for the trip. She will write to you promptly.

* *Red Cavalry*, a collection of short stories, was published in book form in 1926; the stories had appeared singly in various magazines during 1923-1925.

Moscow, December 20, 1925

My dear fool,
    I really shouldn't be writing to you because you never answered my letter, but I'm meek by nature and my pen is wordy. A brief

summary of news: Lyusya is fine and so is the girl. Tomorrow, Monday, they'll be discharged from the hospital and brought home. We are closing up at Sergievo. We have kept only one room there to store the furniture. Some of the furniture will be sent to Moscow. I am just about to finish up my cinematographic business. Possibly I will get an interesting assignment to go somewhere for a month, in which case Mama will have to stay alone in Moscow. There's news about our apartment: Rosa Lvovna is coming back from Paris. That will cheer the place up. Bobrovsky has only one room left. What do you think of my suggestion about coming to live in Russia? I must know how you feel about it because I must organize my life accordingly. It is my ardent wish that, of all our family, you at least should have a permanent, fixed home so that Mama would have a place to rest. Because, in order to accomplish the things I must do, I will have to travel a lot in the forthcoming years and face some other adventures. But that can't be helped. I have picked a hellish trade. Now, if you had a place in Russia where we could all meet, that would make my life so much easier. Try to understand that. From Zhenya, I receive nothing but telegrams. She arrived safely in Paris. So far, I have been writing to her at Sylvia's address: 64, Avenue du Maine, Paris XIV. What a woman—in two weeks she hasn't written me a word. Tell Comrade Shaposhnikov that I have sent him a great number of medical journals and that I bow to him to the ground. And also write me cheerful letters, you jailbird.

Your loving relative and Worker for Enlightenment no. 3929,

I.B.

1 9 2 6

Moscow, January 1, 1926

Dear Mendel,

First of all, I wish you and your husband a happy new year—good cheer, a calm life and persistence in the pursuit of your goals. These three, in my opinion, make for what is called happiness.

Now let me tell you about myself. Today is the day for drawing up the yearly balance sheet. For me personally, the balance sheet is not a favorable one. I must admit very frankly that I have gone backward rather than forward. I haven't done a thing as far as serious literature goes for about ten months, but have simply been hanging around in Moscow in search of big pay-offs, that is, taken the line of least resistance, a road which is loathsome to me. It turned out that I had neither the strength nor the foresight to avoid this odious road, but now I must at least find the strength within myself to stop. There are many unfulfilled obligations weighing on me. If I manage to hand in the work for which I have orders now, during the course of January, then I must go to Paris or to some even more exotic place, where I could straighten out my burdened spirit and do some real work. These considerations, and above all the fact that my only hope of salvation in 1926 lies in my not having to earn money, force us to think of the future, and, above all, about Mama. She and I both consider a journey abroad unnecessary. That's out. And since it's out, it wouldn't be so bad if you made yourselves a home in Russia, where (I and many other sensible people consider) it is possible to arrange one's life better, more honorably and more fruitfully than anywhere else. It would only be possible, however, for you to set yourself up here with my assistance. What can I offer you? A job—for you and for Shap. —right away, that is, a good living wage. Your knowledge of foreign languages, of course, would be a great help. Then, we can offer you a comfortable apartment in Leningrad which certainly would be no worse than the one you have in Brussels. But it is easier to live and to earn enough in Moscow than in Leningrad. I don't think there would be any great difficulty in exchanging our excellent room for two rooms, with very little additional outlay. Thus, by early spring, we could fix you up with two rooms. That's the maximum it would be possible to obtain with the present apartment crisis in Moscow. That's what I can offer you in the material sense, and as to spiritual life in Russia—and *scientific opportunities* —there's no need for me to tell you that they are richer and have a greater future than what you can expect in the West.

Think over this letter. Tell Shaposhnikov in your own words what I have written. Between the two of you, weigh the prospects soberly—East and West—and decide. Take into consideration the fact that I need help to get myself out of the snare in which I am caught and that Mama should be provided with a more meaningful life. In this letter I have only set forth for you the facts of mine and Mama's life and have drawn my conclusions from them. You may have considerations which refute all my conclusions. If you do, please tell me of them. Dear Pupik, since the female heads in our family tend to be narrow and weak, it's quite possible that you will get into a panic. Of course, there is absolutely no reason for panic. It's only that we need to "shorten the front line." And besides, Mama's and my suggestions are only *suggestions*, to which we expect countersuggestions.

Be well now, as a cow,

Your I.

Moscow, February 8, 1926

Oh crazy Maria,

We received your letter. I'm not sure whether it is an answer to what I sent you in secret from Mama. Anyway, what you have to say has greatly depressed me. You write of trips to Rumania and to Paris, but that is all transitory, and right now I am faced with an absolute necessity for a permanent arrangement. Until you and Mama settle down somewhere definitely, I can't move from here. And I must get out of here. With every day, living in Moscow become more painful and unfruitful for me, and to stay on here indefinitely would be to invite both material and spiritual poverty. Please think the matter over and decide at least for the next couple of years ahead whether you are going to return to Moscow or stay in Belgium, or whether you have a third alternative. I must know so that I can organize my very disorganized life. And moreover, we have to think of Mama and to do so quickly. I have very little time before me and you should take advantage of it, for in the future I will have to think mainly of myself and my neglected work. I beg you to listen to my entreaty and to help me, at least by bringing some clarity to our entangled and scattered "state." I'm waiting impatiently for the tobacco. We're having a fierce winter with temperatures of five and ten degrees below zero, but our room is warm. Next month I'll probably have to make a couple of trips—I must go to Petersburg and to Kharkov. . . . Lots to do—boring hackwork, and I just can't get down to real "things."

Yours expectantly,

I.

Leningrad, March 22, 1926

Dear Mera,

Poor Mama forwarded to me yours and Zhenya's letter. If she knew what was written in those letters! I will not enlarge upon the impression this latest news has made on me. Things are shaping up sadly enough as is. If the operation is unavoidable and will cure you completely, then I think it should be done at once. And I don't think it's worth while complicating the matter, that is, going to Paris for the operation; I'm sure there are doctors in Brussels who can perfectly well perform what is not, after all, such a complicated operation. And besides, it's of course very important that Shaposhnikov should be there. I don't know whether I can even dream of coming in time for the operation. As to any plans for the future, yours and Zhenya's letters have left me completely at a loss. In spite of my many letters, you can't even imagine the state of my affairs, which have become catastrophic and intolerable. I can't go anywhere and just abandon Mama to her fate. I can't rush off to Paris for a month or two and then dash back to Moscow for money that I can get only for work, and right now I'm so distracted and worn out that I can't work. It is a matter of completely rearranging my life and I can't depend on you or Zhenya in this matter because each letter I receive from you contradicts the preceding one. I'll be in Moscow this week and once again will try to think what to do next. Write and let me know approximately how much the operation will cost. Has Sh. got a job? All discussion of your moving has to be dropped now. First you must get better. I expect you to write often and in detail. I beg you not to put off the operation. Unpleasant matters must always be got out of the way as soon as possible. I often go to Lyusya's. That apartment is full to the brim with sh-t and anguish—every one of them there is insignificant. Lyusya's nicer than the others but hardly any smarter. I don't think this is intolerance coming out in me, but disgust. And on that, be . . . well, oh, woe to my bones!

What's left of your once-proud brother,

I.

Moscow, March 29, 1926

Dearest Merochka,

I've been in Moscow for two days now in order to deal with all sorts of dismal matters here. Perhaps if I get through with them I'll be able to do some work. Although, to tell the truth, I don't believe that happy time will come when a "writer" will be able to write. Mama knows about your operation. I don't think now that there's any question but that the operation will have to be done without her being there. I am still, as before, in favor of your freeing yourself from that burdensome building material.* How is the situation with the job? When will Mama be able to go to Brussels? For me, this is the crucial question. I am literally shackled—I have only to move somewhere and in a flash, instead of three households, I have four. It's really too absurd for words. Right now your returning to Moscow is out of the question because it's impossible to get an apartment here. They've just passed a law which says one can neither buy nor sell rooms. The only way is to rebuild demolished buildings, but that costs eight to ten thousand rubles and is beyond our means. So there's only one thing left to do—to send Mama to Brussels. But when and how, I just don't know, and I deplore the situation because, locked up here on Preshistenka Street† among the bustle, noise and hubbub, with screaming newborn babies and the neighbors phonograph (I mean all this literally!), it's impossible to work. It's terrible! Mama and I might go down to Kiev—I have to go to Kharkov and I would drop her off there on the way. Today is Passover, the first Seder—sad memories.‡ And on that melancholy note, I wish you gaiety and cheer and faith.

My regards to the learned Dr. Grigory Roux,

Your I.

* "Building material" is a facetious allusion to renal calculi (known also in Russian as "stones"), from which Babel's sister suffered.
† Preshistenka is a crowded street in Moscow where, in 1925-1926, Babel had a room with his mother after leaving Sergievo.
‡ Although Babel's family was not very religious, they celebrated a few of the most important Jewish holidays. Babel himself was an atheist.

Moscow, March 31, 1926

Dear Stone Quarry,

As it is now clear beyond doubt that you ought not to move, we have decided to make the move ourselves. So this very day we are starting to liquidate several unnecessary things (we'll keep the necessary ones), and we'll hand in our application for a passport, etc. So you must let us know *at once* about the renewal of Mama's visa. She will leave May 1 at the latest. During the next few days we will transfer a hundred dollars to Mme. Braude and one hundred dollars to you. Please put this money (which must not be touched) in the bank in dollars and also let me know the *addresses*. You must do all this at once. Enough dilly-dallying. I'm expecting an immediate reply and confirmation of the visa from you. I'm taking the opportunity to send you by registered book-mail my little book *The Story of My Dovecote*.* They sent me from Berlin my book [*Tales of Odessa*] published by Malik Verlag.† It's a very nice edition. I imagine you can buy it in Brussels. *Red Cavalry* is coming out in Russian and in German in April.‡ I'll send it to you as soon as it comes out. Mama has only just passed on to me Grisha's request about the addresses of medical journals. I swear I'll get it down this very day. Write and let me know how you're feeling. As before, I'm for an immediate operation. What does Shap. think about it? I won't be in Moscow for long. I feel restless here and it's absolutely impossible to work. So, prepare to receive guests.

I.B.

* *The Story of My Dovecote* appeared in the magazine *Krasnaya Nov*, no. 4, 1925.
† First German Editions of Babel's works:
    Isaak Babel,
                Geschichten aus Odessa. Berlin, Malik Verlag, 1926.
                Budjonnys reiterarmee. Berlin, Malik Verlag, 1926.
‡ Russian edition of *Red Cavalry*, *Konarmiya*, Moscow, Gosizdat, 1927.

July 16, 1926

Dear Merochka,

Mama's affairs are going well. We reckon she'll leave on Wednesday. We received the telegram about Peters. It's a pity you didn't tell me her first name—without it, it's difficult to send a parcel. We're still quite undecided about whether we should send it. Mama will wire you from each stopping-off point on her way. Before she leaves, I'll send you a hundred rubles. The day after Mama goes, I will also be leaving, most likely for Odessa, where I am obliged by my contract with VUFKU* to be present when my movie† is put on. I'm doing a lot of work now. It is to be hoped the results will become apparent next winter. I feel well, which is something I wish for you too from the depths of my shaken heart. I urge you to go through with the operation when Mama is there with you—there's no reason to go around with that rot in your organism. To the practitioner of black and white magic, I send powerful proletarian greetings.

Your I.

* VUFKU is a Ukrainian film organization.
† This refers to "Benya Krik," a film based on the short story, "The King," which was included in the collection *Tales of Odessa*. The film was at first banned, but later, on January 18, 1927, it was cleared.

Moscow, July 30, 1926

My dear and unforgettable Fenya,

I just received your telegram from Berlin. It made me happier than anything has for a long time. To tell the truth I was very worried about you, but it turns out you've done splendidly. I'm waiting impatiently for a wire that you've arrived in Brussels. I hope I'll get it tomorrow. Please write me a very detailed description of your entire journey from beginning to end. Who did you have for fellow passengers? How did you manage with your luggage? How did it feel being in Poland? How did you spend your day in Berlin? Did you go for motor rides as I prescribed? I suppose that everything went off easily with the visa in the Belgian embassy. Don't stint ink, paper or work on your letter. Now let me tell you what happened the day you left. A few hours before you left, I received an urgent letter from Ada about which I didn't tell you. Ada wrote that the treatment prescribed by Dr. Simonovich (he cured Kolya of malaria and put him on a diet of greens, raw fruit and vegetables) has turned out to be not only mistaken, but criminal and disastrous, for a consultation with specialists has turned up a severe duodenal ulcer. It is very serious; there's not a kopek of money, and no one wants to buy their furniture. Ada asked me to go there and help them out. I couldn't leave at once, so as soon as you had gone I took Katya* aside right there in the station and we decided that she should go to Odessa to help the unfortunate Kushnirs. With enormous difficulty we got a ticket and three hours after you had left, at 7:10, Katya left for Odessa. I gave her twenty rubles for the trip and the same day I telegraphed fifty rubles to Anyuta.† It looks as if I'll soon have to send quite a tidy sum more. Katya arrived in Odessa this morning and I'm expecting a wire from her telling me what she found there. So this is the reason why I haven't sent you the hundred rubles. On Tuesday I'll get my money from Gosizdat [State Publishing House] and then I'll send you the hundred rubles. Without wasting any time (and without waiting for this money to come, of course) you and Merochka must go to the seaside and stay there for at least a month. I insist on this and it will make me really happy if you go. What about the apartment now that you're there? Probably you'll take a bigger one. After my "session" at Gosizdat on Tuesday, I'll know which day I'll be going to Kiev and I'll let you know all about it. All your friends send you their warmest regards and I, I'm ashamed to say, miss you terribly and roam around our room completely lost. Please don't be silly and scatter-brained, and write and tell me about *everything*, since I'm the head of the family.

Regards to our folks, don't do any laundering, eat in restaurants, go for car rides and don't forget your roommate,

Your loving,

I.

Merochka, Buy Mama a handbag and a good dress, fit her out as decently as possible and take her out "in the fresh air."

I.

* Katya was the youngest of the four Shvevel sisters, maternal aunts of Babel. She was married to Iosif Lyakhetsky and was a dentist by profession.
† Anyuta Kushnir was another maternal aunt of the author.

Moscow, August 4, 1926

Dear Fenya,

I received your heart-warming telegram informing me of your safe arrival in Brussels and I also received a postcard from Negorely.

I'm waiting impatiently for a letter from Brussels. At the end of this week, I'm planning to go to Kiev. I'll inform you of the exact day of my departure. Katya is in Odessa. She sent a telegram saying that she found Kolya in a serious but by no means hopeless condition, and since then I haven't had any news from her. I'll send them another thirty rubles today. Everything's fine here. I'm waiting impatiently for the moment when I can get out of Moscow which I have come to hate, and get down to real work. Wittenberg has asked me for a service and I must do it for him because the idiot has been very kind to us. Would Meri please find out if it's possible to get a small portable Remington Russian typewriter in Brussels and how much it would cost. If it is possible to buy one in Brussels, Wittenberg will telegraph the money. It's not a very difficult errand, so please do it. As I'm planning to move around a lot during the next month, I'll let you know my addresses wherever I go. What is your first impression of Brussels? Do you like the life there? How much do their prices differ from ours? Did you heed my request to take a summerhouse? Write, write, write . . . I am particularly interested in the matter of Madame Shap.'s illness and also in whether she's nice and whether she's grown very much stupider, and so on. Regards to you, my fellow citizens,

Your I.

Khrenovaya, September 7, 1926

Dear Mama,

B.V.* sent your letter on to me from Kiev. I am having a great time here, such as, indeed, I've seldom had before. I work a lot, but in an atmosphere I love, and I am thriving on it. Please don't whimper and whine.

After an eighteen-month interruption, I am at work again, which means that soon there will be money. You have never really believed in me, which goes to show what a stuffed fool you are. But never mind, we shall cover up all your gaps with pure gold. I will make good my promise and send the money at the end of September or the beginning of October. On September 1st, I sent Zhenya fifty dollars. Don't worry about the room. Gilevich will take care of it. He has been carrying out all my instructions most punctiliously. He works in my room while I am away. When I got to Kiev, I received a letter from Lyakhetsky asking my permission to spend a few nights at my place. I didn't grant his request so I suppose he must be offended.

I haven't heard anything more from Odessa since Katya's last reassuring letter. I am very worried about Mera's health. I don't know which is better—determination or protraction. But it is no joy to live like an invalid.

Dear Pupik, write to me about your sores. Tell me in great detail what they are and whether they are poisoning your existence terribly. How do you feel about the operation?

Please tame Fenya who sounds quite wild. Explain to her that the ghost of destitution is not yet hovering over us. Shouldn't you take a large apartment so that Mama could have her own room? What do you eat? Do such things as tomatoes and chopped chicken liver exist in Belgium?

Write to me now c/o V. A. Shchekin, State Stud Farm, Khrenovaya, Voronezh Province. If I were a smart man, I'd stay here as long as possible. But good-bye, I must go and join my herd of horses.

Your son and brother who is watching over you two silly geese.

· · · · ·

* B.V. is Boris Venyaminovich Gronfein, Babel's father-in-law.

Khrenovaya, September 10, 1926

Dear Fedoseyushka,

Don't expect any news from me from here in Khrenovaya. I work until dinnertime, then I go and join the horses. Or vice versa. And that is my entire life. I don't know how long this bliss will last. I'll try to prolong my stay here. You have fallen completely silent about the typewriter. What mighty arguments must I use to get through your wooden heads that it is an interesting and profitable business. Give me a clear, straightforward answer—will you do the errand for me, yes or no?

My address is: The Toblinsky House, Stud Farm Village, Khrenovaya, Voronezh Province.

Write to me, you silly geese, both the old goose and the young one.

Yours,
I.B.

Khrenovaya, September 16, 1926

My gorgeous fools,

B.V. forwarded your letter of August 29 to me here in Khrenovaya. I am very glad that you are well in that "spa" of yours. As far as Mama's concerned, I think she ought to go into politics. And you, little Mera, you must do your utmost to get her elected to the Chambre de Députés. There, her violent drive for activity will find an outlet. What a restless old woman! The way she's champing at the bit, there's no holding her back!

I'll stay here until the first or second of October and then leave for Moscow. Adjust your letter-writing to these dates. I work a lot, see few people and many horses. I love it. As soon as I get to Moscow, I'll try to send a few score rubles to Odessa right away. I'll try to manage things so that October is a moneyed month; my relatives seem to be forever asking for something. I have written about twenty times about the typewriter. I am fed up with it. If you understand what it is all about—good, if not, you are a couple of stuffed little fools.

Twice a week I get long and most affectionate letters from Gilevich who is in Moscow. I just about die laughing when I read about the way he's looking after my room. For some reason, Lyakhetsky hasn't written for some time. I have nothing more to tell you about, for, thank God, there can be no news here. I've gotten to like living without news very much.

How is Shaposhnikov? Give him my regards. Please, drink a bot-

tle of wine every day. You ought to live more cheerfully. Good-
bye now. I'll write again soon. My belated best wishes for the Jewish new year. Try to have a better time during it than during the
one just past. May you be happy, my dear, aging little hearts.

Your I.

Khrenovaya, September 29, 1926

Dear Mama,

I was to have left Khrenovaya on October 1st, but will stay here
a few more days because it's really so quiet and such a good place
to work. I received all your letters. I wrote to Lyusya Lifshits about
her things. Don't do anything about it until I let you know from
Moscow. Mama dear, I would have so much liked you to relax a
bit and not look upon the world with such sad eyes. Now I am
living a reasonable life and am preparing—I believe—the chance
for a better future for all of us. You mustn't worry about me. I
have always been very practical about crucial matters. My most
terrible fault (inherited from you) is weakness of character, which
people who do not know me may mistake for wickedness, but now
it looks as if I have become smarter even in that respect.

Like you, I am afraid to write to Odessa. I have no news from
there and as soon as I get to Moscow, I will send them a more or
less substantial sum of money. I would like to help them as much
as I can in their terrible predicament. I wrote to Grigoriev to tell
him to send the money realized from the sale of the chairs to
Odessa; and I wrote a similar letter to Reginin. You've had as much
firsthand experience of Lyakhetsky's sicknesses as everyone else
and so you shouldn't be worried when you get his neurotic letters.
Also, do me a favor and stop worrying about our things in Moscow.
Gilevich writes to me regularly; everything in our room is in excellent order. It is being cleaned, aired and so on. And so you must
think only of what is within your range of activity: see that Mera
gets medical care, arrange your home in Brussels as best you can
for as long as you are there, and remember, dear citizeness, that
you still have a representative in Russia whose head is not yet

dried up and whose drive hasn't yet given out. It is still too early
to despair, F. Babel, so hold your head up, you silly old goose.
Kiss your daughter for me and good-bye,

Yours,

I.

Moscow, October 13, 1926

Dear Mama,

Yesterday I attended to household chores. I sent the wash to
the laundry (a crisis in underpants is threatening, because they
are literally disintegrating). The cleaning woman has washed,
scrubbed, steamed our room. We have so many bedbugs that it
has become a legend among the other dwellers in our apartment.
Just imagine!

I believe I wrote you that I'd found my galoshes. I gave my shoes
—the big ones—to be mended and it turned out that our shoemaker, Prakht, had died. A boil appeared on his neck—septicemia
—and now a younger shoemaker sits on his bench.

B.V. writes to me that Raya is to send you some money very
soon. Yesterday I went the rounds, attending to business, and I
can see I will have lots of running around to do.

I saw Lyusya's and Vesha's little girls. Lyusya's girl is enchanting, Vesha's didn't seem so good.

How are your teeth? Is Shaposhnikov pleased with his work?
What shall we do about Mera? What about the operation? I can't
get that depressing business out of my head.

Boris Mironovich is at home. It looks as though his trouble has
cleared up, but his position is quite unenviable: he works somewhere in an *artel* from morning to night and it is painful to see
the way his wife treats him. Lyakhetsky, as I wrote to you, is a real
pain in the ass. He's a piece of shit, not a man. Will I really be
forced to put him up in my room? It is very hard for a man to
have a lousy mother like you: you have bred up around me so much
melancholy shit and now I am forced to nurse it.

I'll send some money to Sonya soon. Tomorrow I'll see Reginin and Annushka. Feklusha sends you her very warmest. Strange sympathies reside in that proud soul. She remembers you about three times a day. Don't forget when you write my address to put Moscow 34. B.V. writes that he isn't feeling too well. What a gay life! Be well and toothy.

Yours,
Isya.

Moscow, October 27, 1926

Dear Mama,

I am forwarding to you the long-awaited letter from Rosa.* I am going to write to her this very day and tell her what I think of her for not having written for such a long time. Judging by the letter, she is doing fine and that is balm to my heart. I am also sending you the envelope the letter came in, on which the address is written rather illegibly—there's always so much trouble with her addresses—I believe it should read thus: Mrs. R. Edelson, 470 Rockland Str., Lancaster, Penna., U.S. of America. I am not sure about the street, whether it is Rockland or Kockland, but the main thing, the town, is spelled correctly. The Reginin woman has sent Katya twenty rubles; she still owes her another fifteen which she'll send soon. Katya hasn't said a word about the money and so I haven't mentioned it either. Now, although I know it will depress you, I have to tell you that things are very bad for the Lyakhetskys, and he, the miserable jerk, is "ill" of course. He is really quite hopeless. I have decided to be indifferent to what happens to those of my relatives who are rotten and I advise you to do the same. I am still waiting, my dear Mama, for a detailed answer to my previous letter. Meri wrote to me quite reassuring things about her health but I wonder whether you aren't deceiving me. I am very much afraid that you aren't telling me the whole truth.

I am sitting and working now, which means I'm feeling fine. In general, I feel cheerful and inspired as I haven't felt for three years, since Papa's death. I want to hope again that something that makes sense will come of it all. Why didn't you add anything to

Mera's letter? Something must have happened to you again. I beseech you, write to me as often as you can. Write about everything that happens to you in full detail. Then, I would also be very grateful to Grisha if he would send me a *precise and complete* diagnosis of Mera's illness. I would then talk to doctors here and, also, I would be able to follow what is going on.

With a big hug to all of you,

Yours,

Isya.

P.S. Write right away to Rosa and inform her about all this. It is a shameful state of affairs for us not to keep up a regular correspondence with her.

* Rosa Edelson, a friend of the Babel family, emigrated to the U.S.

November 5, 1926

Dear Mama,

I am working a lot now. Besides I have many personal worries. You know that the prerequisite for *my work* is peace. But people and circumstances deprive me of peace. For some of it I have only myself to blame, but the rest is beyond my control. Now you have become one of those who are depriving me of peace. I don't think it's nice; in fact, it's quite callous toward me. If I am not hindered, if I am not tormented, my—and hence, your—troubles will soon be at an end. I'm not asking anything of anyone but it is a depressing thought that the people who are closest to me are driving me to my perdition without realizing it themselves.

I.

P.S. In the course of this month I will send you fifty dollars. I still have work for a month—a month and a half. It is quite possible I'll go to Kiev soon. I am compelled to ask you to write to me about inconsequential things in your letters. I am prepared to give up all except one thing—my work.

November 10, 1926

Dear Mama,

Your letter dated October 29th has reached me after a tremendous delay. Everything is fine with me. I hope you are managing too. There is nothing for us to cry about. So be a good girl. I wrote to you that I had hidden myself from the world outside the city, for otherwise I would never be able to do my work, and do it I must. I am working quite well now. The Lyakhetskys are moving into my room. They have definitely been evicted. Katya says they'll move to Tashkent* where Lyakhetsky has been offered a job. I won't spend more than two or three days in Moscow, during November, so they won't be in my way. Then I will go to Kiev and at the beginning of January—abroad. I have already written to you about that. Please, please, get Ivan Ivanovich out of your head. Soon I will take all the things from him and either store them in Moscow or send them to Kiev as B.V. and I agreed.

Zhenya writes that Lola promised to pay her back the hundred rubles he stole from me. It would be a very good thing.

As I promised, I'll send you one hundred rubles by the end of this month. What's happening to your teeth? You write about the business as if a terrible blow had struck our family. Well, dear mother, you have become very stupid indeed. I've already told you that the Reginins have transmitted the money to Katya. I haven't said anything about it. I couldn't very well. The Lyakhetskys are going through difficult times. I wouldn't mind if they did leave for Tashkent. The fewer relatives, the better. To hell with them. They have been driving me frantic, our damned relatives. One of them's always got something the matter with him. What a bunch of phoneys.

I hope that when I come to Brussels, I'll find you in full glory. Just watch out for yourself when I come.

Be well and may the God of Israel send you new teeth, new cash and, above all, new brains. But even if that no-good old Schemer sends you one tooth once in a while, He'll never do anything about the brains. Kiss Merochka for me and give my regards to my best relative, Shap.—a man who, whether something hurts him or not, keeps it all to himself. Thank him for that from me.

Yours,

I.

* Here and elsewhere "Tashkent" stands for Paris.

Moscow, November 15, 1926

Dear relatives,

I have received your letter of November 2nd. Everything's fine with me. The chances are I'll soon have my play* in stageable condition. The Arts Theater is waiting for it impatiently. I'm working hard, like an ox, a forced laborer, a hired hand, but that gives me real satisfaction. As before, I am living in the House of Rest of the Soviet People's Commissariat—a very luxurious establishment, quiet, separate room, a garden. I am housed free here. Am keeping my address a secret from everyone. Never show my nose in Moscow. I have had enough of idiots. The hell with them. Why shouldn't I, too, live the way I need to for once? Lola promises to pay Zhenya a hundred rubles for Volodka. Merochka's communication depressed me. From the bottom of my heart, I wish her to bear up during these few days—the operation and the few days after it—to be brave and cheerful. Thank God, I have nothing new to report. Anyway, how can I have, being here? Moreover, I don't want anything new to happen. Where will you put me up, when I get to Brussels and what nice things will you feed me?

Your I.

* Babel was then writing the play *Sunset* which deals further with certain of the characters who appear in *Tales of Odessa.*

November 29, 1926

Dear Mama,

Half a word and we understand one another. So I will be brief. In a few days, I am leaving for Kiev where I will stay for quite a while because I would like to work in a quiet, secure atmosphere. Then I'll go abroad for *quite a long* time. I am liquidating the horrible "Moscow period" of my life that has been so painful to me. Don't let's ever talk about it again. I have proved in my past life that it is possible to trust me. So why shouldn't you trust me once more? Don't worry about money. Very soon, within the next few days, I will make good on all the expenses you have incurred recently. I am receiving very nice, cheerful letters from Zhenya. In three days or so, I am going back to the city. I am quite restricted in my movements because Katya and Lyakhetsky are living in my room. That's some pain in the neck I inherited from you. I'll write more tomorrow.

Yours,

I.

Moscow, December 17, 1926

Dear Mama,

Haven't received any letters from you for a long time. I don't know how to account for your silence. I am busy about my passport now—a lot of fuss. I don't want to pay two hundred and thirty rubles for it. A decree has come out according to which, after December 20, there will be a special reduction for artists and writers. They'll have to pay fifty or at the most a hundred rubles. I am waiting for that date. I believe Katya has found herself a room in Kuntsevo and possibly they'll move there tomorrow. I won't write to you about my mood, because I will only be able

to start living once I have shaken the accursed dust of the present
from my feet.

Love to you and Merochka.

I.

1 9 2 7

Moscow, January 22, 1927

My amiable Fenya,

I had to leave urgently for Moscow to get my passport and to
attend to some of my business connected with the theater. It's an
awfully long time since I had a letter from any of you and that
has literally driven me to despair. This has taught me how stupid
I am, since I am capable of worrying about such absurd members
of my family as you. You can answer this letter by writing directly
to the Kiev address. I'll be there by that time. I am very worried
about the state of Mera's health. I have obtained some medical
information around here and, according to our doctors, the operation that was performed on Mera is quite a radical one and should
result in a complete cure. Write to me in detail and ask Mera to
write also about her health. I hope that by now you have received
the hundred rubles I sent you from Kiev. On Monday, January 24,
I will send you another hundred rubles. At the beginning of February, Mera will get fifty dollars. I hope this money will tide you
over. I have done the necessary so that you'll receive one hundred
rubles a month regularly, starting February (that does not include
the three hundred rubles you will be getting at various times before February). Please use this money to raise your living standards. As my late Papa used to say, "I can't, after all, graft my head
on your shoulders"—but I still don't think there's any reason for
you to whine and even less to bemoan those stinking things that

are *of absolutely no use to anyone,* that only clutter up people's lives and prevent them from living. If the need arose, I could always get enough furniture to furnish five or six rooms and, besides, I have kept some of the things. My Moscow address is c/o L. I. Slonim, 16 Varvarka Street. On Monday, I'll go to Sergievo and take all the things from Ivan Ivanovich. Your stupidity makes the simplest matters very complicated. While you are sitting in Brussels, you cannot very well control what is happening to your chairs and bookcases; and anyway, believe me, I am handling these matters with common sense and I am serving and not harming our interests. As to money, our period of financial destitution is over and you will never be deprived of anything again. The matter is settled, as they say. I send you kisses, my beloved old fool, and am looking forward joyfully to our meeting.

Merochka, answer me point by point, about your liver, stomach, brains, etc. Don't forget me and don't think any worse of me than I really am. When I come to Brussels, you and I will go to a beer hall and sit there for three hours or so, and then you will find out more about me and it will be more accurate, more truthful than the shit spread by the world around us.

Yours,
I.

The envelope comes from Anna Grigorievna—don't imagine I am so extravagant myself!

January 28, 1927

Dear Mama,

I will answer your last letter at length, although its purpose remains quite unclear to me. All the valuable things have been packed into two trunks and sent to Kiev to the Gronfeins where they will be quite safe. I put a scare into Ivan Ivanovich and he came over today and, of course, he'll return everything down to the last button. On Sunday I will be in Sergievo. I know people there who would like to buy, and I wouldn't like a chip of wood to be left to Ivan Ivanovich. Of the furniture, I have kept a large cupboard, a sideboard, a writing table, a hat tree, a bookcase and a few chairs. I am sending the samovar to Kiev and have sold the violin. All the linen and also the bedclothes are in Kiev. At Zhenya's request, I am trying to get passports and visas for the old folks who want to spend three months at a spa in the summer. When I have arranged it for them, I'll leave. I have lots of things to do in Moscow and I'll probably spend another two or three weeks here. My literary affairs are in quite good shape. I can't understand why I haven't received notification that you got the money. Tomorrow, I'm sending you fifty dollars through the Torgovo-Promyshleny Bank [Commercial and Industrial Bank]. Write to me c/o Slonim, apartment 54, 16 Varvarka Street, Moscow. Although I try to remain calm and cheerful, your letters are just killing me. What's happening to Mera? Is it possible that the operation didn't help her? Why does she write to me that she is in a desperate mood? If she is worried about material matters, I *swear* that within the next few weeks your financial situation will be radically improved. Now if it is about me that she's worrying, try to explain to her that I am not one of those you can bend into a ram's horn. I feel well and I still hope to do things in this world. So why should she be in a "desperate" mood? Why all this pitiful whimpering? Why all this neurotic imbalance? Keep your chins up, damn you, pull your bellies in, and forward, march! What a moaning crew! There is actually no reason for you to moan. When I go through moments of despair, I think of Papa. What he expected and wanted from us was success not moaning. Remembering him, I feel a surge of strength, and I urge myself forward. Everything I promised him, not in words but in thought, I shall carry out, because I have a sacred respect for his memory. And it hurts me to think you should drown the only sacred memory I have in your needless tears and weakness.

Let me know Aunt's address in Brussels *immediately*.

With love,
yours,
I.

Moscow, February 8, 1927

My Dears,

Your letter made me feel better, but not too much. Apparently Mera's shaky state of health is due to the fact that her organism hasn't yet adapted itself to her new condition. Let us hope that her torments will soon be over.

I was quite flabbergasted to hear from Mera that the money had strayed to Paris and is now on its way to New York. I don't understand what happened to it or whether you'll get it in the end or not. I sent that sum off in the usual way, through the National Bank in Kiev. Today, I have sent you fifty dollars. Hope that nothing extraordinary will happen to this sum too. Please confirm its receipt immediately. I'll go to the bank with the savings book and get the interest. I have sold the things in Sergievo down to the last item. They'll be taken away Sunday. Ivan Ivanovich is all sugar and honey now. I am glad that I'm through with him once and for all. *Benya Krik* was banned (I didn't mind—the film was badly done) but now, they have lifted the ban. It doesn't look as if my departure from here will be delayed, so I'll see you in a month at the latest. Please send me the aunts' addresses without delay. I need them very badly. And please be reassured, my dear ones. I feel quite certain that everything will turn out for the best. Write to Slonim's Moscow address. Lyakhetsky's situation is bad but I have reasons to believe that some time this week I will be able to get him a job. See you soon,

Yours,

I.

Kiev, March 1, 1927

Dear Mama,

Arrived in Kiev yesterday. B.V. is very sick—pneumonia. The atmosphere is only too familiar to us and what's more, it's the anniversary of Father's death. Still, the doctors insist that he is an even bet to pull through. We decided not to send for Zhenya. It wouldn't help anything. Hope everything is all right with you. What worries me is that in March I will have to send you money through the Kiev bank and, judging by past experience, it will take a month for it to reach you. I reckoned to leave in March but now everything is again covered with a film of uncertainty. I will keep you accurately posted on everything. As the result of a family council, I wrote to Zhenya that all was well.

Yours,

I.

Kiev, March 5, 1927

Dear Mama,

This is my sixth day in Kiev. Poor B.V., he is fighting very bravely against his terrible illness. He has pneumonia, a complication of the grippe. The damned grippe had to attack a sick, sixty-four-year-old man. The doctors say it is very critical but not hopeless. To tell the truth, I do not believe in a happy ending. You can easily imagine the atmosphere, because we have been through similar vicissitudes, you and I, and so what can I tell you about my life here? They canceled B.V.'s license to have tenants; he has no money and the entire burden of the huge expenses falls upon me. It goes without saying that I cannot work properly under these conditions and that all I can do is hope that things will get better in the future. Write to me in Kiev for, as you must understand, I cannot tell you how long I will stay here.

Mama dear, write to me at length about your life, about your new apartment and how you and Mera feel. Is Shaposhnikov satisfied with his work? What is your room like? Please do not worry about money. I thought I would send you two hundred rubles this month but in view of the additional expenses I've had to face, we shall have to limit ourselves to one hundred. I will send the money by mail for I don't suppose you are so hard pressed for it.

Warmest kisses to all of you,

I.

Kiev, March 7, 1927

Dear Mama,

Today, at five past five, Boris Venyaminovich died. He died of a grippe that developed into pneumonia. Berta Davydovna is behaving with remarkable fortitude and that helps me greatly in my painful role. In a day or two I'll write in greater detail.

Yours,

I.

Kiev, March 11, 1927

My dears,

I don't remember whether I wrote to you about B.V.'s death and funeral. I think I did. I am staying with the old woman now. Relatives came from Vinnitsa and they are leaving today. B.D. is taking it awfully well really. Once again, alas, I have to deal with matters of inheritance! I cannot leave the place for a single day, because they'd steal everything. I have written at length to Zhenya and Lyova.* Let them decide themselves whether they should come to Russia or whether I should take the old woman abroad and hand her over to Lyova so that then she can go on to America. I will wait for their answer. I was quite ready to leave and had almost got the ticket but things turned out quite differently. I'll be patient. I am anxiously awaiting more cheerful news from you. How is the new apartment? How is Merochka's health? How is your own health, my dear little old Mama?

I.

I don't have your new address. Am very surprised that you didn't send it to me at the time. This is why I am sending this letter registered. Hope it will reach you.

---

* Lev Borisovich Gronfein (Lyova), Babel's brother-in-law, who emigrated to the United States in 1919.

Kiev, March 18, 1927

Dear Mama,

There is no reason why you should cry over me. We are living quietly and comfortably, for the hardships are behind us. Either today or tomorrow, Zhenya will receive "the news." What is to happen will depend on her: either we will come and join her or she'll come here to Kiev. I am working. Just imagine, B.D. is so full of adoration for me that she doesn't even interfere with my writing. In a few days, I am appearing here at a public reading. I am doing it to make some money. Similar evenings will be organized, I believe, in Kharkov, Odessa, Vinnitsa and Yekaterinoslav. If I do go to Odessa I will try to help Anyuta and Sonya. In the lousy local bank here, they have promised me to accept a sum to transfer to you. So it looks as if you'll receive the money at the beginning of April, for money orders seem to travel a hell of a time when sent from Kiev. Well, what can we do? . . .

I am very glad to hear that you like the apartment. And you know, my dear Fenya, there are happy as well as sad days in life, so there's no need to daub black over everything. We should be sad about what is sad and enjoy what is enjoyable. This is a very simple but a very important philosophy.

As far as comfort, peace and food go, I am very well off here. Much of my money went into the medical care and funeral because there wasn't enough Russian currency. According to the will left by B.V., Zhenya is his only heir. Fifteen thousand rubles have been offered for the house, which was renovated, and there are very many buyers. It would be best, of course, to send the old woman over to America. Now, since my life in Kiev is quite bearable, I am waiting for Zhenya's and Lyova's decision without any special impatience. What sort of job did Shaposhnikov get? Is it a solid job? What are they paying him? Please don't grudge yourselves anything. Please remember that you can absolutely rely on the hundred rubles I am sending you. Many kisses for you and Mera. My regards to Shap.

Your I.

Kiev, March 26, 1927

Highly respected Fenya,

I have received your letter of March 19. It takes your letters exactly seven days to get here. As I wrote to you before, there is absolutely no reason for you to cry over me. Up till now, troubles have landed on me like fleas on a dog. But at present, for comfort, food and convenience, I cannot think of anything better. Stepanida* is still here. It is much easier for me to get along with B.D. than I could have hoped. This can be accounted for by her limitless adoration for me which has replaced her previous marked coolness. And since she is a single-minded person, this adoration has something maniacal about it. A new trouble on my poor head! I believe that one of the reasons for it is that lousy "fame" of mine. She opened her eyes wide when she saw how some people kowtowed to me. And now she has come to believe in me once and for all.

A telegram came from Zhenya. She knows everything and has sent a letter instructing us what to do. I am waiting impatiently for that letter. You may rest assured—I am not planning any liquidations. My financial affairs are in good order. As I wrote before, I sent you a hundred rubles from Kiev. Yesterday, I gave the first reading of my new play.† It was a great success—overwhelming, I would have said if it hadn't been for my well-known modesty. How, under those incredible circumstances, I could have managed to compose something that makes sense is quite beyond me. I am sending you a clipping from today's newspaper because these are the first lines about my new child.

I am very pleased to hear that you have a new apartment. *I beg of you*, don't begrudge yourself kopeks and live like a human being should. Now it has become quite clear to me that, for two centuries, we haven't lived properly. I would *feel much better* and would enjoy life much more if I were sure you weren't refusing yourself any of the necessities of life, that you were taking the cures you need at your "spas," not like a pauper Jewish woman but like a lady with a little feather in her hat. *Du courage, ma belle!*

Am expecting a telegram from Odessa about the date of my literary evening there. I'll try to be of some help to Anyuta and Sonya then. It looks as if Mera's condition is getting back to normal. I am very interested to know the opinion of the surgeon who performed the operation about whether the healing process is proceeding normally. I've told you already that the old woman Zeiliger went through that operation twenty or so years ago— which means she was considerably older than Mera is now—and after that all her troubles were at an end. Let us hope that the same thing will happen in your case.

Lots of love,
I.

What is the climate like in Brussels? Do you go out for walks? After some real spring weather, we are back in a rough winter: it has snowed a lot and it's very cold.

* Stepanida was a servant of the Gronfein family.
† The play is *Sunset*. It was later published in *Novy Mir*, no. 2, 1928.

Kiev R.R. Station, March 30, 1927

Dear Mama,

I am about to leave for Odessa. I am reading my stuff there on the first and second of April, then I'll go to Vinnitsa, give two readings there, on the third and fourth, and on the fifth, I'll be back in Kiev. It goes without saying, of course, that I'll visit all our living and dead. As soon as I get back to Kiev, I'll start preparing feverishly for my trip abroad. I got a letter from Zhenya. She asks me not to sell the house and only to get rid of whatever furniture is of no use. Will write to you from Odessa. Lots of kisses. Expecting frequent letters from you and Merochka.

Yours,
I.

Kiev, April 6, 1927

Dear Mama,

I returned last night from Odessa and Vinnitsa. The trip was a great success. I saw Anyuta but didn't have time to go and see Sonya because I only spent two days in Odessa and they were a couple of very feverish days indeed. Materially speaking, Anyuta is quite comfortably off. I am sending them some money from here today. I am beginning to do the necessary about my departure which should be later than May. Here, I'll get rid only of the most useless things, to pay for my journey. So you can see that our meeting is not too far off. Odessa is a dead, cold, bleak city. To tell you the truth, you ought to thank your lucky stars that you are installed in Brussels.

It makes my life much more pleasant to know that Merochka has finally recovered her health. I hope you received the money I sent you, or at least will receive it in the next few days. I hope the time will soon come when I will be able to have peace and go back to my work. This letter doesn't count—it is just a warning of my forthcoming arrival. As soon as I have settled the most pressing matters, I will write to you at some length.

Love and kisses,
Your I.

Kiev, April 17, 1927

Dear Mama,

Best wishes on the holiday. I was at the Zeiligers' for the seder and it was celebrated according to all traditions, just as we used to have it in those far-off childhood years. Deep down, though, I felt very sad for reasons that should be obvious to you. But, generally speaking, recently I have been feeling more cheerful, have been able to work and to see the world in more rainbowy colors. I am busy with thousands of things besides my own private affairs: I must establish Zhenya's rights of inheritance, settle hundreds of formalities, talk to buyers, face red tape and, of course, handle poor Berta Davydovna. I hope you received the money. Do you have matzos at home and do you still stick to the ancestral traditions? What sort of spring are you having? Ours is unspeakable. We are still waiting for a warm day. I trust that we shall see next Passover together in happy circumstances. B.D. will receive her passport for travel abroad very soon. Am waiting for word from Zhenya about the visa. Nothing new to tell you, dear Mama. I am slowly recovering from the painful shocks I have suffered and wish you calm and fortitude from the bottom of my heart. I am still an optimist as before. How is your health? How is Mera's? Does my worthy sister do anything or is she nothing but a housewife—a *heim balabuste?* I send you my highest regards,

Your loving Isai.

My best to Steinbach.

P.S. A few days ago, Lyakhetsky passed through Kiev. He phoned me from the station and told me that he had been summoned because one of his sisters—I don't know which—was ill. I assume that the next thing will be one more trip to the Jewish cemetery. His financial situation has improved; apparently he has managed to bring off some successful transaction.

Kiev, April 23, 1927

Dear Mama,

You mustn't be angry with me for not writing more often. Letters make me sick and literally stick in my throat. Since I am now an "executor of the will," I have to send scores of similar letters in all directions, repeating the same stuff of which I am quite fed up. I couldn't bear to repeat their contents to you. Things are slowly moving ahead here. Taught by bitter experience, I am not hurrying, and the liquidation (a partial liquidation) is going on quite satisfactorily. The main problem is to establish Zhenya's right of succession; the inheritance taxes are huge—calculated in thousands

—and I am expecting lots of difficulties on this score. Next week, I'll go to Lubny where the serious question of denationalizing the house must be handled, and from there to Moscow where I must attend to a great number of things—handing my scenario* over to Sovkino; negotiating with the Arts Theater whose company is leaving on a tour of the provinces in May; getting my passport extended, and so on. I will spend a few days in Moscow, so you can send your next letter to me c/o Slonim, Apartment 54, 16 Varvarka Street, Moscow.

To my horror, I was told at the Gosbank [State Bank] that the hundred rubles I sent you still haven't been transferred. The reason for this is that I had to send money to Zhenya twice this month and so my protector there couldn't send a sum to your address as well. I will insist that the money be telegraphed to you from Moscow on Tuesday. The money has been lying in the bank for over two weeks and I couldn't do anything about it. You can count on getting it and please don't write me any more of those pitiful letters about refusing yourself everything. When I come over, I will bring you the things you need. Despite extremely adverse circumstances, I am working a lot and hence am feeling quite well. My charge is living on laxative powders, thanks to which her stomach is functioning regularly. Nevertheless, she is aging threateningly every day and now looks awfully old compared to her contemporaries. Grisher,† the Odessa impresario, owes me a hundred rubles. I have instructed him to pay them to Anyuta and Sonya. What is Mera doing? Those who do not work do not eat: so what are her reasons for dining?

Your hard-tried but uncomplaining son,

I.

* The scenario for *The Chinese Mill*, directed by Tasin in 1928.
† G. Grisher was the director of *Wandering Stars*, a film for which Babel wrote the script based on themes of Sholem Aleichem.

Moscow, April 28, 1927

My amiable Fenya,

I haven't written to you for a long time. I'm in a pre-travel mood and that is why I don't feel like writing. B.D. got her passport and they'll put the French visa on it here. Zhenya wired that the visa had been granted and so everything seems to be going well. Zhenya has taken a flat in Paris. I am winding up my affairs here and in a week or ten days I reckon to go to Kiev and fetch the old woman. We'll go through Poland and stop over in Berlin, where I have much business to attend to. As to money, don't worry your head—there will be money. I don't want to tell you when I'll send it—I'll just mail it to you. All the things you wrote to me about will be brought to you. Lyakhetsky has arrived in Moscow. We are now awaiting the arrival from Odessa of the manager of the Metals Depot. They are sending Lyakhetsky to work there. Perhaps that's best for him, because it seems obvious that he will never subdue Moscow. If anything, Moscow will subdue him. And with that, good-bye, my dear ones, and see you soon.

Your I.

Kiev R.R. Station, April 30, 1927

Dear Mama,

Am about to leave for Moscow. Out of the frying pan into the fire. In Moscow, I must have a visa stamped on my passport, hand in my play, hand in my scenario. . . . Yes, quite enough to do. Immediately upon my arrival, or, to be more exact, on May fifth (the second is a holiday), I will transfer the money to you. My life in Kiev would have been quite all right—I could even have done some work—had it not been for the unbearable deterioration of relations between Berta and the Zeiligers. How do you like me in the role of peacemaker? And so much the more so in that it is

difficult to conceive of a more evil-smelling soul that Raissa Solo-
monovna's.

. [incomplete]

Moscow, June 24, 1927

Dear Mama,

I am leaving for Kiev on Wednesday 29th. I have wound up all
my business. Did you get the hundred rubles I wired you? Did
Grisha get the books? I've also sent a hundred rubles to Odessa.
This week, I will send one hundred rubles to Mera. I'll bring with
me all the things you need. On my way to Paris, we shall meet
only at the Liége railroad station because, since I'm traveling with
the old woman, I will not be able to stop over at Brussels. I'll wire
you from Berlin when I leave there. Then, in Liége, we'll decide
what to do—whether you will come and see me in Paris or whether
I, after staying in Paris for some time, will come "on leave" to
Brussels. It seems that the end of our torments is near. I am paying
the price for my idiotic softness and the "nobility" of my nature,
but, you, poor thing, what are you being penalized for? Ah, but
anyway, I have faith in myself and I know everything will turn out
right in the end. Love to Merochka, regards to Grisha,

Yours, I.

I have settled all my business *much better* than I reckoned. There
is still powder in the magazines.

Moscow, June 26, 1927

I have five minutes left before the air mail collection. I have
mailed the book. The money order for a hundred rubles was sent
by telegraph the day before yesterday. Am going tomorrow for just
one day—Sunday—to Leningrad, where I will read my play to the
company of the Alexandrinsky Theater and draw up a contract. I
will be back in Moscow on Monday morning. I hope I will be able

to leave for Kiev on Tuesday and, from there, abroad. I will wire
you before I leave. Will write you a longer letter on Monday.

Good-bye, my dear,

I.

1 9 2 8

April 2, 1928

Fenka!

I haven't written to you for a long time. I've had a lot of work
to do and have been very busy. My trip to Italy is still in the air—
I'll know definitely this week. If I go, it will probably be for one
month. When I'm back, we'll put our heads together—I want us to
spend the summer together, the lot of us, and will do my utmost to
see that it happens. In the course of this month also, it's sure
to become clear what Lyova's situation is. This is a very important
point in planning our future existence. You can understand yourself how much depends on it. Now it really looks as if he had
reached a crucial point in his affairs and we must wait for the out-
come without bringing about any radical changes before that out-
come is known. All I know is that the present situation cannot go
on indefinitely—I mean our separation. I'll write to Anna Grigorievna today and ask her to pay Katya fifty rubles out of the very
first money she gets. It is not too easy for me to do it myself now.
Despite everything, my play has been staged in Moscow. By now,
everyone knows that I did *mon possible* but that the theater has
failed to convey to the audience the subtleties hidden in a play
that is crude on the surface. And if it has managed to remain in
the repertory, it is, of course, due to the elements in the "piece"
which come from me rather than those contributed by the theater.
I can say this without being boastful.

Now, here is some news from Moscow. Following Polonsky, Olshevets has been kicked off *Novy Mir* [*New World.*] And guess what for? For drunkenness. He got involved in some sort of debauchery while drunk, and that has cut short his career. What a pity! I've always liked people of his type—a *Yid, a shiker.** But, as they say, the spiciest item is still to come. In Olshevets' place they've appointed, of all people, Ingulov. I received a touching letter from him: we started off together, he writes. He was the first to believe in me and now, many years later, life has brought us together once more, and we are again playing the same parts as before and we'll show the world, etc., etc. It is true that in this return of "the wind in its old circle," there is something symbolic and something that is very pleasant to me personally. . . .

Don't you dare give up your apartment, the increase in rent notwithstanding. If there'll be a bathroom, it's worth paying more. Anyway, I don't expect the increase will be that outrageous—it seems the Belgians aren't all that good at figures.

Today I'll buy matzos and, for your sake, I'll intone praises to that old crook the Jewish God at the seder, because, according to my personal bookkeeping, this Passover is a bit more cheerful than last year's.

As to other feelings, I'm trying to ignore them. I must live more austerely—only then will some sense come of it. In America, negotiations are still going on: the theater I had contacted went bankrupt and folded. Another theater became interested in my play and I'm now waiting for their answer. I don't suppose I'll get it too soon.

Well, that's all there is to report about my affairs. Give my warmest greetings to the married couple I feel so warmly about. It goes without saying that everyone here sends you their regards, love and kisses. B.D. is in full bloom (due to the looming lavatory millions) and bursts into happy laughter on every occasion appropriate and inappropriate. That's the way the world spins.

Yours respectfully,
I.

* Yiddish expression, approximately "Fine Jew, fine drunkard."

April 28, 1928

Idle women! I've just sent Zhenya to the post office to mail you five hundred French francs. My money arrived only *three weeks* late and that thanks to the Currency Control Board's cutting the figure. So I didn't get the full sum I'd been waiting for. Still, it gives me a breathing spell.

We're in an uproar today. A letter arrived from Lyova in which he announces that he is about to sign a contract with some American magnate and hopes to come over to Europe in May. Thus, in the course of May, our modest villa will witness a gathering of people from all parts of the world.

Zhenya has sent you only the first issue of the *Novy Mir* because all the others are being read by B.D.—or to be more exact, by Lyubka the Monarchist.* In the fourth issue, there is a quite sensible piece about *Sunset* by P. Markov,† the best Russian theater critic and the man who is in charge of the repertory of the Arts Theater. It seems as if people have glimpsed something in the play but I'm quite tired of it by now. I'll send you the *Novy Mir* no later than Monday.

For three days, we have been having an enchanting spring here. You must come quickly while the weather is so good. On Monday, Zhenya will go to the Ministry of Foreign Affairs to make some important *démarches*. There is no reason to think that the visas won't be granted.

As to me—nothing is changed: Don Pomeranzo is writing and writing. The sun, now that it has at last shown up, has cheered me up, and so writing is easier and better. Upon that note, goodbye. Write cheerful postcards, give my best to the Belgian proletariat, clap hands and "may everything turn out fine."—*Alevai!*

---

* Lyubka worked for the Babels. The title that Babel gives her is an ironic reference to the rowdy heroine of his story "Lyubka the Cossack."
† See Appendix I for Markov's review.

May 10, 1928

My worthy Muska,

Today I received the stray five hundred francs (from the Germans in Berlin) and thought it my filial duty to share it with you by sending you fifty Belgain francs as pocket money. Any day now I'm expecting to receive my monthly pay and as soon as I do, I'll refresh you in an appropriate manner. Last month we managed to make both ends meet and I hope that they'll send me the money just as promptly in May too. I've heard from Moscow that they're not issuing passports for travel abroad to anyone now (without any exception), and that even sending money out involves incredible difficulties. Still, I'm managing somehow, although quite modestly of course, and not the way I'd have liked to live, especially in Paris where I'm not staying for keeps and where it would be nice to live with more variety—but still we do get along.

I saw Lola and Nadya. They look like demons but control themselves. It's a messy story and there are things, apparently, that cannot be talked about. That poor Spanish woman apparently had the grippe followed by complications which turned into galloping consumption. The poor duchess! She died in the arms of a descendant of Solomon.* Here, it is difficult to say whether love was really that irresistible or whether he suffered a temporary aberration. In any case, the death of these two people who hadn't lived forty years between the two of them is moving and somehow incredibly romantic.

Poor Merochka, all ills seem to be latching themselves on to her. Still, I don't think it's anything, and I think you worry more about her health than is warranted. I am so longing to see her. No news from Lyova at all and I guess the poor fellow will have us mixed up over his arrival for a long time to come. So I've been wondering whether I shouldn't come over to see you for two or three days (and perhaps bring Zhenya along too). That would be the simplest and surest thing to do. We could leave B.D. for three days with Lyubka the Monarchist. Zhenya would stay three days with you and I'd stay a bit longer. There's only one question: will I be able to work there? Are you sure no one plays the piano next door? (This is, as it always has been, my Achilles heel). In any case, get me a visa and then we'll see. I'll try to come as soon as I can and then we could all go to Paris together. If I have to make some *démarches* in the Belgian Consulate here, let me know. I'd like to hope that the Belgians will prove nicer than the Italians and give us the visas.

Would it, in general, be possible to obtain a visa valid for a set period so that I could wander to and fro? As they say, I await your reply. My health is good, I'm working adequately, although I won't see the fruits of the work before three or four months. I think I've covered everything in this letter now. So, my proletarian, class-conscious and comradely greetings,

I.

* The "son of Solomon" was a young cousin of Babel's mother, a son of the "Lyolya" mentioned in the letters. He married a Spanish noblewoman and committed suicide when his wife died very young of galloping consumption.

Paris, May 21, 1928

Mother!

I've sent you one hundred *belgas* today. They've given Zhenya an appointment at the Ministry about your French visas. Tomorrow we'll also start doing the necessary about our own trip to Brussels. I didn't do anything about it before this because anyway I couldn't leave Paris before June first. Tomorrow we'll let you know whether there'll be anything for you to do about it in Brussels.

We've received news from Kiev that Zhenya's rights of succession have been confirmed but that she'll have to pay more than a thousand rubles in taxes. It is a very important and complicated business; I won't be able to move until I have seen it through and it is urgently necessary to get it over with.

A collection of articles* about me has just come out in Russia. It makes very amusing reading—quite incomprehensible. It was written by frightfully scholarly fools. Reading it, I get the impression that I'm reading about a dead man—what I am doing now is so different from what I did before. The book is adorned with my portrait by Altman and it's quite funny too—I look like a cheerful pug. I'll send you the collection tomorrow. Please don't lose it—I must, after all, make a collection of that sort of thing. I haven't done a thing for three days. I had put too much pressure upon my brains and got overtired. Now I seem to have recovered and tomorrow again, *je me remets au travail.*

No news at all from Lyova. This is so much the worse in that, sooner or later, Zhenya will have to go to Kiev to sell the house, which is important and cannot be postponed. And what complicates things is that once she is there, there is absolutely no guarantee that they'll give her back her passport for travel abroad. But, after all, her trip is still quite far off. We'll have time to think about it.

I have read that you're having glorious weather in Brussels, while here it is raining, *mes amis,* raining every day, in every form—downpours, fine drizzles through a heavenly sieve, and on Sundays, to mark the holidays, rain mixed with hail. And this is called *la douce France* and *Ville Lumière.* Ah, give me Odessa any time.
. . . And on that note, my lovelies, period and until tomorrow.

Yours,

I.

---

* This refers to the book called *Articles and Materials,* published by Akademia, 1928, which included the autobiography of Babel and the following critical essays: "Babel and the Short Story," by N. Stepanov; "Babel," by P. Novitsky; and "Sunset," by G. Gukovsky.

Paris, September 30, 1928

My most amiable ones!

We intend to leave on Tuesday. We'll let you know definitely tomorrow. Yesterday, went to the consulate and they gave me forms to fill out. I'll send them to you registered tomorrow, with the instructions. Have taken note of Grisha's specifications concerning the apparatus. I'll try to do everything. I spent the whole day running around saying good-bye to people. It's hard work. It's real fall weather here. I can imagine what it's like in Brussels. I am very pleased you are getting a good apartment. And whether it's necessary or not, once a week you'll have a bath. Until tomorrow.

Yours,

I.

Kiev, October 17, 1928

Am leading the life of a businessman, so active that I forget where I am. I have my own "manager" now, Boris Markovich, and sit at a desk the way poor B.V. used to. I hope I'll manage to bring these sickening affairs to a successful conclusion. I'll let you know the results when and if they materialize. Write to me c/o S. A. Finkelstein, 30 Krasnoarmeyskaya Street, because I intend to move out of the hotel where I am now, but still don't know where I'll go. Good cheer and good health to you.

Yours,

I.

Kiev, October 20, 1928

Dearest little Mama,

Yesterday I got an on-account payment of five hundred rubles in fees from VUFKU. I immediately sent fifty to Anyuta and twenty-five to Sonya. On top of that, I sent a special letter to each of them. I would have liked very much to send some money to Uncle Grisha but I still do not have his address. Mera promised to find out about the addresses for me and I implore her to make every conceivable effort in that direction. For my part, I will do the necessary. I am busy from morning till night with all kinds of business—literary, commercial, taxes. I rush from one office to another, hollering, begging, hoping for the best. Despite all this hustle and bustle, I feel fine on my native soil. There's poverty here, much that is sad, but it is my material, my language, something that is of direct interest to me. I realize more and more that with every passing day I am getting back to my normal state, while in Paris I felt as if there was something pasted on inside me that was not my own. I don't mind going abroad on vacation but I must work here.

I'll have to remain in Kiev for quite a while. In the first place, the business here is quite complicated and in the second, I must wait for my suitcases with books which the Paris office of the Soviet Merchant Marine—damn it—not knowing that the Kiev customs office had been closed down, sent to the wrong destination. I am looking for a room where I can stay two or three weeks and it's possible that I'll get one at the place of some friends of Doctor Finkelstein's. I am obsessed with one thought and filled with one desire now—to work and to organize my existence securely and peacefully, but that existence is quite inconceivable without you (I would like Mera to remember that). Next spring I'll do my best to drag you back here, but we'll get to that later. Still, the notion is firmly planted in my heart.

Now, since I am now a free, independent and relaxed person, I'll be writing to you quite often. My regards to all. I shake their paws and send them my love and kisses.

I.

P.S. Tomorrow, Sunday, I'll write to Iosif and Katya.

Kiev, October 28, 1928

Today is Sunday—the day of rest. I slept late, went to an eating place and had excellent tea there with the heel of an excellent black loaf and butter, read Budyonny's letter to Gorky in *Pravda*,* was terribly tickled by it, even swelled up with glee and, now, am writing to you out of sheer fullness of heart. Everything would be so nice if it were not for Mama's illness. Write soon to reassure me.

Yours,

Is.

* Semyon M. Budyonny (born 1883), Marshal of the Soviet Union since 1935. During the Civil War he was from November, 1919, Commander of the First Cavalry Army to which Babel was attached as a correspondent. When the first *Red Cavalry* stories were published in 1923-1924, Budyonny expressed his outrage in a short letter addressed to the editors of *Krasnaya Nov* and published in the magazine *Oktyabr*, no. 3, 1924, under the title "Babism Babelya." (Budyonny's play on words cannot be translated into English. The sense might be rendered by something like "Babel's womanism.") An article of Gorky's entitled "How I Learnt to Write" in which he defended Babel's portrayal of the Cossacks in *Red Cavalry*, appeared in *Pravda* on September 30, 1928. Budyonny countered by writing an open letter to Gorky which appeared first in *Krasnaya Gazeta* on October 26, 1928.

See Appendix II-a and II-b for Budyonny's open letter to M. Gorky and for Gorky's answer to Budyonny, which appeared in *Pravda*, November 27, 1928.

Kiev, November 5, 1928

I have completed my first twenty-four hours at Stepanida's. I am wallowing in bliss. I couldn't have wished for better surroundings. We are living in a workers' settlement, in a warm, low house, in quiet, orderliness and peace. I expect to enjoy living and working here.

I have already written to you several times to tell you that Uncle Grisha received the hundred rubles that were coming to him. I am waiting for further word from him. I am seriously considering whether it wouldn't be worth while for you to go and take a cure in southern France. It is so important to restore Mama's health that perhaps it is worth making the sacrifice of going to live with B.D. Now, can you get enough money for it? For my part, I am prepared to do everything to enable you to go, but you must realize that it depends on Mera rather than on me. But, as I wrote to you before, I expect great things from this month. I finally got a letter from Zhenya. Lots of love. Until tomorrow.

I.

Kiev, November 16, 1928

Dear Mera,

I have received the notification that they're sending twenty-five dollars to Mama. Please let me know when she gets the money. So far I have no news from the Moscow Bank but I hope they'll do it there. Please remember that I don't want you to count every kopek—you must make your life as comfortable as possible. I beseech you to take an apartment that has a bathroom, and in which Mama could have a good, dry, light room with a window and a nice bed. Also, if possible, it should be close to some public park.

I concluded the business with the house here and, with the money I got out of it, I bought government bonds. The next drawing is on November 20, so perhaps we'll win something. [The bond issue also constituted a national lottery.—Tr. MacA.]

I am having a great time with Stepanida. I have recuperated in both body and soul and my work is going well again, and perhaps it will get somewhere some day.

I received a very cheerful letter from Iosif. He's made some money, doesn't need any assistance now, and is full of jokes and witty remarks. Best of luck to him. Write to Zhenya as often as you can. I wrote to tell her that she ought to visit you and that you should all have a good time together, and that would do you all a lot of good. You can write to me as before to the post office box.

As for you, Merochka, I can't tell you how happy I am that you are feeling well. I could never believe that your illness would not yield to treatment and time. If only you could consolidate your present good state of health and—most important—get rid once and for all of the maniacal notions that prevented you from living and working. As you can see, you too must now widen your interests and become more active. I don't suppose Mama has too much to do now so ask her to write more often, without bothering too much about what she writes. I don't expect any literary pearls from her. Regards to Grisha. *Je vous embrasse*, my little old women,

I.

Kiev, November 19, 1928

Dear Mama,
 You already know that things are not going well for Ilyusha.* I sent him sixty rubles today upon his request and I wrote that if he needed more, I'd send it to him any time. So that you shouldn't think that only you and Annushka are worrying about him, while we here just sit with our arms folded, I am enclosing the money order receipt. I promised you that while you were abroad, Ilyusha would never be in dire material need and now I am keeping my promise and will keep it in the future. All this is being done to give you complete peace of mind.
 Your last few letters have been more cheerful, although I still cannot see what actual efforts you are making to achieve a more comfortable life. Why have you still not taken that apartment? You ought to get yourself a *femme de ménage* who would come in every day. When you get well enough to go out, I insist that you be driven by taxi to some park and spend an hour or so in the fresh air. After all, why should you live all the time in a state of constant alarm, privation and idiotic—yes, really idiotic—worry. A professor I know has left on a brief official visit to Prague. He promised me to transfer twenty-five dollars to Mera. Please ask her to send me confirmation of receipt of that sum. Congratulate Grisha on his smoking revolution for me—or I should say, rather, evolution. I myself, although I don't really inhale, am trying to smoke as few cigarettes a day as I can. I am working a lot now and so I feel wonderful. The fall is lovely here. We are having some sparkling sunny days. And Stepanida's house is just the house I need. I am about to leave for the post office now to find out whether there aren't any letters from you. Please write to me

General Delivery so as not to get things mixed up for you or for me—I go to the post office regularly.

Au revoir, mon vieux,

I.

* Ilyusha and Annushka, referred to in subsequent letters, are names previously agreed upon to signify the dispatch of money. It should be noted that the transfer of funds is often referred to as shipments of books (Pushkin, Sholokhov, etc.) and literary magazines. The financial needs of the two families are also expressed as a wish for reading materials.

Kiev, November 23, 1928

Am very pleased my parcel reached you so quickly. Next month will send fresh caviar again, for it shouldn't go bad in December. Hope you received my registered letter in which I inform Mama that money has been sent to Ilyusha. I can just imagine Mama with short hair! It's a good thing that horses are tending to disappear from the streets abroad, otherwise they'd rear at the sight of that clipped-haired citizeness. Give my best to Annushka and tell her that she can always rely on me when she needs something. With that, good-bye. The weather is so nice that I've decided to walk all the way to town. So, until our next little pow-wow,

I.

Kiev, December 4, 1928

Dear Merochka,

The misunderstanding about Ilyusha is due to your confused way of writing. My—or rather your—mistake will be corrected tomorrow morning (as I wired you). I hope Ilyusha will be able to go on with his studies. Please write about it to Zhenya who is specially interested in the matter; I would like Ilyusha to give her back half of the money he has received. I am indescribably glad that the misunderstanding has been cleared up and that I'll be able to be of help to Annushka.

Now as for you—although Zisman is tough, I don't think you should quit your job. He isn't really as bad as they say and you may find another boss even worse; anyway, you're not all that sure to find another job. You write that Mama is terribly nervous. What does that dream mean? Is it possible that on top of a mad mother-in-law I'm now to be afflicted with a *mishuggene* mother? What is it all about, I ask you? Some kind of leisure-class complaint, or what? Mama, please, if you can manage it, don't be an idiot. Try to amuse the poor little old woman, feed her wine, champagne, fruit, asparagus, cauliflower, wash her hair, give her hot and cold baths, buy her a flannel shirt and woolen stockings, drive her around in taxis, read humorous stories aloud to her and cure her *à la fin des fins*. And besides, write to me sensibly what sort of nervousness it is and why so much buzzing with all those doctors. I'm sure it's a lot of fuss about nothing.

Fads, nothing else. . . . All right, a joke is a joke but you've got your tails between your legs. Tell me, how long will you have your tails between your legs? Cheer up, you silly old goose, everything's for the best in the best of all worlds! And write to me about something silly, about something homey, like tomatoes with onions.

Yours,

I.

Kiev, December 15, 1928

Dear Mendelevich,

Your last letter was more cheerful than the preceding one and that cheered me up too. You write that Mama is feeling better, but I wish you would be more specific and would pinpoint for me what exactly this improvement consists of, whether she can go out, and whether her condition has changed very much in comparison with when we parted? I consider that things are going well for all of us now and that soon they'll be really good (as you know, I'm a strong-willed man and don't just scatter my words to the winds), so that all Mama has to do now is to live, enjoy life and abandon these "Jewish ailments," along with her fidgeting, worrying her head off about various relatives, etc. Really. And you should tell her so. We must decorate our houses with gaiety not with *tsores.* But how can one convince people of that?

I was very glad to be able to be of service to Ilyusha. As you know, Zhenya has been quite unable to set herself up and her financial situation is quite lamentable, although there is some hope that she will get a good job. Nevertheless, I would ask Fenya, who is more energetic, to bring her efforts to bear in that direction too. It would take a considerable load off my shoulders. I'm planning to go over to Khalzhonnov's to find out from him what has become of the twenty-five dollars I sent to Prague. They should have reached their destination long ago.

I don't share your apprehensions about a car for Grisha, but perhaps it really would be better to get it toward spring. In any case, I would recommend that you two lazy people enroll in a driving school and learn to drive. That will help you to become fully European, and besides, it's great fun in itself. I would be positively jubilant if you ordered yourselves that bit of movable property and would be prepared to partake in the expense, provided, of course, that Annushka doesn't object. Fenya should thoroughly impress it upon her that it isn't a luxury but, in your circumstances, a first essential. My dear, please try and rent the bath from the jockey again. It is only here at my saintly Stepanida's that I understand what a bliss it can be. I lead the philosophical life of a sage here, but I miss my ablutions. But then, everyone has the same trouble here. You people, and Mama especially, pay criminally little attention to that aspect of hygiene. You should take a bath, my friends, every day, and although I mostly bathe in eau-de-cologne, I offer you this bit of advice with a clear conscience. What state are your clothes in? Is Mama still strutting around in her prehistoric sweaters and gaiters? Has she made herself a new dress?

I've already written to you about the "business" letter which Katya and Sasha Lyakhetsky burst out with. But what can you do? They won't let you live, but I've trained myself to regard these explosions with unruffled calm. Of course, there's no one to blame in this. The letter was dictated by dire need and I answered them that I could let them have a hundred rubles, but that to talk of thousands, and what's more, other people's thousands, was out of the question. I want to send fifty rubles to Odessa for the holidays. I'll do it three or four days from now, so that they get the money around the 21st or 22nd of December.

Well, there doesn't seem to be anything else to say. I'm expecting pleasant communications from you, comrade bookbinders.* I hope you're leading a more scatterbrained existence than before. You should try to see to it that Annushka widens her circle of acquaintances. My regards to Esculapius and Mama, upon whom I call to close ranks and march forward with a song.

I.

* Babel's mother and sister had taken up bookbinding in the hope of adding to the family income. They did not persist in this undertaking.

Kiev, December 23, 1928

Haven't been to the post office for several days. I sat the whole time in my warm, quiet burrow and worked, and so I don't know the news from Brussels. I would like to believe that everything's fine with you. Katya sent Zhenya a parcel of caviar, etc., on the 10th of this month. I hope she'll get it all right. We're having a wonderful winter here—snowy, sunny clear. From my window I can see a clearing glistening in the sun and trees in snowy caps. It's very pretty. Today is Sunday and so I am going out for a walk. Tomorrow I'll go to the post office. Spend the holidays gaily and greet the new year with whatever—well, with champagne in your hands! Good-bye, or, I should say, until tomorrow, because I'll write from the post office.

Yours,

I.

1 9 2 9

Received a "thank-you" letter from Anyuta. Sonya too, of course, found use for my forty rubles. Katya also sends us her blessings. She, the sinful soul, still had my hard-earned two hundred rubles stored away somewhere that were destined to be sent to you and Zhenya. I assume that she is nibbling away at them bit by bit. Well, what can you do? And, of course, God forbid that you should let out a squeak about it. Katya wrote to you about the mineral-baths cure—well, what do you think of it? Have you asked the doctor?

I was awfully pleased with the news about the car. I'm counting on your driving me all over Belgium. Now, if you buy a car, in my opinion it should be a Fiat. But you must start taking driving lessons well beforehand—it takes several months to become sufficiently sharp at it. You must start right away. It will be lots of fun and I don't see why you shouldn't do something pleasant for once; life is full of unpleasant business and so we have to invent things that are fun for ourselves. On my instructions, Katya has subscribed to that newspaper for you. Let me know when you start getting it. I'm very sorry that Annushka has left, but you must do your utmost to find someone to replace her. Zhenya had quite a large order but I don't know whether she has handed it in or not and am waiting very impatiently for further reports from her on that subject.

I'm really quite put out that you still haven't received my twenty-five dollars; I'll do my best to speed the business up.

As to me, my dear, discreet relatives, I have no news. And that, intentionally. My wishes have been fulfilled. I have swept out of my way all my stinking acquaintances, got away from the hustle and bustle, and am living on a chipped-off bit of the world, in philosophical solitude and work. I think up something and then, slowly, unwaveringly carry it out, for, as you know, if there's one thing God didn't grudge me, it's doggedness. As usual, I have lots of secret plans, and all that makes my life full, good and intense. It's real heaven for me here at Stepanida's. I have to run three miles to town and am happy about it. And I have decided deep down in my heart that I won't have any news for a long time to come. We all—me, Zhenya and the lot of us—must start leading a regular life; we must train ourselves to do so. Only that silly B.D. sticks in my throat like a fishbone. Still, I'm sure we'll think up something.

Oh, Beatific Feodosya, why do you write so seldom? Is it because you have no strength? Do you have proper glasses? It is outrageous that you can't find time to go to an oculist for prescription glasses and are still primitive enough to try to fit yourself up with a pair of "suitable" specs from some flea market. And how are things with your choppers? You'd better get yourself fixed or you'll go to pot, you old fool, and we'll miss you. So long, *mes vieux*. Don't forget your loving,

I.B.

Kiev, January 7, 1929

My dear relatives, who in turn have relatives of their own, and may they perish! Haven't written to you for some days because Katya landed her latest blow on me from which I still haven't quite recovered. I have already written to you about that request to "borrow two thousand" from me, a request that I rejected. Well, I thought, that's the end of the business. But then, one fine day, as they say, namely, last Friday, I received a heart-rending telegram: Beseech you to save us—let us have eight hundred rubles for a couple of weeks. What was I to do? I do not have that kind of money. So I sold five-hundred rubles' worth of Zhenya's bonds and wired them to Katya. Of course, I haven't said a word about it to Zhenya and I feel very mixed up about it all—I am trying to preserve my own kopeks as long as possible to be able to work quietly without depending on the publishers—this is my life-blood—and if later I have to pay back the five hundred rubles to the Gronfeins for the Lyakhetskys (and to think that she still has my other two hundred rubles lying around somewhere unless she's already put them into circulation)—then business will really be lousy for me! I've been trying to hold on to the money for you and for my own board—and now look what's happening to my plans for the future! It looks as if it is a real crime to have a character like mine, that is, never to moan, complain and all that. Everyone around you decides that there is nothing more natural than to pounce upon such a "lucky" fellow! It's both a misfortune and a joke. To make the picture complete, there's a postcard from Iosif from Odessa in which he playfully writes that if I have "the means and the opportunity" I should send him thirty or forty rubles. He's probably starving. So what do you expect me to do with all these *malheureux*—may they get lost! Please, don't let out a squeak to Katya or anyone else about this letter: I've simply told you in my own words the story of a small opera libretto based on the drama *Members of an Artel*.

My mind feels so oppressed that I no longer know what to write. The only thing that consoles me is the weather—we're having a magnificent, sunny, clear, invigorating winter. Ah, my poor dears, how nice it would be if you were here!

When are you moving? How is Mama's heart? Mama's teeth? Mama's eyes? Mera's tummy? Grisha's car? Zhenya intends to go and visit you in February so try to have a "wonderful time."

For my part, exhausted as I am by the blows landed on my head by our relatives, I cannot write and I think I'll go to see a traveling menagerie instead. There is a monkey there and a redheaded clown and, since I am forced into it, I might just as well have some fun. So good-bye, my respected relatives who, in turn, have . . . etc., etc.

I.

Kiev, January 22, 1929

Beatific Feodosya,

Katya wrote to me that she will return me the money by the promised date so that, for the time being, there is no need to worry.

Lyakhetsky passed through Kiev but he didn't get to see me because no one knows my address here and he couldn't find me. He spent quite a long time in Kiev, for we now have snowdrifts and the trains are delayed. Perhaps his arriving in Moscow will spoil the chances of the debt's being settled, although I don't think so, for the money was mostly for Sasha who used it for his business. In any case, it is still a bit early to worry about it. God forbid you should write a word to Katya about all this. Please don't do so!

My trip to Odessa has not yet been decided on definitely. I have drawn up new conditions for the film studio and am awaiting their answer.

I am receiving gay and cheerful letters from Zhenya; she often mentions you and says she intends to go and pay you a visit. I don't understand why she doesn't communicate directly with you —I suppose it's just out of laziness. I have already told you that she got a large order in her painting line*—and so, for a few months now, she has no need to worry about work or money. That's very nice.

I'll be very sorry if I have to leave Kiev, because of my apartment —I'm sure I wouldn't soon find another one like it—and because of the wonderful, poetic Kiev winter. Only in the countryside around Kiev can one fully appreciate the beauty of the Russian winter. I hope to send you some of my snapshots soon—I am so delighted with my camera.

Well, I guess that'll be all for today. It's eight o'clock in the morning now and I've already had my tea. Outside, snow is falling on the clearing. I must earn my daily bread. Good-bye. I have asked you so much about your and Merochka's health that I don't wish to repeat myself and will just wait for a proper answer.

Love,

I.

* Babel's wife had begun to restore canvasses. She was a gifted painter.

Kiev, February 6, 1929

We are having freezing weather. I have even got a chilblain on the tip of my nose and Stepanida is putting goose fat on it. I seldom go to the post office in town and that's why I write less often.

Judging from Mama's letter, she really feels better and that has cheered me up a great deal. The management of VUFKU are trying to convince me not to go to Odessa but to try to work for the Kiev studios. If we agree on terms, I'll have to remain in Kiev for another month or so. I had already got used to the idea of moving to Odessa and it makes me quite sad to abandon it, although, of course, working in Kiev is in every sense more advantageous, particularly from the money point of view. Anyuta informs me that she'll be happy to take the trunk and so I'll send it to her before I leave Kiev. I have made a list of the things the trunk contains and so there is no danger that anything will get lost. I received a letter from Katya in which she informs me that she can send me the money but that if I don't need it just now, she would like to have a bit more time. I wrote and told her that although I didn't have a present need for the sum, I might receive a letter from Zhenya at any moment demanding it. Therefore, I wrote, Katya should be prepared to send the sum to the address I give her as soon as requested. In Moscow, the cold is even more severe than here and it appears that Katya's apartment isn't a particularly warm one. But, in any case, it is wonderful that she should have an apartment of her own.

I have already written to you that our mirror was taken away from Borev. Didn't you get that letter?

Poor Zhenya has been ailing for almost a whole month now. She had a very bad case of the grippe and it seems there's a very violent flu epidemic in Western Europe. When she recovers, she will be able, with her improved material situation, to take her mother to southern France to pay you a visit. It's just such a shame that her health hasn't been too good this past month.

I received an inquiry from Tashkent, from Merochka, about

whether I could get her any translating to do from French and English from Gosizdat. I was forced to write and tell her that there are so many translators that they could use them for fish bait and that the best thing for her would be to try to get herself a job in Tashkent. Let the poor thing fend for herself.

In a couple of days I'll let you know what the VUFKU's final decision is and, consequently, what the plans are for the forthcoming month. So far, thank God, I have nothing new to report. I am laboring with "long-range plans" in view. My health and the state of my nerves are infinitely better than they were when we were last together and I feel as if I were regaining my former writing form. Living surrounded by snow and proletarians has always had a beneficial effect upon me.

Now, let's change the record and ask you: how is Mera's health? How are the tummy and the nose? I, can you imagine, haven't had a single head-cold since the beginning of the winter and that despite trotting to see . . . one particular fellow. And upon that, goodby,

I.

Kiev, February 20, 1929

My dears,

I write seldom because I really do not have much to write about. I've already told you that I'll do the work I was supposed to do in Odessa in Kiev. This way, it will be much more profitable. I'll probably stay here until mid-March and then take off for the northern Caucasus. I am due for a change of air and longing for it. My stay in Kiev is the only instance of industriousness and "worldly wisdom" in my existence. I didn't think I'd be able to submit to a routine that is outwardly so boring and monotonous. But I find now that this routine has been as good for me as a cure in a good sanatorium and that it has restored both my mental and my physical balance.

I haven't received anything from Zhenya since her letter about her grippe—she's such an awful letter-writer. I wired and got an answer that everyone was in good health and all was fine. Now I am waiting for a letter from her. They were supposed to go to southern France but I don't know how all that came off. Each time, Zhenya has mentioned her intention of taking a trip to Brussels and I hope you'll soon get together.

How do you like your new apartment? Describe it to me in greater detail. It's a shame Mera has no work; perhaps Zhenya could help her in that. Ah, we certainly could do without unemployment.

The apocalyptic cold has abated and the weather, although still quite cold, is pleasant once again. The cold wave apparently swept over all Europe and I've been told that in Paris the temperature went as low as 5° below zero.

Well, I suppose that's all. "Guard your dear health," as they say in the Ukraine. What is the situation with Mama's mobility? For how long is she allowed to walk? I still haven't received an answer to my query about Mera's health. I am waiting for it.

Veuillez, mesdames et messieurs, agréer l'expression de ma sympatie [sic] *la plus profonde,*

I.

Kiev, February 28, 1929

Dear Merochka,

Your tearful letter is, I believe, tearful mainly because you were ill when you wrote it. If we stop and think that the cold wave swept over all Europe, causing countless disasters, how can we complain—in such a world even death looks pretty.

The news about Annushka is serious. It should be well understood by now that I am quite powerless in the matter. But there is hope that there will be work and I think Zhenya will send her the order during the first half of March. I'll do my best, but it is more a matter of luck than of effort spent. I am sure that everything will be all right in the end, so let's keep calm.

I believe Zhenya will come to see you very soon. She didn't take her mother to southern France because the cold wave had spread and it was hardly worth going all that way only to find the cold there too. In every letter, she tells me that she is longing to go and see you and it looks as if her wish is soon to be realized. I am expecting any day to receive an announcement of her departure.

The bitter cold has abated a little and the weather is tolerable now. In any case, my stay in Kiev is coming to an end. I must leave for the Kuban on my exotic literary business, if and as soon as I get a telegram from Mitya Schmidt, the director of the Krasnodar Cavalry School. The work I was supposed to do in Odessa I have completed in Kiev and so I am able to choose where I wish to stay. If you get a telegram from me announcing my departure for Krasnodar, write to me at the following address: c/o D. A. Schmidt, Director of the Krasnodar Cavalry School, USSR. I am expecting a lot from this trip and am very pleased about it. Please, *mon vieux*, try and emulate my unwavering—*inébranlable*—optimism. Cheer up, it's not yet time to despair! I'll write to you again tomorrow because, according to my sources of information, I should get a message from my worthy wife. *Zeigezind*, which, in translation, means good health, and enthusiastic regards to your and my relatives. I'll write to you soon,

Your worthy brother,

I.

Khrenovoye, April 15, 1929

My dear ones,

Life here would be like paradise for me if I were not ceaselessly thinking of you. I wake up at night covered with cold sweat. Unfortunately I won't stay here for very long but will have to go back to Rostov. So keep writing to the same address. For some days I'll have to live without letters from you and that fact is causing me unendurable worry.

Here, it is still winter, a snowy film covers everything and only now has the spring sun started to thaw it. The mud is impassable but the horses and colts and the whole way of life at the stud farm are such a delight that I can forget everything except for your troubles which I cannot get out of my head.

I'll write to you often because only in that imperfect communication am I able to find a semblance of peace and satisfaction.

I plan to go back to Rostov on the twentieth or twenty-first.

Lots of love,

I.

Rostov-on-Don, April 27, 1929

Am sending you two Russian books to read and an English translation of my things,* that I received from London yesterday. It is nicely produced but the biographical note is wildly hilarious—Mama is promoted to a Moldavian Jewess.

Mama's scribblings on your letters are balm to my heart. What have you decided about Royat? Of course it makes more sense for you to go to Zhenya's than for her to come to see you. As for me, I'll never manage to get out of here before the end of the summer, however hard I try. I know what it implies but still I cannot leave before August. I must think for all of us, organize a solid, stable life for every one of us, and I'm sure that if I gave up this work, it would be the end of everything. And so I cannot do anything before I have finished the task on hand. I know, my dear little old ladies, that that sounds hard and callous, but I have grown smarter now and I won't be chasing ten hares at the same time any more. Besides, I feel responsible for all of you and cannot afford the luxury of rushing around in all directions. Zhenya knows about my affairs. When you get the fifty dollars I wrote to you about, please wire me just one word: "Received."

I've had a lot of trouble with Katya. She has only now started paying back her debt. Her unreliability (of course, they have had all sorts of difficulties—one of their associates was arrested, Sasha left for somewhere and still hasn't returned after five weeks, etc., etc.) has made things extremely painful for me. I am writing to you about it only now that the business is coming to a happy ending.

Dear Mama, I laughed a lot over what you wrote about my having no apartment and about malaria or something. Since Sergievo,

I've never had an apartment like the one I have now and, in general, I am surrounded by "admiration," attention, consideration and comfort such as ten poor old Jewish mamas wouldn't be able to give me. No, my dear, I am very comfortable in Rostov and the road toward my "own" family home lies through Rostov. If only your health were all right, I am sure the rest would take care of itself. Do your best to spend the summer in Royat with your daughter. I want to believe I'll find you completely recovered. Urge Mera to write frequently to me for then I feel that I am participating in your life.

Don't be depressed because you're having a sad Passover—they have been trying to console us for the last few thousand years by saying that "everything will be better next year in Jerusalem." And indeed—a person with courage should always find the inner resources to overcome sad thoughts.

Good-bye, my dear ones,

I.

Merochka, the most convenient way for me to receive my mail is at General Delivery, Main Post Office.

* *Red Cavalry* was originally published in Nadia Helstein's translation by Alfred A. Knopf, Inc., London and New York, 1929.

Rostov-on-Don, May 5, 1929

My dears,

Owing to the fact that your letters have become cheerful, my spirits have risen. Besides, the weather has turned so wonderful now. We're having lovely summer days. This evening I'm at last moving to the summer quarters (they couldn't get the room ready earlier) and there I'll plunge into work. I have a week's work to catch up with—all Soviet employees have from the first to the sixth off and I've got into the general routine. My plans are simple: I must arrange my financial affairs by next year; am now engaged in negotiations on that subject and hope to conclude them in the course of May; secondly, to work; thirdly, to come and see you not later than August. I won't be able to make it earlier. I say this, fully aware of the meaning of my words—I will be *unable* to leave before August.

Toward the end of July, Lyova should arrive in Paris. I am very happy about it. If Mama's health enabled her to move to France, I would really be infinitely grateful to the Creator.

Zhenya writes that everything is all right with her. Her apartment is at your disposal. What is the result of the ray treatment? How is your health, Merochka? With all the other tragedies, you must have quite forgotten about yourself.

Well, that's all there is. If we use our brains, everything will be fine. And it looks as if I have gained a tiny bit of wisdom.

I.

Rostov-on-Don, June 1st, 1929

By itself, Mama's handwriting on your letter was quite enough to make me happy. "God grant that everything should be all right."

After a long silence, have received a quite reassuring letter from Zhenya: everything is wonderful with her and she seems to be in an excellent mood. Her doctor says that her pregnancy is progressing ideally and he only hopes that everything will continue the way it's going now. Zhenya is living with Ira [Irina] and apparently they will stay together till the end. Unfortunately, Lyova's arrival has been delayed because of certain difficulties at his factories. I am placing great hopes on his arrival because I would like to settle the question of B.D. once and for all. One way or the other, it must be cleared up.

As to your sister and my aunt—she has stuck her quill you know where in me. There is complete silence about the two hundred rubles and I will have to cover them myself. It is such a disgusting way to act that if they don't settle their debt I'll break off all relations with them. That will clear the air and I'll feel easier. And that's not even mentioning the money she managed to wheedle out of me before. So good luck to them or, rather, let them go to hell, it won't be a great loss to us and they won't get a bagel hole from me in the future.

I have asked you before about Mama's appearance—please write and tell me about it. Zhenya has sent me snapshots of herself. She looks great. There's no more room left to write. Be good, *Zeigezind,*

Isya.

Rostov-on-Don, *June 29, 1929*

Am leaving for Kharkov today (I have to work there in the archives of the Russian Civil War). Then I will go to Kiev where I'll settle my financial accounts with the Film Studios. I expect to be back in Rostov between the tenth and the twelfth of July. I'll wire you when to write to General Delivery, Kiev.

Poor Zhenya is now counting the days. She is, of course, going through the most difficult period now. But her pregnancy on the whole has been very satisfactory and there is every reason to assume that the confinement will also go well.

I am very disappointed to hear that you never get out of the city. Of course, if Mama's health makes it impossible, there is no point in talking about it, but my heart is longing for you to graze a bit on the grass in the sunshine.

Despite the fact that Raya is now helping Fenya, it would seem like a good thing if Mera thought of work too. How is Annushka getting along? Why is there no news from her?

Here, it is very hot and there is nothing pleasant about travel in dusty railroad cars. But since I move around in "soft carriages" it is quite bearable. I will write you again from Kharkov, my lovelies, and in the meantime, I press you mentally to my broad chest and pray to our private God that everything is all right with you,

I.

Kiev, *July 15, 1929*

It is the fifteenth already but still no wire from Zhenya. I wrote to her that the world has never yet seen a more circumspect woman.

I am quite worried and rush to the telegraph office three times a day. The last news I had that Zhenya was fine and well is a week old. Nothing since then. She, poor thing, is just as anxious to wire us as we are to get her wire.

I have wound up my business in Kiev but am staying on here because I am afraid to miss the telegram. Write to my old Rostov address. How do you like being out in the country? You'll get your money this month. When are you going to resume your ray treatment? You must go on with it if it does you any good. Today I will drop in on the old Zeiligers, who need a moral shot in the arm each time. I'll write more in the evening, for I can't say all I want just now, being in a feverish state. My best to you,

I.

Rostov, July 20, 1929

Dear Grandma, Aunt and Uncle,

She turned out to be a girl. Wise people say that a devoted daughter will provide for the old parents better than a lazy son. So let us thank the Creator and try to live the best we know how. Ira's wire was very comforting. Zhenya and the baby are doing very well. I am anxiously awaiting further news. Ah, I had a terrible time waiting for that wire, with the unhurried temperament of my spouse manifesting itself to the full. She carried that child for eleven months, unless it is the progeny of a railroad conductor.

As soon as I received the wire, I rushed to the railroad station, got onto the train and was off, because I had nothing else to do in Kiev. So now my center of operations until I leave to join "the family" will be Rostov-on-Don. In Kiev I saw to it that the old folks will get the money regularly and that is a considerable achievement. I got here last night and am feeling quite tired. I'll write in greater detail tomorrow.

I.

Rostov, July 23, 1929

Just got a wire from Zhenya. Both ladies are doing fine so everything's marvelous. The wire was sent by Natasha. Natasha is a nice name, although her patronymic will spoil it somewhat. I had asked Zhenya to give her a Hebraic "label" (I like Judith very much) but she didn't heed my request. I don't resent it—she is in a better position to see what is needed.

I was really elated to receive the news that you are in Spa. This month as well as next, you will receive money from Volodya. What worries me is that you may have forgotten to notify the post office to forward the money orders to Spa.

Please don't think, Merochka, that I forgot about your birthday. I was, however, in such confusion that day that I couldn't raise my hand to write a congratulatory message. I was sure that something terrible had happened to Zhenya with all possible time limits past. I don't suppose that in the past century any woman has had such a long period of gestation. But all's well that ends well. Write more often and I will keep bombarding you with letters.

Please, be well,

I.

Rostov-on-Don, August 1st, 1929

I am so sorry for poor little Merochka. Why should such a horrible thing happen to her? Is it possible that she has to go through that trouble without end? Don't you let me down at least, Grandma, stay well, will you?

Nothing from Zhenya except that one letter written after her confinement. Then she wrote that everything was progressing perfectly except that for four days there had been no milk. I don't know whether milk will appear at all or whether the baby will have to be bottle-fed.

I have come to town to pick up my mail and to do some shopping and will leave for the country in the evening. It is unbearably hot. Compared with the town, my place is real bliss. The more I live here the better I'm getting to like the northern Caucasus.

Fenya should have received her money long ago. I am waiting for word from her about it.

I am doing a bit of work and soon I will take some energetic steps to obtain a leave of absence. I want you to stay at Spa as long as possible for, after all, it's much healthier than Brussels. Try to take advantage of all the cures.

I cannot go on writing, my dear Mama—the seventh layer of sweat is dripping off me, there are millions of people in the post office and everyone of them is stinking and dripping. I'll write a better letter at my leisure when I get back home. Above all, look after your health. Is Grisha with you? Give him a cheerful greeting from me. Until tomorrow then, my sickly ones,

I.

Lipetsk, August 31, 1929

A.K.* has changed a lot. He has shrunk, grown quite wrinkled and, in general, is a very sick man. It looks as if he is seriously ill although the doctors cannot agree on what it is. Some say it is a kidney inflammation, others that it is appendicitis. My impression is that a serious disease is taking its toll inside him.

His conversation is, of course, unchanged. He is still as much in love with literature as before, still as ardent and naïve.

This is a magnificent spot, the countryside is lovely, cool, reassuring, so Russian, a landscape without bright colors, a quiet river, groves, oak woods.

Am leaving, probably for Khrenovaya, tomorrow. Write me as often as you can at the Rostov address.

I.

* A.K. and Al. Konst. refer to Alexander Konstantinovich Voronsky (1884-1937?), the founder and editor of *Krasnaya Nov*, refuge for the "Fellow Travellers." He was expelled from the Party and exiled to Siberia in 1927, then permitted to return, but he "disappeared" permanently in 1937.

Khrenovaya, September 4, 1929

Hope Mama's back is all better. Ah, everything was going too well, something like that had to happen. I am very happy to hear that Lyova has come—that will distract Zhenya a little. I am bombarding them with letters, for they must after all make definite plans for their life. I am firmly determined to bring "my family" home, and in order to do that in the more or less near future, I must start working on it right away. Besides, Lyova is there now and it is the best time to decide. I am waiting for word from Zhenya on that subject.

If Mama's health will allow it, the best thing, of course, would be for her to wait for my arrival. Especially as, since Zhenya is not in Paris, there is nowhere for her to go. But Merochka needs to go to Paris even more than Mama, and, once there, she should concentrate on attending to her liver, if need be in a sanatorium. That is the central problem.

For the second day now, I am wallowing in bliss in Khrenovaya. I don't know how long I will remain here—it will depend on how I feel and how much work I am able to do here. I am very happy that my work has entered a propitious phase and some of its outlines are becoming recognizable. And now, living at Khrenovaya, I feel that I can no longer do without the countryside. Nature is, after all, the only inexhaustible source of hope, freshness and work. Please write to the Rostov address. Eat, drink, and be merry. My best regards to our dear Esculapius,

I.B.

Khrenovaya, September 12, 1929

Maria, my sister!

Send me the following parcel to General Delivery, Rostov: six pairs of *fil-d'Ecosse* ladies' stockings, rather light colors, size nine to nine and a half; one pair of ladies' kid gloves (or light-colored leather), six or six and a quarter. I need these things very badly for a benefactress. Throw in some chocolate for me this time, unless the customs duties are too large. I would very much appreciate it if you would do this. As for cash, we'll settle somehow, God willing. You could get the sum from Zhenya who is prospering since her brother's arrival. She has already taken the young creature to a spa, so, as you can see, my daughter has started out in life in a well-organized way. I have inquired about how things stand with Lyova and about their financial and family affairs but thus far haven't had any reply.

Haven't received Mama's personal scribblings for a long time and miss them very much.

I.

Rostov, October 2, 1929

As I wrote to Blyuma, I believe we shall meet, but the waiting period must be measured in weeks rather than in days. It has never even occurred to her what difficulties must be overcome to attain it. I have never missed those close to me as much as I miss them now, but there are circumstances that are stronger than my will and I am not willing to do something that is incompatible with my dignity in order to speed the happy day.

Willy-nilly I have come to think that it is easier for the mountain to come to Mohammed than for Mohammed to come to the mountain. Of course, there is hope, but waiting is still a matter of *weeks*. One good thing is that I have a safety valve—my work and the regular life for which I have always longed and am now achieving. But then poor Blyuma has no such safety valve. Nevertheless, I cannot be sad, for I know that happier times for us are not too far away and that I, for one, am preparing properly for those better days.

This is the end of my sheet. Further tender outpourings, *mein Liebchen*, will have to wait for the next opportunity.

I.

Rostov-on-Don, November 2, 1929

Isya left a couple of days ago. As you can see, he looks like nothing on earth and that after spending some time at a spa. His life isn't easy—he has tons of worries and little money. I felt like a real pig, I was very tired that day and inflated myself like a turkey cock. *Parole d'honneur*, by nature, we are better, more attractive, more spirited.

Tomorrow or the day after, will let you know the answer from the University of the Don concerning Grisha.

Am waiting to be summoned to Moscow. If only you knew how much I don't want to go there. But it looks as if I'll have to. I must go the rounds, as they say. Until tomorrow,

I.

Rostov-on-Don, November 23, 1929

Dear Fenyusha,

This is my last letter from Rostov. Am leaving for Moscow tomorrow morning. I think everything will turn out all right. My personal affairs do not bother me: things always take care of themselves as far as I am concerned. But I am worried about Merochka. Wouldn't it be better to move to Paris first and only then to go through the course of treatment. You were quite right to keep the money. It is a shame that you can't get a bit more cash so that you could get on more energetically with the treatment. What effect is the ultraviolet-ray treatment having? With my inexhaustible optimism, I still believe that Mera will be able to rid herself of that damned illness.

Katya has a nice place in Sochi. For the first time in many years, the poor thing can breathe more freely. I believe I have already written to you that I sent twenty-five rubles to Anyuta. I remind you once more of the Slonims' address: Apartment 12, 13/15

Mashkov Lane, Pokrovka. No matter how long I have to stay in Moscow, I'll live outside the city so as not to interrupt my writing. I am very partial to writing. It gives me strength and enjoyment and I hate interrupting it. I already have a room outside the city waiting for me so that I can't complain that I am not being looked after.

You should go to Paris as soon as possible, my dear ones. Lyova writes that Zhenya *klube nakhes.* Well, that may be so but it doesn't look as if anyone intended to take the old woman. That is something I am prepared to fight about to the last.

How is it that your apartment has become warm? Maybe the overhaul of the house has had its effect. I assume then that now you have a very adequate place to live in.

I am leaving tomorrow, and with pleasure. Although I've greatly enjoyed my stay in Rostov, my nomadic nature is pushing me on. Anyway, all my friends have moved away from here.

I will write to you from Moscow as soon as I have the layout of things.

Look after yourself, Mendele Pupik, get better and give me a chance to heave a sigh of relief.

I.

P.S. Am receiving daily postcards from Iosif. The word "shit" is an unfailing feature of each of them.

[Written above the date.] The best thing would be to write to General Delivery, Kursk R.R. Station, Moscow.

Kuskovo,* December 2, 1929

I hope very much that this letter doesn't find you in Brussels and that you will have already made the acquaintance of the little supplement to our family. I am expecting a full description of that person from you. Because of my moving, all my correspondence has been thrown out of gear and for a fortnight I haven't had any of your worthy messages to read.

Moscow has become more beautiful, more businesslike and noisier. Faithful to custom, I am staying outside the city—in Kuskovo, formerly the property of the Sheremetevs, about twenty minutes from Moscow by train. And I am going on with my work. I have hardly seen anyone yet and, anyhow, I don't even feel like doing so. Life in my little house surrounded by a century-old garden and by immaculate snow is full enough without any of my idiotic acquaintances.

Still, I went to see the Lifshits. Strictly speaking, nothing's changed for them. Their daughter looks so much like Isya that I had the impression that I was having a hallucination. I dropped in on them in the evening and she got out of bed, rushed over to me in her nightdress and reeled off a list of the presents I had sent her from Rostov. I had time to notice that this little Jewess has, like every other little Jewess, very short legs, and that her little behind sags very low over her legs—so she'll be a girl like all the others.

As to Sasha's daughter, she is very ugly. Her mother is monstrously fat. Sasha has his feet solidly planted on the ground and is prospering in the job I got for him three years or so ago. Tomorrow or the day after, I'll go to see Iosif. I believe Katya is still in Sochi.

The friend from whom I expected to find out about the results of my business has left for a few days for Leningrad and is due back any moment now.

Merockha, please get control of yourself and take advantage of your stay in Paris to look after your health and also, of course, to take your mind off your worries. This Paris trip ought to do you good and bring you some relief.

The Lifshits told me that Lyusya was expected to come to Moscow for a few days from Leningrad. It seems she has turned into a lady with a great deal of poise and composure. For her sake, I'll break my proud isolation and go and see her.

When I am in the city, I still have my room with the Slonims, who treat me with the same tender adoration. For the twenty-four hours I spent at their place, I felt as if I were with my own Mama. Their apartment is magnificent: four rooms with the latest modern comforts. And one of those rooms, from here to eternity, belongs to me. . . . There's friendship for you.

Al. Konst. is in Moscow. He is taking a treatment—now I want you to be all ears and attention—of injections of pregnant women's urine, and it seems he is thriving on it. They say that this is the latest medical discovery and that it is extremely "effective." In the train, when I told a Jewish lady about that remedy, she grew thoughtful and said: "I don't really expect *they* charge too much for it. Why, it's a quite readily available item."

And with that, good-bye. As you can gather, so far my impressions of Moscow are not overabundant. This is due to the fact that I am trying to go on with my work rather than hunting for impressions. Be well, damn you.

Je vous embrasse de tout mon coeur,

I.

I repeat, in case, the Slonims' address: Apt. 12, 13/15 Mashkov Lane, Pokrovka, Moscow.

* Kuskovo is the splendid eighteenth-century palace of the Counts Sheremetev. After the Revolution it was converted and served for a while as a rest home for writers.

1 9 5 0

Moscow, January 16, 1930

Your last news, that Merochka is feeling better, cheered me up a great deal, but now you have fallen silent again. How am I to account for it? Is it possible that in all this time Mama hasn't managed to get away to Paris? Who is responsible for the delay? I asked Zhenya to be quick about getting the passport extended. "Toss" her a wire—that will shake her up.

My affairs are progressing little by little: I am working and waiting for my vacation. I hope the vacation is not too far beyond the mountains, but it is quite beyond my power to bring it any closer. It is very warm here, not really like winter at all, and I do a lot of walking, all over Moscow which is completely transformed. Today, I'll go and see Katya whom I haven't seen for a long time.

Did you get the money for December? Write to me c/o Slonim, Apt. 12, 13/15 Mashkov Lane. I am living in great luxury here and am enjoying bodily comforts after my provincial existence.

I.

Moscow, February 4, 1930

Dear Grandmother,
I still insist that the foundling girl cannot resemble me for the good reason that she's plain. As soon as I get to your town, I'll lodge a complaint with *la chambre correctionelle*. Do you still know how to look after children and do they let you? Do you shove a grimy pacifier into your granddaughter's mouth as you used to do with your son when we lived on Dalnitskaya and Balkovskaya streets? Do you chew a day-old bagel with seeds on it with your gums and then give it to her wet with saliva as you used to do to your son? for which he will never forgive you. And then too, you begrudged me diapers, you didn't give me orange juice, you rocked your son in a cradle, killing his self-reliance, and if the stuff I am producing turns out badly, I shall know who to blame.

I.

Kiev, February 9, 1930

I didn't have time to write to you from Moscow. I got here in the middle of the night, seven hours late, because of snowdrifts. Kiev is buried in snow and it's very beautiful. It is all the consequence of a snowstorm that swept over here. Today or tomorrow

I'll find out how long I'll have to remain in Kiev and will do my best not to make it any longer than necessary. I have just written to the three generations of my womenfolk in Paris. Please keep addressing your letters to me at the same Moscow address.

Regards to Grisha from the Mother of Russia's cities.

I.B.

Kiev, February 16, 1930

Dear Merochka,

I've been in Kiev for six days and have completed all my business here. Today I'm leaving for the country, for the sector where what is called "total collectivization" is being carried out. For we have a complete transformation in agriculture and in village life here now. I would never have forgiven myself if I had missed seeing this process with my own eyes—both because it is interesting in itself and because it has a significance transcending anything we have seen.

By the way, I will soon be going back to Moscow, so send letters, as before, to the Slonims' address.

Regards to Grisha,

Yours,

I.B.

[A postcard depicting the Dnieper in flood.]

Dnepropetrovsk (formerly Yekaterinoslav), April 1, 1930

I've spent three days here visiting the huge iron-and-steel works. Am leaving for the Dneprostroi tomorrow and from there am going on to Moscow. Am not sure this postcard will find you still in Brussels. In fact, I'll be very glad if you are already in Paris when it gets to Brussels. Write to Slonim's address.

I.

Moscow, April 27, 1930

Leading beauties *du royaume des Belges,*

I've really had enough of your worries. A young man whose mental and physical gifts are in full bloom has better things to do than keep up a correspondence with retired Odessans. Writers' funerals alone take up so much time. You should have thought of that yourselves! ! !

V.M.'s death completely bewildered me.* His main reason, as they say, was an unhappy love, but of course, years of accumulated weariness played its part too. It's difficult to make out because the letter he left doesn't provide a single clue. Mama probably remembers him, huge and blooming, when he came to see us back in Odessa. . . . A monstrous death.

Did you send my letter to Volodya? I don't know what to do. Now that the secret is out, you'd better not count on his coming up with it too regularly. For this reason, I have taken steps to obtain a certificate from the consul in Paris which will make it possible to send Mama 20-25 dollars a month. I hope that Zhenya will carry out my instruction and go to see the consul. This would be the best solution, because it is sure, permanent and reliable.

My dears, of all the sorrows that you manage to think up with such liberality, there is only one real grief—Zhenya's illness. Of course, she is young and her system will overcome this acute crisis, but she should be watched and taken care of untiringly. As things stand, this is impossible. I understand that better than anyone and, at last, I feel the need for a corner of my own. This need has come over me later than we might have wished, but once I have my mind set on something, I don't deviate from it. In order to go to Tashkent, I will have to do a lot of work. I will do it and sooner or later (and certainly not later than this summer) I will make the trip a reality, all difficulties notwithstanding. My extremely simple plan is to bring Zhenya back with me. I've written to Lyova about it and I can't give it up—I see no other way of establishing a home. Zhenya and I will talk it all over when we see each other, but I am already making preparations. Besides, I must bring peace to her poor soul. You mustn't complain because she seldom writes. She has to carry on the fight on several fronts. That sort of battle has always strengthened and tempered me, but unfortunately our strengths are not comparable. Zhenya is my main concern and, in general, I will do everything to bring us all physical and mental calm. Her letters are full of admiration for our daughter. Apparently, of all our family, only that little Weeweeki and I have any talent for gaiety.

It would be very good for Mama to go to the country. Try to arrange it. But then, how could she be left alone with the real, native Belgians? What sort of deaf-and-dumb language would they use to communicate? So you'd better go along too.

About a week ago, in Moscow, the spring sat picking her nose for a while, then decided to come out into the street, but yesterday she got fed up with it, and now we have wind, cold and leaden clouds, and in Orekhovo-Zuyevo it's snowing. Until I take my trip to Tashkent, I won't move from here. The preparations demand my presence here. Write more often to Zhenya without making any special demands on her. We must be considerate of her.

And on that note, good-bye, my played-out old drummer.

My warmest kisses. I think there's nothing to be dejected about and that the flag is flying high. I sit at home every evening now, sip tea, work and dream. I see only three or four "tried friends" and have become solid and unbending, like an old Englishman.

I.

* Babel is referring to the poet Vladimir Mayakovsky, born in 1893, who committed suicide on April 14, 1930.

Moscow, May 10, 1930

Dearest Merochka,

I have an unshakable faith in the future and so cannot share your sad thoughts. Life is complicated, especially for a man of my profession, a man who pursues his profession with such fanatical demandingness toward himself. I've never before felt such strength, confidence and inner calm (in spite of everything) as I feel now. My relatives should be glad of this, but instead they pour a stream of tears over me. Come to your senses. You shouldn't be such neurotic wet blankets. After all, how can one distort the simple things of this world? Wake up! Zhenya is ill. She is young and she will get well again. She is under treatment. She has other things to think of than writing to you. It's no tragedy, good God, really it's not. Perhaps because I am not asleep, because I don't sit still in one place, because I putter about among the enormous events that are taking place here, because I go forward toward this life's triumphs, because I look at them with open eyes—perhaps because of all this, I have *la vision nette* of many things which to you seem insurmountable. I have changed a lot, my dear, since we last saw each other. I have become steadier, calmer, harder, and I am ripe for family life. Perhaps you will think it's a bit late in the day, but that's how things have worked out and you can't undo what's done. And then, perhaps the course of my development in the past was natural and inevitable. That course of development has been especially hard for Zhenya and for my immediate family because they were not pursuing their own objectives but were dragged along behind a wild horse. Now the wild horse has quietened down and the spiritual obstacles—the only obstacles *qui comptent*—have been overcome. And now, in the first place, I must get a refill of new impressions, a thing which is very important to me, and then rest and be refreshed before I start on a decisive phase of my work. When I get back from here, I will have to rewrite a few things for publication and only after that will I be able to take that journey to see Natasha. I reckon to see her when the warm days come round. I'm hoping to get a letter from you tomorrow and am waiting for it with a beating heart.

Whatever is my poor Fenyale doing? I have no words to express my ever-present anxiety for her. Merochka, write to me as often as possible even if it's only postcards, even if it's only a few words. As before, I'll let you know all my addresses.

The frost seems to have burst a gut and today it is noticeably warmer. I have a hope now that I will be able to travel in bearable weather. As to Molodenovo, I will go back there in March. By then, perhaps, the snow will be melting already.

It's time for bed. Tomorrow morning I have to go to the station. Good night to you too, *chers enfants de mon coeur.*

[A postcard with a view of Moscow: The Kremlin from Kropotkin Quay.]

Moscow, May 13, 1930

The chances of my being sent on a mission in the middle of the summer are improving and as a result I am full of cheer, a thing which I wish for you too, my dear wailing women. I have written to Uncle Tomgorsky. I'm expecting the very pleasantest possible communications from you. I can't remember whether I wrote and told you that I had sent a small piece to VUFKU in Kiev.

Moscow, May 26, 1930

Respected Fellow Countrywoman,

A few days ago I wrote letters to Lyova and Zhenya with roughly the same message. I wrote that my mission cannot be a long one and that I consider the only sensible thing to do is to bring my little (although enlarged) family back home with me. I would have liked to receive word from Zhenya so that in the meantime I could look around for some kind of a home for us. I don't think there's any need to be too hasty about it all, but I feel we should move in that direction. It could be realized, say, early next spring. My letter should disperse all Lyova's fears. Never in my life have my family feelings been as sloppy (spiritually speaking) as now. And it's probably for good. On that count, at least, you can shed your worries. Just so long as Zhenya gets better.

Her financial affairs have improved this month and I think she'll be able to send you something. You really must put yourselves out to pasture. You haven't mentioned anything about your plans for the summer in your letters. It's no use just letting your hands fall helplessly (and mostly for no reason). You must go and bask in the sunshine. I too am probably going out of town this week. In the next few days, I'll pick myself a spot.

I think that yours and Mama's habit of "worrying" is becoming a mental sickness. Really, it's monstrous. Apparently you cannot stand the barest contact with life, or otherwise you have no idea in general what life is like and how to separate happiness from sorrow. You don't know how to gauge sorrows or how to differentiate between them. Every occurrence in life takes on a disproportionate importance for you and one of my first concerns when I see you will be to restore your sense of reality. I know better than you how difficult it is (and one of the most difficult things in life is the work of self-perfection), but my *joie de vivre* never deserts me and I've seen a few things in my life. Nature hasn't done me any special favors, but I'm not lazy about developing courage, doggedness and calm in myself. Really, Merochka, you have to either decide that our vegetating here on this planet is something unbearably sad, or—or to come to your senses and put things in their proper perspective. For the last few years I have only taken a passive part in your lives but now, you see, I intend to cut short this snivelochondria with an iron hand. People get old, sick, but why blot out the sun with your open palms? I must ask both you and Mama to exclude me and everything connected with me from the sphere of your worries. In our house there will be both peace and work—and we'll all be together. It will all be done. There's no need to let out a lot of sobs and sniffles, sniffles and sobs. I'm telling you the truth—I've never felt in such fine fettle, never stood so firmly on my feet as now, and for this reason, all your ohs and ahs over my person seem to me simply stupid, astonishingly stupid. To me, fool that I am, it seems that you should consider yourself lucky to have a son with such an indestructible philosophy, but it's nothing but sniffles and sobs. Pooh, it's stupid. And I admire Natasha more and more. I'm sure I could come to terms with her.

We're having wonderful summer weather and people have somehow become gayer, smoother-tempered. I often go to see Katya, These days I work in the mornings and evenings and during the afternoon I go for walks, and sometimes I drop in on her, stuff myself to the gills with the food of my childhood, sleep a couple of hours, and then have "family tea." I don't need much to be happy. Or rather, I ask a little contribution from others and then process whatever it is within myself.

Go and wash your face. I remain yours, filled with great respect. Heartfelt greetings to my little old woman. I feel that you two should be separated and locked in different cells, because the younger fool plus the older fool make an average stupidity high enough to drive the flies to despair and make them migrate to the neighbors.

With lordly greetings,

I.

P.S. Have sent money to Uncle Ilyusha. To reassure Mama, I enclose the receipt.

[A postcard with a view of Moscow: Bolshoi Theater, Sverdlov Square.]

Moscow, June 7, 1930

It's still winter here, except that it has stopped snowing. Is it true that it's the same where you are? I still haven't been out of town, but I'm longing to go—I just can't decide on the right place. Why haven't you written? I've finally received a telegram from Zhenya saying that everything's fine with her. That has put me in an absolutely iridescent mood, a thing I wish for you too. Write, *mes amis*, more often.

I.

Molodenovo, June 14, 1930

I am living in a village thirty miles from Moscow, near Zvenigorod, in an area often referred to as the "Russian Switzerland." I couldn't have come at a more opportune moment. It's as hot as Egypt here—over 85 degrees. The Moskva is close by and one can swim there, although the river is so shallow that it can be forded at any spot. Tomorrow I will take up my interrupted work. Oh, and I forgot to say that there is a stud farm two-thirds of a mile from my village—the main attraction for me.

A couple of days from now I'll go to Moscow, especially to see to your business, to send you a little dough. Worrying about you people is making me itch all over. Apparently traits inherited from my mother's side are beginning to make themselves felt. I pray fate to let us live through these final weeks in some sort of relative peace, and spend them in work—which at this juncture is decisive for me—otherwise, because of this eternal anxiety for you, I can't even gather up my thoughts. I beg you, *mesdames*, to try to subdue your whining a bit for a while.

Merochka, please do me and yourself a favor and go with Mama to take a long rest. I'll write more fully about this from Moscow, but please remember that if you want to give me courage then you must do something right away for your own and for Mama's health.

Regards to Grisha. I'm hoping that a letter from you will be waiting for me at Anna Grigorievna's. Katya has gone to Odessa. Ada is about to bear fruit. I've sent forty rubles to the aunts. Today I went swimming for the first time. (N.B. It's impossible to drown.) I feel wonderful.

I.B.

Moscow, July 6, 1930

This is the continuation of my letter. I proffer this saying: "I'm a picture, you're a portrait." And I hope to hear the same from you.

They have operated on Lev Ilich. He is recovering slowly.

Tomorrow morning I'm going to Molodenovo where I will probably stay until the 13th. Ilyusha will bring me my letters. Write more often and, Mama, *write in your own hand.* Cheer up, old woman. How can I instill wisdom and calm in you? Your notion of the devil is all wrong, or rather, the way you daub him. As everyone knows, he's not as black as he's painted.

What I hear about Zhenya is good, and as to the fact that she's not much of a letter-writer—that's an old fault. In the autumn we'll begin to live like normal human beings, then those old faults won't matter any more.

I couldn't be happier about your going to Spa. Merochka, you shouldn't begrudge yourself everything; I've already told you several times that your former situation, when you had some kind of a purpose and a foundation, must and will be re-established.

I don't understand your question about Ilya Grigorievich.* I saw him quite a long time ago because Annushka asked me to, and since then haven't heard a thing from him. I wrote to you about the time I did see him, so what is it you want to know now?

I'll write from Molodenovo. Bliss is awaiting me there and my only regret is that I cannot share that bliss with you. We will strive for that.

Good-bye, my doves—*meine tambalekh.*

I.

* The Soviet writer Ilya Grigorievich Ehrenburg had frequent occasion to travel abroad and thus could often see Babel's family—convey messages, etc.

Moscow, July 22, 1930

I came here yesterday for the horse races and spent such a full day that I didn't manage to write to you—and now I'm about to leave to catch my train. I faithfully swear I'll write from Molodenovo this time, with due consideration for your rank and importance and the place which you, *mes petits*, hold in my heart.

All that nasty business with the "interview on the Riviera" has ended in triumph for you and me. The *Literaturnaya Gazeta** [Literary Gazette], which in its impatience (impatience to read my worthy works) went beyond permissible bounds, got the rebuke it was asking for. All's well that ends well. But this fever surrounding my work (as to the temperature this commotion has generated, you can't even imagine) would have worn to shreds any man less inured than me. But I'm holding up under it heroically and proudly offer myself as an example to you. Just don't get sick, and you'll see, everything will be wonderful. Now you can understand why my holiday has been put off so long, and now it is already in sight.

So, until Molodenovo. The burden of years piles up, but I don't feel it, a thing I wish for you, Fedosya, too. I didn't congratulate Merochka because I was involved in that mess with the *Literaturnaya Gazeta*. Let's put off my congratulations till my tomorrow's letter from Molodenovo. I embrace you with all my heart and expect, indeed demand, cheerfulness from you.

Until tomorrow. I have to go to the station now to go to my beloved retreat.

I.

* Bruno Yasensky in *Literaturnaya Gazeta*, no. 28, published a polemical comment on an interview that Babel allegedly gave while on the French Riviera with his wife. (The interview signed by Aleksander Dan, had appeared in the Polish weekly *Wiadomosci Literackie*.) According to the interview, Babel said that it was impossible for him to work freely in the Soviet Union. The matter provoked a good deal of trouble for Babel and he wrote a disclaimer to *Literaturnaya Gazeta*. At a meeting of the FOSP (Federation of Soviet Writers Organizations) the question was discussed and Babel was cleared.

The article by Bruno Yasensky from *Literaturnaya Gazeta* and the press release issued after the FOSP meeting will be found in the Appendix, III a and III b.

Molodenovo, August 12, 1930

This is the very best time of the year in the country—mowing and harvesting time. In Molodenovo they still use sickles for reaping. I have learnt the knack and handle one with infinite delight. It provides gymnastics for body and soul. The weather is hot and I run off to the Moskva for a swim, often twice in the same day. (For Mama's information, I've already told you that it is impossible to find a place in the above-mentioned river more than waist-deep, and only chickens and cigarette butts get drowned.) My work is also going along at a more lively pace. Keeping my aim in mind —seeing Mera and Natasha—I'm driving myself as hard as I can, but in hurrying there's a danger of overspicing it, and one can bring to nought the fruits of many years of effort.

I've written to Katya and Anyuta and I reckon that letters from them and from you must be waiting for me in Moscow. If it were only half as nice in Spa as it is in Molodenovo, I would be happy. Just what kind of treatment are you undergoing in Spa? Give me the low-down on it.

I don't remember whether I've already told you that Zhenya came through with a long letter and some very good photographs. All's fine and dandy with her, apart from her loneliness. As I've already suggested to you many times, all our misfortunes are geographical in nature. There's a very simple solution to the problem but Zhenya doesn't agree with me about it, so we just have to wait.

In her photographs, Natasha looks blooming and a mite Jewish. I assume that Zhenya has already bridged the four-hour gulf between Brussels and Paris. She's very pleased with her new apartment.

Did Grisha go with you to Spa?

On about the fifteenth, I'm going to Moscow for a few hours to receive my money. I'll write from there.

As far as "refurbishing" goes, I'm placing great hopes in Spa. I beg you to justify them and I beg you to take a cure like the Lithuanian Jews used to do in Odessa—from Doctor Zilberberg's into hot sea-water baths, out of the hot sea-water baths into a tent to take a grape diet, from the grape diet into Goberman's kosher restaurant, from Goberman's into the hydro-helio-psycho-therapy sanatorium, from the sanatorium to Doctor Zilberberg, from him to the Khadzhibeyevsky Estuary . . . and so on—*ad infinitum.*

The spirit of my ancestors has risen up in me against one of Papa's rules—to stay clear of nature—and I'm quite prepared to spend the rest of my life in the country with all my loved ones. We have to expect that Natasha's nose will keep peeling throughout her youth. She'll blow her nose in her fingers and mispronounce words like a peasant.

I've nothing more to write about and remain,

IB.

Molodenovo, August 19, 1930

Received a letter from Ada. Everything's fine with her. They say the little girl is sweet. Ada is going to join her husband in Darnitsa at the end of the summer. Apparently the exodus from Odessa will start in September.

I was very happy to get a postcard from Zhenya. She is driving to Arcachon by car with Ira, to look for a place to live. They have got as far as Bordeaux. She left the child in Paris with her nanny and they will join them by train. That worries me a little, but apparently the nanny is quite trustworthy. You write such rubbish about Zhenya's letter-writing that it makes my ears wither. She's just lazy about it, Mama dear, and then too, she's probably ashamed to write now after not having done so for so long.

You're right, Fenyasha, it's better in Molodenovo than in all the spas in the world. I have to go to Dnepropetrovsk on business, but I don't have the strength to tear myself away from here. It's very hot now and it would be a difficult journey, so I've decided to put it off. I'll stay in Molodenovo and do some more work.

The main reason for my happiness in the last [. . .] is that I've started working as I've never worked before—and that is the basis of everything. If I could just get my "little family" over here, then I wouldn't give a damn about anything. If you only knew how much I miss you all. I miss you excessively because I've drifted apart from everyone—from all my acquaintances, from all my friends, the fickle ones and the true ones, which leaves me with only the stablemen and the horses at the stud farm. Good company, *ma mère*, very good.

Well, get better, get better without fail and without let-up.

I.

[A postcard with a view of Leningrad: The Peter-Paul Fortress.]

Leningrad, September 8, 1930

I returned yesterday evening from my "war" campaign, had a good night's rest after many labors and am now about to start my Leningrad day. I'm going to see Lyusya Brodsky. I'm leaving for Moscow a couple of days from now. It's autumn here already but the town is as irresistible as ever. I'm feeling very well.

I.

Moscow, September 15, 1930

This is my third day in Moscow. I'm attending to practical matters (money, food, clothes, underclothes) so that I can be off to Molodenovo again. The cold weather has already begun here and household affairs have to be seen to. I came to Moscow with Lyusya Brodsky and her little boy. He's a nice child. Lyusya came here to visit the Lifshitses for a few days. I'll do my best to sit tight in Molodenovo for the next few weeks, so that I can prepare something for publication, otherwise I'll never get anywhere. I'm very glad about Mama's two kilos and beg you to hold on to them and not give them to anyone. Zhenya's last letter came from Arcachon, but now it's ten days since I received anything from her. I guess one will come any day now.

I saw Annushka. She has a vacation now and she is sewing and ironing for me and keeping me clothed. Katya isn't here yet. She went to Kiev with Ada and apparently has been detained there. The only trip I have to make is to the Ukraine, to my old village. But I must put it off because I simply have to get on with my work.

Because of my peregrinations, I haven't written to you for a long time. Now I will write regularly again. I hope you will do likewise.

Warmest kisses, *mes enfants,*

I.

[A postcard with a view of Moscow: View of the Kremlin from Sofiskaya Quay.]

Molodenovo, September 25, 1930

One o'clock in the morning. The working day is over. The entire village is in darkness and only in my window is there a lamp burning. Complete quiet, darkness and calm. Around here the autumn is beautiful and cold. In my free time I go in for photography. I'll send some pictures soon. Good night.

I.

Molodenovo, September 29, 1930

I'm expecting the mail from Moscow this evening. So I'm taking advantage of the opportunity to send you a few lines. After a ten-day stretch of work, I'm having a rest today. I'm going for a walk through the stud farm and across the meadows by the Moskva. The weather is delightful, Indian summer in all its splendor.

My decision as to what date to go to Moscow will depend on my correspondence—I'm going for two days at most—I have to see the Zeiligers and other relatives, get in some food supplies and visit some plants for material I need for my writing.

The photo I'm sending is an unsuccessful one—just for a change. Some better ones will be ready soon.

In Molodenovo, aside from secret thoughts, absolutely nothing new happens—unless you count the fact that they've already harvested the potatoes and are finishing carting the beets too—and so I have nothing more to write to you about. All the news occurs in Moscow and so I'll write from there.

Your most respectful,
Hermit crab

P.S. Mama, do you have any news from America—about Rosa?

Molodenovo, October 13, 1930

Zhenya has grown lazy and doesn't write. I sent her a detailed letter today informing her of our plans for the immediate future. I hope it will calm and gladden her and that her ire will turn to graciousness.

Here at the stud farm, the home-grown amateurs keep taking snapshots of me and they flood me with unusable photos, one of which I'm sending you.

Before I left I saw Katya and Iosif. He has a job and so everything's fine with them. The only thing is that he's planning to have his hernia operated on because it's started bothering him. They have wonders to tell of little Sashur. He's walking already and beginning to think of getting himself work.

In Moscow, as always, there was a tremendous lot to do, but I'm now provided with all the essentials and can sit in Molodenovo without stirring. My happiness here is limitless and if only I didn't get tired, if only I didn't have to interrupt my work—then I would ask God just to send me my four women and I wouldn't need anything else.

As to the passport, I'm doing the necessary. I have established a more regular connection with Moscow. They'll bring me my mail more often and so I'll answer your questions as they arise. That's all for today.

Mamachen, write to me—independently of Mera—your uncomplicated thoughts.

Your I.

Molodenovo, October 21, 1930

For several days I just couldn't get hold of my mail. They finally brought it yesterday. I got letters from you and from Zhenya. The good turn Lyova's affairs have taken makes me doubly happy—

both for him and for all of us. If B.D. leaves this winter, the horizon will be considerably brighter and everything will become much simpler. It's about time. I'm only afraid that this good fortune won't last long, because there's a crisis in America. I've told Zhenya my views about the immediate future and I'm awaiting her answer. The news that my female progeny is flourishing is balm to my heart. I hope you'll be seeing each other soon.

We're having Indian summer here with warm and often sunny days. I don't want to leave. I live less comfortably here than in Sergievo, but from every other point of view I am better off. My work has got into its stride here and I think that here it is much more fruitful than in Sergievo, and then my nerves have become much stronger, I sleep very well, and my health is better than it was then. If only I could get my women together, then I could go further. I know and I feel, Fenyale, that time is fleeting—but you can't stop it with your hand. We must bring this separation to an end in a worthy manner. And that's why you must hang on, old woman. Please, hang on!

Why didn't you people take part in the celebration of "the independence of the Belgians"? The pretext that your feet ache won't do. Brussels isn't Molodenovo (last night I lost one of my overshoes in the mud and it was lost for good, sucked into the mud. That's the way things are over here. My landlord, Ivan Karpych, trotted all down the road, but just the same, he didn't find my overshoe) so Brussels isn't Molodenovo and it would be possible to find a means of communication if it weren't for laziness, petty provincialism, fear of man and of any shelter (even an outhouse).

I'll have to go to Moscow soon—to hand out "gratuities." I'll write all the news from town.

Isai Imuilovich (That's what they call me in Molodenovo).

Moscow, November 8, 1930

No letters from you for a long time. I keep wondering whether it isn't because Mera is ill. She hasn't written anything "in her own hand" for a long time either. *Ma soeur,* be proud before this bitch of a life with its sicknesses, and don't give in. If you gather up your whole will, then nothing can stand against it. Buy a bottle of wine for dinner and drink it between you to the health of your near ones and those far away.

I.

Moscow, November 9, 1930

Mama's long silence alarmed me very much. I sent her a telegram and received a reply saying that all is well and a letter follows. Now I can go to Molodenovo feeling more or less reassured. I think about it with joy, although my life in Moscow is little different from in the village. I work until two o'clock, then go out to make the rounds of "official establishments," then come back and spend every evening at home. Nevertheless, my stay in the city has somehow poisoned me and I don't have the same ability to work —and that just when my writing has reached a decisive phase.

I'm expecting to have some news very soon and will pass it on to you immediately. Good-bye, *mes chers enfants.*

I.

Molodenovo, November 17, 1930

Arrived here on the fourteenth. For three days I've been recuperating spiritually, relaxing physically and getting down to work. After sleet, rain and damp weather, today we have frost and it is possible to go out for a walk. It's warm in my little cottage, too warm even. It looks as if it'll stand up to whatever frosts may come.

Had a difficult time in Moscow. Dealings with the old Savrasovs are becoming more and more troublesome. The old man has become altogether frantic. I had to wait three weeks for him to part with the things for the Zeiligers. That's the way he is now, and I'm sure he would like not to part with them at all. He's a man who was never remarkable for his angelic character, and now, in his old age, his stinginess and penny-pinching are becoming a real joke.

And my distress was further aggravated by Zhenya's protracted silence. The thing is this—in the middle of last month I consulted my friends about whether I should join her at once or wait. People who are very much in the know were of the opinion that the trip would certainly be interpreted as a flagrant case of desertion and that I shouldn't budge under any circumstances before the winter is over. Their arguments are irrefutable and it is impossible not to agree with them. With hope and despair battling in my heart, I suggested the following plan to Zhenya: that she should come and join me for a month or two, leaving Natasha in the care of her Mama-in-law and sister-in-law. The money for the trip back, the tickets, are all prepared already. Zhenya remained silent for three weeks and then answered that she isn't well enough to make such a journey. I am trying to change her mind. I was so longing to see at least one of the family in the next few weeks. I reckoned that her mother-in-law would understand my situation and would look after Natasha for a couple of months, and at the end of the winter, I would have replaced her. In the meantime, Zhenya seems to be difficult to budge. What do you people think about it all?

Mamulya dear, write to me more often, write to me at length and I will answer in kind. Here, where my spirit has room to expand, I can think about you more clearly and I want to talk to you more than ever.

I.

[A postcard with a view of Moscow: The Park on Arbat Square.]

Moscow, December 14, 1930

Dearest Mamura,

I have devoted a few days in Moscow to practical matters, to all sorts of negotiations, running around and such-like fuss, and so I am unable to produce the philosophical missive for you which the situation demands. Let's leave it for Molodenovo. Meanwhile I must remark in brief that you are a stuffed fool and that in that narrow skull of yours there's a real mix-up going on of all sorts of notions about good and evil, a complete distortion of notions of happiness and unhappiness. Let's proceed in order. However amazing it may seem (!), I feel very well and, for example, am standing this winter (today it's 6° below) with incredible ease. For five or six years now (knock on wood!) I haven't had even a sign of an attack. The main thing is for me not to make abrupt movements, not to walk too fast, then I feel completely all right—if you'll forgive my saying so. I am living a more normal, hard-working and intelligent life than I ever have before. This is the incontrovertible truth, and as a result, my nerves and my ability to sleep have been transformed beyond all recognition—if you'll forgive my saying that too. As for the apparent misfortunes in my literary life, up till now I have brilliantly allayed the fears of my short-sighted admirers and it will be the same in the future. I am made of a dough that is a mixture of stubbornness and patience and it is only when these two elements are strained to the utmost that *la joie de vivre* comes over me—and that's what I'm feeling now. And in the final count, what do we live for? For pleasure understood in its widest sense, for the affirmation of our personal pride and worth. What's wrong then? The only thing that's wrong is that I'm far from my family, for whom my affection becomes more and more shattering with every day. This separation is caused one hundred per cent by circumstances beyond our control and if I want to maintain my dignity, integrity and pride in my work, I can't do anything about them. I have also continued to accept these circumstances because I know we will not have to remain separated for much longer. By all indications, we should be seeing each other not later than next spring—that will be done.

I'm so sorry for Mera. Anna Grigorievna Slonim suffers from the same nettle rash. Injections of atropine have helped her a lot. Have you tried that? And then they say d'Arsonval's currents, or rather, d'Arsonval's cage, have a very good effect. Please inquire about the atropine.

Whatever happens, send the passport to Zhenya. I'm sure she'll do everything. And go to Paris soon. All your conjectures about

Zhenya's silence and about her indifference toward you are the most preposterous rubbish I've ever heard. She writes about you very affectionately, but you know how passive she is when it comes to doing anything, and that's the only reason for her silence. When they do not touch on the question of our separation, her letters are cheerful and calm and she writes about Natasha amazingly well, and *klubt naches*.

And another absurd thing is what you write about Raya. Seeing old women affords me real pleasure and the pity you suddenly display for the Californians is unwarranted. . . . *Mon amie,* let's worry about ourselves. Raya will get along without our pity.

Moscow, December 15, 1930

Gosizdat just informed me that the latest edition of *Red Cavalry* has been sold in record time—something like seven days—and that they are going to put out yet another printing, which means a new payday for me.

I have written to Zhenya to say that it looks as if this horsey will keep pulling us along until spring. And to think that it is just a second-rate horsey! But then, just try and understand readers.

With that, I wish you good health! Yes, please don't let me down—be in good health.

Isaac Spinoza

Molodenovo, December 28, 1930

Dear Maryushka and Fedoseyushka and dear Fedoseyushka and Maryushka,

I've just scribbled off "a missive to the Parisiennes" full of thoughts for the New Year. You certainly wouldn't want me to plagiarize myself, so I will limit myself to sending you *l'expression* of my love and devotion and longing to be with you—but then, of course, that's all I have in the world. I have already written to Zhenya that I've never in my life had a year in which I worked on myself so much and so tenaciously, without allowing anything to distract me, as this last year. It seems to me that it was the most crucial period of my life. I feel that I have become a better husband, a better son and brother, and perhaps, a better craftsman than I was before. We cannot fail to spend the year 1931 together and then, perhaps, you will tell me that my self-confidence was justified.

You to whom I am attached body and soul, be happy and try to muster all the strength of your souls and bodies for your happiness. Good-bye, see you in the course of the coming year!

I'm afraid this letter will reach you too late because we have no [illegible] and it is twenty-five degrees below. I went for a walk this morning and was unable to take my eyes off the magnificence of the sparkling snow, the snow-covered woods and the villages shimmering in the blinding, steel-cold sun.

Communications aren't so terribly good these days and this letter may very well be delayed.

It is a matter for real amazement the way the Russian peasants build their cottages—it's so warm in my place, even hot, with the fire burning all the time in the stove. Besides, about four times a day I have tea, and with black currant jam to boot.

I.

[A postcard with a view of Moscow: Sverdlov Square.]

Molodenovo, December 31, 1930

I've been told that letters from you have arrived. I phoned Anna Grigorievna in Moscow. Probably I'll get the letters in a couple of days. Here, the temperature drops to twenty-five below and lower in the mornings, but the beauty of the place takes my breath away. On these moonlit nights the snow is blindingly bright. I'll meet the New Year at the stud farm as is fitting, in the company of simple and therefore good people. Sitting among them, I will be thinking of you. All the prayers of my soul are concentrated on wishing that this year may be a happy one for you and that you may be in good health. Are you in Paris? If not, do you intend to go there soon?

Salut, mes enfants, salut!

I.

1 9 3 1

Molodenovo, January 2, 1931

From twenty-five below, the cold has abated, and now it's between five below and zero—but you should see how beautiful it is! Sometimes when walking at night, I stop in the woods as if stunned. The nights are at their brightest at this time of the year —a tense, dazzling moon, snow, cottages. The whole wood sparkles with a really magic light. I have to go into town for a day— to get presents for a wedding that is taking place on the eighth. In Moscow I will be able to read your long-awaited letter and to answer it. Once more, my best wishes for the new year—and may it be intelligent, purposeful and full of determination.

I.

Molodenovo, January 14, 1931

I just can't gather my wits again after Vanyukha's wedding. These five days of deadly drinking (I didn't drink myself) have pulled me out of my rut and now I just can't make myself get down to work—oh well, it'll come back by itself.

Nature is being kind to us. The weather is amazingly mild and calm. Early every morning, while it's still dark, I make my way through the snowdrifts to the stud farm, and there, under the direction of a stableman, I am learning a new profession—the handling of horses. It's a delight that isn't comparable with any other. They are prize horses, real whirlwinds. And so, having filled my lungs with oxygen, I return home a completely new man.

They brought my mail from Moscow yesterday. It turned out to be rather meager. Zhenya hasn't written for a long time and there are no letters from you either. I would be very "interested" to know how your Paris trip is working out, and then I worry when I don't get frequent bulletins about your health.

I've nothing more to write about. I've fenced myself in so thoroughly against any news-and-events, that sometimes I'm even surprised at myself. This gain of wisdom is a bit of a bore. And since it is the generally accepted opinion that you're stupider than I, you should be the ones to write more often. You absolutely must —a thousand devils take you—be well. Do you understand or don't you? Better watch out now!

With regards from Molodenovo,
Isai Imuilovich

Molodenovo, January 27, 1931

Isn't Zhenya right to insist that Mera be treated in Paris? And moreover, don't you think something more drastic should be done, such as a trip to the south, to some spa, for a few months? I understand the inconveniences such a decision involves, but just the same, your health should have first priority. Aren't you contenting yourselves with half-measures and palliatives when really drastic remedies are needed? I would have pawned my soul to achieve some sort of success. And, really, don't you think that the climate has a pernicious effect? Please, please answer me about these matters, because they torment me. And as you women have no sense, give my regards to Grisha—it's a long, long time since we last wrote to each other. Today it's only fifteen instead of twenty-five below zero and I'm thawing out in Molodenovo. Mama is all wrong in imagining that one suffers from cold in the country. It's just the other way around—here they have the most effective devices, such as felt boots, sheepskin coats, and mittens; in town, with shoes and feeble steam heat, it's much colder and much less comfortable.

I.

Molodenovo, February 4, 1931

I have decided to give myself a rest and have been lazing around for several days. But, because of the bitter cold, I'm not having a very exciting time. My other function—as assistant to the stableman at the stud farm—is also in abeyance, because in this cold we don't dare exercise the horses. I'm thinking of taking a little trip, most likely to the south, to refresh my brains. I'm going to Moscow in a few days and I'll decide definitely then.

I sent into Moscow for my letters yesterday and I'm counting on receiving some sort of a scribble from you.

One bit of news I can pass on to you is that both our cows have calved. It's impossible to keep the calves in the barn in this cold, so, following the local custom, they've been taken into the cottage. So, when I go to get my meals, I hear them moving about and lowing softly behind the big Russian stove. That was all that was missing from my varied experience of life. Now I think there is nothing left for me to wish for. Diogenes in his barrel didn't roll much farther than I.

I've received a postcard from the Lyakhetskys. They're still in Moscow and have jobs. On this trip, I'll drop in to see them for sure. I've already written and told Zhenya how difficult it is for me to tear myself away from Molodenovo. Here I have come to know the bliss of absolute quiet, work and concentration. This place has spoiled me, so that I really find life rather hard in other places. Now I'll wait till I hear something from you and then I'll write in my turn.

Yours,
Ivan Karpovich Babel

Molodenovo, February 8, 1931

What shall I say? To whom shall I confide my sorrow? To whom recount the tale of my days and nights full of unquenchable anxiety and heartache? If all that could help, then you, my poor Mendele, and Mama would be skiers, bicycle riders racing in the *Six Jours*; you would fly across the ocean with Coste and Bellonte.* I received both your letters at the same time and was a little relieved as a result. Mendele, warm days are coming and I will replace you in your duties as guardian over our restless old woman. Everything is being done toward that end. My whole way of life —hard-working, solitary, single-minded—is subordinated to that end, and if you don't count my professional thoughts, then my thoughts of you engulf me entirely. *Mon amie*, if one is going to acquire relatives, then one should pick them from among peasants; if one is going to pick a trade—make it that of a carpenter and house painter; if one is going to marry, it should be to a pockmarked cook. But as you and I have fulfilled none of these recipes for happiness, then we must, first, develop *bonne mine*, and second, struggle, break our way out, surmount our troubles, *quand même et malgré tout*. I dare to give you advice from my sublime distance because every hour, every moment, I share your misfortunes. I share them in spirit and wish for nothing so much as to share them physically. You see now what a classically Jewish "family man" I've turned into.

The absence of letters from Volodya shouldn't worry you. It must be an accidental delay for, to my certain knowledge, everything's all right with him and he has probably already written to you. I am sending Mamenka two bad photos (my admirer wasn't too successful), but they'll do for her collection.

I embrace Grisha with all my heart. Service in the eyes of the Tsar and friendship in the eyes of God—they are never wasted.

Yours, pining for you,
I. Diogenov

* On September 1-2, 1930, D. Coste and M. Bellonte completed the first nonstop flight from Paris to New York in 37 hours, 18½ minutes.

Molodenovo, February 11, 1931

I am writing this to you deep in the night. It's almost dawn, so I should have dated it the 12th rather than the 11th. All night I've been sorting my things and my papers, because tomorrow, for a little while, I have to take leave of Molodenovo where I have spent so many solitary and fruitful hours.

My program is the following: I spend a few days in Moscow and then go to the south, via Kiev. In Kiev I have to go to see the administration of VUFKU, for whom I do some nondescript work from time to time, and then I also want to go to unforgettable Velikaya Staritsa, of which I have retained one of the sharpest memories of all my life. Then I'll go farther south for a few days to the new Jewish "peasant" colonies. Then back to Molodenovo. I'm taking this trip with two purposes in mind, I, [End of letter missing].

Moscow, February 19, 1931

I have become accustomed to peace and comparative serenity and as a result, in Moscow, I find myself unable to raise my hand to write. Yesterday I tried to pay for my sins by sending a telegram. I've been detained in Moscow longer than I expected. Business gets done slowly these days. I expect to leave for Kiev on the 21st or 22nd. The branch of Komzet* there will point out the very interesting Jewish colonies to me. I've already written to you many times about my plans and I don't want to repeat myself. When I have seen the Jewish peasants, I expect to return to the Russian peasants in Molodenovo, where I will rewrite a certain piece of work and give it in to be published, and after that I'll set off to see Natasha.

I've been very worried all these last days because of Mama's illness. I specially sent you the telegram two or three days before leaving so that I would hear from you sooner in Kiev.

We're having a real, official winter this year. It never gets warmer than five degrees, but my clothes and footwear are helping me to stand the bitterest colds without falling sick.

Today I will see the Lyakhetskys. I'll write in more detail before I leave. So, until tomorrow.

I.

* KOMZET, OZET, commissions responsible for the rural settlement of Jews, were established in 1928 to incorporate the Jews into the new economic structure of the U.S.S.R. In 1939, five "national Jewish districts," or agricultural colonies, existed in the Ukraine and Crimea. See also Babel's letter of March 15, 1931.

Kiev, February 25, 1931

Arrived here the day before yesterday. To my great disappointment, it's as cold here as in Moscow, and it's windy to boot. I saw Katya and Lyakhetsky the day I left. Both brothers are working—that's good, but the conflict with Annushka has reached the breaking point. You will easily understand that I can't and don't want to get mixed up in that dirty business. Sent Anyuta twenty-five rubles.

I am staying with friends. They are taking good care of me and I am experiencing all the charm of "home life." I am busy searching for an "appropriate" village where I can stay. I haven't been to get my mail yet but I'm reckoning on receiving a letter from you today or tomorrow. Tomorrow I'm going to see the old people. I'll write often because I miss you all very much.

I.

Kiev, February 27, 1931

Today the weather has turned warmer and I reckon that in the next few days it will be possible to leave for "my service post." I haven't yet selected a village to go to, but I've had some interesting offers. Besides, I want to wait until I get letters from you and from Zhenya. I'm going to the post office today. From one point of view, my stay in Kiev is turning out differently from what I had expected; from another, as foreseen. My lodgings and the landlords are adequate and I simply work for three-quarters of the day, i.e., the same routine as in Molodenovo: bedroom slippers, a piece of string in my hands* and about six miles of daily movement within the confines of one room.

I.

* Babel had the habit of twisting a piece of string between his fingers when reflecting or writing.

Kiev, March 5, 1931

A snowstorm of quite incredible violence raged here for two days. The trolleys stopped running and the streets were turned into a mass of frozen, snowy mounds. This annoys me very much because it means my trip to the village has to be postponed. You know that my every action is subordinated to one end—seeing Natasha —and every delay depresses me. I'm trying not to waste the time here and am going ahead with my work the best I can.

I've only received one letter from you here in Kiev. As eight-tenths of a person's misfortunes are imaginary, I cherish the dream, day and night, of finding you in relatively good order. Learn strength of will from your descendant and we will surmount everything, even the sore spots.

I.

Kiev, March 6, 1931

My Dearests,
    Yesterday I sent you a few books to read. It was very difficult to choose something for you. Our fiction writers write very badly and one just doesn't know what to choose. My only hopes rest with

myself. I've sent Zhenya a few manuscripts. Perhaps she'll share with you.

Winter continues without let-up—apparently it's no use waiting for spring here. I'll give up waiting and leave *quand même*, because I have to hurry. Zhenya sends me joyful news about Natasha —the maiden is blooming and that is why I have to hurry—in order to find her in such good form.

You people be damned—I dream of you a couple of times a week. May the sun warm you a little. May you go for a little walk in the park. My dear ancestors, if you want me to finish out my term of life, try to have yourselves a good time.

Yours,

I.

Kiev, March 11, 1931

It has grown warmer and tomorrow I'm leaving for my village. There, I'll try to wind up all my jobs. Although I've tried to do some work, this trip has made me waste quite a bit of time—a thought that causes me pain. I'll try to catch up in Makarov and only hope that my lodging and other physical conditions are favorable.

While in Kiev, I got only one single letter from you. That's very little. Worry is sneaking into my heart again.

I.

Makarovo, March 15, 1931

Once again, I lose contact with you, became badly worried, couldn't stand it and sent you a cable. Will wait for your reply with my heart in my mouth. Although it is very interesting here, I'm sorry I got involved in this latest trip: it has taken up a lot of my time and quite exhausted me. But now I must see my OZET [Obshchestvo Zemleustroistva Evreev Trudyakhshikhsya— Society for the Resettlement on the Land of Working Jews] business through because, as the saying goes, "Wanting is worse than slavery."

I have got myself a nice little cottage and I'll be able to work. Write, as before, to General Delivery, Kiev—people from here often go there and your letters will reach me quicker than if you sent them here directly.

The spring is being very shy in presenting its claims and today, for instance, it snowed.

Kiev, March 17, 1931

Makarovo was certainly an extremely interesting place, but as soon as I got there, I realized that quiet literary work was absolutely out there—living conditions ruled it out—and I saw that each day spent in Makarovo was taking me further away from Natasha. So for the first time in my life, I gave up and returned to Kiev, where I immediately pounced on my scraps of paper. No, it looks as if, under present circumstances, I mustn't disperse my efforts in too many directions at once; the only thing for me to do is to go to reliable old Molodenovo and wind up my work there. For the time being I am working in Kiev because my lodgings here are quite tolerable.

You don't write. You're knifing me and I can find no place to escape from my worries.

I.

Kiev, March 24, 1931

Having come back from Makarovo, I've decided to take advantage of my stay in Kiev, and while going on with my usual work, try to make some extra money. Will find out tomorrow whether this plan will work out and will then decide accordingly when I'll leave for Molodenovo. I'd like to leave on the 27th or 28th at the latest. Once in Molodenovo, I'll pounce on my work with the bloodthirstiness of a tiger, in order to get it finished.

They say that the Kiev spring is delightful. This year it has started rather late. There was an unusual amount of snow this winter, so now it's thawing hard.

Are you preparing for the holiday? I've already seen this year's matzos and, who knows, perhaps I'll have an opportunity to taste some. I want you absolutely to be in good health and beseech you not to dodge this request of mine.

If I don't manage to write to you tomorrow, I'll do so the day after without fail.

I.

Kiev, March 28, 1931

Payment of the money due to me has been delayed and so I'll have to stay here for a day or two longer. I hope you've already written to Moscow. Got a letter from Zhenya in which she tells me about Natasha so vividly that it seems to me I can see the girl before my eyes. She really seems to be *une brave fille*. I never cease to remind Zhenya about the passport.

Yesterday, with great emotion, I went through our family trunk, thinking of all of you and of those who are gone, and my heart contracted with sorrow and painful enjoyment. I took Papa's medallion and cufflinks, his old tobacco pouch and a few pictures, wanting to keep them with me. I hope that this trunk, the companion of our existence, will yet return to our family hearth. I'll look once again at the pictures and possibly send you some.

It is quite impossible to imagine anything more disgusting than this year's spring but, after all, to hell with it—weather is a transient matter.

Yours,
I.

Moscow, April 5, 1931

Haven't left the house for several days and can't leave for Molodenovo for a quite childish reason: I have a strep throat. Today, the white spots are almost completely gone and I reckon I'll be able to go out tomorrow. My confinement to the house has coincided with a cold wave that is quite unheard of for April. It's like a curse—wherever I go and whatever place I return to, although the season advances, I find the same thing in every place: streets sheeted with ice, deep snowdrifts, bitter cold. Like you, I miss the sun and warmth terribly.

Zhenya writes to me quite often. She is feeling more cheerful than usual and can never say enough about how pleased she is with Natasha.

À *demain,*

I.

Molodenovo, April 12, 1931

I found a funny picture of me in our Kiev trunk. And since they say that laughter helps the digestion, I'm sending it to you.

I have the honor to inform you that today, on the first day of Passover, a fierce snowstorm is raging and, fearing to drown in the drifts, I didn't venture out to the stud farm. Looking out of the window, I have the impression I never left here: still the same snowy expanse without end or measure, still those bare trees and still Ivan Karpovich trudging out of the barn with an armful of hay. For the first time in my life, my whole body is clamoring for sun and warmth and I dream of enjoying those bounties in your company.

Molodenovo remains faithful to itself. The peace here has a healing quality and, after a month and a half of wandering—and quite senseless wandering to boot—I am returning to normal.

Am writing this in the middle of the night, before going to sleep after a hard day's work, simply out of a need for a heart-to-heart chat, which will enable me to think of you more clearly at the end of this day.

Regards, my dear ones,

I.

Molodenovo, April 16, 1931

My charming courtesans,

I consider it necessary to warn you that my correspondence with you may be interrupted for a week or perhaps even two. Spring has been with us since yesterday. I've never seen it from so close before and I'm happy to be spending these days in the country. A great deal of flooding is expected after the long and incredibly snowy winter. Our Molodenovo sticks out of the side of a mountain and we'll be surrounded by water on all four sides. The sole means of communication with the outside world will be by boat. The stud farm has promised to let us have them but nevertheless I have to assume that letters won't be delivered.

We're not afraid of the siege of the elements. Spring has brought with her an abundance of milk and eggs and we will be "full to the gills," as Ivan Karpovich puts it.

My heart tells me that there's a letter from you waiting for me at Anna Grigorievna's. I'm trying to find a way of getting hold of it. I reckon that the day after tomorrow I'll manage to dispatch a courier.

Since the "big day" is approaching, I'm working hard now, day and night. Molodenovo is loyally helping me.

You should quickly go away somewhere, to the mountains, to the valleys, to the sunshine, to your granddaughter. Don't put off the trip. It is quite out of the question to think that Zhenya would not do her utmost to get you a visa.

Owing to the fact that (it's a whole week since I last went out of our courtyard) I have absolutely no news for you. You know yourselves that Alfonso XIII has taken to his heels and left Madrid and Don Cascara Sagrada* has taken his place.

Until tomorrow,
Your loving
I.

* A jocose reference to Niceto Alcala Zamora (1877-1949), who became the

[A postcard with a view of Moscow: The Triumphal Arch (1826)]

Molodenovo, April 19, 1931

I have spoken on the telephone to Anna Grigorievna. There's a letter from you waiting for me, and some other business to attend to besides. I've decided to dash off to Moscow for a day while it's still possible, because if I don't do it now, I won't be able to move an inch for ten days or even two weeks. The water is still rising. I hate to tear myself away from Molodenovo, where I have got into my routine, but I console myself with the thought that it's not for long. While I was traveling around I kept catching colds, but now I'm fine.

Until tomorrow,

I.

Molodenovo, April 24, 1931

My comrade here is willing to take the risk of going to the station and can't wait, so a few lines only. Zhenya writes that the business with the visa is at last under way. She has entrusted it to a lady we know who I'm sure will do it.

We're having an unprecedented flood here. From our mountain, it looks like a boundless watery expanse. You have to go to the stud farm by boat. Spring, an enchanting spring. I've never lived at such close quarters with winter as I have this year and never been so happy to see the spring.

I.

first president of the Republic of Spain after the triumph of the republican cause April 14, 1931. Zamora remained president of the Republic until 1936.

Molodenovo, April 25, 1931

Spring appeared here three days ago, but then it's a wonderful spring. Before the windows of my cottage stretches a vast expanse of water. To get to our village you have to go by boat. I had great difficulty getting here yesterday. I started out in an automobile, changed to a cart, then to a ferryboat, and had to go part of the way on foot, but it was really worth it. To work, as I'm doing here at the moment, is extraordinarily good. It peps me up in body and soul; apparently it's hard for me to get along without sunshine.

We must wait for the passport from Zhenya now. I think she'll do it this time. She has very sensible plans for the summer and I would like—have a burning desire—for you to have a part in them. You absolutely must get in touch with each other at once—and leave very soon, so that you will get every possible scrap of sunshine. There is no need to take my tastes into consideration—I will join you wherever you are. I only ask one thing—hurry up about it.

Received two pictures of Natasha (dating back to November). In them, she looks terribly like Vitya Zeiliger and, nevertheless, extraordinarly sweet.

This time Katya saw me off when I left for Molodenovo. She's jubilant—the court of second instance has confirmed the ruling on Annushka's eviction.

There's such a nice combination of smells here that it's hard to sit still inside. I'm going to join the cows, the pigs, the chickens—they are all bellowing or clucking, each respectively using the voice granted it to greet the sun.

I.

Moscow, May 3, 1931

Came to town for the May Day celebrations. They went off very well, with the shining cooperation of the sun. We've seldom had such a wonderful spring. Molodenovo is a delight. I'm going there today and as I don't do any letter-writing in Moscow, I'll write at length from the country. You mention my going to a health resort. Well, I never leave my resort—but I'll be with Natasha to celebrate my own and her birthdays.* I just mentioned it to you vaguely in order not to worry you with dates, but if I've set my heart on it, that means I hope to carry it out.

I.

* The Orthodox Church celebrates the name days of St. Isaac and St. Nathalie on August 3rd and 26th, respectively; hence, Babel hopes to be in France by summer. More than a year will pass, however, before he obtains a passport.

Molodenovo, May 7, 1931

We're having very fine days here. We didn't have anything like them last summer. In the woods the nightingales sing unceasingly as if by command. There's no need, Mamachen, to go to a resort from here. If only it was summer for ten months of the year. I withstood the northern winter like a cow in a cowshed, but then, I delight in the grass no less than a cow.

How do matters stand with the passport? When will you get moving? Keep in mind that it must be done quickly, as quickly as possible.

I.

Molodenovo, May 12, 1931

There was a slight interruption in the spring but now she has come into her rights again. Although I have to go to Moscow, I will try to hang on here as long as possible. It's really too lovely. And then, my work is at a crucial point too. I've loaded myself down to the very limit of my strength, because I'm reckoning on a rest.

Tomorrow I'll send someone to see whether there are any letters—I reckon there should be something from you by now. As before, I couldn't be happier over the effect the warmth is having on me—I've become a completely new man. On my day off, I'll write you a detailed letter.

I.

[A postcard: Mokhovaya Street, First Moscow University.]

Molodenovo, May 15, 1931

Phoned to Moscow and found out that there's a letter from you, but they'll only bring it to me on the 17th. Yashka Okhotnikov* came to see me yesterday. He made me an offer to go—under excellent conditions—to Magnitogorsk, to spend some time there with the engineers at the construction site. The temptation was great but I withstood it. I have reached a point in my work where it mustn't be interrupted and I still reckon that my well-earned rest is in sight.

As before, it's good here in the country. There's no need to tell you how good.

Until the 17th then, my old women,

I.

* Okhotnikov was on the staff of the magazine *Oktyabr* [*October*] which was organizing two "brigades" of writers. In May, the first left for the oil fields near Baku; the second, comprising authors Fyodor I. Panfyorov and V. Ilyenkov, went to the metallurgical centers in the southern Urals.

Molodenovo, May 19, 1931

Supplies have run out altogether—have to go to Moscow for reinforcements. Expecting to leave tonight. It's hard to leave your own place even for a day or two. I've never lived in such splendor, brightness and serenity. Everything's flooded with light, the meadows have turned green, the sun is shining as in summer. I haven't received my mail. The cart belonging to my landlord, Karpych, has broken down and so there's nothing to drive to the station in. Without news, I become alarmed about you, lose my peace of mind, and that's why I've decided to go without putting it off. I'll write you the news from Moscow right away. After my winter-enforced immobility, I do about seven miles a day now and enjoy this freedom of maneuver. Now it is clear beyond doubt to me that the winter should not be spent in a warm climate. I'm becoming a completely different man.

I.

Moscow, May 21, 1931

Dear Invalids,

Have come to town to see Gorky. I hope to be back in my enchanting Molodenovo tomorrow night. I must hurry for my old women. I've asked Katya to come and see me tomorrow. I spoke to Sasha on the telephone. Everything seems to be fine with them.

It makes me sad to think that Mama is still without "feminine company" in ungodly Brussels. Remember that this summer you must self-sacrificingly attend to your health.

I met Volodya's father.* He told me that his son's affairs have deteriorated and that he (the son) wants to cut his allowance by half. I don't know whether it's definite, but I was very sorry for the old man and for Fedosya. The only consolation is that Kirill's presence will make things easier. I will try to find out more precise information on the subject. Writing this, I have a thousand other things to do and so I will limit myself to a few lines. Merochka, I will be waiting with a quivering heart for your description of your niece.

Until the day after tomorrow,

I.

* Volodya Zeiliger was the husband of Babel's sister-in-law, Raya. The family had emigrated to the United States in the early 1920's.

Molodenovo, May 24, 1931

I phoned Anna Grigorievna today and learned that yesterday, a few minutes after I had left, a letter from you arrived. They will only bring it to me here on the 27th. That was very bad luck. Katya equipped me for the trip, sewed things and obtained all sorts of provisions. The long-awaited moment of liberation from Annushka is approaching. Looks like she's being evicted today.

I spent the 22nd out of town, at Alexei Maximovich's* [Gorky's]. We felt all our former affection on meeting each other. My impressions are so complex that to this minute I can't sort them out. But, of course, the old man is one of a kind in this world.

My confinement to Molodenovo this time will be protracted and important. The next trip I make I'll have to present myself at the publisher's. So there you are.

The spring—or rather summer—we're having would be suitable for Nice. The apple trees are blossoming in front of my windows. And it all makes me even happier because I can breathe easily and walk without difficulty. Today I went swimming in the Moskva for the first time—the water temperature was 60°, not more. There's nothing for Mama to worry about—to drown yourself here or to commit suicide, you'd have to stick your head under the water because it's no more than neck-deep anywhere.

Quickly scatter to your health resorts.

With greetings from Molodenovo,

I.

* Alexei Maximovich Gorky (1868-1935), who was still living in Sorrento, was making one of his annual visits to the U.S.S.R.

Molodenovo, May 28, 1931

Most Gracious Mamulya,

I've received from Zhenya a few enchanting snaps of Natasha and one mother-daughter picture. I suppose you've received them too. I hadn't imagined Natasha like that at all. She doesn't display a classical beauty, but her face is full of charm, expressiveness, concentration. A very sweet girl. Try, *mon vieux,* to spend the time you're without Mera as sensibly as possible, sensibly for your health. It's a pity that you couldn't go off to some resort while she's away, even if only to Vichy again. Why wasn't this done? Zhenya writes that the passport has been extended. Better late than never. I knew about Volodya reducing his parents' allowance. I put up a fight about it, but there was nothing I could do. His affairs appear to have deteriorated.

Until tomorrow,
I.

Molodenovo, June 1, 1931

Fedoseyushka,

I am working under such pressure that I've even begun to neglect my most sacred and pleasantest duty—writing to you. And that's not all—I don't even notice the amazing beauty spread out around me. Flowering meadows, sprouting fields. It's a beauty such as, alas, you'll never see either in Spa or Nice. The last two days have been stormy ones—yesterday was Pentecost and today is Whit Monday, a Molodenovo church feast-day. On such an occasion there's plenty of drinking. Accordion playing and songs all night.

Did Mera leave? Have you received the passport from Zhenya? I wrote to you before about how distressed I was that Volodya's affairs are bad. The only thing that makes me feel less bad about it is that in the not-too-distant future I will be able to intervene more effectively in the matter of their welfare.

Regards to Grisha. I'll write to him separately.

I.

Molodenovo, June 5, 1931

Fedoseyushka,

I have a couple of days more of urgent work to do, after which I'll have to go to Moscow for a week at least, for the time has come to take care of financial, literary and, above all, family affairs. If I am detained in Molodenovo for more than two days, I'll write to you again from here. Probably there are letters from you sitting in Moscow, but I won't send for them since I'm going there myself. Today, before starting on my two final days of work, I have given myself a day off, but I've had no luck. It's rained the whole time. The peasants would pay "plenty" for it, but it's forced me to sit in my cottage, drink tea and read an old copy of Turgenev. Last night was an agitated one here—we had a fire. It's particularly frightening in a village and particularly magnificent. It is frightening because it might spread through the whole village. Luckily, it was a farmhouse right next to the pond that caught fire, and although everything was destroyed, including the animals—two cows, a pig, the sheep—the other houses escaped. We didn't sleep all night. I got completely filthy and exhausted and almost got my physiognomy scorched. But then, to make up for it, I drank tea from a big samovar with the peasants at four o'clock in the morning and we gabbed about the fire.

Even at this point I don't know whether Mera has left or not, but I suppose she has and am expecting letters from her from Paris.

Aside from the fire and my imminent departure for Moscow, I have, *mon amie* Fedoseyushka, no news, for the simple reason that all the news is ahead of us. It's two o'clock in the morning—time to sleep. Good night.

I.

Moscow, June 17, 1931

As you can see, I'm still in Moscow. I'm combining rest from work with all sorts of financial transactions. I would like my next trip to Molodenovo to be the last, and for that reason I'll sit tight here until I have completely cleared up all my affairs, above all, my family affairs. I hope that the next week will decide what and when.

I'm mostly busy here with negotiations with publishers, because I'm handing in certain material. I'm handing it in to cover the advances. It'll be published later, in August or September, by which time I shall have to add a few more stories to it.

According to the verdicts I've heard, I'm writing better now than before, so everything your Slonim* said applies to the past and has no significance for me. Incidentally, you should give me credit for one thing—I'm entirely self-possessed when it comes to criticism, whether it's damning or ecstatic. I know what it's worth —and mostly it's worth about a five-kopek piece.

I've received a letter from Mera, from Vichy, with a full report on Natasha. You can understand how fired-up I was by it all—although I'm already so incandescent that it's impossible to make me any hotter.

I'm very sorry that I've written to you so seldom lately, but it would be no exaggeration to say that they are literally tearing me apart here. Everyone's longing for my humble company and I can't possibly escape, so I have no time left at all.

I know Volodya has halved his allowance to his parents, but his salary too is only fifty per cent of what it was. Of course, it's all very regrettable. It's all because of the state of affairs for musicians there. He probably doesn't work a full week.

I've already told you that Katya got rid of Annushka. I often see Katya. She is a help to me in many things, does all sorts of errands for me, fixes up my uncomplicated wardrobe. She should be coming again today. If so, I'll sit her down to write a letter to you. I still think you could have arranged things differently; instead of stewing in Brussels, it would have been much better to be spending this time in Spa. Of course, it wouldn't be convenient for Grisha, but couldn't he arrange to stay in a boarding house? Quickly, quickly, *mon vieux*, get off to Spa.

My heartfelt regards to Grisha. My very first day in Molodenovo I'll write to him. I'll send the money to Sonya. The weather's been dismal all week. I'm selfish enough to be pleased about it—I'm not missing anything in Molodenovo.

Until tomorrow, dearie,

I.

---

* Marc Slonim, author and critic, born in Russia in 1894, who lived in Paris at the time.

Moscow, June 20, 1931

I keep collecting material to write to you at length, and in the meantime I'll confine myself to scribblings, greetings, bows down to mother earth herself. Katya and I are putting together a small parcel for Odessa because Sasha is going there for his vacation. I've seen the old Zeiligers. All's well with them. I would have had a chance now to send your regards to Ilya Lvovich if I hadn't lost his address. Send it to me right away. I'm writing simultaneously to Mera. I'm longing for you to go to Spa as soon as possible.

I.

Moscow, June 26, 1931

Fenyushka,

Tomorrow I'm going to Molodenovo for 8-10 days and from there I'll start tearing off some notes to you. And in the meantime, to give you some soul-saving reading, I enclose Katya's letter. I can't stay away from Moscow for long because I've got some things under way and I have to keep them going. I had reckoned on seeing Natasha on her birthday, but apparently it won't work out. I have given the publishers some manuscripts and the editors are demanding that I add some more. I won't fix a time for you because I don't know, myself, but if I've "set my heart on it," I'll do it and, of course, I'll pick the moment when it will be most convenient and most effective. You can understand yourself that there's no need to keep reminding me and nagging at me. I'm so caught up in family matters that I can't think of anything else—unfortunately, and I pay less attention to my work than I should. But no doubt it'll all work out. My efforts are directed toward assuring the future as well as the present, and that explains my diabolical patience and caution.

I'm very distressed to hear that Mera is returning from Vichy already. What's the hurry? What can have been achieved in such a short time? I don't understand a thing. Where and how does she expect to go on with her treatment? Where are you going away to and when? All these questions bother me greatly and I would like an answer to them as quickly as possible. I don't believe it's possible to restore one's health using resorts so parsimoniously.

Are you getting letters from Volodya?

I.

Moscow, June 29, 1931

Received a letter from Zhenya giving an enthusiastic description of La Bourboule. Why did Mera refuse to go there, if only for a few days? God knows, I don't understand a thing. Anyone would think that Mera was running at least ten corporations. I still can't get over the fact that her course of treatment turned out to be so short. Is she in Brussels? What about Mama's trip to Spa? I feel that it shouldn't be put off any longer, and that the best thing of all would be for the whole family to go together.

I'm leaving for Molodenovo today. My editors have become so greedy that they are clamoring for more and more material, and so I have to write it. I have no objection to work, but thoughts about the family distract me from it.

Until tomorrow in Molodenovo,

I.

[A postcard: Dorogomilovsky Bridge.]

Molodenovo, July 1, 1931

I'm in the country once more and working once more, and everything would be great and all the Spas and Vichys in the world wouldn't be worth one Molodenovo cow, if only Fedosya and the other absent females were here. You, they tell me, haven't earned them yet—work a bit more and then you'll get them. With that hope in mind, we are scratching away.

Until tomorrow,

I.

Molodenovo, July 3, 1931

They're haymaking here—a romantic time. The summer weather might have been made to order—hot and dry, and when it's needed, it rains. The grass is lush. There's twice as much hay as last year. The wheat is coming on superbly, everything is breathing, growing. The peasant won't admit it, but you can feel the satisfaction in him. Just now, before dawn, I went out into our farmyard. The village is asleep, the woods and fields are sleeping; over the river hangs the huge, orange disk of the moon, the watchman beats his gong and, for some reason, it seems to me that nowhere else in the world is there such beauty—and then my heart contracted at the thought that you were not here to see it all. Nature here—her beauty and serenity—could really be a consolation for everything. Here, I've recovered right away, after Moscow, and am at work again with my former enthusiasm. I've managed to hand in some manuscripts, but the editors are demanding additional material. They're right. The stories were very topical when written and, for publication, some more up-to-date material should be added, and that's what I'm doing now. Well, the editors may be right, but the time has come to look far ahead, not just ahead to the next two weeks, and it costs me a great effort to overcome my growing impatience. I'm lucky to have two defenses against misfortune—work which I like and Molodenovo, my fortress.

They'll only bring me my mail on the 7th. Until then I'll be without news from you. It worries me to think of Mama sitting in Brussels and of Mera's lightning return.

Judging by her first letters, Zhenya is very pleased with her stay in La Bourboule. It's beautiful, comfortable and healthy there. After all, I'm rather sad at not being able to spend Natasha's birthday with her, and I've promised myself that in future years I'll never miss that day.

It's growing light and I've written myself out. Enough. There's great peace and quiet in my heart.

I.

Molodenovo, July 7, 1931

They didn't send me my mail today. I'm expecting it tomorrow and, in the meantime, don't know which of you are "at hand" in Brussels and which have left. Here the summer is in gorgeous full bloom. It's very hot. Haymaking. I am spending these days in the most ideal environment you could possibly imagine—in quietness and work, amidst grass, trees and fields. People who come here are amazed to find that, thirty-five miles from Moscow, our Zvenigorod Switzerland still exists. Life has become much gayer for me than before. I don't remember whether I've already told you that Alexei Maximovich [Gorky] has settled down less than a mile from Molodenovo in the former Morozov house. (They picked the best of the places around Moscow for him.) And since, for old times' sake, the rules that regulate the stream of people around him do not apply to me, I sometimes go to visit him in the evening. There's no need to tell you how instructive it is and what an unexpected pleasure to have him for a neighbor. It brings back my youth, and the good thing about it is that our relationship, formed in my youth, hasn't changed to this day.

Soon it'll be a birthday for our whole family. I have devised a present for the day—simply the work that I have set myself to finish by the time our birthday comes round. How nice it would be to present myself and my dependents with this gift. I reckon to get letters tomorrow.

À demain,
I.B.

Molodenovo, July 9, 1931

They brought me Mera's letter yesterday. I'm sorry to hear that she didn't go to [La] Bourboule, if only for a couple of days. I'm selfishly glad at the news about the *voiture* because I hope to take advantage of that blessing some day too. I wish Mama would leave right away for Spa—perhaps with Ilyusha's help. Could she spend a long time there? Please consider it. Once the question about Paris is settled, it would be a very good thing. I think it's worth making every effort to achieve it.

I am thriving in the country. My colors are exhausted—I can't describe the splendor here. It's terribly hot (for me, it's a curative heat) but here it's easy to bear and I work easily and with zest— and perhaps we'll receive a reward for this work—"a benefit to the family involving a journey . . ."

I.

Moscow, July 15, 1931

I've come to town for a day. I've got a lot of things to do with all sorts of papers—taxes and so on. I have to keep them in perfect order and that's what I'm trying to do. I'll leave here this evening and come back again on the 19th, because that's the day of the races.

I'm terribly glad that you're in Spa at last. How are you doing there? Just what does your treatment consist of? Write in detail. Do you have company? Mera writes that there are other Russian ladies in your boardinghouse.

I'm very pleased with my last visit to Molodenovo. I made great progress with my work, which is very important to me. I've already told you that they're making me do some additional work on it and that's what I'm doing now. The only thing that bothers me is that I'm not doing it with sufficient eagerness. For, just the same, weariness is making itself felt. It's true, Molodenovo will cure me of everything and help me overcome my tiredness.

It's much better here than it was last summer.

Until tomorrow,

I.

Moscow, July 15, 1931

I've come into the city for a day on all sorts of bureaucratic business, all sorts of taxes, documents and so on.

I'm very glad that Mama has gone to Spa. I'm writing to her simultaneously. It bothers me to think, just the same, that you stayed such a short time in Vichy. Shouldn't you repeat the treatment in the autumn? Couldn't Uncle Ilya help you? And by the way, let me know his address. I think I've already told you that I've lost my old notebook with all my addresses in it. I'm leaving Moscow this evening and returning on the 19th. There are the races on that day.

I'm having to work beyond my strength and tremble to think how it may affect the quality, but then the reward is gleaming ahead of me. Anyway, without Molodenovo, I wouldn't have been able to get through with all my tasks. I'm expecting a detailed report on the sea from you.

Heartfelt greetings to Grisha,

I.

Molodenovo, July 18, 1931

I had wanted to start working today, to add the "final touches" on my publisher's demand, but apparently my brains aren't sufficiently rested from the great effort I've had to make. Tomorrow I have a legal holiday—the trotting races. I'll return to the village on the 20th. The races come at just the right moment. I'll rest a little. Our granddaughter is an adult already. She is entering on her third year today. Have you written to Zhenya? She's probably in Paris now.

I'm very sorry that I couldn't send Mera a telegram on her birthday. I just don't happen to know where she is now.

How is your treatment going? Write more often, Fedoseyushka.

Yours,

I.

Molodenovo, July 22, 1931

Mamachen,

How are you getting along in your health resort? It's sunny here now, just like in our home town. After lunch I sun myself and swim. The river has really become so shallow that you lie in it like in a bath. It's true I need a little rest, but I mustn't even think of it at this time because every day of lazing around separates me for that much longer from my family. And that's why I'm driving myself. Physically, I feel wonderful, only my brains would like to take it easy, and then too, surrounded by such beauty, you want to enjoy it. Starting today, I've introduced an innovation—I work only until lunchtime, and not the whole day as I did before.

I'm hoping to entice Katya to Molodenovo. They've invited her to Odessa but she quite rightly supposes that she won't get a chance to rest there. If she goes, it'll be a real loss to me. She is my guardian angel and, most important, my wet nurse.

I.

Moscow, August 3, 1931

Yesterday came into Moscow on business that could not possibly be put off—the races. After the races, went to the jockey Semigov's place. Spent the night there. We both got up at four o'clock in the morning and went to the stables. Such things give all Moscow grounds for saying that I'm the biggest sham in the world—but I do it because I really want to, from an inner need. Now I'm about to return to Molodenovo.

When I got home I found Mama's letter with the picture in it, and for several hours now I haven't been able to take my eyes off it. Fenyale, *ma mère*, you have afforded me today the greatest pleasure a man can experience. In my opinion, Mama doesn't look bad at all. Only I can't make out what's the matter with her mouth. Does she have teeth or not? Or does she need to get a set? one of her lips looks swollen.

It's ten days now since I had any news from Paris. I don't know where Zhenya and Natasha are. I'm beginning to be worried and I shall bombard them today with all types of postal communications.

Thanks to the fact that I allow myself short but frequent rests, I feel fine. I have no words to describe the summer we're having: Odessa, Yalta, Sukhumi—we're having all that here. While the poor things, chased by wind and rain, have once again moved toward your winter quarters. On my knees I beg you (although you must ask Grisha too) to get yourselves *une auto*. I think the thing would give you more strength, fresh air and energy than a health resort. Wouldn't it be good to take advantage of the end of the summer? What are the chances of your doing so? I'm writing in a rush, as always in Moscow.

Until Molodenovo, until my village heaven.

I.

Moscow, August 17, 1931

I am writing from Katya's house. On the table in front of me there is a real gallery of our relatives, those who are still alive, those who are long since dead, and those who vanished recently: this distracts me a great deal and induces thoughts that take me far away.

I received from Zhenya a collection of delightful photographs of Natasha, a beguiling damsel. I am asking Zhenya to send them immediately to you, too. They were all taken at La Bourboule. Natasha—Zhenya writes—is sick. Her stomach doesn't tolerate milk, and when this substance gets into her food, she is covered with a sort of eczema. I don't think this is anything serious and the doctors assure us that it will pass without any after effects. You can write to Zhenya in Paris. The last letter came from St. Jacut de la mer, but Zhenya was about to leave.

The news about the phonograph and the radio make me rejoice. The radio leaves me indifferent, but I nourish a real passion for the phonograph: in my opinion there can be no more poetical and exciting relaxation than listening to good records. You should get a phonograph of the latest design: you will feel genuine pleasure.

What about the car? How long will you continue hesitating? You should take advantage of it before the end of the summer.

I don't understand whether Katya intends to leave or not. Now all the family is reunited but they say that Iosif is getting ready to go to Odessa. Though Katya needs a rest, her departure doesn't please me. My main support in Moscow, she collects money for me, does my errands, takes charge of my food and clothes ration cards, cooks for me, and sends provisions to Molodenovo. It is true however, that this is compensated by the fact that my ration cards are of a special and superior category, so that what's allotted to me is actually more than enough for everybody. Without me, of course, they would not have seen so much of God's mercy. Right now we want to go out to buy a little linen and shoes, perhaps we will be able to buy something for Odessa also . . .

Even if I were to fall in your esteem, I—begging your pardon— feel good. You can not imagine how beautiful Molodenovo is, and what a beneficial influence a stay there can exert, better than any (climatic) resort that I know of. Now and then, it is true, I get tired of it and really bored, but it's easy for me to stand as there are compensations ahead. Unfortunately it is not in my power to hurry them along as much as I would like—to make them appear tomorrow or even today. I will not be able to stand a long wait, nor do I believe I will have to. Enough now with this long letter, it's time to get busy with my affairs. I'm about to go out with Katya.

Your,

I.

Moscow, October 6, 1931

Arrived in town. Spend whole days sitting at the publisher's, reworking, and dictating my brainchild. The quiet life is over!

I've received from Zhenya new pictures of the child—charming pictures. I've issued a stern "command" for copies to be sent to you. Everything's fine with our Parisians, and I'm very glad about it. The only thing is that, as a result of the general crisis, Lyova's affairs seem to have deteriorated.

Tomorrow I'll be seeing Katya. I spoke to her on the telephone. It seems Iosif hasn't left for Odessa yet.

Until tomorrow,

I.B.

[Marked: 1931?]

⋅ ⋅ ⋅ ⋅ ⋅

I'm sending you my favorites from among the latest pictures of Natasha. There's no need to tell you how dear they are to me. I like to immerse myself in them from time to time, so send them back to me quickly. Simultaneously with this, a reprimand is flying off to Zhenya—it's just impossible to get her to address one more envelope and send the pictures to one more person. The photographs in which Natasha is wearing a little white coat and the one in the armchair are particularly enchanting, and especially moving is the one where she is standing by a bench with her arms folded. It's a fairly early picture—taken in April.

Don't be angry with me for sending postcards. They're reminders of me because I think of you constantly—but my life is poor in outside events. One can only note the rain and the sunshine, the ploughing or the potato harvest, and the prowess of the stud's horses at the racetrack. And as to my inner life, don't be disheartened. At least, *quand même*, you will read the stories.

I've already told you that I handed over the things for Uncle Ilya to Iosif. I hope he's already left for Odessa. It was a great pleasure to me to send the things. It was no inconvenience, absolutely no inconvenience, to me. I only regret that I have so few uncles to worry about.

Zhenya's last letter said that she and Natasha were well, that Natasha is coming along very nicely, that they were planning to move to Paris. They must be there by now.

Please, *je vous supplie*, be sure to get a car. You'll take youthful Fenya and her guardian, that is, me, for rides. Don't put the matter off. I'm convinced that with a little effort this plan can easily be carried out. I seem to have "elucidated" all current affairs. I must also add that my postcards are a result of the fact that my correspondence is nearly always one-sided. You see, I'm not answering a letter, but just writing. Good night. It's beginning to rain, one o'clock in the morning, delightful warmth and quiet, and my only heartache is over you.

I.

[*Marked: September or October 1931?*]

. . . . .

the man who wrote two years ago and I think the present man is better, firmer, and gayer than the former one. There's no need to explain to you that now, in these last weeks in Molodenovo, it would be senseless and criminal to change the plan and pace of my work. The past years have their own logic and they dictate it to me. I have about a month and a half left. In November, whatever happens, I must see Enta and Fenya. I'm using every ounce of my strength and ability to bring it about, while keeping a constant eye on the future all the time, unlike before—that is, I'm trying to prepare everything, to make sure that there will be work, money and all that. It has all moved along terribly slowly. The damned sicknesses won't wait. But you know how difficult general conditions are and, on top of that, there's my wilful, whimsical trade and my respect for it—that I can't help.

Molodenovo, October 14, 1931

Before leaving I asked Katya to send you and Zhenya each a copy of the magazine *Molodaya Gvardia*. In it, I make my debut, after several years of silence, with a small extract from a book which will have the general title of *The Story of My Dovecote*. The subjects of the stories are all taken from my childhood, but, of course, there is much that has been made up and changed. When the book is finished, it will become clear why I had to do all that. This month, two stories will appear in *Novy Mir*—one from that same series and the other, a country story.* Everyone who's heard them has liked them, but . . . but peace has vanished from my life. And that's why I have to thank heaven for Molodenovo. After a long interruption, I've been in contact with the literary market place again, and there's much that disturbs me.† Back in the country, I am recovering and getting down to work again.

Fenyushka, once you've set out to do a thing, never give up. There's no going back now. I must toe the line. Those who are dear to me and I myself will have to pay dearly because of that line, but I know that soon I shall be atoning for my sins before you. As you can see, the last act of the tragedy or comedy—I don't know which to call it—has started. Don't jog my hand, *mes enfants*. If you only knew how much that hand needs to be firm and steady.

Nature is being very gracious to us this year. After a few unbearable rainy days, it's warm and sunny again. From my window I can see "the woods garbed in scarlet and gold." Yesterday they heated my room and I had to keep the door open all day. I've reread what you wrote about "the horrors" of the Molodénovo winter and again couldn't help smiling. It's very nice here, *mon amie*, very nice. My little cottage looks quite exotic—it's quite buried in hay and in the sunshine it sparkles and gleams.

I hear regularly from the old Zeiligers—everything's fine with them. I told you long ago that they had brought up the old man's salary to one hundred rubles. I haven't written to them in October yet—I'll do so very soon. Katya told me before she left that she had written to you. Did you get her letter? They are supposed to bring my mail tomorrow—I'm very anxious to find out what you thought of the pictures of Natasha. I already have a new set. The summer did both mother and daughter good. Zhenya's latest letters have been very nice and calm. Her news about Lyova isn't too cheerful—in the general crisis, his affairs have been tottering and how can that fail to have a disadvantageous effect on Berta Davidovna's situation?

What are the prospects of getting a car? Although you're going through a time when you have other worries besides buying one, you could have done it quite easily earlier.

I will wait for your letter and then will go back to messing up paper.

Be smart, happy and healthy—try hard.

I.

* The story "Awakening" was published in the September issue of *Molodaya Gvardia* (*Young Guard*), while "Gapa Guzhva" and "In the Basement" appeared in the October issue of *Novy Mir*. See also the letter of November 8, 1931.

† This was a stormy period in Soviet literary circles. VSP (Union of Writers) underwent a purge and expelled twenty-five per cent of its membership; violent articles appeared, attacking the activities of RAPP (Russian Association of Proletarian Writers) which had been formed in 1928. The ferment, culminating in the resolution issued by the Central Committee of the Party on April 23, 1932, led to the dissolution of the proletarian organization in literature and the arts. The Union of Soviet Writers, which is still in existence, was then formed; it was to prove to be much more malleable, adhering to the tenets of Soviet socialist realism.

Molodenovo, October 16, 1931

Fenyale darling!

I beseech you to go to Paris. It will distract you. There's nothing much to argue about—it's only a four-hour trip! All the proceedings over the visa can be got through with in three days. You'll make me very unhappy and take away my peace of mind if you don't do it. I shall wait with my heart missing beats for news from you about this. Things are quiet and calm with Zhenya at the moment. They are well. You couldn't go at a more opportune moment. I name Natasha my political representative where you are concerned. What can you do, if your infant was chosen for a profession which is more concerned with descendants than with ancestors? But the hour of the ancestors is also in sight. "Hang on," Fenyale, as they say here in Molodenovo.

If you only knew how much I have worked on myself during these years in which we haven't seen each other, how much has been accomplished, how my entire being has been regenerated for the better, you would be proud of your son. I am experiencing a greater exaltation than ever in my life before and I feel that there is a strength in me which I never suspected. Sometimes a stupid thought comes into my head—it would be good to give birth to an unbending and full-blooded warrior such as my mother gave birth to. But it is the misfortune of that mother that her warrior fights along the line of greatest resistance and he would be terribly depressed if he had to act otherwise.

Fenya, I have never needed to waste a lot of words on you. This year will not have fulfilled its cycle before I tell you face to face a couple of interesting things. By the way, talking of faces—yours in the picture I got leaves a rather sour impression; Mera doesn't look like herself at all, but much better; and Grisha there, in my opinion, is that Morgan fellow who, according to today's newspapers, has arrived in Paris to hold discussions with the Prime Minister about a billion-dollar loan.

I tremble: you write nothing about the pictures of Natasha that were sent you. Can they have got lost? By now I should have had your acknowledgment of their receipt. Zhenya writes that she derives great joy from the maiden.

So then, you are going to Paris, just to please me. I rarely ask for anything concerning them, and rare requests should be fulfilled.

What's happening about the car? If you had a car, you could buzz back and forth between Paris and Brussels.

As I write, sunshine is filling my whole window. The rays of light lie on the paper; in the stove birch twigs are crackling. This year the weather has definitely gone over to the side of the Bolsheviks.

Write, go for walks, drink tea and dream. That's the whole list of my amusements and they're not so bad as they seem, and perhaps they're even better than any others.

And so you are going to Paris.

IB.

[A postcard from the series "The USSR at the Construction Site."]

Molodenovo, October 31, 1931

My darling relatives,

I haven't written for so long because my feeling of guilt before you makes me numb. This month, I've wasted ten days attending to all sorts of practical matters. Well, it's all done now, but I've got behind in my work. The thought that I am laboring for you gives me strength. Without that, despair would invade my heart. I've dug myself in, in Molodenovo this time until the victorious end. I returned here from Moscow four days ago. During November I will be obliged, against my will, to take two days off—the 7th and the 8th [the anniversary of the Revolution in the old-style calendar, October 25th. Tr.—MacA.] The holidays coincide with the day of Molodenovo's patron saint and two bottles of vodka have already been bought. Everyone's relatives will ride into town and it'll be impossible to work anyway. And on top of that, they'll force me to drink vodka.

Because of all this, I had thought of going to Moscow for these two days. But then, I was sitting and writing, I raised my head— outside the window the snow was sifting down. I like Molodenovo more in autumn and winter than in "blossom" time. It's quieter, more solitary, sterner, the tea tastes even better and the pleasure of a country stove is more inspiring.

I have sternly and severely ordered Katya to send you the magazines with my scribblings in them. I hope she's done it. The scribblings are rather trivial—they've been padded in order to cover the advances. I am keeping back more important things. In general, my writing has only now got into its swing. I've finally trained myself. It's a good feeling—to find you know a trade and to believe that there's no power on earth that can deprive you of that ability.

Merochka's latest letter showers me alternately with hot and cold water. What a pity she didn't undergo this latest treatment several years ago, but nevertheless I'm glad to know that there are measures to be taken against that cursed sore.

But what's the matter with Mamasha? When all's said and done, my heart has gone through great pangs of anxiety. There hasn't been a minute when I haven't prayed to my God for her.

Unrolling the scroll of the years, I see that in my life there has been one true, unchanging and indestructible love—and that's for Fenya. It's even becoming obvious to everyone around me now. Well, all right.

Will anything come of the plan for Mama to go to Paris?

Until tomorrow. The snow is growing thicker. The ground is getting covered with a white film.

I.

I wrote to the old people a couple of weeks ago. I'll send them a line or two again in the beginning of November.

Moscow, November 8, 1931

Arrived here yesterday for the holidays, and, fittingly, strolled around, even, as they say in Molodenovo, overdoing it a mite. Today, I'll settle my affairs and tomorrow I'll go back to the country again. The October number of *Novy Mir* is out with two of my stories. I like one of them—the one about childhood. The other is the beginning of a new series. I arranged for that number of the magazine to be sent to you a long time ago—I suppose it's been done by now. I feel I must warn you that all the things being published now are insignificant compared with some other stuff I've done. I'm holding my heavy artillery in reserve. You'll see that there was good reason for my slowness—but now that I know my own character, I will arrange my family affairs differently. To separate in order to start on some new work is impossible for me—

that way, my whole life would be spent away from my family. But I can't go back now—I must write the last lines, and then we'll all start the new page together.

Katya is going to Baya's now, but the sum of money she is taking with her—forty rubles—is so miserable that I really feel ashamed. My affairs are in good shape right now and I could have given her much more, but I don't like to do so without first asking Mendele's advice. I will try to go and see her.

Until tomorrow, with "ever so many" kisses,

I.

Moscow, November 14, 1931

I will be detained in Moscow until tomorrow. I have to do a lot of work in the Archives and the public library, collecting material.

For me, as always, life in town is unpleasant, and that's why I'm so parsimonious with letters during my stays in Moscow. I'll get into my full letter-writing swing when I'm back leading the good Molodenovo life.

With Baya, it was a quite unpleasant business. Katya took her some winter things; she was very polite but didn't take them, saying that she had parents who could help her in case of need and that, so far, there was no need to bother me.

And with Volodya, it was even more lamentable. I think it's all the old people's doing. That must be why they haven't written to me for so long. What can I do? I will leave the matter up to you, but I think the best thing to do would be to throw oneself on the mercy of the conqueror. I'm expecting an immediate reply from you about this.

I found out yesterday that they still hadn't sent you the copy of *Novy Mir*. I bawled them out and they've probably done it now. Please send Zhenya the *Molodaya Gvardia*. I think her copy must have got lost.

I often see Katya. She helps me devotedly and takes care of the practical side of my existence. She said she was going to write to you.

Iosif is in Odessa, but there's been no news from him as yet. Neither of the Lifshitses is in Moscow. They have their vacation now and each of them has gone his separate way.

I'm off to my Archive, where I'll stay till night.

I reckon that tomorrow's missive will be sent from Molodenovo.

I.

[A postcard: The Moscow Soviet.]

Molodenovo, November 18, 1931

After a rather stormy visit to Moscow, I have come back to the country quiet, work and solitude. The business with Volodya greatly distresses me—what should I do about it? The issue of *Novy Mir* came out very late, but by now it should be on its way.

No news of Zhenya at all.

I'll write to you about all our affairs tomorrow. Physically, I feel very well.

I.

Molodenovo, November 27, 1931

Received a letter from Zhenya. Everything's all right with her and evidently she is well, since she doesn't mention her health. The only thing is that her financial situation, just like Mendele's, is quite lamentable. All eyes are turned to Kirill, but in my opinion, he is powerless in the matter. I'm planning to go to Moscow for a day or two in the beginning of December to get my dossier moving, and I'll see Kirill and consult with him. Although I'm not convinced of it, maybe there is something to be done.

Cheerful news about Natasha. She speaks well, is healthy and feels wonderful. How I would like to see her! I console myself with the thought that there's not long to wait. You sent me three pictures, but I think there were many more—I won't give you a chance to appropriate them. Please send them all.

Winter has paid us a visit. The first snow fell the day before yesterday and from the window I see a cover of snow which may be threadbare but which is white at least.

I went out yesterday evening. Full moon. Molodenovo was magically beautiful. Except for family affairs, I am fine and I have a feeling that my work is more productive than before. It's a very pleasant feeling. In general, as a result of painful and persevering training, I have made a really skilled workman of myself and life is easier and more secure once one has a trade.

I'm going to Moscow on the second—to take a breather, to find out about my war book and the tax collector. I'll be finishing my "assignment" in Molodenovo and at the same time will be going to Moscow to do some running around the offices, so that, when the time comes, everything will be ready.

Did you receive Zvezda [The Star] and Novy Mir? I believe they were sent out long ago.

With greeting from Molodenovo,

I.

Molodenovo, November 30, 1931

With delight, I am watching the snow fall—real snow. For these last weeks we have been cut off from the world—it was impossible to get through to us by wheel or sled. Frost closed our typically Russian roads with their holes and hillocks (yesterday toward evening it fell to five below)—and all that without any snow. The village is full of broken wheels and damaged horses' legs. Now it looks as if a sled track will be established in a day or two and people will be able to get through to me here. Otherwise, really, I'll outdo any hermit. Reginin* was supposed to bring some page proofs, but apparently he couldn't face the cold. I waited in vain for him all day.

We have met the winter (which arrived suddenly in the wake of a warm autumn) as thrifty, seasoned peasants should—in full preparedness. We have everything—sheepskin coats, felt boots, mittens, caps with earlaps, and warm, hand-knitted socks. In general,

Babel's fifth birthday photograph.

Babel posing with his father in his first uniform of the Nicholas 1 Commercial school of Odessa.

LEFT TOP: *"I rested in school."*

LEFT BOTTOM: *The occasion for this picture was Babel's first pair of glasses.*

Babel in 1922. *"You know all. But what's the use, if you still have spectacles on your nose and autumn in your heart?"*

1925: *"Babel is the rage of Moscow.*
Everyone is mad about him."
—K. Fedin

LEFT: 1924. *Evgenia Borisovna*
Babel (Zhenya).

RIGHT: *Babel's mother,"Amiable*
Fenya."

Babel's house in Moscow.

Summer 1928: Babel and his wife at the beach of Saint Idesbald in Belgium.

Summer 1928.
Babel and his sister
in Saint Idesbald,
Belgium.

Babel's mother and sister, Brussels, 1930's.

Babel with his daughter Nathalie. "She now calls me mon petit papa *more often than* cochon."

Babel with his daughter. "I have sired a tiger . . ."

ABOVE: *Molodenovo, January 1931. "I am learning a new profession—the handling of horses. It's a delight that it isn't comparable with any other."*

BELOW: *Molodenovo, July 1931. "The wheat is coming on superbly, everything is breathing, growing."*

Evgenia Babel in Paris, 1932

A contemplative Babel.

Babel and his sister, Belgium, 1935

Evgenia and Nathalie, 1936

U.S.S.R., 1936.
From left to right:
Babel, Malraux,
Gorky.

Babel in the U.S.S.R.,
late 1930's.

1938. Babel's "villa" at Peredelkino.

Winter 1938, Peredelkino. "It is located in the middle of a wood where the layer of snow is quite thick."

1939. Babel shortly before his arrest.

in town I never knew what it meant to be protected against the cold. The peasants keep warmer than we do. I don't believe the temperature ever falls below about 60° in my cottage. It's very possible that my attacks have vanished without a trace just because for several years now I've lived without steam heat. You heat the stove with good birch wood (and there's no difficulty obtaining it, God knows) and you feel fine.

I am working hard, eagerly, and it would seem, productively. But actually, future generations will be the judges of that.

I have no peace worrying about yours and Zhenya's financial affairs. I've sent several letters to Moscow on the subject and am planning to go there myself—but, frankly, I haven't any very great hopes.

Please—whatever happens—be well! ! !

I.

* The journalist V. A. Reginin was editor of 30 *Dnei* [30 *Days*], a magazine in which several of Babel's short stories appeared. Babel is here referring to proofs of his story "The End of the Old Folks' Home," published in the January, 1932, issue of 30 *Dnei*.

Molodenovo, December 4, 1931

Going to Moscow tomorrow; will probably stay until the 7th. I have to find out how the business with the documents stands—and then there are lots of other things to attend to. Have been notified that the Writers' Union has mobilized me to take charge of *udarniki** with a gift for writing. In view of the fact that I live permanently in Molodenovo, I will have to ask them whether there isn't some other way in which I could acquit myself of my duty as a citizen.

I've worn myself out working during the last three weeks. My trip to Moscow comes at a good time—I'll have a rest. I've gone completely cracked with my thirst for "work." I want to work every hour of my life and am only held back by my limited strength, and, then, my imagination can't keep up.

I called Anna Grigorievna today and she told me there were letters from you and Zhenya waiting for me. I'll answer them tomorrow when I get there. For two days we've had temperatures of 10° below zero. Otherwise, the weather has been remarkably steady —sunny and clear, only with very little snow, which makes travel difficult.

Until tomorrow,

Yours,

I.

* *Udarniki* means "shock workers," i.e. workers who try to attain very high production. In 1930 RAPP (Russian Association of Proletrian Writers) began a crash program design to integrate literature into the proletarian movement chiefly by training the *udarniki* or cream of the proletariat to write, thereby producing truly proletarian literature. It was resolved to require every established writer to work with *udarniki* study circles and to give individual consultations to novice writers. By 1932 it was generally admitted that the program, while producing a number of new worker-writers, had failed to overcome the backwardness of proletarian literature so deplored at the Sixteenth Party Congress.

Moscow, December 7, 1931

My second day in Moscow. Yesterday I arranged a little outing for myself—I drove out of town with some friends in a good car. We dined luxuriously and listened half the night to the latest Parisian and Spanish records. Today, back to business. You cannot have the remotest idea how complicated it is. The publishers are tearing me to pieces and I can't keep up with their orders.

Can you really still not have received the October number of *Novy Mir?* I have had the literary magazine, *Zvezda* sent off to you. It was absolutely essential to send Zhenya the *Molodaya Gvardia.* I am simply amazed at your passivity. With communication with Paris being so easy, how can Merochka still not have taken advantage of it? You simply must go—and as soon as possible, and I beg you to send me a wire when you leave.

The documents are making their usual slow progress—I keep hoping.

Going to Molodenovo the day after tomorrow. I'll write from there about the results of all my efforts.

Saw my secretary, Katya, yesterday. Iosif has arrived and I hope to go and see them today.

I am well—the winter is clear and cold and there's little snow. Until the day after tomorrow,

I.

Molodenovo, December 12, 1931

I've received a new German edition of *Red Cavalry* and *Odessa Stories* in one volume from Berlin. It's been magnificently done. I'm told that the book is a success and has sold out already.

I wrote to the old people in Kiev and got back a rather unintelligible reply from them. They write that they know nothing about Mera's disagreement with Volodya and ask me to write to him directly and assume there will be a return to the "old norm." I just don't know what I'm supposed to make of it.

I had to stay in Moscow quite a long time—I'm doing the rounds of the offices more and more energetically as the time is drawing near. It's such a pity that I can't work in Moscow—conditions aren't right for it. But I have to hurry because everything depends on my handling in the new stories. I'm doing what I can. I'm in a very exalted state, for, one way or another, the change in my private life is imminent and so, in thought and feeling, in fact with all my heart, I am living in the future.

At long last we've had some real snow. Nevertheless I managed to get all the way to Molodenovo by car. I should think it will be the last time, because soon the road will be covered with snowdrifts and then I'll have to change over from the car to a sleigh when we leave the highway.

What about Mera's trip to Paris? I do so wish it would come off.

Don't forget to send me the rest of the pictures. The first lot reached me all right. I have lots of business letters to write now and so I'll leave any further chitchat with you until tomorrow.

I.

Molodenovo, December 16, 1931

It's very nice here now. The snow is deep and the temperature is around fifteen degrees. It doesn't bother me in the least, which just shows how one gets used to things. Even when it's fifteen degrees, I don't have to wrap myself up or even turn up my collar. I experience greater serenity, wisdom and keenness for work in Molodenovo in winter than in summer, when, after all, one does get distracted.

I'm doing a lot of work. I'm on my "third assignment." In the first two there's little that can or will be used for publication. But my further work will be better, I hope. I have big plans and make a multitude of rough drafts and sketches. And that's where I've got my tail caught. In my lifetime, I've produced very little work—a wretched amount. I've banked everything on the "quality of the output," and now I have to puff along and catch up.

I have to be in Moscow on the 25th or even a day or two before that. By that time I shall have received an answer from the Administrative Department. They've given me reason to hope that the answer will be yes. In any case, I'm working on it in all directions. Of course, the one thing that would help me most would be to complete the "third assignment" promptly, but, alas, I am an animal with a long period of gestation.

I've sent a messenger to Moscow today for provisions and letters —is it possible that there won't be anything from you again?

As I have no outside news and am trying to transfer my inner feelings to paper for public consumption, we'd better wait for tomorrow's mail for fresh material. Did you get the October number of *Novy Mir?*

Have my prayers been heard and Mera's trip to Paris by car been arranged? How is your collective health? Aside from an inevitable tiredness as a result of my work, which is sometimes excessive, I feel wonderful. I think it's the discipline of work in Molodenovo which keeps me in such good form.

Until tomorrow,
I.

Molodenovo, December 21, 1931

Yesterday they brought me your letter at last. Katya repented her sins and sent a lot of all sorts of goodies—goose, sturgeon, some good canned foods and so on. My landlord's son brought fifty pounds of it from the station, which is 6 miles away, in the dead of night. I shouldn't have lost my temper with Katya. The poor thing, she never manages to get to the shops or the trolley in time and she never feels her best in the winter.

Talking of winter, so far it has brought us only beauty, without any of its discomforts. After several icy days, we're having mild, snowy weather. Yesterday when I went for a walk in the snow-sprinkled woods, I gasped in admiration. The countryside around Sergievo can't compare with our Switzerland here.

I can't tell you how glad I am that Mera has gone to Paris. If such an opportunity presents itself again, she should take advantage of it as often as possible. I'll be waiting for her "report."

I got the pictures. It's a long time since there have been any new ones. Perhaps Mera will bring some. Have you really not received the magazines yet? I was informed long ago that the *Novy Mir* and *Zvezda* had been sent to you.

I'm going to Moscow on the 23rd. As you know, I have to be there on the 25th. I hope that the New Year will bring us a gathering-pin of the "scattered temples." For me the worst is behind—the painful search for new paths in my work, and temporary sterility. Now I've more or less worked things out and feel I'm standing more firmly on my own feet. And this feeling of self-confidence brings all the qualities . . .

I'll send my next letter from Moscow. Regards to Grisha. How's his business doing? Has the crisis seized his branch too?

Whatever you do, be well.

I.

1 9 3 2

Dear Mother and her direct and indirect descendants,

I sent you my best wishes for the New Year. Now, since there is no God, it is up to us to make the year a wise and a fruitful one. On the 31st, the last day of the old year and six days after the date fixed, I had a conference with my superiors. I wired you about the favorable results of that meeting. My efforts, as you can see, are beginning to show results. The main difficulty will be with money. The Currency Control Board has summoned me to appear before it on the 15th to discuss the matter. But even at the very best, I will only receive a wretched little sum. I suppose that literary and bureaucratic business will occupy the entire month of January and so I won't start on my journey before February.

It is a matter of considerable surprise to me that the foreign press should be interested in such insignificant things as "Karl Yankel." * The story isn't too good to start with and, on top of that, it has been horribly distorted. I believe I've told you before that what was published was a rough, uncorrected version, and all the mistakes completely distorted the meaning. In general, what's being published is a quite insignificant part of my work—I am writing the main bulk of it only now. It is too early to shower me with praise—we'll see what there is to come. The only thing I know I have gained is the feeling of having become a professional writer and a will and eagerness for work such as I have never experienced before. All this, however, is not yet sufficiently obvious in my writing. It still depends too much on luck, and some of it is too messy and isn't presented in the proper order. But after all, everything will be taken care of in its turn.

We are having an exceptionally mild winter. For a whole month now, the temperature hasn't once dipped lower than twenty-five degrees. Moscow is very beautiful. Tomorrow, I'm going to Molodenovo for a week. I haven't done any work for ten days or so and that causes me unbearable torment. I need those hours spent each morning with a piece of string in my hands like a real sedative: without them I feel a thoroughly broken man, whereas on the days when I do work, I feel reborn both physically and morally.

Tomorrow, I'll write from my village. I send you my love, my dear ones, and promise you that I'll do more to gladden your hearts than I have done in the last few years.

I.

* The short story "Karl Yankel" (first published in *Zvezda* [*Star*], July, 1932) concerns the legal action brought by a husband against his wife who had their infant son circumcised and who was charged with preferring the Jewish name Yankel to that of Karl Marx. The story naturally lent itself to partisan criticism. Babel's irritation over the furor the story aroused is evident here, as is his apprehension about the difficulties that could easily ensue for him. (See also letter of January 7, 1932.)

Molodenovo, January 7, 1932

I seem to have managed to wind up my business in Moscow and I've come to Molodenovo for a few days to do a bit of work. I have to return to the city for a final talk about money. I expect it will be difficult, although they have promised to let me have some. I don't feel like going over and becoming a dependent of the American uncle who, anyway, seems to be cracking up.

Today is the first day of [the Russian] Christmas, but it's so warm there's water dripping from the roof. The winter is being kind to the poor. Life in Russia has changed so much that, in the village, you would never guess it was Christmas. Nefedovna* has baked some stuffed cabbage and that's that. The son is working like on any weekday and Karpych, the master, is running around in circles wondering whether to get drunk or not. The very fact that he is hesitating proves that the holiday's roots have been severed.

I have a very busy day today so I will be brief.

We are aware here of the articles they write about me abroad but, unlike Mama, I don't see anything pleasant in them and, in fact, am quite furious. But it's of no importance. After all, it's impossible to gag a mug you can't reach.

Until tomorrow then.

I.

Did you get my New Year's telegram telling you that they were giving favorable consideration to my request?

* Nefedovna was the wife of the peasant Karpych, the owner of the house where Babel lived while in Molodenovo.

Molodenovo, January 11, 1932

I was waiting for Katya's parcel today as if it were manna from heaven. But the messengers arrived empty-handed. For the umpteenth time, that whimpery old slut missed the train. I am furious at her imbecility and now I will have to alter my plans and take off for Moscow just when I am getting warmed up and into my work. An agent like her ought to be fired on the spot but I am reluctant to do so after all this time. They get their supplies on my ration cards—cards such as they couldn't even dream of otherwise—while I have to sit here feeding on dried beans.

I am writing all this now in a fit of rage but really it is painful to have to have anything to do with that fool.

Nevertheless I'll stick it out here until the fifteenth, for I really can't see what I could do in Moscow before that and, besides, there is no place in the world where I can work better than here. Winter rather than summer is the blissful season in Molodenovo —it is a time of privacy, quiet and the beauty of nature. And this winter is an exceptionally mild one.

I.

Molodenovo, January 12, 1932

Dear Mamulya,

I want to take back now all the nasty things I wrote about Katya. She got mixed up about the train schedules and today she sent me the food with her cleaning woman. So now I am living in plenty again with halvah, preserves, caviar and other such victuals.

Yesterday and today I worked a lot and have drafted a story that strikes me as poetic and simple, and is on a quite unexpected topic. I haven't yet given a thought to practical considerations concerning it. I know I ought to have done so. But still, I've derived moral satisfaction from it.

Tomorrow, I will phone to Moscow and find out when I am to leave, on the fifteenth or the sixteenth. I feel that every extra day in Molodenovo strengthens our moral and financial foundations.

Sent off my tax-assessment for 1932 today, proudly filling in, in the box for "family dependents": Babel Natalia, age—two and a half.

I cannot get my fill of the charms of nature surrounding me here. We haven't seen any winter weather—there's a lot of snow but it is very warm.

Until tomorrow then,

I.

Molodenovo, January 15, 1932

Today I called Moscow on the phone. It turns out that the meeting of the Currency Control Board has been postponed till the twentieth. A good thing I didn't leave. I'll stay in Molodenovo another three days.

Yesterday, I exerted a tremendous effort and drafted a rough version of a short story and today I feel very tired. I went for a long walk before lunch—went to the stud farm and walked as far as the next village—slept when I came back and now, as evening is approaching, am sitting down to write some letters. The weather is still wonderful, between 25 and 30 degrees, and the air is a delight to breathe. Spent three hours or so in the forest today. Even my peasants realize that my health has greatly improved since last year. I think I will always remember Molodenovo with affection. On the twenty-second we're having another wedding—my landlord is "marrying off" his second son. He returned from service last year, was sent by me to a training school for mechanics, got himself a job in a factory and now is getting married. So, on the twenty-second, we're going to have a party at the fiancée's house and on the twenty-third, another party here in Molodenovo.

Today I called the Lifshitses on the phone. Lyusya Brodsky is in Moscow and she promised to come here for a few hours one day before the nineteenth. The last time she was there she stayed with the Lifshitses and, being a great enthusiast, she was tremendously enthusiastic about her stay.

When I get to Moscow, I'll take out a subscription to *Pravda* or *Izvestia* for you and Zhenya. In doing so, I'm thinking of myself too. On the twentieth, I'm going to the French consulate to find out if my visa is still valid or if it must be renewed.

I'll write again before I leave. I have already announced my forthcoming departure to the peasants and a great lamentation arose.

I.

Molodenovo, January 25, 1932

At first, the Currency Control Board refused to grant my request. Then they reconsidered. The matter is being pursued and I hope that it will end satisfactorily. I've been crushed by endless things I must get done and have had no time to write. I will send you a detailed letter tomorrow.

I.

Moscow, March 4, 1932

I'm still stuck in Moscow, stuck here for personal reasons, one of which is a quite unexpected one. I am still trying to get permission from the Currency Control Board, correcting proofs, doing some urgent additional writing and, above all, breaking in my new apartment.

A few months ago, I put in a request to the Writers' Union in which I declared that, in view of my forthcoming trip abroad to get my family and bring them back to the Soviet Union, I needed an apartment. A few days ago, I was called in by the Union and they offered me two rooms set apart in a small, quiet wooden house in Krasnaya Presnya. It is a temporary arrangement, they said, until larger quarters can be found. It would have been crazy to reject the two rooms which, in view of the present rush to Moscow, represent tremendous value and a steppingstone toward our future establishment. After the most necessary work and cleaning was done, I moved in with Katya's help and approval. I brought Karpovich's daughter along with me from Molodenovo and have been living in my new place for several days now. I can honestly say that I am quite pleased with it. I only wonder to whom I should turn over the apartment when I go. I must choose carefully and find a trustworthy person. I am thinking of Sasha Lyakhetsky (he would like to break off) and of Vera V. who isn't too happy either, living at her sister's.

Did you get the new edition of the *Odessa Stories?* Since I am watching out for my interests and am not interested in my old writings, they have messed me up accordingly on the cover. They issued ten thousand copies of the book and it sold out almost entirely within a few days, so my disgrace is not being displayed in the windows of the bookstores. I am working hard, getting further and further away from outside hustle and bustle and so am feeling well. I still have to do some more work in Molodenovo (the final touches) and after that I'll hasten my departure. The only thing that saddens me is that life is now a thousand times more interesting, significant and active here than it is abroad and, aside from family matters, I have nothing to do there. Our climate has awakened with a start and the winter, a quite severe one, has descended upon us.

I.

Moscow, March 8, 1932

I didn't wire because there's nothing to boast about. It is harder than it looks from a distance, as you must realize by now. The setback doesn't mean that there's no hope left of course—that family state of mind must be done away with. Taught by bitter experience, I'll continue my *démarches* and still hope to succeed. The annoying part of it is the delay, but that, of course, can't be helped. I've only been up and out for two days—like everyone in Moscow, I was down with the flu during which I was devotedly cared for by Katya. Now I am completely recovered.

I am terribly depressed because, with all sorts of business keeping me here, I can't go to Molodenovo. I badly need a spiritual rest. And, as though to spite me, there has been a terrible snowstorm. All the country roads are buried in snow and it will be quite impossible to get there for a few days at least. Do not be angry with me for my long silence—I like to write of deeds, successes and "achievements," as they say here. So, since I haven't any to report, I'll just have to wait until there are some. And I intend to do my utmost to have something to show.

Yours,
I.

Moscow, March 16, 1932

I sent you a telegram two days ago and yesterday I was going to write to you but got sidetracked by other business. I went to see the Currency Control Board and, as you must have gathered, the prospects for the future seem a bit brighter. They told me that it wasn't a question of rejecting my request but simply of a necessary delay, and they gave me an estimate of how long it may last—two months. They reckon that permission will be granted at the beginning of May. I had no alternative but to accept. As to how I feel and what I've been through in all this time—that's another question. I'll try to use the remaining weeks to do some work in Molodenovo, work that requires great concentration and in which I'll use the materials I have collected. For in Moscow I only collect material and jot down mere sketches, and am quite unable to do any serious writing. I'll come up to Moscow for one day each week. Taught by bitter experience, I'll press my business constantly and without letup.

While the first half of the winter was exceptionally mild, the second half has come down upon us furiously, bringing with it bitter cold, snowstorms, mountains of snow. I have read that the cold wave swept over western Europe too. How has it affected your collective health?

As a result of the events of recent days, our correspondence has been completely disrupted. I was under the impression that I was just about to meet you and so was unable to write. Now I'll try to do so more regularly but will postpone the outpourings of my heart until May. So don't hold it against me if by chance my letters arrive a bit irregularly. Still, I will write to you often enough from Molodenovo, because everything there is conducive to it.

I see Katya quite often. She is still in charge of my food supplies, of my ration books and so on. She worries a lot about the poor aunts who stayed behind in Odessa, and keeps sending parcels to them.

Recently, while I was sitting at Tretyakov's listening to all sorts of yarns, he snapped a picture of me with his Leica without my being aware of it. It looks quite pale but *tel que je suis*. Ilyusha Slonim is modeling a bust of me in clay and it is coming along superbly. When it is ready, I'll send you some pictures. I'll decide today exactly which day I'll leave for my village. Will write to you in the evening or tomorrow morning.

I.

Moscow, April 5, 1932

I presented my papers again yesterday, this time in a more hopeful atmosphere than before. The case will probably be given special attention and sped through. I have declared that I must leave no later than May. In case of further difficulties, I'll go to Alexei Maximovich [Gorky] who is now in Moscow.

Received a letter from Kiev, from the Zeiligers. They now rent what was the drawing room of the Gronfeins' former apartment. They asked me what to do with the furniture. I wrote and told them to send it to Moscow. We now have somewhere to put it and must collect all our scattered belongings and all our scattered people. Spring, or rather summer, has arrived and caused a physical transformation in me. There is absolutely no doubt that the healthiest thing for me is to live in a warm climate.

Katya has a guest from Odessa staying with her—Dora. I need her like a dog needs a fifth paw. Katya will write to you separately. I will keep you posted on all developments.

I.

Molodenovo, April 9, 1932

In these few days in the country, I have caught up with my sleep and am working away. The spring floods are approaching Molodenovo and will soon cut us off from the rest of the world. For the next eight or ten days, it will be impossible to get to Moscow. The starlings and wagtails have appeared. From here—from Molodenovo's hill, one can watch God and His works.

Although my requests must wait until the beginning of May, I have decided to repeat my *démarche* the next time I am in town. As I wrote before, the omens are more favorable than last time.

Have received a letter from Zhenya. She is fine and is about to move to a new apartment. The main thing is that she doesn't complain about her health. Our young maiden is thriving. She received a doll as big as herself from her American uncle and was greatly inspired by it.

In my Moscow apartment—and I can call it that now without blushing—they are making some repairs and the stoves are being rebuilt. My Germans will certainly succeed in making my abode shipshape.

I have become somewhat estranged from my village landlords. The old grandmother has been left paralyzed by a stroke and she now lies in the main room next to the dinner table. And I, despite my coarse, hardened state, still cannot eat with the murky, glassy stare of the dying woman directed at me. She was a good old woman but all the peasant members of the household are clamoring for her end. She is well past eighty. I take all my meals in my own little hut now and my landlords sometimes come over to visit me.

The Reider publishing house in Paris has offered Zhenya a contract and an advance for a translation of my newest stories* but I prefer to wait.

It's night. Spring rain is falling. Please be well.

I.

* Babel's first published work in French was *Cavalerie Rouge*, Reider, 1930, Paris. The work was translated by Maurice Parijanine with the collaboration of the author. This work was reprinted in 1959 by Editions Gallimard.

[A postcard with a view of the Dneprostroi from the series "The USSR at the Building Site."]

Molodenovo, April 12, 1932

The floods are beginning here. The hill on which we sit will be surrounded by water and, except for poetry, I'll have nothing to do. I won't be able to get to Moscow before the 20th but, anyhow, I have nothing to do there before that date.

My stay in Molodenovo has had its favorable effect upon me and I am quite fit now. I am enjoying my work, the quiet and the proximity to the earth. If you get no letters from me during the coming week, blame the floods.

I.

Molodenovo, April 23, 1932

Managed to get to the village with incredible difficulty. A horrible flood. The water has been falling but now it has risen again and flooded over the banks. We haven't had any spring this year, nothing but mud, cold and gloom. Makes one sick to look at it. I betrayed the South and now I remember it with regret.

Our Moscow apartment is undergoing repairs. The Germans are working furiously, rebuilding the stoves for next winter, painting and repairing. I'll be back in Moscow by May 1 (I'd like to attend the May Day parade this year) and by that time the apartment is sure to be in perfect order.

I went to see Katya, had her attend to one of my teeth, ate some home-made matzos. She bakes them every night and it takes her almost until dawn. How are you celebrating the holidays? With matzos and the synagogue or without all that stuff?

On the 30th offices are closed and May first and second are holidays, so I'll hand in my request on the third. And this time there can be no question of retreat—all my plans are based on my leaving in the second half of the month.

Stepan Kuznetsov, the actor, is dead. Does Mera remember him? He was so remarkably good in A *Nest of Gentlefolk* and in *The Inspector-General*. The greater part of his career was spent in Odessa and Kiev. He had a very special talent which made him very attractive.

There is some very sad news from our home town, from our aunts. I have just written to Katya to tell her to transmit them a little money. Katya sends them parcels ceaselessly.

Since, while I am in Molodenovo, I belong to no one but myself, I'll write to you quite often. For some reason, you seem to have lapsed into silence. Do not forget one who is devoted to you, body and soul.

Yours,
I.

Molodenovo, April 29, 1932

I can't feel too pleased with my latest stay in the country. My head has kept aching. It may be the approach of spring or that I am overtired. For this reason, the results of my work are not up to the standard I'd hoped for. I'm going to Moscow tomorrow. I want to watch the May Day parade and then, on the third, I'll start on the new—and I hope the last—lap of my calvary.

Once or twice the sun has put in an appearance here, but it is raining again today and it looks very much like fall.

I hope to find a letter from you when I get to my palatial new apartment—you haven't written to me for a long time. How did you spend Passover? I had nothing but a taste of Katya's home-made matzos.

Do not expect any lengthy communications from me from Moscow, although I'll keep you posted on the latest developments.

I.

Moscow, May 6, 1932

Yesterday I sent you a postcard giving you a summary of the most important developments. Now I am just sitting and waiting. Your excuse that you dare not write to the new address is ridiculous—it will be my home base for a long time to come and the best place to write to me. I've already given you the address many times but I'll repeat it once more: Apartment 3, 4 Gorbinsky Alley, Vorontsevo Field. Send me Natasha's pictures immediately— I'll give them back to you when I come or send them back any time you ask for them.

I am very happy to hear that you celebrated Passover according to the rules. I, for my part, didn't see anything of it except for Katya's home-made matzos. The news about Lyova's coming over is very important for I must have a talk with him on various family matters and, above all, about Berta Davydovna, because I have firmly decided to gather my scattered family—I refuse to go on living alone.

I didn't know about Lyusya's son's death. Wretched woman.

I.

Molodenovo, May 11, 1932

Even Zhenya has managed to find time to write to me at my new address, but from you—nothing still.

Katya is in Kiev. Iosif is up to his tricks again: he suddenly entered a sanatorium.* It took the intervention of his nephew to extract him again. They'll be in Moscow in a few days.

Before leaving for Molodenovo, I went to see Gorky. I am expecting my "case" to be settled within the next week or ten days. If difficulties arise again this time, I'll push Gorky into action. My case is now "impending."

Zhenya has been in her new apartment, 10 Avenue Pasteur, Paris, XV, since the 10th. She is very pleased with the new apartment but I'm sure she has nothing on me—I'd bet anything my place is better.

Freken and Agafya are working for her as before and I am very happy about it.

I hope you've sent me the photographs. I'll try hard to return them to you personally in the not-too-distant future.

Gorky will be living within one mile of Molodenovo as he did before, so, in going away from there, I am losing a very nice neighbor.

Spring has arrived here. From my window I can see the same wood, the field with peasants tilling it. Everything is so familiar but I may be seeing it for the last time.

I'll write soon. When I'm in Molodenovo, I'm always very punctual.

See you soon—and I believe that with all my heart.

I.

* Babel is here implying that I. Lyakhetsky has been arrested.

Molodenovo, May 19, 1932

I went to Moscow last evening to see somebody and came back at four this morning to do a bit more work. My friend gave me hope and asked me to come back in a few days to finish the business. In general, it seems to me that the outlook is much more propitious now than it was in March. So I am awaiting the reply to my request in an optimistic mood.

Yesterday Katya and Iosif came back from Kiev. Their nephew has ironed out all the difficulties. Iosif doesn't leave his room. He has a badly neglected hernia that must be operated on.

Our trunk is safe and unmolested and it will be sent along with the furniture when the Zeiligers get around to it. That trunk is very dear to me. No one will steal anything here—never in my life before have I had such an apartment, such order, such grandeur.

Molodenovo is very nice just now. The fields will soon be covered with flowers, the apple trees are in bloom before my windows, a nightingale has come to live in a wood a few steps away from me. But my thoughts are elsewhere.

My neighbor Gorky has returned to these haunts and came to pay me a visit the day before yesterday. I had sent someone over to him to borrow some victuals. He sent me a whole armful of wonderful things.

And so, I hope to write soon from Moscow as they should summon me there in a few days.

Yours,

I.

I am very sorry you didn't send me Natasha's pictures in time. It's not worthwhile bothering any more now.

Molodenovo, May 27, 1932

I've just come back from Moscow. In the first stage, my request has received favorable consideration. The next stage remains and I cannot say whether it is the more or less important of the two.

On the 30th, I have to go to Moscow to read on the radio and, by the 31st, I hope that the second stage of my request will be decided. I must act with determination—it's now or never.

I've received Natasha's pictures, but no letter dated from the 10th. Could you have got the address mixed up? My daughter belongs to the same "type of beauty" as I do, but her face, as I wrote to Zhenya, is very lively and expressive. In one picture I detect a resemblance to Zhenya.

I.

Moscow, August 5, 1932

From my silence you will have realized yourselves that I have nothing cheerful to report. My *démarches* constantly stumble against formidable obstacles. I waited to write to you in the hope that I'd be able to give you some precise dates; I kept postponing it from day to day, but now I see that further delays are very possible. Now, since I am not in control of my movements, you shouldn't include me in your plans. I would be very happy to know that you'd left for Spa and am waiting impatiently for word from you that you've done so.

We are having an "unheard of" summer—it looks more like a Nice or an Odessa here than Moscow. Unfortunately I spend most of the time in the city. My neighbor is on leave of absence in Vienna and I am all alone to pace the six large rooms here. The garden attached to this house is a great consolation though.

All the Lyakhetskys are at hand. They often have visitors from Odessa, from the "fiancé's side," staying with them. Katya receives these guests without any special enthusiasm. She should really be sent to some health resort but I have so many things to think of now that I can't give her the attention I should.

Lately I have been doing a lot of posing for pictures that will be included in various books of mine and I'll send you some photos and prints.

Having broken the seal of silence now, I won't use it again and will keep you *au courant* of my difficult affairs. I'll manage to see things through somehow and I only hope that your summer isn't wasted through my fault. Actually, for purely selfish reasons, I don't want to have that additional load on my conscience.

I'll write again very soon. I would like to receive a letter with the Spa postmark on it from you.

Yours,

I.

Moscow, August 17, 1932

I seldom write for quite obvious reasons—I keep waiting for the day when I'll have some good news* for you. It's still the same alternation between hope and despair, and I feel it's not worth while entertaining you with all these tidal ebbs and flows. And so I just wait. By all divine and man-made laws, this waiting, which has been going on for so many months, must soon come to an end.

I have spent the hottest months in Moscow, my only consolation being my nice apartment and the garden attached to the house. I have showers three times a day. My Germans are on leave in Vienna and I am alone to pace the six rooms and two floors. I am looked after by a cook and a maid so that, from the viewpoint of physical comfort, things are better than they have ever been and rather make me think of the life of a misanthropic Parisian bachelor as described in certain novels. But, of course, you know about my mental state. My only *Ausflug*, except for my trips to Molodenovo, has been visits to my friend Semigov's stables. There, among the magnificent race horses, I have recovered a relative peace of mind, and I believe that the laws governing a stable of race horses have advanced my understanding of human limitations.

I am very glad that you are out of Brussels. And since I am now nothing but an "adviser" and "well-wisher," I would like you to stay out of the city as long as possible.

Katya has two guests staying with her now: Zhenya Hoffman, who is really *inénarrable* in his blessed denseness (he would like to be transferred to a Moscow job) and Misha Potetsky, also a fool, but this one, an athletic type.

Let me have Rosa's address. I always remember her with affection and I would like to write to her. How is she getting along? Zhenya doesn't write to me for the same reasons that I don't write to her. I expect that everything is all right with her, considering.

Yesterday I sent you a wire ending with the words: "Letter follows." I can use them again to close today's message. I have nowhere to look to but my little family and I cannot fail to be dogged on this point.

I.

* The "good news" will be that on August 17th, *Literaturnaya Gazeta* will announce that the Organizational Committee of the Union of Soviet Writers had nominated Babel together with other writers—Vera Inber, the critic Zelinsky, and the poet Selvinsky—for membership on the national commissions of MORP (International Organization of Revolutionary Writers). The nomination rekindled Babel's hopes of being sent abroad and he was indeed able to go the following September.

Moscow, September 4, 1932

Yesterday they gave me my passport for travel abroad and I sent you a wire. I reckon to leave before the tenth. I still have many things to do here, including attending to my financial affairs. It now looks as if I will have to stop over for a whole day in Berlin to get my Belgian visa. They don't issue them in Moscow. I'll wire you when I leave Moscow and then from Berlin to let you know what train I'm coming on. Perhaps we could meet in Liége.

As soon as I get to Paris, I'll start taking the necessary steps about

Mama's passport so that she'll be able to go back home. When you get this letter, wire me immediately in Moscow to say whether we can meet in Liége. I've sent off two telegrams to Zhenya, one to St. Jacut de la Mer and the other to Paris.

I feel tired now. See you soon.

[Written in a different hand.]

My dear Tatunya,

Tell Papa that Grandpa is crying. I suppose everything is going so badly that he doesn't feel like writing. I miss you very much, my dear girl.

St. Jacut de la Mer, September 19, 1932

We are living in a very romantic spot now. I found Zhenya in excellent form: she looks better than ever and her coat is glossy, as they say of horses. I still haven't recovered from the shock I received at the sight of my daughter—I never expected anything of this sort. It is really quite beyond me where she could have got so much cunning, liveliness and cupidity. And it is all full of style and charm. That, at least, is my impression. I haven't been able to find one ounce of meekness or shyness in this tiny tiger cub. I'll send you a detailed report when I've had a closer look at her. We will stay here a few days longer. We are going to Dinard today to buy me certain things. I'll write when you should send me my passport. Until tomorrow then, my dear ones.

St. Jacut de la Mer, September 22, 1932

We are having a great time. Yesterday we went to a fair in the neighboring town and I looked enviously at the horses and cows they had there. Today I went to see the fishing boats returning from sea. This is a fascinating place. I ought to go to Paris but I would like very much to spend a few more days here. By my Russian standards, they feed us fantastically well. Natasha displays a constant and unwavering appetite that makes me wonder what gluttons in our family she takes after. In general, she is a very sly creature, quite full of worldly wisdom.

I.

St. Jacut de la Mer, September 25, 1932

I have sired a tiger. Without consideration for age and position in life, she showers French obscenities on all around her. She called me *cochon* today, and her appetite is such that a special decree should bar her from entering the USSR. Now, inasmuch as she was born ten days after the time limit and inasmuch as Makhno* resides in Paris, I no longer have any doubt left that it is he who is her father.

It is so nice here that we keep postponing our departure. Still, we shall be in Paris on October first at the latest.

I.

It's all a lot of slander: a person is entitled, after all, to eat her fill and give a piece of her mind once in a while. My regards to the whole family,

Zhenya.

* Makhno was the leader of an anarchist band of White Russians who fought against the Red Army in the Ukraine during the Civil War; he had a reputation for great ferocity. He emigrated to Paris and died there in 1934. Babel later refers to his three-year old daughter as "Makhno."

Paris, October 2, 1932

Arrived here two days ago in the evening. Your young relative is more likely to cause death than to give life. Yesterday she called me *cochon* and punched me in the mug, making my glasses fall off.

How is your collective health? I was surprised not to find any message from you here. My best wishes for the [Jewish] New Year.

Did Mama go to the synagogue? How is she? Can she move around? While our trip to Brussels is being decided upon, couldn't she come over here? Send me the passport. The apartment here is excellent and we could all fit into it very nicely. Yesterday, I saw Berta Davydovna. She is not too well. Today, I am arranging a room for myself and tomorrow I'll get down to work.

I.

Paris, October 4, 1932

I am getting installed in the apartment or, more exactly, am arranging a room for myself to work in. I have no time to waste. Your silence is beginning to worry me. Can something have happened, by any chance? Why don't you send me that passport? I am longing terribly to see you all and hope to find out in the next few days how that longing can be satisfied. We must first make financial estimates and work out a program, then we can decide who'll go to see whom first.

In the last few days, Makhno has quieted down and sometimes displays such meekness and reasonableness that my heart melts. The Russian lessons take place amid a lot of shouting and unpleasantness—she doesn't want to learn the language, which, however, doesn't prevent her from often calling me *dyurak* [the Russian word *durak*—fool—pronounced with a French accent.—Tr. MacA.].

What date does Yom Kippur fall on this year? .

I have received a letter from Lyakhetsky. Katya is leaving to take a cure in Kislovodsk. He is leaving for the Ukraine. Everything is all right with them.

I will have to take part in an evening devoted to Gorky at the Soviet Embassy here. It seems quite impossible for me to get down to work here and that depresses me very much.

I must ask Grisha for a favor, a quite *brulant* request, I dare say. It seems to be quite impossible to find Capstan pipe tobacco here, the *mild* sort, in the red wrapping, which is the weakest there is. I am in great need of it. Could he get some for me and send it the first chance he gets to give it to someone, or by mail if the excise duties are not too great. I would be very grateful indeed.

Don't remain silent. Write.

Yours, I.

Paris, October 6, 1932

Yesterday, I sent off my letter to you and this morning I received yours. It's just as I thought—Mama is sick. Still, I hope she'll be able to move before the month is out. Send me her passport and I will have it extended, and I'm sure I will be able to send her the visa at any time. I have made the acquaintance of [Anatole] de Monzie and I'll have no difficulty with it.

Starting tomorrow, Zhenya will have a Viennese maid who's been recommended to her by Madame Birkham. Then she won't be so tied down in the house.

I have ordered a full wardrobe at a good tailor's: two suits and a winter coat, and bought myself a few more things, so very soon I will look like a prospective cabinet minister.

My relations with Mademoiselle Nathalie are improving with every passing day and it looks as if it will wind up in a solid friendship. I can make out her sly character a bit. No doubt about it: she's an outstanding maiden all right!

We must do our utmost to get together as soon as possible.

Mon très cher Grisha, please don't forget about the *mild* Capstan.

Yours,

I.

Paris, October 12, 1932

I've got the passport. In a few days our Ambassador is arriving and I'll go over to the Embassy then. Besides Mama's passport, which is a simple matter, I have to deal with Zhenya's and Berta Davydovna's, and they are not a simple matter at all.

Natasha is blooming; her health has improved here and she seems to have become accustomed to me. Ah, if only we could all get together quickly! We are having a good time. I have visited *le Salon de l'Automobile* and have attended a lecture by the Grand Duchess Maria Pavlovna. The only snag is certain financial difficulties. Our expenses for this month have reached the figure of ten thousand while both Zhenya and I are expecting to receive most of our monies in the course of November. Zhenya has asked me to ask you whether, since you are thrifty, lower-middle-class people, you couldn't let us have a thousand francs or so until November? Is Shereshevsky coming?

Above all, how is your collective health and when do you think Mama will be able to travel? The apartment is ready to receive her.

I.

[A card with the beginning missing.]
. . . she is always ready to fight but in Paris she has become *plus maniable* and her looks have improved immensely, which surprises Berta Davydovna no end. And also, she now calls me *mon petit papa* more often than *cochon*. Yesterday morning, she came to wake us up and said in a very matter-of-fact tone: *"Eh bien, levez-vous, mes enfants."*

The measurements for *le chandail*: length 51 cm, waist 98 cm, chest 100 to 102 cm, sleeve 61 cm. You see what to do. You must make allowance for the fact that it may stretch a tiny bit.

I.

Paris, October 20, 1932

Received the things yesterday. They're excellent. Now I'm sure that *le chandail* will be a beauty. Natasha is crazy with joy. Yesterday, I puffed on my Breton pipe all day. How is Mama's health? I'll send you your documents very soon—the Ambassador hasn't arrived yet so I'll arrange it some other way. I'd have very much liked Mama to come by the end of this month.

Will she be able to manage it?

I have been working all the time up till now. Now I'll give myself a rest and will look around Paris for a couple of days. Zhenya is writing separately. And so, for today, I'll restrict myself to the above.

I.

Paris, October 28, 1932

I went to the post office to send you my letter and, when I came back, found your letter waiting for me. Zhenya had a bad night but feels much better today. Still, she will have to go on wearing the bandage for a few days. Your passport is ready and I am sending it to you with the visa attached. I would like it very much if you could come before the 15th. Your granddaughter is in full bloom. Financially, October has been a very hard month for us because Zhenya had to pay several debts, then we had to pay for the apartment and for my suits—which, by the way, are magnificent and come from a first-class tailor—and for other wearing apparel. But I hope that, starting in November, we shall be able to balance our budgets and have no deficit.

I only managed to write to Lenya Trayanovsky today—his mother came to see me before I left and asked me to give him her regards. I'll write to Katya. I have received word from Iosif that he has now been cleared of all charges of criminal dealings, and word from Moscow that my favorite horse has won the Prize of the Republic. These two pieces of news have made me very happy. I am very sorry that I never thought to send Natasha's pictures to Rosa. I'll do it next time. I am anticipating the joy of wearing that *chandail*—I gather Mera is a past master at such things. Good-bye, then.

Your impatiently waiting,

I.

[A postcard with a view of Parc Monceau, Paris.]

Paris, October 30, 1932

Yesterday Dr. Marshak had to remove the pus that had formed in the wound. After that there was a great improvement and things are moving toward recovery. Before that, we had a hectic day—I acted as nanny and cook, and I have been doing the shopping (and rather enjoying it, I must say) for over a week now. But from Thursday on, we shall have a new maid, a Swede.

Today is the beginning of the *Toussaint* holiday and the ministry will be closed for three days, so I'll send you the passport and the visa at the end of this or the beginning of next week.

Yours,
I.B.

Paris, November 2, 1932

My pictures have arrived from Moscow. They photographed me shortly before I left, for an anniversary collection of my writings. I am sending you one.

After Marshak had cleaned up her wound, Zhenya felt better and she is now recovering nicely. Tomorrow a new maid is coming to work for us and she will put the house in order. Some friends take Natasha for walks to the *Jardin des Plantes* or else she is in a Danish "home."* Her appetite is still awesome.

I am very glad you reminded me about the telephone—I'll call you up one of these days. We'll have a phone installed in our apartment soon—the whole procedure has been simplified now and it is a cheap affair.

I'll go to the *Ministère des Affaires Étrangères* with Marshak who has connections there. We'll do it at the end of this week or at the beginning of next. I would appreciate it greatly if Mama were to leave for here as soon as she gets the visa. When the maid gets here, we shall have order and bliss.

I am continuing to lead the lower-middle-class life, working at regular hours, going for quiet walks in Paris, and brightening those walks a bit now and then with a modest *apéro*.

I.

* The "ladies club" of the Danish colony.

Paris, November 6, 1932

Got your second wire today. What does that dream mean? About three days ago, I sent you a letter containing two snaps and reassuring news about Zhenya's health. Is it possible that it went astray? Today, I abstained from going to the central telegraph station, assuming that you'd finally received my letter. In case you didn't, though, I'll send a wire tomorrow.

Starting yesterday, Makhno now spends three hours a day in a kindergarten (run according to the Montessori method). She is taken there and brought back by car.

And now we have a maid. She is a huge, twenty-year-old Swede, beautiful after a fashion, unable to understand a word in any language, a slow, dumb, attractive creature.

Since Marshak cleaned it, Zhenya's wound has been healing rapidly and she is getting better. I hope to end all the formalities connected with Mama's visa in the very near future so she should get ready to leave.

I'll be in the Ministry tomorrow and will try to find out more accurately how things stand.

I.

[A postcard: Les arènes de Lutèce, Paris.]

Paris, November 8, 1932

Zhenya sends you her regards and swears that she mailed the letter. I can't make out what happened. In any case, I think you were out of your mind to send all those telegrams. Here, everything is as well as can be. For two days we have been celebrating the fifteenth anniversary of the Revolution at the Embassy and at the trade delegation's quarters, so I have rather neglected my duties. In the next few days I will devote myself to the passports of all members of my family, and also get my own visa extended, etc. With my next letter, I'll send you all the papers. Am awaiting Mama's arrival with impatience.

I.

[Letter without a beginning, postmarked November 16, 1932.]
. . . In general, they have been dragging me to all sorts of meetings, luncheons and dinners. I am trying to do lots of work but feel considerable mental weariness, which comes at a very wrong moment, because some things absolutely must be finished. I hope I'll manage though. Mama will bring me the jacket. Just about all of Natasha's wardrobe was made by Mera's hands and I too am becoming her dependent. So long, *mes enfants*, as Natasha says. My best regards to Grisha.

Yours,
I.

Paris, December 11, 1932

Mama's passport has been extended to December 15, 1933. I went yesterday and on Saturday to the *Ministère des Affaires Étrangères*. I hope they'll give me the authorization and I can send it to you together with the passport. They were supposed to inform the French consul in Brussels about it. I see no reason to delay Mama's trip any further. This is a very convenient time and Natasha is in full bloom. I enclose a few pictures. Last Sunday, she and I went to the Jardin de Luxembourg and a friend snapped a few pictures of us.

I hope I'll be able to send you some money before Mama leaves —this month has been good for us in the financial sense, but, as far as debts go, Zhenya's spending has made a hole in our budget. Besides, we have equipped Natasha and myself for the winter.

I'll write to Katya today. The news from Moscow isn't gay. Here, unlike in our homeland, there is nothing new. Still, I am up to the neck in my work as a newspaper correspondent. I'm hardly managing to keep up. And so, wait for my telephone call. When Mama is here, we shall have a real talk about Brussels.

Salut de tout mon coeur à Grisha,

I.

Paris, December 15, 1932

Dear relatives,

It looks as if Mama's documents are in order at last and you'll only have to wait for notification from the consul now. I am sending the passport tomorrow. After a period of very hard work, I took two days off. Today I am picking up the yoke again. Anyway, I have no time to myself because I must escort my daughter: tomorrow she goes to some birthday party; on Saturday, she has a Christmas party in her kindergarten; on Sunday, another Christmas party in the Danish Embassy. *Voilà.* And so, we must have a Christmas tree too. After Russia's austerity, such a soft life is strange to me.

Did you get the snapshots of Natasha?

My money vanishes as soon as it appears but, this time, when it comes, I'll hide the fact from Zhenya and send you some by special delivery. I have nothing more to write to you about and, anyway, I'm sick of pushing my pen all day long—it's graphomania, this endless correspondence with all corners of the world. With all my strength, I am longing to communicate directly.

I.

1933

Happy New Year. This year, we will try to *faire de notre mieux.* The day before yesterday I sent you a hundred belgas. What's happening about the visa? I would like Mama to leave as soon as she gets it—while the Christmas tree is still starring in the house and the holiday mood has not yet flown away.

We greeted the New Year in a strange and pleasant way. We refused all invitations and spent the evening with a friend and his wife, just the four of us. We went to a movie on the Champs Elysées, where we saw Marlene Dietrich, then had supper on the Boulevard St. Michel, visited Les Halles, and returned home at five o'clock in the morning.

Zhenya has asked me to remind you of the following: since our "trousseau" is not quite complete yet, Mama is authorized to bring a pair of sheets with her.

I'm expecting to hear from you and to receive telegrams informing me of your departure.

Regards and best wishes from our family to Grisha,

I.

April 5, 1933

Mon vieux,

Received another telegram from Gorky asking me to leave at once. I have visas for myself and for the family. We will travel separately, because we don't have enough money for all of us to go at once. I received ten thousand francs a few days ago with which we reckoned to pay the debts and put all our affairs in order, but yesterday we suffered an unexpected catastrophe: Lyova notified us that there'll be no money from him this month, and it's precisely this month that we have to meet the quarterly bills, so all our plans have turned to dust. Zhenya should receive a certain sum of money after I leave from a movie firm for which I have done some work —that'll pay for her trip and settle what we owe you "with interest." I reckon to get some more money still in Sorrento and then I'll send you a "supplement" myself.

I have your tribulations constantly in mind. *On va arranger ça.* It looks as if I'm leaving on Saturday. There are a great many formalities with the *aller et retour.* Everything's all right here. I've had myself a summer suit made and fitted myself out a little for the trip. We would have completely freed ourselves of debt if it hadn't been for the snag with Lyova. And in general, it sounds quite a gloomy story.

Natasha is in great form and tells us fairy tales.

I'll write again before I leave.

I.

Naples, April 13, 1933

It appears that everything they write in the geography books is true. There are places here of glorious, unlikely beauty. I'm not really myself again yet. We'll sort ourselves out bit by bit and then I'll write in more detail.

My address: Poste Restante, Sorrento, Italy.

I'm waiting impatiently for news from you.

I.

Sorrento, April 15, 1933

The earthly paradise, I suppose, must look about like the Capo di Sorrento. The emerald sea is spread out before the window, olive, orange and lemon groves grow right up to the door. It's only now that I'm recovering my senses after so much blissful beauty. I must work so that I can quickly drag my ladies over here. Our grand old man is well, cheerful and unwearied. He's planning to go to Moscow in the middle of May. Received a letter from Katya. She's in a much better state of mind. Why isn't there any news from you?

I.

Sorrento, April 18, 1933

They've found me a room "out of the way," here. It has a terrace looking out over the Bay of Naples. The weather is really magical. The lights of Naples, Castellamare, Vesuvius. An uncanny beauty. Gorky is leaving some time in the second half of May and has invited me and my family to stay in his house. It's tempting and very convenient. As there's an incredible mess here, I don't want Zhenya to come with Natasha before the beginning of May. I wrote to her to that effect today. I've already started work and little by little am getting into my stride. Working conditions here are such as I've never had in my whole life.

Why have there been no letters from you for such a long time? Write me proper letters in envelopes, not postcards. Did Sonya get the money? Has Mama recovered from her Paris impressions? There are some new pictures of Natasha. Will you demand them from Zhenya? Write to me at length about how each of you is faring.

I.

Sorrento, April 24, 1933

Have received a letter from you at last (which is more than I can say for Zhenya). We've been having bad weather here all the time, but today it looks as if it might improve. I am working with pleasure here under such conditions—quiet, solitude, peace—as I have never had in my life before. I miss Natasha very much. Financial matters are holding them up. I'm hoping they'll get here at the beginning of May. In a few days I shall read a "story" I have written to Gorky and his advice will determine all my future plans.

He and I have been to Capri and today we're going to look around Naples. He knows every stone here. There are two more excursions I have to make—to Vesuvius and to Herculaneum and Pompei (all these places are very close by) but I want to wait for Zhenya and we'll go together. Katya writes to say thank you for not forgetting the aunts. Apparently the translation was received. But, nevertheless, it's strange that there's been no confirmation.

Sorrento, May 2, 1933

The sirocco, a suffocating tropical wind, is blowing. It's a grand picture—"trees bending low," the sea wrapped in an oppressive, milky fog. . . .

Received a letter from Zhenya. Everything's in perfect order. She has kicked out Sonya and is busy sewing summer dresses which are not yet ready. I've pointed out ways whereby money can be got. I'm hoping that financial matters will be settled and she will be able to leave. Zhenya tells me that Natasha is in better form than she was. She's very well and is as mischievous as ever. I would like them to come here very soon because I miss them.

I've completed a Herculean task—a play. As, of course, it does not fit in with the "general Party line," it can expect rough going, but everyone wholeheartedly acknowledges its artistic qualities.* The setting and the characters are new ones, such as I've never used before, and if it comes off I shall be happy. In a few days, when I start typing it, I'll ask for advice.

* Babel was finishing the play *Maria*, which was ultimately published in the March, 1935, issue of *Teatr i dramaturgiya* [Theater and Drama]. What he foresees here was fully confirmed; the drama aroused a great dispute and was eventually banned.

Sorrento, May 5, 1933

Yesterday, I spent the whole day in Naples with Gorky. He took us to the museums, showed us ancient sculpture (I'm still breathless with admiration), paintings by Titian, Raphael and Velasquez. We had lunch and dinner together. The old man drank, and he drank plenty. In the evening, we went to a restaurant located on a hill above the town (a fairy-tale view from there). Everyone in the establishment has known him for thirty years and they all got up when he came in. The waiters rushed to kiss his hands [sic] and immediately sent for the old-timers who sing Neapolitan songs. They came running—seventy-year-olds who remembered Gorky well—and they sang in their cracked old voices in a way I will never forget. Gorky wept unrestrainedly, drank constantly and when they tried to take his glass away from him, kept saying: "It's the last time in my life." For me, it was an unforgettable day.

I am trying hard to speed Zhenya's and Natasha's coming. I hope that they will arrive in ten days or so.

I have been advised to send my play by mail. Of course, I really ought to take it myself. I haven't decided yet what I will do. The Gorkys are leaving on the ninth—there's a Soviet ship going from London to Odessa and it is, of course, most convenient for them to take it. Besides me, there'll only be Marshak,* our superb children's poet, in the house, and I hope he will take to Natasha. Marshak also has a sister in Brussels and possibly we will all go to Belgium together.

Gorky has taken three of my new stories for his almanac. I am really quite pleased with one of them—I only hope the censors will pass it. Gorky has promised to send me my fees in foreign currency.

It is very sad that Brussels water is bad for mother. Can that fact be properly established and if it really is so, perhaps she should switch to mineral water. Now, since Zhenya is keeping her apartment, I begin to wonder seriously whether Mama shouldn't move to Paris for the winter.

I wrote Zhenya about the pictures; hope she will react. They must be very good ones. My room has grown dark and they are calling me for supper. I must stop now. Till tomorrow then.

I.

* Samuel Jakovlevich Marshak, born in 1887, poet and translator best known for his children's literature.

Sorrento, May 11, 1933

The Gorkys left on the 8th. They took a train to Genoa where they caught the Soviet boat that will take them straight to Odessa. I saw my "master" off as far as Naples, stayed there a couple of days, then came back here yesterday evening. Now, I am alone with Marshak in the huge stone villa and wish Zhenya and Natasha would come very soon. They are, of course, held up by financial difficulties that I hope we shall be able to overcome.

I have started copying my play and hope to send it to Moscow in a few days.

Gorky has asked me to write a few pieces on Naples—it is a thing I would like to do very much and I'll have a go at it.

I.

Naples, May 18, 1933

All plans are changed. I am urgently summoned to return to Paris. The film that was to be made before mine has been scrapped and the director wires me that we must get down to work immediately. My interests in the matter are too great for me to let it slip. I'm leaving for Rome today and for Paris in a couple of days. Zhenya also insists that I should finish with the film first, before I attend to other things. As soon as I get to Paris I'll begin to do the necessary to get a Belgian visa. It is my dream that our whole family should come and see you. I'll write in greater detail from

Paris after I've seen my director. I'll send the play from Paris because I haven't been able to type it up yet.

I.

Rome, May 20, 1933

I'm dizzy with all these Coliseums, Forums, Sistine Chapels,
Raphaels, Pantheons. I meant to leave today but can't tear myself
away. How do I know when I'll get to come back here? At last I
have a chance to see all the things about which I've read hundreds
of books since my childhood.

I'm leaving for Paris the day after tomorrow.

I.

Florence, May 24, 1933

This is the crowning touch. In all my life I've never seen anything more beautiful than Florence. I'm walking around in a daze
after all these Michelangelos, Raphaels and Titians. I'm leaving
for Paris tonight and should get there at 10 o'clock tomorrow evening—there, unfortunately, all sorts of things will land on my
head. Right now I'm going to buy a present for Natasha.

I'm sending you a "Loggia" with a Benvenuto Cellini statue in
the foreground.

I.

Paris, May 29, 1933

Florence eclipsed everything else that I saw in Italy. The impression it made on me will last all my life.

At home everything's in order. Dire misery. Lyova hasn't sent
any money in May. Zhenya is hoping that things will work out in
the future. Natasha has changed a lot in a month and a half. She
speaks Russian excellently (it's several days now and I still haven't

recovered from my surprise). She's less naughty, greeted me with real joy, talks unceasingly about her Grandma.

We must make every effort to meet very soon. It seems I am going into the film business in earnest; I hope to see more clearly what's what by the end of the week.

The negatives of Natasha's pictures were left lying around and I only sent them to a photographer to have prints made yesterday. The pictures will be ready for you in a few days. I'll also send you my photos of Florence.

What can I tell you about Katya? I forwarded some of her messages to certain people in Sorrento and perhaps they will do something about it.

In Italy, I found a translation of *Red Cavalry*.* Of course, I didn't get a kopek out of it, but the book is nicely produced as you can see from the enclosed copy.

This is now the very busiest time for me—as soon as there is a brief lull, I'll write to you at greater length.

I have just read a few issues of Moscow's *Literaturnaya Gazeta*. The reviewers all shower praises upon me and I wonder whether this is not due to Gorky's influence. I am still very curious to know whether the censor will pass my latest stories.

I.

* * *

* *Armata a Cavallo* was originally published in Renato Poggioli's translation by Frassinelli, Turin, 1932.

Paris, June 18, 1933

Seized by remorse, I called you up last night at nine o'clock. But it proved to be in vain—there was no answer.

Here, everything's fine. I haven't written all this time because I've been hellishly busy. I got bogged down with the screenplay, as the work turned out to be more difficult than I had bargained for. I have to read a lot of stuff and on top of that they keep hurrying me, and I have never known how to hurry in these things. But I must finish this work by the end of June for otherwise I won't be able to move away from here or do anything else. And so I just sit working day and night, getting very little pleasure out of it, because it is "on order."

I have bad news about Gorky. During the crossing from Constantinople to Odessa he caught a cold that turned into pneumonia, and for two days was, as they say, on his deathbed. I don't know how he is now and have sent a telegram to inquire. It is all very sad.

Mlle M. has been here and we've had a talk with her. The dresses are very nice. Natasha is now in full bloom and it is a shame you can't see her.

All these considerations make it even more necessary to get on with the scenario. It looks as if Lyova's business is very bad for there hasn't been any word from him for the past two months.

It seems Lyakhetsky has been packed off to some town in the north. I think that is the best thing. This way, I'll be able to do something for him when I get back to Moscow.

Yesterday I spoke at an antifascist meeting. Both Germans and Jews clapped. In Germany I have been put on the list of forbidden authors and *Red Cavalry* has been solemnly burned there.

That's all I have to report for now, and as you can see, nothing much has been accomplished. In a few months, I hope, we shall be having a much gayer time.

I.

Paris, July 2, 1933

There's still nothing "definite" to report and that's why I haven't written. I have to present my outline sometime this week. I am forced to work with a director who is a pedant and full of bad taste, and am constantly seething with rage. Besides, I am in a hurry to get rich for your sake, for the aunts' sake and for my own sake. Gorky is recovering and they're sending me very tempting offers from Moscow which make it necessary for me to go there. On the other hand, I want so much to live with you for a bit. And so I am in a tizzy. I hope, however, that all these problems will be solved this coming week.

We've received a letter from Lyova that is, in a way, reassuring: it seems he has understood that he must give up pie in the sky and the chase for millions and get himself a normal, steady job. He promises to send some money in July.

We are having poor man's weather here—it isn't hot at all and the town is very pleasant. Natasha went for a walk today in the Luxembourg, wearing her new dress and a new white hat; she looked quite irresistible. At last, she has learned to speak Russian and sounds like a real little Russian girl. She constantly mentions Grandma Fenya and threatens to set out for Brussels on foot. She is considerably better behaved now, and although she is still rather naughty, it is more bearable. When they next meet, I'm quite sure that Grandma will have a much easier time with her.

Recently, I tried to call you on the phone again, and once again without success—there was no one home.

> A bientôt,
> I.

Paris, July 10, 1933

The main trouble is that the scenario they commissioned me to write is somehow failing to come off and I don't know whether I'll be paid for it or not. I don't believe rushing things would do any good. I think the best thing would be the following: if the situation has not cleared up by the 15th, Mama should come here by herself (I hope that by then her visa will be ready) and then we will all decide together what to do after that. We should also do the necessary so that Grisha and Mera can spend their vacation in France. It's all a question of *sous* and I'll do my utmost in that respect. In the meantime, Mama Number One should start preparing herself for the trip. I'll try and send her money for it. I'll soon either phone or write to you by air mail. The date of my departure hasn't been set yet but we must hurry. I absolutely must see Gorky who, in August, is going back to Sorrento, for I must make it sure that they will let me travel abroad again. I have masses of things to do and we'll talk about all this when we meet.

I'll write to Sonya today and, in the course of this month, will send her whatever I can spare without fail. Poor Odessa! According to the news from Moscow there is a considerable improvement in the food situation there. In general, the government policy is more liberal and I feel certain that material conditions will be better in the coming year than they have been during past years.

Here everything's fine, except for the heat wave. Natasha is in great form and yesterday she suddenly demanded that I tell her a tale about a little girl who has a Papa, a Mama and a Grandmama in Brussels. I enclose some pictures.

Moscow, September 1, 1933

I got here safely and without trouble, except for being pulled off the train in Warsaw because the last remaining stub of my railroad ticket had been canceled by mistake. I spent a very pleasant day in our embassy and then resumed my journey. I saw the two Lyusyas. They are in good order or should I say, rather, in good disorder?

They had a hard winter here. Katya keeps drowning me in her tears: she's had heaps of trouble. I am looking around me. *Es war höchste Zeit* for me to come back. All sorts of absurd but sinister rumors have been circulating about me. I've managed to attend the horse races.

And so, life goes on,

I.

Moscow, September 3, 1933

Dear Mendeleev,

I'm gradually getting acclimatized and beginning to think about work. Am sending you, registered, a few copies of the new edition of *Red Cavalry*. Keep one—or as many as you need—for yourself and send the rest to Enta. She needs them. What are the plans about Mama? How is her health?

I.

[In a different hand.]

My love and kisses and thank you for the medicines.

Katya

Moscow, September 21, 1933

Life is getting back to normal. I've given a lecture about my trip abroad. It wasn't as good as I might've made it. And then, the newspaper reports got everything mixed up. But that's inevitable. I am now rewriting the "work" I wrote in Paris, because the ending didn't come off. I wish I were through with it for that would leave me free to get down to thousands of fascinating things. I'm being sent on an assignment to the Caucasus and the Ukraine. I may have occasion to visit Odessa. I hope that by October I'll start working "for export" and so be able to help Mama and Zhenya. So, except for the dire need in Paris, everything's fine.

We are having a monstrous fall: every day it rains; it's midday and dark. It never stops pouring. This year's phenomenal bumper harvest is suffering quite a lot.

Yesterday the Lifshitses and the Semigovs came to visit me. We drank, ate and played some records.

A very nice engineer from Vienna is staying in my house. During meals we conduct small talk in the Viennese dialect, then we smoke cigars and sip Viennese coffee. My *palazzo* is in good order.

I found Katya's affairs in a lamentable state. We're gradually putting them straight. Write. I haven't received anything from you yet. What memories have you kept of your niece? I miss you all badly.

I.

Nalchik, October 21, 1933

I've had a marvelous trip: Rostov-Sochi-Gagry-Sukhumi-Nalchik. The weather has been enchanting all the time. I reckon to stay in

Nalchik for some time, being here on an assignment from *Pravda*. It looks as if I'll find quite abundant material to write about here. I feel fine, having been bathing all this time. Am awaiting news from you with great impatience. Address your letters to me here. I have already wired you my exact address. I repeat it here once more: c/o General Delivery, Nalchik, Northern Caucasus. Write more often—I feel terribly isolated without your letters.

Salut,
I.

Nalchik, October 29, 1933

Am living in a blessed land—and am traveling with its master* through hills and dales. We flush out wolves and hares and catch salmon in the Terek. Everything breathes abundance here, such as there hasn't been for many years. The harvest is a fabulous one and building is in progress everywhere. It's a joy just to live here. I'll try and stay as long as possible—it's quite possible to collect unusual material here both for home consumption and for abroad. Because of all my wanderings, I've somewhat neglected current business. I'll try to catch up with it. Moreover, I've completely lost contact with all my correspondents and am very worried—how are you all, all three generations of you? Did you receive my telegrams telling you my address? Where is Mama? I'll wait one more day and then wire again. Don't leave me without news of you. I repeat the address: General Delivery, Nalchik, Northern Caucasus. I've taken root now for a while and will write to you regularly because I think of you constantly.

I.

* Betal Kalmykov (1893-1958), a man of exceptional vitality, organized Soviet authority in the north Caucasus area. He was a permanent member of the Executive Committee of the U.S.S.R. His assistant was Yevdokimov.

Nalchik, November 8, 1933

Don't know what can have happened to my Steiner in Moscow —not a word out of him in spite of my repeated telegrams, and he hasn't sent me my mail. I only heard about Zhenya from you.

I'm still tearing up and down Kabardino-Balkarian Province, a pearl among Soviet provinces, and cannot be too pleased that I came. The harvest here is not only huge, it is also most efficiently gathered—and it is very pleasant to live in Russia amidst plenty at last. I've been in the mountains, to the foot of Mt. Elborus (it makes me weep to think that my family isn't here to see such beauty). I am wandering across the Cossack steppes and am planning to settle in one place soon so that I can re-establish my lost contact with the world. I think if I take full advantage of this trip and do some serious work, it may produce major results and even lead to my reunion with my family in the end. Write.

I.

Nalchik, November 2, 1933

The telegrams I sent Zhenya have come back marked addressee unknown. For this reason I've just sent off a telegram to you. I've at last heard from my Steiner. I hope he's sent all the mail that's been received for me in Moscow. In any case, I feel horribly isolated from you.

I haven't started working yet, because I'm still roaming about this wonderland.* Today I'm leaving to visit a German collective farm—one of the richest and most modern collective farms in the region—and I'll set my mind working there. Went hunting with Yevdokimov and Kalmykov. They killed several wild boar (I didn't take part, of course) 6,000 feet up, among the alpine pastures and with a view of the whole Caucasian range, from Novorossysk to Baku. We spent a few days in a Balkara settlement at the foot of

Mount Elborus, at an altitude of 9,000 feet. I found it difficult to breathe the first day, then I got used to it. I enclose some snaps of these places (there was a photographer with us).

I feel fine physically, as might be expected under these circumstances, but I miss my family terribly. I find it hard to live without Natasha, and worrying about all of you has become a full-time occupation for me.

They have given Katya the passport and now I'll have to see about getting her an apartment. *Je vous supplie,* write to me as often as possible, otherwise I feel altogether alone.

I.

* Kabardino-Balkarskaya, from 1936 an Autonomous Soviet Socialist Republic; its capital, Nalchik, lies to the north of Caucasian Mountains. This mountain chain is the highest range in the U.S.S.R. and in Europe, and Mt. Elborus, 18,481 feet, is the highest peak.

Nalchik, November 26, 1933

Do you get my telegrams? I intend to stay at a collective farm for some time. There, I'll try to sort out the mass of new impressions that have rained down on me. I suppose Zhenya must be having a hard time now. I'll try to write a few articles for the French. Moscow doesn't attract me at all. The winter here is mild and, physically, I feel wonderful. There are astonishingly beautiful spots here (I'll send some snaps in my next letter).

Katya has received the passport but now she's whining because she doesn't have an apartment. She demands my immediate return. She imagines that I am all-powerful. People are strange really. . . .

Now that I have managed to settle down, I will write often, because I think of you every day and every hour of my life.

I.

Nalchik, December 4, 1933

Invaluable Mamashenka,

I received your letter of November 25th with the enclosed like-
ness (quite successful). As to the middle-agedness—it shouldn't
get you down. It's fashionable here nowadays. Tomorrow, for instance, the second province conference of old men and women is
opening. They are the prime movers now in the organization of
collective farms—they supervise everything, show the young people what to do, walk around wearing badges with "inspector" written on them and, in general, are greatly honored. Such conferences
are being convened all over Russia now. The music thunders and
the old people draw applause. All this was thought up by Kalmykov,
the secretary of the province Party committee here (with whom I
am staying). He is a Kabardian by descent and by nature a great
New Man—a type unknown heretofore. He has been famous for a
decade and a half already, but all the stories are easily outdone by
the reality. With iron determination and farsightedness, he is turning this small, half-wild mountain country into a real jewel.

I have also decided to inform you that even in Nalchik (a spot
with a climate that allows you to breathe like a fish in water) the
temperature is five below zero, but the air is so clear and in the
house I am so surrounded by stoves and every comfort, while outside I go around in a Lincoln—that I don't feel the cold at all.
I'm waiting impatiently for the day when I'll be able to move to a
collective farm thirty miles or so from Nalchik, where a warm hut,
snow and very interesting surroundings are waiting for me. For
the moment, my address will be the same as before.

No letters from Zhenya for a long time, but I know from other
sources that she's all right. My wanderings have caused my correspondence to be interrupted, but now, as you can see, I've settled
down and sorted myself out and am writing regularly. As to our
seeing each other, I can't share your pessimism. There is nothing
except my work to hold me here, and everything depends on my
work. I won't let anything drive me off my course now. I'm going

to live where it's convenient for me to work and where I can do so without letup. That may ensure both our seeing each other and money for you. I've already sat down to my writing table and my thoughts are moving a bit, in fact better, I think, than they have in the last few years.

I don't need to tell you how much I miss the family. It's hard sometimes and I try to make myself feel better by working and by maintaining a determined resolution to put an end to our separation once and for all. Someone's waiting for me so I'll end here. *Je vous embrasse, mes enfants,*

I.

Nalchik, December 9, 1933

Today I'm moving to a Cossack settlement thirty miles from here. There's a post and telegraph office there. Letters will be delivered regularly. Write to my former address—my mail will be forwarded to me. The winter here is extraordinarily mild and pure. I feel wonderful and walk miles and miles without tiring. This may be due to the state of exaltation I'm in—at least as far as work goes, I'm in "form" now such as I haven't been in for many years.

I write to Zhenya regularly (when I'm settled, I'm always punctilious), but I get no answers. It's all because of that damned address. If it hadn't been for you, I still wouldn't know it to this day. I'll settle down in the new place, then I'll write.

Salut,
I.

Prishibskaya Cossack Settlement,
December 13, 1933

I'm living in an old, pure-blooded Cossack settlement. The change-over to the collective farm system was not easy here and they have suffered hardships, but now it's all going ahead with a great deal of bustle. In another couple of years, they will be so well off that it will overshadow anything that these Cossack settlements have seen in the past—and they didn't have much to complain about. The collective-farm movement has made great progress this year and now limitless vistas are opening up—the land is being transformed. I don't know just how long I'll stay here. It is both interesting and essential for me to witness the new economic relations and forms. Use my Nalchik address as before. They'll forward the mail from there.

I can also tell you that I've finished the play. In the next few days I'll copy it and send it off to Moscow. The most remarkable thing about all this is that I've already started on another one, and it looks as if I have stumbled on a gusher. I've learned from my previous efforts.

The winter here is extraordinarily mild and beautiful. There's a lot of snow. I feel well. We eat roast pheasant for dinner and drink young wine supplied by the German collective farms.

I.

Prishibskaya Cossack Settlement,
December 19, 1933

From Nalchik, I've moved to an even more isolated place: letters are brought here by coach and horses and it takes them an extraordinarily long time to get here. Try to write often. Thank you for forwarding Zhenya's letter. Materially, the only way I can help her is through my "output." I have finished the play—I was mostly thinking of Zhenya in working overtime on it. I'll send it off to her as soon as I can and I hope she'll be able to use it. It is quite difficult in my business to foresee how much money will be coming in, but I must send as much material as possible.

The change of environment after my return from abroad, and the fact that things went forward in this country while I was away, means that I have had to make a considerable effort of adjustment, both emotional and intellectual, in the past few months. And so, I couldn't just sit down and start writing straight away. But now I am working with great zeal. And I believe now that, after the play,

I will be able to send Zhenya some more stuff in the course of January. It all weighs on my heart and I will do my utmost.

Compared to the way my relatives live, my life here is very pleasant—quiet, warm and interesting. The winter is amazingly mild, snowy and sunny; my Ukrainian landlady is stupid and frantically eager to please. She roasts geese for me, bakes doughnuts, and cooks Ukrainian borscht. I spend half my day working and the other half with the Cossacks on the collective farms or touring the neighboring villages. One of these days, I'm going to Nalchik, so when you write to me, use my former address there.

About the passport—I'll write to our Ambassador and it will all be done in a trice. We must do our best to see that Mama goes to see her granddaughter very soon. Let's work out how it can be done.

I am leaving now for the poultry farm, an extraordinary and fascinating institution about one mile from the railroad station. It is the largest—as things are getting to be here nowadays—poultry farm in the world. It has an incubator capable of handling 160 thousand eggs, and scores of thousands of sitting Leghorn and Rhode Island hens. Tomorrow a huge—[illegible]—is being inaugurated, capable of feeding millions of chicks a year.

I.

Prishibskaya, December 28, 1933

It is quite possible that this card will reach you on New Year's Day and so please accept best wishes from your relative, who keeps thinking of you every minute of his existence wherever his unquiet spirit may be.

I am living in peace and warmth, am surrounded by people worthy of interest and am inspired—more than ever—by all sorts of ideas. I am recopying the manuscript now and will send it to Moscow in a couple of days. Then endless fuss and literary bargaining will start for me. But as long as it hasn't started, I feel happy. The only thing is that I can't get my daughter out of my head.

I.

Nalchik, December 29, 1933

I got here from Prishibskaya on the evening of the 26th and spent two lovely days hunting (very successfully) with some friends —the toll being fifteen wild boar. Am leaving today for Gorlovka in the Donets Basin. I have to go there on business and reckon to return to Prishibskaya afterward. Perhaps I'll have to stop over in Kharkov. Within ten days from now, I hope I will know when I am to return to Moscow.

Got a letter from Zhenya in which she writes that Natasha is still beset with stomach troubles. I have also received Mama's latest letter. I'll write from Gorlovka. I'll let you know my address by telegram. Please, do me a favor and live well in the forthcoming year.

I.

1 9 3 4

Gorlovka, January 8, 1934

Under the avalanche of new impressions I have not been able to write. Not to have been familiar with the Don Valley was a real gap in my life. To go down into a mine, to the end of the tunnel, where they are hammering coal, moved me deeply. I need to return there again. Everyone here—workers and engineers—bears a special stamp which greatly attracts me.

I am expecting news from Moscow. It's possible that they won't call for me until the end of February, in which case I'll take another trip in Kabarda, to Nalchik, in order to go on with the investigation . . . If this is so, I will cable you. Here I live in the house of the local "authority," an old and trusted friend. Unfortunately I have always stayed in the neighborhood of Gorlovka; snow storms have made it impossible to push on any farther in my car. The cold is severe and above all accompanied by wind, but I am enduring it well. I suppose I got in condition in Kabarda. Nevertheless I remember that climate with nostalgia.

I.

Gorlovka, January 20, 1934

I'm leaving today for Moscow via Kharkov and Kiev, and expect to reach my destination on the 27th or 28th. So, as I wired to tell you today, my address is Moscow. I've just heard that on the 12th they held a reading of my play at the Vakhtangov Theater and that the actors liked it very much indeed. I don't like such thundering send-offs, especially since the play isn't topical and when I wrote it I deliberately broke the laws of playwriting. In any case, I must go to Moscow and deal with it.

I'm sitting on my suitcase and that's why I'm making this short. I was quite right to visit the Donets Basin—it's a region it's essential to know. Sometimes it can drive one to despair trying to take in, artistically speaking, this boundless, forward-streaking, never-before-seen land called the USSR. The spirit of hope and triumph here now is greater than at any time during the sixteen years since the Revolution.

I.

Moscow, February 13, 1934

It's such a long time since I wrote to you that yesterday, in a fit of remorse, I sent you a telegram to say I was well and everything was all right. The Paris events [the February '34 right-wing riots.

—Tr.—MacA.] worry me very much and I have sent a wire asking whether my family are all right. I think of Natasha a thousand times a day and my heart contracts.

I'm still busy with theater matters. Rehearsals are starting simultaneously in the Vakhtangov Theater and in the Jewish Theater. I'm negotiating with some provincial towns too. The play that I have completed is really only a trial work. I am writing the next one at full steam and attach much greater importance to it.

My Molodenovo is finished for me. I'm going to look over a country house outside the city where I could work, because I just don't know how to refuse people and in Moscow I'm so encumbered with other people's affairs that I don't have a moment to think of myself. There's enormous animation in all fields of endeavor here—feverish activity.

I still live with the same ghosts—I miss all of you and I want to work. Good-bye, my dear ones,

I.

Moscow, February 18, 1934

Bagritsky was buried today.* He was an old friend from my home town, a marvelous poet, whose growth I watched and helped wherever I could. His weakened body was unable to survive an attack of pneumonia.

Received a telegram from Zhenya saying that everything's all right with them. Tomorrow a Frenchman is going there and I'll send them my love through him.

My itch for the drama is still with me and I'm trying to find a new Molodenovo of sorts, to work there, because in Moscow if it's not one thing it's another. My completed play will be put on in two theaters simultaneously—at the Vakhtangov and in the Jewish Theater, under the direction of Mikhoels.† As to the fee, I'll try to see to it that Zhenya gets it by March.

Despite myself, I'm living a "worldly" life here. People pour in, in streams and, since many of them are very interesting, I have very little time left, and that's why I'm trying to find myself a cell.

I'm very tired after these three days of vigil—I went through the full ritual with the Bagritskys. I need a rest.

Until tomorrow, my dears.

* Bagritsky (1895-1934) was the pseudonym of the poet Eduard G. Dzyubin, born in Odessa of a poor Jewish family. His most important poem, "Duma pro Opanasa," ["The Song of Opanas"] (1926), deals with a Ukrainian peasant forced into service by Makhno.

† Salomon Mikhoels (1890-1948) was a well-known Russian Jewish actor and director.

Moscow, February 25, 1934

You shouldn't take an example from me and should write more often. I beg you to. I'm being torn apart by all sorts of things I have to deal with. I'm coping with Bagritsky's legacy and at the same time am looking for a room outside town so that I can get back to work.

Yesterday, the famous French architect, Lurçat, left Moscow.* I sent with him a doll for Natasha and the manuscript of my play for Zhenya—we have to see about getting it translated and start negotiations with theaters in Paris, Czechoslovakia and other places. Perhaps something will come of it. Here rehearsals have started in two theaters simultaneously—at the Vakhtangov and in the Jewish Theater (under the direction of Mikhoels). I received quite a large sum for the performance rights. I paid off a large part of my debts, helped a multitude of people, and now feel released—and can concentrate all my concern on Zhenya.

Tomorrow, I'm going out of town for a couple of days to visit Gorky. He was sick but he's better now.

There's a really unprecedented epidemic of grippe raging in Moscow. There are sick in every house, and our house help is down with it. So far my former God has had mercy on me. . . .

I.

* The French architect André Lurçat, born in 1894, took part in the 1934 Exhibition of Modern Architecture in Moscow.

Moscow, March 2, 1934

Honorable Fenya and the next generation too,

In the name of the Russian proletariat I express my sympathy for your severe loss and hope that you will help the new young man to carry out his grave responsibilities.

And now let me go on to tell you that I got through with current business the day before yesterday—read a piece of mine in public—and am now looking for a solitary spot out of town. I received, I may say, a delegation from the Molodenovo peasants begging me to return, but it's become too crowded there. In a few days I shall be getting down to a good job—writing a scenario for Bagritsky's poem "The Song of Opanas." We want to set up a real memorial for him and it was with pleasure that I accepted the offer to do the scenario. The movie will be produced by Ukrainfilm, which is now being transferred from Kharkov to Kiev. You've probably read that the Ukrainian capital is being moved to Kiev and that there's a great deal of building going on there. It's a very opportune moment because Kiev has grown shabby, while Kharkov has had an incredible spurt of growth in the last few years.

I'll have to go to Kiev in April about the scenario and perhaps I'll be able to slip down to Odessa. I'm very happy at the prospect because I miss the Ukraine.

As to the passport—you will get it.

Moscow, March 3, 1934

Katya has left to go to see Iosif. I had to supply her with money. In general, I have to bear the full moral and financial weight of the business.

As before, I'm doing things for numerous people and there's little time left for myself, and yet I have an endless quantity of work before me.

I've handed over the play to the Vakhtangov group, and by fall another one has to be put on in the Arts Theater, and then I have to write the scenario and a lot of stories. I still haven't found an apartment outside Moscow, although I need one badly.

Today, for the anniversary of Papa's death, I'm sending some money to Anyuta and Sonya in Odessa and I'll ask them to go out to the cemetery and see what state his grave is in. I reckon I'll be able to visit Odessa this spring. I want to visit the places I knew as a boy.

This evening I'm having a gathering of fellow-townspeople from Odessa—old colleagues from the Odessa *Izvestia*, where I started out, and old friends who used to come to our place way back when we lived on Reshelevskaya Street. It'll be an evening of reminiscences and the gentile cook has made gefilte fish of which Grandma would have been proud.

I.

Moscow, March 7, 1934

Received a letter from Zhenya. Natasha is well and is growing. I've been told that their little town—Plessis-Robinson—is very snug and quiet. Natasha is out in the open air all day. Zhenya describes the sort of wordly wisdom she picks up from those damned eight-year-old little Parisiennes very amusingly. I sent Natasha a big Russian peasant doll with a Frenchman who was passing through. She should get it in a few days.

I'm bogged down in Moscow. Ahead of me I have an untouched mountain of work; I lost touch with a lot of things in my isolation and now I have to catch up. I'm looking for a country house quite close to town because in the next few months it is essential for me to be in Moscow. And besides, I'm following in Mama's footsteps and having all the bridges rebuilt that were erected by that fat crook [a dentist] on *rue de la Convention*. As I've already told you, in the spring I'll have to go to Kiev and Kharkov about the scenario.

The passport will have to be sent either to Zhenya—drastic measures will be taken—or straight to the consulate, the address of which will be given to me in the next few days. As soon as I get it, I'll wire you.

The rehearsals for the play will begin at the end of March. I'm holding back the work in every way possible because I want to be ready with my next play by the time this play is put on. I believe that I'm in a fertile period and so I must develop my graphomania.

I've had my hands full with Bagritsky's family. I was able to secure them financially for the year ahead and I'm very happy about it.

With that, good-bye, I have heaps of things to attend to.

I.

Moscow, March 15, 1934

I've moved to a country house and begun work. I come into Moscow on business and to do research. There's a struggle raging around my play, battles and arguments, which just shows that it contains a live seed. I'm very glad that I'm not in town at this moment. I'm still engaged in the art of playwriting. "The inner search" is no longer in fashion nowadays—I need facts and knowledge, and so I have to go back to the source a lot. I'm also starting work on the scenario for Bagritsky's poem "The Song of Opanas." Frankly, I must bend my back to it and keep it bent.

I've written to the consulate in Paris about Mama's passport. You can send it to Zhenya and I'll tell her what to do with it. I'm sure they'll attend to it in ten minutes.

I've sent the play to Zhenya. I'll ask her to have copies made and send you one. This play will have a sequel, in fact.that's what I'm working on now. I can't be away from Moscow for long because of the rehearsals at the Vakhtangov Theater. I wish I could find another place like Molodenovo. I keep looking around. The Molodenovo people send me delegation after delegation. I managed to get them five horses for the spring sowing.

In Moscow the weather has broken and it looks like spring.

I'm terribly drawn toward the Ukraine and to the country, but I must wait.

How is your collective health? As before, things are moving at a feverish pace in our country here.

I.

[A postcard.]

Moscow, April 5, 1934

Am enjoying the spring. We've had several days of sunshine by now. I stroll around Moscow which is all torn up like a field of battle—they're building the subway. The first line should be opened in November of this year.

I've started work on the scenario based on Bagritsky's poem. When the libretto is ready, I'll take it to Kiev. I hope to be able to insist on their moving the production to the Odessa film studios. If they did, I would be able to live in Odessa for a while. At the same time, I'm working on my play. I would very much like to finish it by the fall.

There's been some improvement in Iosif's "case." I am trying to arrange for him to be allowed to come back to Moscow some time in the course of this month. I ate up my matzos. My maid has gone to the store to get the flour, cottage cheese and other things which go to make up *kulich* and *paskha* for Easter.

You write very seldom. Without news of you, I am miserable.

Moscow, April 14, 1934

Darling Mamasha,

I'm absolutely fine. The paradoxical thing about it is—and I've often spoken to Zhenya about this—that in our country, which is still so poor, I live in greater comfort and *freedom* than you and Zhenya. When it comes to apartments, food, services, warmth and peace—I can have it all, as few people anywhere can (of course, having Steiner for a neighbor, receiving supplies from abroad, and so on, makes a big difference); so there's no need for you to worry. But I have to do a lot of work this month and it's hard work. In a sentimental moment, I took it upon myself to write a scenario based on Bagritsky's "The Song of Opanas" by the first of May, and now I'm not at all happy about it. The poem, alas, affords hardly any material for a movie, and so I have to invent some and, what's more, invent some that is in the spirit of the poem—which brings us to a new misfortune. The Civil War is out of date as a subject and would not interest today's audiences, so I have to take all that into consideration and approach it from some new angle. That's for one. Number two—I have to hand in the text for another scenario, also by the first of May. This makes me spend my days in continuous (and purely mechanical) work, from which those both near and far try to tear me away as hard as their strength will allow—and their strength is considerable. If I manage to finish these jobs all right, I will get a considerable sum of money for them which will go entirely to paying off debts, mostly the Paris ones. I have already met many of my personal and literary obligations, but there are still quite a number left. I want to get clear of them in these next months. As soon as I'm through with the movies, I have to write a play for the Arts Theater and put some stories I wrote long ago into shape for publication.

I was very glad to hear you had moved. But what the hell do you need that elegant district for? You'd be much better off with more light and air. How much will you be paying for the new apartment?

A friend of mine, the chairman of the Moscow cooperative, is leaving for France at the end of this month and has promised to take parcels for you and for Zhenya. I want very much to send something for Natasha. I'll let you know when he leaves.

Jascha Heifetz is giving a series of concerts here. I went to one on the 11th. It made an indelible impression on me and brought back my boyhood. There were many people from Odessa among the audience. I'm going again on the twentieth.

Our papers are becoming more and more interesting as the results of fifteen years of effort grow clearer. Great news today—all the Chelyuskin* group have been taken off the ice floe. That shows how good Soviet aviation is.

I still haven't picked myself a "summer residence."

Don't worry if you don't get letters from me. It will be because I want to be able to inform you all the sooner that I have finished my cinematographic labors. I'll write in a few days about my other affairs.

I.

* The shipwrecked survivors from the *Chelyuskin* were transferred by Soviet planes from their drifting iceberg to the mainland.

Moscow, April 29, 1934

I'm working hard on the scenarios in order to finish them quickly and leave myself free for further work. I absolutely have to finish the play for the Arts Theater by the fall and to write a few articles for Natasha.

Natasha, as I've already told you, misses me and her Grandma very much. I would like at least to send her a representative in the person of Mama. It's nice in Robinson in the summer. I realize that all difficulties stem from a shortage of funds, but perhaps things will be a little easier at Zhenya's now. What do you think of the matter?

In what capacity are the Zismans going? It's time Mendele managed to make such a trip. In general, it's time to gather in our scattered family. Such a passionate son as I should be given first priority with his mother—she's stayed long enough with her daughter. If there were something I could do to help Mendele from here, I'd beat myself into a pancake for her sake.

The day before yesterday I gave what is called a literary talk to some Young Communists. I met Zhenya Troyanovsky there and she asked me to send you her regards. Unfortunately, her daughter is ill—looks like bone t.b. Except for that, they're fine. Vera is as cheerful as ever. She's been living for several months with Lyuba who combines in her person a collection of different diseases, but who keeps squeaking just the same. On that, I will interrupt my letter. I want to find out about the parcels so that I can let you know exactly.

The spring seems to have come for real. It's hot today. The town is preparing for the May Day celebrations. I, too, will go to Red Square.

Why do you have your pictures taken so seldom? It would be very nice to get some photos from you. If you have any, send them.

Yours,

I.

Moscow, May 13, 1934

My main walks are the same as before—to the cemeteries or to the crematoriums. Yesterday Maxim Peshkov* was buried. His death was a monstrous one. He wasn't feeling very well, but in spite of that went swimming in the Moskva and was struck down by a lightning attack of pneumonia. The old man could hardly get to the cemetery. It tore one's heart to look at him. I had become very good friends with Maxim in Italy. We drove thousands of miles together, and spent many gay evenings over a bottle of Chianti. . . .

I've only just received your letter of May 7. I'm very glad to hear that the apartment is a good one. I'll send the magazines and newspapers in a day or two. Because Lyova's affairs are so spasmodic, Zhenya's mood has not been too good. I have taken a few steps which I hope will have results, then she will recover her spirits. I'm writing today to her and to the Embassy so that they can act independently over there. I expect you've already heard from her.

I've already finished one urgent piece of work. Since I took on the job—"The Song of Opanas"—I'll finish it little by little. When I'm through with it, I'll be able to make proper plans for travel. Ukrainfilm very much want me to go to Kiev and Odessa. The temptation is great.

We were having summer weather up till yesterday, but today it's overcast. I greatly regret that I have little spare time for walking around Moscow. The city is a very interesting place right now. It is full of life and is being thoroughly rebuilt. And culturally, we are becoming part of Europe. Concerts by eminent musicians, and so on. Materially, our life is incomparably better and, if it weren't for Berta Davydovna, I would put the question of Zhenya's and Natasha's coming here in the sharpest way. I think about it all the time now. If they came, nine-tenths of all my difficulties would fall away.

With that, good-bye. Now the way for us to achieve our common happiness is for me to work harder, especially now that the very nature of my work has changed—I have to study and travel around. There's no doing anything now by sitting in one's study and meditating. . . . I hope that in my next letter I'll be able to tell you that the film is finished. After that, the road will be open for me to do the work my heart is set on.

I.

* Maxim Peshkov, the son of Gorky, born in 1897.

Moscow, May 26, 1934

Chlenov* has come here for a few days and is returning to Paris on May 29. He'll take a parcel for Natasha with him and has promised to get Mama's passport extended at the consulate immediately. Well, that's got that rolling properly.

So far, no word from Zhenya that she received the books. I wired her today to ask about them. I'm sure they must have arrived.

I'm winding up my Moscow affairs and the day after tomorrow am going out to visit Gorky at his country house. I'll stay with him for ten days and then move to my own place. My work for the movies is coming to a happy end and I'll be going to Kiev in June.

I have concluded a contract with Gosizdat for the publication of all my presentable writings in one volume. Some new things will go into it too. The book will come out in the fall.

We have general contentment here now—it's raining. The drought had become threatening but now prospects for the harvest have improved sharply.

I'll be very glad not to have to deal with the private affairs of so many people once I go away; they prevent me from working.

I've passed on to Gosizdat the order for the books for you—the *Akademia* editions and others. You'll get them at the beginning of June. With that, good-bye. As the movie director has arrived, I must work.

I.

* Chlenov was a member of the Soviet Embassy in Paris.

Uspenskoye, June , 1934

Dear Mamashenka,

I will certainly make my trip to the Ukraine but I cannot specify the exact date yet. Every time I think of going, I get more work to do here. And, moreover, I'd like to find a replacement for Molodenovo first. A man who has an apartment in Moscow simply must have one out of town as well, where he can isolate himself to work. On the 12th I'm supposed to go and look at a little house, at a place on the Kursk railway line. It's special advantage is that the station is five minutes' walk from Nikole-Vorobinsky Lane [where his Moscow apartment was—Tr.—MacA.]

A very interesting evening yesterday: a Jewish Mama brought her nine-year-old son to see Gorky.* He is a literary *wunderkind* who writes adult verse—and on political subjects to boot . . . The boy isn't just precocious—he's a freak—and he has been horribly brought up. As he read his poems, he kept banging his fist down for emphasis—and he was full of professional, literary preoccupations. If the boy could be restored to childhood, something might come of it.

A trip is being prepared for tomorrow for a whole group to go to visit the building site of the Moskva-Volga Canal. I'll write when I get back. Right now, I've snatched a few minutes in which to jot down these lines. Today, I have to do my own writing and besides edit a whole bunch of material.

Je vous en prie—be well.

I.

* Gorky wrote a short piece about the *wunderkind* Babel mentions, which appeared in *Pravda*, August 8, 1934; see Appendix IV.

Uspenskoye, June 18, 1934

I'm still living at Gorky's. As they say in Odessa—a real thousand and one nights. My memories of this will last me my whole life. I'm still looking for an isolated place outside Moscow. I have a few in view and in the course of the next few weeks will decide on something.

Have been busy doing some editing for Gorky all this time and so neglected my work on the scenario. I'm taking it up again now: I want to finish it quickly and take it to Kiev, otherwise it'll be in the way of my further work.

A selection of my writings will appear in a G.I.K.L. [*Gosudarstvennoye Izdatelstvo Khudozhestvennoi Literatury*—State Publishing House of Belles Lettres] edition in the fall.

The Ehrenburgs have arrived. Hope they've brought greeting from Zhenya and Natasha. I'm going to Moscow in two or three days and I'll see them then.

I've sent money to Odessa. I'm still trying to arrange things for Iosif. It was all fixed up and then it was postponed again. Nevertheless, we'll make it in the end. We're having a bad summer: rain and cold. Yesterday they had the heating on here.

Spent a few hours with Schmidt* yesterday. He told me many things about Chelyuskin. I'm going to see him tomorrow. He lives not far from here.

With that, good-bye. From my window I can see meadows, woods and flowerbeds. Before me, I have a day filled with work. I must get a move on with these jobs. I'm writing this early in the morning. I reckon to find a copious missive from you in Moscow.

Mama's letters are my great consolation.

IB.

---

* Professor Otto Yulevich Schmidt (1891-1950) was a Russian mathematician, physicist, and Arctic explorer. He led the unfortunate *Chelyuskin* expedition in 1934, and another to the North Pole in 1937.

Moscow, June 20, 1934

Taras's trail has been uncovered. Zhenya writes that she has invited you for June and July which leads me to the conclusion that your passport is in order. In any case, I've phoned Glenov and he will do the necessary. All Zhenya will have to do is to take the passport to the Embassy. I want you to go to Plessis-Robinson immediately and without fail. If for no other reason, do it for my sake.

Zhenya writes that Natasha must have her tonsils out. It's a quite uncomplicated operation but still, I'd prefer you to be there. So I am waiting for a telegram announcing that you are on your way.

I've come into Moscow to see the Ehrenburgs and Malereau [sic] and shall spend two days here. Gorky has loaded me down with tons of editorial work which has caused me to neglect my scenario. It doesn't look as if I'll ever catch up.

Mama is right in what she says about nerves and literary work. But, in so far as my nerves are fairly good, all the rest is in order.

Yesterday was a solemn day—the arrival of Chelyuskin's men. They were given a reception reminiscent of a triumphal procession in ancient Rome: flowers were strewn in their path, the town was decorated. All Moscow, they say, was asparkle.

I'll go to buy the books for you tomorrow and will write to you again then.

I.

Uspenskoye, July 9, 1934

Dear Mamachen,

Lately, I've been running around in circles all the time and that's why I haven't written to you. I've had tons of editorial work and screen writing and, then, along came those Swedes with their greetings. They cost me a lot and also take up much of my time.

They are still in Moscow so that, even when I'm out of town, I still have to see to it that they're all right, straighten things out for them, telephone and so on.

In general, there's no end to the visitors—the Ehrenburgs, Malraux [this time the name is transliterated.—Tr.—MacA.] . . . Not one of them is like me, that is, each of them needs something or other and so I have to tear myself into little pieces. In the future I must arrange my existence differently: keep sending my material to Enta instead of fussing about my guests. Otherwise, it is too much for me.

I have heard that Enta has received a subsidy for July and am waiting for confirmation.

All my visitors tell me that Zhenya has a nice house, that she and the child are looking well and that they wouldn't mind going to a spa in August. But I don't see why they should go to so much bother since the house they live in is a villa anyway. With the money I've earned that has been spent on them recently, we could have built a house here and lived superbly for a whole year. But as things stand, the benefits derived from it by them are quite meager and, as for me, neither my personal life nor the conditions under which I work are as good as I could wish.

I don't dare to give too much advice at a distance but I think that the best thing would be if you went and joined Natasha and they just stayed where they are; that way you could spend the summer together.

Now that I am in the summer house, I'll write to you more regularly. I cannot get my teeth into serious work, although I have a desperate longing to do so.

Until tomorrow,
I.

Moscow, November 14, 1934

My worthy distant relatives,

If I write seldom it is not because something untoward has happened to me but simply because of the complications of life.*

These complications arise from three causes: one—literature, two—the fact that I must get hold of more money than what's coming to me and, three—the softness of my character because of which I get weighed down with all sorts of requests and am forced to run around for other people.

I am working more than ever before but, as you can see, I have nothing tangible to show for it. Life refuses to linger at my desk, be it for five minutes only. It is a rewarding assignment to express the philosophy of this stormy movement in my art, but it presents difficulties such as I've never had to face before.

I am incapable of compromise, be it internal or external, and so I have to suffer, retreat inside myself, and wait. Much of my time is taken up by all sorts of nondescript jobs done for money and I receive enough of it to have built myself a house in town and a villa in the country, to have bought a car and go driving all over the Crimea, the Caucasus or wherever. But instead, it all goes to pay the old Paris debts and to send money to Enta, to whom it is just a drop in the ocean, while here it is a whole fortune. And so, I am even deprived of the moral satisfaction of really helping her. All this should be radically changed, and if I could have a breathing spell, lay aside the money jobs and turn to short stories (for translation), it would make more sense. But it seems quite impossible for me to get the breathing spell I need. All this means that I haven't a spare minute for myself.

Nowadays, writing doesn't mean sitting at one's table. It means rushing all over the country, participating in active life, doing research, establishing close contact with some enterprise, and suffering a constant feeling of impotence at one's inability to be everywhere one ought to be.

I have already told you that material conditions are improving here with amazing speed. I am sure that Natasha could be incomparably better brought up here than in France and it is becoming senseless to remain there.

Now, with winter approaching, I cannot demand that they come over here right away, but I'll start a real campaign in January or February. The stumbling block in the business is, of course, B.D., but I shall explain to Lyova in no uncertain terms what I think about it all.

With all sorts of people staying in my place, there's been a lot of talk; but now, they're gradually dispersing and they will all be gone by December 1st.

As soon as they have left, I'll go to Kiev, a trip which is long overdue and has been postponed several times. Generally speaking, I am longing to make myself a foothold somewhere around Odessa, because the tempo of life in Moscow is so fast that, with my habits and my need for lengthy meditation, I am having a very difficult time. Today Moscow is one of the noisiest of European cities, and in the scope of its development and the revolutions that take place daily in its streets and squares, there is no doubt that even New York is no match for it. Yes, I must say that now, every day, we can see the outlines of a country of unprecedented might more and more clearly and, by now, there is no doubt in anyone's mind as to the realizability of the slogan "to catch up and surpass."

I'm going to take two days off and will then send you some books and the newspapers, which are becoming more and more interesting. Now, since you have more time on your hands than I, do not keep any accounts in our correspondence in the form of credits and debits—just write as often as you can. I miss you very badly. I won't write about Natasha but the fact that I am forced to live without her will soon cause an emotional explosion. I feel it coming.

So long, my dear ones, write and tell me when Mama is coming over here.

Your reinforced-concrete son and brother,

I.

* "The complications of life" seem to be reflected in the unusual speech Babel made at the "Congress of Soviet Writers" in Moscow, on August 23, 1934. The speech, which was printed two days later in *Pravda* under the title "Our Great Enemy—Trite Vulgarity," follows in Appendix V.

Lionel Trilling in his introduction to Babel's *Collected Stories* (op. cit.) comments perceptively on this speech: "Beneath the orthodoxy of this speech there lies some hidden intention. . . . It is as if the humor, which is often of a whimsical kind, as if the irony and the studied self-depreciation, were forlorn affirmations of freedom and selfhood. . . ."

Moscow, November 26, 1934

I finished the screenplay only two days ago and now I'll have a bit more time to myself. I sent you the books. Please let me know whether you got them.

Natasha has been ill. I didn't want to write to you about it at the time, but she's fine now. The doctor said it was German measles. Zhenya says it was scarlet fever. If so, she recovered very quickly, but I'm skeptical about it.

A friend of mine is going abroad and I am sending Natasha a little fur coat. They've promised me to transfer the money to Enta on the 27th. I hope I'll be able to send a small sum to Mama in the course of December. Am doing my best. I must remind you that, by the spring, I am expecting Mama to come and stay with me. The apartment is quite empty. In view of the fact that my most innocuous words and movements cause sinister gossip, I insisted that the females who were living in my place be moved elsewhere, so there are no outsiders left here: we are just the two bachelors, Steiner and I, two house helps and one electric samovar which never leaves the table.

I am feeling well. It has snowed for the first time this year and it's very beautiful outside. I am longing to do some writing but, alas, I am smothered in an avalanche of jobs I have to do. I'll turn in my screenplay in a week. I want it to lie around for a while. When I hand it in, I'll find out exactly when I'll be going to the Ukraine.

Why have you fallen silent? I consider the matter of Mama's coming here as settled irrevocably and without appeal. Your silence on the subject worries me no end.

How is Grisha's business? Are you satisfied with your apartment on rue Alphonse Hottat? Your staying abroad is a constant sore for me. Real miracles are taking place in our country. There is an incredibly rapid rise in the general welfare and the world has really never seen such an outburst of energy and cheerfulness. Everyone with a living soul in him is trying to come here. You must give it very, very serious consideration. Yes, it is no exaggeration to say that there is no town in the world where life is more interesting than in Moscow.

I am a man weighed down by business, study, work, waves of people, so don't try to keep books on incoming letters from me, just write more often yourselves. I send you my tenderest kisses, my dear ones.

I.

Moscow, December 13, 1934

My amiable little Mama,

Just today, a lady I know left for abroad with a fur coat for Natasha, and a small sum of cash. It's a very pretty squirrel coat. In a few days Slonim's brother is going too and he is taking along some toys and other things. Whoever does has the same message for Zhenya—to convince her to come to Moscow where, according to the general consensus, life is much more interesting, better and, if you wish, more secure than abroad. And on top of this, her coming here would immediately remove all the material load from my shoulders. As I have written before, it is senseless and criminal, but above all senseless, to keep sending money from here.

A neighbor of mine is going over in January and he'll hand you something to take care of your most pressing needs. Later I'll wire you the exact date when he is leaving.

The break in my work wasn't a long one and I must get down to it again and labor, mostly for the French market—work on one more scenario. It looks as if I'll never get rid of the debts incurred during my last trip abroad and in the course of the past autumn. Of course, I enjoy my work, but I wish I had to think less of the material results and was able to plan my time in such a way as to devote the best hours to the things that are close to my heart. I am held in Moscow by the necessity of doing some research in the archives of certain establishments, otherwise I'd have rushed off to the countryside or left for the Ukraine. Here, I cannot dodge visitors and am forced to arrange the affairs of too many people. Just take Lyakhetsky for one: I am having to work hard now to obtain an authorization for them to stay in Moscow. Of course, they are stupid, helpless people, but now, when I have an extensive and serious work before me, I cannot spare them so much time. Also, some people sent a pale, long-legged, tow-headed Swede to visit me; he came and then suddenly decided to go nuts, so now I'm forced to have him moved into a lunatic asylum—and I couldn't possibly give you a complete list of things of this sort that I have to cope with. And that without even mentioning the graphomaniacs who line up at my door loaded down with their fifty-pound manuscripts. Am reading Hecht's very long novel for the third day now, without, alas, getting any aesthetic kick out of it. And then I am pestered by all sorts of horsemen, warriors, criminal investigators, conferences at the Writers' Union (but, to tell the truth, I manage to dodge those) and other innumerable nuisances.

In three days I'll send money to Sonia and to Anyuta.

Still, the possibility that I'll soon be in Kiev and Odessa is not to be ruled out. I am sending you the books. During recent months, they've taken lots of pictures of me, so I'll have to select some and send them to you too.

Katya has written to you herself. They're installing themselves in their old apartment. To my great surprise, Iosif doesn't look bad at all, even younger if anything. But he is just as stupid as ever.

As to the passport, it is a very simple matter—there's nothing easier than getting it extended and I can't understand why such an uncomplicated step should cause so much fuss. Yes, the passport must be extended without fail and I believe we must start moving by spring. It is my opinion that we have been doing things in the most difficult way for long enough. Could you send it to the Embassy directly from Brussels? Those Belgians of yours are trying to outstrip the whole world in pigheadedness—I believe Brussels is the only capital where there is no Soviet Embassy!

I am very pleased, though, that I can resume my filial duties which I never forget for a minute anyway—but my arms are a bit short and I cannot reach out to you. . . . Have as good a time as you can, my dear ones. I shall write regularly now.

I.

Moscow, December 23, 1934

Received Mera's irate letter and have just sent you a telegram. Natasha is fine, everything's all right. The girl only had one of those numerous childhood sicknesses. Well, I can't get a straight answer about whether she received the fur coat I sent her either. Zhenya has never been much of a letter-writer but I know that she always lets me know very promptly if something goes wrong and that silence on her part is a sign that everything's fine.

I'm not surprised at Katya's imbecility—there are not many things that surprise me—but I am quite furious nevertheless. Those miserable people, who are of no use to anyone, have poisoned one year of my life: every morning on waking up I saw the same humble, begging figure before me, a sight that automatically deprived me of the ability to work for the rest of the day. It cost me tremendous efforts and I have had to swallow my pride too to rescue these people from the bottom of the abyss, and it is no exaggeration to say that if they are still alive it is only thanks to me. And after all that, it turns out that the healthiest thing to do is to keep silent about me. My patience and indulgence toward so-called relatives are really unparalleled. But this time my patience is at an end.

I am feeling fine. Life here is terrifically interesting. However, my chosen trade, my tastes and my rule of thumb—all or nothing —have never given me any grounds for believing that my personal life would be an easy one, that I would go forward along a path strewn with roses or that every step of mine would cause jubilation in my friends and relatives. I never took on any obligation to lead an easy life when I was born. I am no braggart and that gives me the right to say that I take what people generally refer to as hardships in my stride, that I bear them with an ease and courage such as is seldom met with, and that if I don't mention them it isn't because of my fortitude or any peculiarity of my character, but only because of my legitimate distaste for such an uninteresting and insignificant topic. You are inventing all sorts of dangers threatening me, when there are none. The only thing the matter with me is my separation from Mama and the rest of you. So, instead of moaning about me, help me, come here and live with me.

I.

1 9 3 5

My delightful Mama and her progeny,

We are having temperatures of twenty below zero, windless and very invigorating weather. The streets are beautiful. The schools are closed. Yesterday the temperature slipped down to thirty below; today it's warmer—it has gone up to ten below.

A few days ago, Slonim—the one from Tashkent—left for Paris and I sent Natasha a dress and a Russian peasant doll with him. I also have a tea cozy with a peasant doll on it and am waiting for the first opportunity to send it to you. And perhaps I'll manage to send Fenya a small sum of money too. I am sending you some books. I will transfer some money to Odessa.

Went to see the Lyakhetskys. They are installed in their old apartment. I met Hoffman there. He is still wrapped in his blissful stupidity—*quand on est bête c'est pour toujours.* Probably he will move to Samara and work in the Meat Combine there. That would be very good; there's the Volga and many beautiful spots and the town which, because of the construction of the gigantic electric station, is growing very rapidly.

I have finished most of the writing I had to do on order, and feel I can live a life that is natural for me. I would like to convey to the world what I know of the old Odessa, after which I could move to the new Odessa. I dream of seeing you, all or separately, in the spring, and I shall do everything in my power to see that that dream comes true. I am not good at reaping financial benefits from my literary efforts at the time and the place of my choice, but I hope that this time things will work out by themselves.

In our apartment, the fires are burning in the stoves, the samovar is boiling and my German is keeping the place clean. I am now the owner of an eight-cylinder Ford just received from America, which we share equally. We have a chauffeur. That makes life much easier and more pleasant. It would be hard for you to imagine how thick the Moscow traffic is, even thinking of Paris. In a month, the first line of the subway, between Sokolniki and Devichie Polye, will be opened. That will ease the congestion a bit, although we really need ten lines rather than one. The subway is being built at a feverish rate.

I am so absorbed in my work that I've had to postpone all the trips I had been contemplating for the time being. I'll let you know if there are further changes in my plans. I make a wish—that we should meet in this coming year. It is my principal and most ardent wish. The rest will take care of itself.

Your friend,
I.

Moscow, February 3, 1935

The [All-Union] Congress of Soviets is taking place in Moscow. Comrades of mine have come from every corner of the country— Yevdomkimov from the northern Caucasus, Kalmykov from Kabarda and many friends from the Donets Basin. I am giving them lots of my time. I don't go to bed till around four or five in the morning. Yesterday, Kalmykov and I took the Kabarda dancers to Gorky's place and they put on an unforgettable performance.

I am getting along all right, except that I'm so soft by nature that I'm forced to spend a great deal of time and effort with a multitude of useless people because I haven't got the courage to kick them out. Lately I have been swamped by all sorts of old Odessa Jews who come to ask for donations for worthy causes and claim to have known my "late Papa." And then, one of them

named Fraenkel—would he be related to the Fraenkels of Niko-
layev?—took advantage of my absence and swiped a wallet containing 450 rubles that belonged to a friend living here. A very
venerable patriarch.

Sent a hundred rubles to Sonya recently. Lyakhetsky is about
to start on a new job. I am writing a comedy for which I have
great hopes, but unfortunately much of my time is spent earning
money by semiliterary means. Recently they have published a
complete collection of my stories. The first printing of fifteen
thousand copies sold out very quickly and now they are putting out
a further printing of fifty thousand. All this brought in a substantial sum, the lion's share of which went to pay off debts incurred
during my trip, from which I have been still unable to disentangle
myself.

I can't tell you how busy I am, how besieged I am by people
and work. I am seized by despair when I think how much is still
undone, how many books I have to read, how much traveling I
have to do. . . .

My health is satisfactory, except for my sinusitis last winter. I
want to get it punctured. From the above it is obvious that *Moi,
je suis très pris* but is that any reason for you not to write?

At Zhenya's everything's the same. Natasha is growing, in my
absence, alas. What makes it especially painful is that, under present circumstances, a writer is not free to dispose of his person and,
besides, I have the urge to write (here also, I must say alas) and in
this too I am unlike other people. If I manage to finish my comedy
by spring, I suppose that will set the ice in motion. I'll try. I beseech you with tears in my eyes to write more often. Worrying
about you and those in Paris is one of those bitter feelings that I
find harder to bear than anything.

I.

[A postcard.]

Moscow, February 4, 1935

Am torn apart by thousands of things I have to do and that's
why I haven't written to you. I'll have more time in a couple of

days and then I'll start bombarding you with letters. The Party Congress is taking place now. All my comrades are climbing uphill and so am I, little by little. They are starting to rehearse my play and it has already gathered some ardent fans. I hope to be able to arrange things for Katya and intend to send something to Zhenya. Will write to you in the nearest future,

I.

Moscow, February 18, 1935

Greetings, amiable Mother,

I am alive and well and am even attending to my nose: they are making punctures in my Highmore sinus cavity. I cannot say the operation is very pleasant, but it makes me feel better. I would like to get rid of my nose colds once and for all because I've really had enough of them.

Lately, I've been leading an extremely social life—I've been attending the Congress sessions and sat through four days of a conference of collective farmers in the Kremlin. It has all left an indelible impression upon me.

Karpych, my former Molodenovo landlord, came to stay with me here. He has been doing the following things in Moscow: for the first time in the sixty-five years of his life, he spoke on the phone, for the first time went to the movies (we saw the marvelous Soviet film, *Chapayev** and he was one of the first Soviet citizens to take a ride on the subway, which will be open to the general public in two or three weeks. Now they are doing trial runs and it takes a lot of pull to get a pass. It is a fantastic affair that can't be compared either with the Paris or the Berlin subways, and I even think it's rather too luxurious.

I will soon be finished with the orders I have received. The film in which I had a hand will be shown soon. It was extremely warmly received at the previews. We'll see what will come later. I am working on a new play. It looks as though they will soon publish *Maria* and, who knows, perhaps stage it too.

Iosif has got a job and has left for the Donets Basin.

A lady I know is going to Paris on the 22nd. I'll put together a package for Zhenya and Natasha. I would like to send something really nice.

I'll send the books off to you tomorrow. A lot of interesting new things have appeared.

People are being a nuisance—they come in a continuous stream. Old Odessans come in detachments and, on the strength of having known Papa, demand money and clothes. I give them some sometimes but it affords me no pleasure to do so. Yesterday a certain Dunovets turned up who claimed he was a telegraph messenger twenty years ago. And in fact, I did recall his face and so I gave him something. Fancy the famous Fraenkel stealing 450 rubles—there doesn't seem to be any comprehensible reason for it.

The day before yesterday there was a meeting—the anniversary of Bagritsky's death. Olesha,† Paustovsky,‡ Vera Inber § and I made speeches; the Lifshitses were sitting in the first row. It was all very moving. Yevdokimov and Kalmykov are urging me to go to the Caucasus, a region which we may say we own nowadays. I haven't decided as yet what I'll do. Dear little Mother, write more often since you are a lady of leisure. A collective farmer's regards to Mera and Grisha.

Your adoring,

I.

* *Chapayev* was a Soviet film directed by Sergei and Georgy Vafilyev (1934). The film was based on the novel of the same name by Dmitri A. Furmanov (1891-1926) which has become a classic of Soviet literature. The book is set in the Civil War period and focuses on the partisan leader Chapayev. The thing that perhaps interested Babel so much in the work was that it draws a sharp contrast between the strong but emotionally undisciplined revolutionary feeling of Chapayev and the controlled, calculating rationalism of a Bolshevik commissar.

On March 5th, 1936, there was a meeting of the Writers' Union in Moscow to honor the tenth anniversary of Furmanov's death. Babel made a speech entitled "Self-discipline in a Writer." The tone of the speech reflects the general atmosphere of the late thirties in the Soviet Union and the predicament common to all Soviet writers of the time. See Appendix VI for Babel's speech, which was published in the magazine *Moskva*, no. 4, 1936.

† Yuri Karlovich Olesha (1899-1960), whose most famous book is *Envy* (1927). Olesha disappeared from the Russian literary scene in 1938, then reappeared during the Thaw. A one-volume edition of his *Selected Works* was published in 1956 in Moscow.

Moscow, February 24, 1935

My nice Mama,

I am sending you the most precious of my possessions—the photographs. They are amazing. Please let me have them back without fail.

The day before yesterday they were at my nose again—they punctured it and cauterized it, hurting me. The doctor treating me is excellent and I feel that my nose is getting better with every passing day. I have decided to get rid of this affliction of mine at any cost. I have already gone through four minor operations.

A piece of news for you: they've decided to publish *Maria* and the play will appear in the March or April issue. This gives it a good chance of being staged.

The comedy I am working on is progressing, although slowly. It would be great if I managed to finish it by May.

A strange change has come over me—I don't feel like writing in prose. I want to use only the dramatic form.

Iosif is in the Donets Basin. Things will get into a groove and be all right. The Odessa aunts are clamoring for money once again. I'll have to send it to them.

Our eight-cylinder Ford is serving us with distinction. Perhaps one day it will appear at your doorstep and bring you back home.

Spring has arrived here—everything is thawing and, with the arrival of the warm weather, I am turning into a different and cheerful man.

This will have to be a short letter because I'm dying to sleep.

Today, my Kabarda hero, Kalmykov, left. We talked from eight o'clock in the evening to seven in the morning. I saw him off to the station and then went to a private showing of the American

---

‡ Konstantin Georgievich Paustovsky, Soviet novelist born in Kiev in 1892, whose *Memoirs* have been published under the title *The Story of a Life*, Pantheon Books, New York, 1964.

§ Vera Mikhailovna Inber, born in Odessa in 1890, is a lyric poet and short-story writer.

film *Viva Villa* and so haven't slept one minute since the night before last.

A lady friend of mine is leaving for Paris on the twenty-eighth and she's taking some presents with her. She has promised to send me a detailed description of life in Robinson.

Why doesn't my sister make a mark in her own hand on the letter to me? How is Grisha's work?

It breaks my heart to part with these pictures—*send them* back. Good night, I am going to bed.

I.

Moscow, March 14, 1935

My beautiful Mama,

Why haven't I received a letter from you for such a long time? I am very worried and intend to send you a telegram.

I am living in a country house near Moscow now, where I both work and rest.

Professor Slonim, who has just arrived from Paris, is absolutely crazy about Natasha. He says he has never met such an enchanting creature. You can imagine how I feel, listening to it all. The professor in question is a renowned medical authority and he finds Natasha very nicely developed physically and says she seems to be in very good shape. And Zhenya seems to be growing a little more receptive to my arguments—she says she would like to become a bit more proficient in her trade so she wouldn't have to be idle over here.

Did you get the pictures of Natasha? I remind you that you must send them back to me. Do you get the newspapers I send you?

Three days ago, I sent Natasha a dress and some candy with an acquaintance of mine.

Moscow streetcar riders are greatly excited by the opening of the subway. People who have been away from Moscow for a year wouldn't recognize it. And now that the warm season is approaching what do you think about coming back to your native land? I miss you very much.

I am longing to take a trip to the places of my childhood, to

Odessa, to the Ukraine. Everything hinges on the results of my writing. But in these things, everything, in the final analysis, depends on the ex-God.

Am going to Moscow tomorrow to get some books and, while I'm at it, will send some to you too. I have partly renounced my old principles and am collecting a small library for myself.

In the nearest future, I'll take advantage of the quiet of the countryside to work out all my plans and then I'll communicate them to you. The only thing I ask of you is to let me know as often as possible how you are getting on. Please.

I.

Moscow, March 23, 1935

I am very worried. Yesterday I sent off a telegram and am expecting an immediate reply. Do you get the newspapers I send you? Everything is all right here.

Guess whom I met yesterday? Stolyarsky. You must have read that there has been a contest of musicians in Warsaw and in Leningrad. As usual, Stolyarsky's pupils reaped the honors. He is now a famous professor. Yesterday there was a concert at the Conservatory performed by the participants in the Leningrad contest. I decided to go for old times' sake. We met in the foyer and fell into each other's arms. He is fresh, red as a ripe apple and was wearing a bright necktie with a pin in it, and spats. He was accompanied by his fat, heavily made-up daughter who wore a beauty patch.

Just as before, Stolyarsky is mass-producing child prodigies and supplies violinists for the concert halls of the world. I am the only one he cannot boast about. He remembered everything—our dining room, our courtyard on Tiraspolskaya Street and my determined resistance. I'm going to give a solemn dinner to mark this occasion. He recognized me right away and in his first outburst of enthusiasm declared that I hadn't changed in the least.

My work is progressing, although rather slowly. All sorts of people with all sorts of problems take a lot out of me. My former landlord, Dr. Finkelstein from Kiev, came to see me one day. At first I was delighted to see him but it soon turned out that I was expected to intercede for him, as I have to for so many others. I escape to Zvenigorod now and only come to Moscow from time to time. My latest trip here has been poisoned by the fact that I didn't find any letters from you. You are leisurely female persons, in fact housewives, so what would it cost you to scribble a few lines from time to time? Do it very soon, I beg you!

My regards to Grisha. How is his business? I would greatly appreciate it if he wrote to me about it.

I.

Moscow, March 31, 1935

My dear little Mama,

I felt in my heart that you weren't well and for some days I couldn't stay quietly in one place. I hope by the time you get this letter you'll be well again. You're my great love on this earth and so I must firmly ask you to remain in good health.

Today, a Frenchman who had taken a dress to Natasha returned from Paris. I spoke to him on the phone and tomorrow he'll come here to make me a lengthy report. He's already told me that he found everyone fit and well in Plessis-Robinson. After Mera's letter, that made me feel a bit better. I'll write to you tomorrow after I've talked with him directly.

I've received a letter from Zhenya in which she informs me of her plans. She is now taking a course in ethnography, is very much involved in it and will come to Moscow when she has completed her lectures. So that's when the weight will roll off my heart.

As to Natasha, you can judge for yourselves from the pictures what sort of a creature she is. I am a terrible fool not to have thought of getting them copied here. Tomorrow, I'll hand in a whole lot of photographs to be retaken and will then send them to you. So, please send me the pictures I sent you immediately and you'll receive copies of them instead.

I am not sure what the Frenchman will tell me tomorrow, but I have good reason to believe that Zhenya's financial situation is a difficult one. It would seem that I could easily have put it right by sending articles to France. But, not to mention the fact that that sort of writing is not my forte, something seems to have put a spell on my hand: I can no longer write prose. This has happened to me before and I know that the only thing I can do is to wait for things to change. The only form that attracts me now is drama. And so, for many months, I've been sitting over a play which I haven't been able to bring off, but now, only a couple of weeks ago, to my great joy I saw a flash of light and it looks as though I'll be able to finish it. Anyway, there's no going back now—too much effort has gone into it as it is and, besides, the theaters are waiting and are hanging over me like a heavy storm cloud.

As you already know, *Maria* is being published; as soon as it is out, I'll send you a copy of the magazine.

Mikhoels—from the Jewish Theater—has decided to put on *Sunset* after the big success of *King Lear*. They are looking for a translator now and will start rehearsals in the summer. In addition, *Sunset* will be staged by the Jewish Theater of Byelorussia and it looks as if the Russian theaters may give it another run.

And "to topple all this," as Stolyarsky, whom I saw a few days ago, would say, a very funny business is going on now, in which I secretly have a part. I believe I wrote to you that I was given an order—to rewrite an unusable screenplay. Well, I rewrote it very thoroughly but, since I didn't believe that the film would have any success, I demanded that the movie producers should not mention my name. But now that film, *Pilots*, is having a success approaching the reception meted out to *Chapayev*. Well, those involved know what's what, of course, but for me it's too late to back out of my decision. So the whole story is causing a lot of excitement and merriment among the movie people and the writers.

I have written a small piece on Bagritsky and am awaiting the hour when I will again be able to write prose. There's something beginning to seethe inside me and, who knows, perhaps it will come off.

Spring is coming. Friends are trying to drag me off to Kabarda, to the northern Caucasus, to Pyatigorsk. Schmidt wants me to go to the North Pole. But I think I'd better stay put and work, for that is the only way I can help Zhenya and you. If I could gather in my scattered tribe, my heart would recover its peace. Physically and mentally I feel I am better fitted for work than ever before.

Above all, be well.

I.

Moscow, April 17, 1935

My uninteresting relatives,

It's the first *seder* tonight, a fact that I am bringing to your attention with a special telegram. I have managed to get matzos, and not from Katya who . . . [illegible] . . .

I'm going to a certain patriarchal house tonight. Three days ago, sent a hundred rubles to Sonya. My trip abroad has brought me to the brink of bankruptcy and, to this day, I cannot get rid of the debts, humiliations and unpleasantnesses, and there's no telling how much of my energy, nerves and spirit have had to be spent on hack work. And so all I can do is send short stories, especially since we know that there is a demand for them. In recent years, however, my stories haven't been coming off too well—certain mental and literary changes have taken place within me that are beyond my control, changes that take no account of publishers' requirements and that aren't interested in whether Lyova's business is good or bad. I have started to write articles again that might help Enta and Mama, but one can never be sure of anything in this business. And then my literary endowment is such that I can only handle ideas that I have thoroughly worked out, ideas that, on top of that, must be original, otherwise they don't interest me, and even if my own life depended on it or my child was dying before my eyes, I would be unable to get results by trying to force myself.

That's one thing, and the other is that if I do nothing here in Moscow I have an income that would enable my family to live not only passably but regally in comparison with their present life, as far as clothing, food, housing, summerhouses, medical care, seaside places, Natasha's education, etc., etc., go. And besides, I would be free immediately from having to humiliate myself over money matters, I could do some serious work, go to the places I must go to (it is indispensable now for me to travel all over the Soviet

Union and study life intensively, in order to be able to write about it) and I would at last accomplish what I can and must accomplish in my writing. So why is it a matter of vanity on my part? It is a matter of logic, it is a desire for moral and material stability in life. And, after all, why must Natasha be brought up in French lycées among an alien people, struggling through the depression and misery besetting the Western world, when she happens to be a citizen of a young and flourishing country full of sap and vigor, and with a future! Well, do I have the right to wish for it or not? In my opinion, Natasha belongs with all her being to Russia and her severance from us will cripple her. I am afraid that this will be realized only when it is too late.

Now for point number three. Let us assume that the cycle of short stories I am working on now comes off. Then Zhenya and Mama will receive a sum of money each. But what after that? The same situation again? I have already sent many messengers to Zhenya and they have told her that from the material viewpoint my life is something quite beyond her dreams. Well, shouldn't that convince her after all? I haven't written to her because I feel miserable and I don't want to make her already gloomy life even gloomier. And so I'll work in a very unpropitious mental state and, although I'll do my damned best, I really don't know what I fear more—to write successful short stories and thus prolong our dispersion or to fail in what I am trying to do. I am not really afraid of the latter because in these things my doggedness and energy are inexhaustible. I am longing for privacy, for meditation, for a life organized according to my own recipe, and that is all possible here. But I am being pulled out into the public market place, into the world of fuss and business and bargaining, into which I don't fit.

I am not writing all this to make you feel bad. On the contrary— I'll use whatever strength I have to make a better life for my family.

I am enclosing a copy of my published play.

Next time, I'll write a lighter and more cheerful letter.

I.

Moscow, June 13, 1935

Dear Mama,

My series of throat infections is over, my organism seems as good as new, and I am enjoying the first summer days granted to us. I spent a few days in Molodenovo. It is really lovely there. When I lived there, private enterprise was winding up its existence and the village was full of discontent and misery; but now, everything is sprouting at an incredible rate, and that includes people and trees, grain crops and children.

I put off writing to you from there because the Molodenovo post office is a tiny one and it is never in much of a hurry. As to my sickness, well, I fell victim to something like an epidemic. At the turning point of the spring, many people came down with a disgusting combination of the grippe and a throat infection, just as I did. Speaking of medicine, I am leading an exemplary life now and in a couple of weeks or so I'll have completed a thorough overhaul of my mouth and will then leave for the Zheleznovodsk spa where I'll spend a month attending to my hypersensitive mucous membranes.

When I think of the life I'll lead in the northern Caucasus, I feel ashamed before you, because it'll be a palatial one. The supreme chief of the northern Caucasus is an old friend of mine and the preparations made for my arrival will be such that I don't even feel like going—makes me feel rather awkward. After the cure, I'll visit Nalchik, Pyatigorsk, Dagestan and other enchanted places. . . .

Katya came to see me before I left for the summerhouse. At last, everything is all right with them. I managed to get a job for the old fool [her husband, Iosif Lyakhetsky] in Kislovodsk (where, as is well known, some people live on for a hundred and twenty years). His papers are now in order and he is here on official duty. I only hope he will behave like a human being, because I am sick and tired of having to look after these elderly babies. I imagine Katya must have written to you about it all.

On my way to the Caucasus I'll break my journey in the Ukraine and, whatever else, I'll stop over in Odessa. Kiev is going through a period of feverish growth and they say that soon it will be the turn of our home town.

My nice Mama, if I write seldom it is not because my life is hard —compared with millions of people, my life is easy, happy and privileged—but because it is uncertain and this uncertainty derives from nothing else but changes and doubts connected with my work. In a country as united as ours, it is quite inevitable that a certain amount of thinking in clichés should appear and I want to overcome this standardized way of thinking and introduce into our literature new ideas, new feelings and rhythms. This is what interests me and nothing else. And so I work and think with great intensity, but I haven't any results to show yet. And, inasmuch as I myself do not see clearly how and by what methods I will reach these results (I do see my inner paths clearly, though), I am not sure myself where and in what kind of environment I ought to live if I am to achieve my goal, and that is what causes my reluctance to drag anyone along behind me and makes me the insecure and wavering man who causes you so much trouble.

I am not worried about myself. I have faced trials of this sort before and finally triumphed over them. But the thought of you hurts me.

Paris, June 27, 1935

So far, we haven't made any definite plans. Zhenya had thought of sending Natasha to the seashore with her school for a couple of months but now all that has been scrapped. I'll try to arrange a trip to Brussels as soon as is practicable. Possibly I'll manage to get a visa here. Please, will you try to get it for me on your side too?

The Congress actually ended yesterday. My speech, or rather my ad lib talk (delivered under awful conditions, at nearly one o'clock in the morning) went down very well with the French.*

I'll spend the short time assigned to me in Paris in roaming around the place in search of material like a hungry wolf. I will try to make some systematic notes of what I know of *la Ville Lumière*, and perhaps have them published one day.

I wrote to you when I was still in Moscow that everything was fine with the Lyakhetskys.

I found Natasha at her shining best. She hasn't lost any of her charm and seemed very pleased to see me again, but she keeps extracting *dix sous* from me that she claims to need for the most varied purposes. Zhenya has put on a little weight but is feeling fine. The old woman has completely deteriorated physically but has grown quieter and less cumbersome. She just sits and sits in her corner and only comes to life when it's feeding time.

The things for Natasha arrived today and had an enormous success with one and all, filling the household with gladness.

My heartfelt regards to Grisha. I'll write and telephone.

Am waiting for the passport. When it comes, I'll take an armful of passports and see to it that they are put in order.

See you soon, *mes petits.*

My best to Grisha from the bottom of my heart.

I.

* In 1935 a Congress for the Defense of Culture and Peace took place in Paris. Ilya Ehrenburg in his *Memoirs* writes: "The Soviet Delegation arrived, without Babel. The French writers who had organized the Congress requested our Embassy to include the author of *Red Cavalry* in the delegation. Babel arrived late, on the second or the third day, I think. He was due to speak immediately. He reassured me with a smile, 'I'll find something to say.' This is how I described Babel's speech in *Izvestia*: Babel did not read his speech, he spoke gaily and in masterly French for fifteen minutes, entertaining the audience with several unwritten stories. People laughed but at the same time they realized that under cover of those amusing stories the essence of our people and of our culture was being conveyed to them; 'this collective farmer has bread, he has a house, he even has a decoration. But it's not enough for him. Now he wants poetry to be written about him.' "

From I. Ehrenburg, *Truce, 1921-1933*, vol. 3 of *Men, Years, Life*, published by MacGibbon & Kee, London, 1963.

Paris, July 1, 1935

I have made my application for the visa. They've promised to give it to me within the next few days. We'll come to see you after the tenth and then we can celebrate the three birthdays at the same time. But, alas, we shan't be able to stay very long—I don't expect I could stay with you beyond the end of July because my main work—the work for which I may get paid—is here in Paris. But we'll see about it when the time comes.

I feel great. I find I am the father of an infant who is notorious for her criminal activities within a range of ten kilometers.

I only had a chance to have a good look at the things sent for Natasha after mailing my letter to you. They're really excellent and are already in full use.

As I watch the girl, I cannot help laughing. Her heredity comes out mostly when she organizes dramatic scenes for her own benefit: each morning she puts on a violent quarrel with her parents, but she is only play-acting the quarrel scene, since she has no real reason for the outburst except as an excuse to pronounce the words: "*Andouille, va!*"

What saddens me is that Zhenya insists on speaking French to her, which makes her Russian very lame.

I'll let you know as soon as we get the visa.

I have to be off now. I have loads of things to do.

I.

[A postcard.]

Paris, July 4, 1935

The passports, including Zhenya's and Berta Davydovna's, will be ready on Saturday. For the first time, Natasha has been entered on a passport and thus becomes a Soviet citizen. It looks as though everything is settled and you won't have to go to the trouble of getting us the Belgian visas.

I am leading a hectic existence here and spend most of my time running all over Paris, with very little left to spend at home.

Today, most of the members of our delegation left for home and things will be quieter. I feel fine, although my daughter bullies me. I took her to a doctor who said she should have her adenoids out. Any day now, I will let you know the date of our departure for Brussels.

I.

Paris, July 11, 1935

Mama's passport is in order. The next time, I believe, you'll be able to extend it in Brussels since Belgium is expected to recognize the USSR any day now. Then we'll have to give some thought to Mera's and Grisha's passports, but we'll discuss that when we meet. The prospects of my family's settling in the USSR are very bright now and I enriched the Soviet Union with a new citizen when Natasha was entered on Zhenya's new passport.

I haven't called you on the phone because it is quite expensive. I reckon to get the Belgian visa on Saturday. I feel that I should stay in Paris as long as possible, because the town presents an exceptional interest these days—the atmosphere here is truly prerevolutionary and I see and feel what's going on around me infinitely more acutely than I did on my previous visit; it is as if a sort of clairvoyance had descended upon me. And if it wasn't for my ardent desire to see you as soon as possible, I'd remain here for a little longer.

I'll send you a cable when we leave. Zhenya has found a woman with whom she could leave Berta Davydovna. The woman seems quite experienced and it looks as if she'll stay on for good.

Yesterday we went to a concert given by Iza Kremer.* She sang better than ever before. Memories of my youth overwhelmed me. I couldn't restrain myself and after the concert went over to talk to her and Kheifets (the former publisher of the *Odessa News*). A very touching scene ensued. If she doesn't leave town right away, we'll meet again. At the concert, I saw many former Odessa citizens who have aged a good deal.

I walk around a lot. I wish I didn't have to work just now, but I do.

Our daughter is already a grownup with plenty of cunning. She keeps asking me for *dix sous* to buy herself some candy and leads a private life of her own. You'll soon see her for yourselves.

I'll let you know as soon as I get the visa.

A bientôt, mes enfants,

I.

We cannot sufficiently admire the clothes sent by Mera. She seems to have become an expert in that sort of thing.

* Iza Kremer, born in Bessarabia in 1885, died in Argentina in 1956. She was a singer of Russian, Yiddish, and German ballads.

[A postcard.]

Plessis-Robinson, July 15, 1935

My very worthy Sister,

The day before yesterday I managed to conceal from *tout le monde,* including my own family, a very sad date. But I feel I must remind you of it and ask you to drink to our collective health tomorrow. The serviceable woman is coming on the 18th and we'll be able to leave on the 19th or, in any case, no later than the 20th. We'll wire the exact train time.

Tomorrow is Natasha's birthday and we're organizing a children's festival here. You must promise us to repeat it in Brussels.

Yesterday we had an unforgettable day—we attended both manifestations. I'll tell you all about it when we meet.

I.

Vilshanka Village, September 4, 1935

I have been to the post office in Kiev every day to see whether there was anything from you. Nothing. I am surprised and depressed. I am traveling around the countryside in Kiev Province and am now staying on a collective farm not far from Belaya Tserkov. It is the first time in my life that I have seen our remote native town. I sent you a telegram from there. I feel fine, am seeing interesting things and visiting collective farms; they are becoming the mainstay of Soviet life. I am going back to Kiev in a few days and from there shall move on south. I will inform you of my new address by wire. I hope to find a letter from you in Kiev. I have no idea what sort of a time you had in Spa, where our Es-culapius is, etc.

Salut,

I.

September 11, 1935

I am sailing along the Dnieper on a steamer. I left Cherkassy yesterday and am on my way back to Kiev. The weather is fine. I've had an amazing ten-day trip through the settlements and villages of Kiev Province. I have been to Korsuna, Belaya Tserkov, Cherkassy and many other places. It would be no exaggeration to describe what I found there as miraculous. Some villages already have two or three schools, a hospital, including a maternity ward, a movie theater and a hairdresser's, and many of them have electricity. And you must remember that they stand in places where four or five years ago there was emptiness.

I am enjoying my voyage on the Dnieper immensely. Not long ago we passed the places where the Gronfeins come from—Pereyaslav Rzhishchev. The boat is very comfortable and it doesn't rock a bit which makes navigation of the Dnieper very suitable for a seaman like me.

I am already worrying that there won't be any letters from you in Kiev but am trying to hope that I'll be spared that trial.

I.

Odessa, September 19, 1935

I am in my home town. They say that contact with their native soil gives people new strength. I am wallowing in delight. I am staying in a villa and go swimming in the sea. The villa is in Arkadia and is very comfortable. I came to Odessa on the sixteenth and stayed at the London Hotel where I lived like a lord, then, yesterday, I moved to Arkadia* which is quite unrecognizable now with its palms, neat walks and umbrellas on the beach.

In other respects Odessa is lagging—she is poor and provincial, but as beautiful as ever. I haven't been to see anyone yet, haven't announced my presence here, just roamed around the town. The houses at 17 *Reschelevskaya* Street and 12 *Tiraspolskaya* Street are just as they were, even the name plates of Natanson and Gurfinkel are in their places, so probably they still live there.

I am delighted that there aren't many new buildings nor many that have been altered, for this way I recognize everything right away.

Today I'll put in an appearance at the aunts'; they'll bring me up to date on the news and I'll send you a complete report. I am waiting to get Tobnash's address which I have lost.

While in Kiev I attended the war games and saw a few things that other mortals haven't seen.

Some vague business is demanding my presence in Moscow but I'll try and stay here as long as I can, for I feel I am being resurrected both mentally and physically. I'll go to the post office today to see whether there's any mail from you. Now there are two big post offices in Odessa, one on Sadovaya Street, the other where the little post office used to be on the corner of Post Office Street and Yekaterina Street.

The Odessa talk is still as colorful as before: "And so I drank *this* vodka . . ." "Give us those there t'ings . . ." The guardians of the peace are referred to as "Dem folks."

I missed a great event by a few days—unprecedentedly huge schools of mackerel were driven inshore at Odessa, hunted by pilchard; the fish were jumping ashore and people were catching them in their bare hands. Boys fought for them in the streets.

As I accumulate information, I shall keep you briefed.

Today, I'll arrange with Anyuta to go to the cemetery.

I.

* Arkadia: a Black Sea resort near Odessa.

Odessa, October 9, 1935

In this amazing town the sea-bathing season is still on. The weather is radiant. I am living in retirement in a villa by the sea and doing a lot of work. My landlady, a fisherman's wife, prepares delicious Odessa dishes for me. I think with horror of going back to Moscow. I keep putting off the things I have to do in town, waiting for bad weather, although each visit provides rich food for thought and emotion. Take my visit to Stolyarsky alone! I spent the night at his place. The Maestro walks around in gaudy pajamas with checkered pants, with his long mane floating. There is a violin school named after him in town and he is considered the greatest violin teacher in the Soviet Union. Child prodigies drop from his hands like peas. It is a picture of perfect bliss—he is loved and spoiled by everyone and his daughter even got married recently, although she is stuffed heavily with years. He asked me to send you his best regards.

I demand categorically that Mama recover from her illness. I wish she could see the way Sonia runs around; she leads a full life and looks great. Anyuta looks much better and younger than Katya, and all her girl friends, such as Sonya Feldstein, look the picture of health.

I reckon that my work in Odessa will bring the day when we meet again considerably closer. I have received a touching letter from Natasha.

Keep writing to me at the Odessa address. When there is a change, I'll inform you by wire.

In Odessa I have rediscovered the existence of God and pray to Him for Mama's recovery.

I.

Odessa, October 13, 1935

I went to the post office today and was very disappointed to find nothing from you there. Am very worried.

I am about to move into town from my villa and shall keep a great memory of the time I've spent here. This morning, I swam in the sea as usual but toward evening an autumn wind blew up. I am writing this between two and three in the morning, listening to the breaking of the waves and the whistling of the wind. There's only me, the caretaker and his wife in this huge villa. There's a full moon these days and the nights are so beautiful that it even makes me feel sad. I often stand on a cliff above the sea and am unable to make myself go home.

I see the aunts quite often. They and E. Ya. can expect rich gifts in the nearest future.

I'll try to stay in the South until the end of October. I won't be able to stay on beyond that because I have some quite urgent business to attend to in Moscow. In the meantime I am trying to store up my energy for Moscow and am undergoing a course of treatment at the Lermontov Sanatorium—a wonderfully equipped place—under Professor Kalina, the brother of the late Kalina (a cheerful stuffed fool, but a very good doctor who has become a professor now). My treatment consists of nasal inhalations and sunbathing which, in my opinion, is the only proper cure.

I.

Odessa, October 19, 1935

My enchanting Mama, my flower divine,

I hope you take first prize in the forthcoming football championships. In our country, citizenesses of your kind practice parachute jumping and qualify as "Voroshilov Sharpshooters."

The matter of my further travels will be decided in Moscow. My stay in Odessa has done me a tremendous amount of good—my soul and my brains have been thoroughly refreshed. Perhaps I am also enjoying living here so much because I'm liked by the people. Completely unknown street cleaners, news vendors and what not, come up to me in the street, say hello and engage me in the most incredible conversations. The other evening I went to the Sibiryalovsky Theater. At one point, I was asked to say a few words. Then, when I left, there were thousands of young people thronging about in Kherson Street. They barred the road to my automobile, shouted, hollered and prevented me from leaving. As you can see, the nice Odessa people are still there.

I've met many of my old schoolmates. They are all bookkeepers or something of the sort and all look henpecked and subdued. I seem to be the only one unaffected either by place or time.

Well, above all, you must remain in good health, both of you, and give my love to Grisha.

I.

I don't think I know who the [Soviet] ambassador [in Brussels] is but it'd be easy enough for me to make his acquaintance.

Odessa, October 23, 1935

My highly respected relatives and preceptors,

Urgent business demands my presence in Moscow but I'm stubbornly ignoring it. There is food for my spirit in Odessa and I must come back here. As before, it is a town all on its own. I must go to Moscow about matters of literature and international affairs—I must find out whether the congress will take place in Paris in November. And while in Moscow, I'll find out who is our representative in Belgium. I'll inform you of my departure by wire so you can keep writing to Odessa in the meantime. I see the Aunts constantly and when I get my money from Moscow, the appropriate gestures will follow.

I live like a sage here: I inhale all sorts of alkalis and oils through my nose, warming my snout under a Bakh Lamp, and on top of that, have some blissful things thrown in free of charge (so much is free of charge in this wonderful land) such as sea and mineral baths followed by showers that promote my circulation. I do all this at the Lermontov Sanatorium. It seems like a continuation of spring here except for brief reminders of fall which come and then vanish without leaving a trace.

I have nothing more to write about. I must go and run around a bit and do some work.

I.

Odessa, October 30, 1935

For the first time, it looks like fall today—it's raining. I must leave for Moscow, for my business can't wait any longer. I'll stop over in Kiev for a couple of days or so and reckon to be in Moscow on the sixth. So, from now on, address me at Bolshoi Nikolo-Vorobinsky Lane. . . . I must go around and pay visits to everyone now.

I've been told that Lyakhetsky has arrived here but I haven't seen him and my whereabouts are so secret that I'm sure he won't find me. I'll try to see him before I leave, though. I expect to get my money today or tomorrow and will then shower my bounty upon the aunts and Lyakhetsky.

I can't convey to you completely how pleased I am with my visit to Odessa. I have rested and relaxed here both in body and in soul and I have been able to work a lot, with the enthusiasm and freshness of youth. From this experience I must draw the conclusion, once and for all, that Moscow is not the place for me to live in, although I must always keep a foothold there.

Before I leave for Moscow, I will inform you of all my affairs and movements.

I.B.

Just received your letter of the 24th. I'll send you your "share" from Moscow as soon as I get there. It's quite easy now.

Moscow, November 13, 1935

I saw Lyakhetsky in Odessa and he had his usual rather dopey look. Once more his is loaded down with powers of attorney and authorizations, once again he is repairing old machines and showing an enviable resilience. Naretskin has had another bit of his leg cut off. I didn't go to see him but was told that he lives on money given him by his son who is in the merchant marine and was on a trip abroad while I was in Odessa.

The German who lives in my house is going abroad in a few days and he'll take some caviar for you. I'll try to send you as much as possible—it's a good thing it's turned so cold now for that will give the caviar the best chance of reaching you. I'll also try to send you something with Ehrenburg. I've seen him and am organizing a big dinner party for him tomorrow.

I am feeling very good after my stay in Odessa: I have repaired my nose and am now attending to my teeth. As soon as that's done I'll be able to become a world traveler once more.

Lyubov Mikhailovna Ehrenburg told me that she had seen Zhenya and that she looked absolutely gorgeous. The Paris congress that was to be held in November has been postponed for a while.

I've been told that I'll be able to see my family any time I have some "output" to show, so that is the only thing I should concern myself with now. Having had my fill of traveling recently, I find it a joy to sit by a hot stove in the felt slippers I got in Brussels and unhurriedly squeeze something out of myself. . . .

I will send some children's books for Natasha today. Should I go on sending books to you too? Have you read the last batch?

And now, I close with Odessa greetings and remain yours very respectfully,

I.B.

My dear little Mama,

Write more often, and since it is a well-established fact that Pushkin could write better than you, you needn't be ashamed and can just put down whatever comes into your head.

Moscow, November 21, 1935

Everything's as good as it can be. In Moscow, it's winter already but I am so well equipped for the cold that I could leave for the North Pole. My rooms are light, warm and quiet and I am working.

I have received confirmation that the Odessa Film Studios have paid 250 rubles to Anyuta; they were supposed to pay Yelena Yakovlevna at the same time. I hope they have done so.

Yesterday Katya came to see me. She looks surprisingly well. We shall try to get Anyuta to come to Moscow.

I haven't heard a word from Zhenya for quite a long time. A few days ago I sent some excellent books to Natasha. All I've heard about Zhenya was from Ehrenburg's wife, who told me that she saw her swaggering around wrapped in silver-fox furs. Do you get the books I send you? Do you really want them? I'll send some caviar for the Doc [Shaposhnikov] and Collier. I believe a good opportunity is about to present itself.

That will be all for today for I have a mighty desire for food and am being summoned to dinner.

Yours respectfully,

I.

Stalino, December 5, 1935

My nice Mama and my lovely relatives,

I am off on my travels again. Last night saw the closing session of the congress of Donets Basin Literary Clubs at which a reader of mine assured me of his love in terms that would've made you spout tears like whales. My program is a tour of government offices, mines, factories and state farms of the Donets Basin (for I've been held up in my work by a shortage of factual material), after which I'll move to the Kiev area and will visit some of the collective farms on my list. I reckon to be back in Moscow by January 1st. Address your answer to General Delivery, Central Post Office, Kiev, for I am sure it takes a very long time for a letter to get all the way here. I'll keep you informed of all my movements by wire.

Before I set off on this trip, I tried desperately to get through to you on the phone but, alas, Brussels seems to be the only European capital with which we have no telephonic communication. I could've called Zhenya but then she has no phone. And, of course, I haven't heard a thing from her and Natasha.

It took some courage on my part to go on this trip for it was so cozy, quiet and warm in the Nikolo-Vorobinsk house and I was decidedly reluctant to rush out into the uncomfortable world. But I had to.

I'll write to you very often because I think of you constantly.

I.B.

Stalino, December 9, 1935

My lovely Mama and my charming Shaposhnikovs, hail!

I am still in the Donets Basin and am still enjoying it. My headquarters is located in Stalino—formerly Yuzovka. I take trips to Gorlovka and Maneyevka, and intend to go to Mariupol. I can't convey to you the mighty energy and vigor seething in this region which is the real steel, coal and electric heart of our great country.

I'll stay here for another eight days or so and then move on to Kiev. Address letters to Kiev for I'm sure it'd take the mail an impossibly long time to get here. It looks as though I'll be wandering about until the end of the month. The last leg of my trip will be to Kabardino-Balkara.

After that, we'll be able to think of other countries.

I am very depressed at not having any news from you. Everything's fine at the aunts'.

With greetings from the Donets Basin,

I.

Stalino, December 13, 1935

My stay in the Donets Basin has had to be extended. But I'm in no way sorry about it. The only trouble is that I'll only get your letters after a long delay, when I get to Kiev, which will be around the 20th. But anyhow, the mail is so slow that I don't suppose they'd arrive before that.

Luckily the weather is warm and travel is very pleasant. I am finding out things I need to know and I have the feeling that I am leading a useful life. Ah, if I could only do without Moscow altogether!

My life here is very comfortable—I'm lodged by factory directors and share their fare, and I have an automobile and horses at my disposal. In Maneyevka, my life is particularly luxurious. I stay there at the house of the director of a really gigantic steel plant. To give you an idea, there is a winter garden next to my bedroom.

I.

Stalino, December 15, 1935

I'm still functioning quite energetically in the Donets Basin. My center of operation is the Maneyevka Steel Plant. Today I'm leaving on a tour of the countryside and will stop at some quite out-of-the-way places. After that, I'll return to Stalino and from here will go on to Kiev. It takes over twenty-four hours to get there and that's a bore.

The winter around here is quite puny and I am still going around in my autumn overcoat. I'm staying with the publisher of the local paper. I'm very comfortable and it's for free—not quite though: my landlords wish to converse while I wish to remain silent. Yesterday I spent my day in a blast-furnace shop. It's an impressive, fiery sight.

I miss your letters and reckon to find a pile of them in Kiev when I get there.

I.

Stalino, December 20, 1935

Am leaving for Kiev the day after tomorrow. It's very hard for me to live without news of you. I've been moving around these last few days, visiting two state farms and then Artemovsk (formerly Bakhmut) and Gorlovka. This time, I didn't go down into the mine. The whole Donets Basin is seething—the Stakhanovite movement is in full swing. Leaving for my Maneyevka headquarters this evening and from there going directly to Kiev where I hope to find lots of mail from you. How is your collective health? My heart is full of memories of the trips I've made this year: Brussels and roaming over the old familiar places in Odessa.

I.

Moscow, December 30, 1935

My wonderful relatives,

Returned home this very day. It's a lovely winter here, lots of snow and an even, windless cold. In the South there was rain and mud, and the climate there seems to be getting milder every year. The Odessa cure seems to have had a tremendous effect upon my nose, for whatever conditions I found myself under in the Donets Basin, I didn't have anything remotely resembling a nose cold. I must repeat the cure once again in the summer, whatever else I do. The repairs on my teeth are also nearing completion—it'll be all done in January. I have been undergoing the dental treatment with great zest since it is free of charge and I have the services of the best specialists available in Moscow.

When I read in your letter that you were in relatively good health, I danced with joy. I wish you, in the course of 1936, to cover yourselves with glory as prize fighters, weight lifters, javelin throwers and parachutists.

I'll stay in Moscow for a while now—or rather, just outside it— for I must, in the end, produce an opus. I'll also send you some caviar. I asked someone to do it for me, but nothing was done about it while I was away.

I can't find a trace of Zhenya in the whole world. I'll send telegrams to the four corners of the earth. I know my poor daughter has been ill. My New Year's wish for myself is to work well and to see all the members of my family.

I am making this very brief for I am tired after my journey.

Should I go on sending you books?

Well, a happy New Year to you, my dear ones.

Hold on, Mama. . . .

I.

1 9 3 6

Moscow, January 7, 1936

Am living in warmth and comfort. No news from my progeny. Katya has left for Odessa loaded with gifts. Anyuta and Sonya have received some money from me during the past month. A Frenchman will deliver some caviar (for presents) to you in the next few days.

I have gained in wisdom and spend my days quietly working, smoking, pacing my room in my slippers, strolling slowly through narrow side streets. There's rather little snow, it's warm and the winter, in general, is quite mild.

Around me a tide of prosperity and enthusiasm is foaming and the population of all the Russias is bounding forward like a tiger . . .

What must I do about books and newspapers? I'm writing briefly just not to leave you without news of me, although there's nothing new to report, and I wish you'd do exactly the same for me. Whenever I lose contact with you, I immediately feel lonely and depressed.

I.B.

Moscow, January 28, 1936

Everything's fine. There's been no winter this year. It's warm and I find it easy to breathe. I'm working hard and have to do lots of running around. By March first, I'll have paid up all my debts and filled all the orders I've received and will be able to devote all my time to "pure literature." Yesterday, I received a present from the film studios—a marvelous Tekin rug worth two thousand gold rubles. Some present! If they are satisfied with my work, I am certain they'll send me on assignment at the beginning of the summer and I'll have a chance to see Fenia and Enta. It is very hard for me to watch over Natasha's destiny at a distance and so the only thing is for her and her mother to come and live here with me. This matter must be settled at our next meeting—it cannot wait any longer. None of us will be able to stand any further uncertainty. I personally am quite absorbed in my work here and that helps me keep my mind off it. But that's not what really matters. Natasha is my main concern.

On top of all my work, I have a lot of people coming to see me: Kalmuks from Kabarda, miners from the Donets Basin, old pals from Kiev. . . . And all these people must be fed dinners and entertained until four in the morning. I just don't have the physical stamina for it.

Zinaida Lvovna—remember, the youngest of our landladies in Obukhovo Lane—is in a situation similar to Lilya's: she too fell passionately in love at a ripe—even overripe—age and he too is a sick man and that marriage is also a heavy load now and I must bear it too.

Unlike in past years, I'm leading a disciplined, austere, hardworking life. However, despite all my efforts, human waves come breaking against my monastic cell and it shakes like a tree in a storm [Babel's mixed metaphor.—Tr.—MacA.]. Well, I hope I'll still manage somehow.

I recall with elation the weeks spent in Odessa. Ah, what a nice life that was.

And on that, see you later. I'm writing this during a brief break in my work. Will write a longer letter on my "day off." I expressly demand that you all remain in good health.

Your second cousin,

I.

Moscow, February 2, 1936

My dear and highly respected Mama,

Haven't a spare moment for writing to you, haven't a spare moment to look at my newspaper. I have taken on an important pledge: to clear myself of all debts, to give up all other work and to devote myself exclusively to "pure art." That alone can take me into clear waters—in the dignified sense—and enable me to see my dear ones. I have assigned two months—January and February—to this great effort of freeing myself. I'll fulfill all the assignments I have taken upon myself, although I have accepted rather more than I can reasonably cope with. Still, I'm sure I'll finish everything by March 7.

It's lucky that I'm feeling fine physically just now; it would seem that hard work is good for the health: so far I haven't had a cold this winter. I bless my Odessa cure and that fool Kalina for that.

We hadn't had any winter weather until three days ago when the cold got back at us a bit. Now, for the third day in a row, the temperature has remained around 15 below zero, but it's windless and beautiful. I am sitting on a sofa by a hot stove with my feet tucked under me and admiring my rug. I wish Papa could see it— it's a real work of art and must be worth around three thousand gold rubles.

Am sending you a batch of papers. We'll turn our attention to Robinson in March. I've asked Zhenya to take your granddaughter to see you.

Good-bye, my dear ones,

I.

Moscow, March 1, 1936

The first of March. . . . But it's snowing and windy here. I have been feeling fine for five days now, but am still keeping to my room. I intend to venture out into the world tomorrow—I'll go to Gorky's place and will call you from there on the phone.

Financially, I am doing rather well now. I keep driving myself and am working *comme un nègre*. I hope that by the end of March I'll be clear of all my debts and will be able to work without thinking about tomorrow.

I am sending some books for Natasha. What you write about her fills my parental heart with joy and also with bitterness because I must live apart from her. I'll do my utmost to make the separation short.

Have sent money to Sonya. Write to me more often so that I may derive some joy from my family.

Akademia has entrusted me with the editing of Sholom Aleichem's works.* I read him in my spare hours and roll around with laughter; it brings my young years back to me.

Write quickly about the books.

I.

Grisha, as far as photography goes, my main hopes lie with you. Please, take Natasha at all possible angles and send me the pictures.

Salut,
I.B.

Natasha, my sweetie,

I hope I will be able to talk to you on the telephone tomorrow. I am very glad that my Mama is coming to see you. Please, don't be too rough with your grandma, she's a frail piece of pottery; but with your aunt and uncle, you may be firm and see to it that they do not misbehave.

I am sending you some books. Write and tell me whether you like them. I suppose they are selling flowers on every street corner in Brussels now, while here in Moscow I look out at a six-foot

---

* The great Yiddish writer, 1859-1916. *Akademia* was preparing a complete edition of Sholom Aleichem's works for the celebration in 1939 of the eightieth anniversary of his birth.

layer of snow in front of my window, reaching as high as the janitor's toolshed, and it is still snowing and snowing.

Good-bye, my dear one,

Yours,

I.

Moscow, March 5, 1936

Unexpected news: am leaving for the Crimea this evening, to go and see Gorky with Mikhail Koltsov* and Malereau,† who is here from Paris. I'll return on the 11th. I'm very sad at not having managed to get through to you on the phone—Malraux's [transliterated] arrival has disrupted all my plans. I have been going out for a few days now and there is no trace of my grippe left.

I hope that this letter will find Zhenya in Brussels. I've received confirmation from old man Gaikis.

Kiss my rowdy daughter for me.

We're traveling in a special car. Will write to you tomorrow.

I.

* Mikhail Koltsov, Soviet writer and journalist, 1898-1942. He was the *Pravda* correspondent in Spain in 1936-1937, and published a *Spanish Diary* (see the letter of October 25, 1938). He was not heard of after 1938, probably for political reasons.

† Babel's spelling of Malraux.

On March 22nd, 1936, Gorky wrote as follows to Romain Rolland: "Malraux came to see me. He is obviously both intelligent and talented. We agreed on some practical questions which should help to unite the European intelligentsia in the fight against fascism." (*Sobranie Sochinenii*, vol. 30, p. 435)

Moscow, March 18, 1936

Am scrawling this in a hurry. I've taken on so many urgent orders that I have no time to breathe. This mad race will go on for another couple of weeks and during that time, I'll be talking to you on the phone.

Annushka is leaving today and she will transmit the books to Enta and Fenya—books that I consider very interesting. I didn't have much time to give to Annushka; I'm frightfully busy and anyway, they only spent three days here. We are dining together tonight. Last night, I got them tickets for the Arts Theater.

I am very sorry to hear that Zhenya and Natasha have left. I am very happy to know, though, that materially they are much better off now, because, in that case, the father of the family can at last attend to his own duties.

I did get the neckties and the gloves. Thank you. Katya has gone to the store to buy some caviar and I'll give it to Annushka for you. Don't worry too much if it gets lost.

I have thousands of errands for Annushka and I hope she will make a very complete report to Fenya whom I reckon to see in the summer. And on that, so long until tomorrow, for all sorts of characters connected with the movies and literature have come and are clamoring for my soul.

I.

Moscow, April 15, 1936

I intend to ring you up tonight, so I'll be very brief now. Rain mixed with snow is coming down. We've only had two sunny days. I think of Odessa with longing. I have handed in the most urgent and pressing work. I am expecting an easing-off toward the end of the month and hope to devote May to affairs dear to my heart.

What are your plans for the summer? I think you should give the matter serious thought. I would like you to spend this summer in the countryside. I hope you'll be able to arrange it.

Have received a thank-you letter from the Odessa aunts. They're fine. How is your combined health? I have been eating matzos all this time.

And so, until this evening,

I.

Moscow, April 26, 1936

Most honorable Citizeness née Shvevel,
  We are gathered here around the dining table: Professor of Dentistry Etraordinary Ye. A. Lyakhetsky [Katya], hers and your nieces, Ada Gofman and her offspring Zinaida, and the floor-polisher, I Babel. We send you our greetings. Besides veal and hominy, we have also been served gefilte fish here, the sauce for which was stolen by our neighbor, and matzos. Before handing the pen over to Ada, I wish you good health and prosperity and that you may remember to write to me more often.

I.B.

  It seems so strange, my dear ones, after ten years of absence, to find myself at Katya's with Zina. Sitting here at Katya's with your favorite son and my only male cousin and having eaten some Jewish fish, we are saying just as many nasty things about your life as he has been saying about ours. Katya and I will write to you at greater length. Our love and kisses,

Ada.

[In a child's handwriting.]
Dear Aunty Fenya and Merochka,
  Zina.

Moscow, May 27, 1936

My ravishing Mama,
  More than a month ago I gave Steiner the books you asked for but I only received word from him that he was about to send them on yesterday. I sent him an irate message today for I am afraid he may keep reading the books till eternity. But he has never done anything of this sort before. Please let me know by airmail as soon

as you get them. They include a Pushkin, a Gorky and a very nice edition of Sholokhov.

I am very displeased to learn that you are paying off Zhenya's debts for she's had many more opportunities for doing so herself than you have. She hasn't written to me at all since Raya's arrival. I would have so much liked to have Natasha's picture. I'll write all this to her today.

Summer has descended upon us at last (we didn't have any spring). I feel fine and have got rid of most of my debts and completed most of my assignments. I am working on my own stuff now and it would seem that, after all these years of painful deliberation and search, I have found my road and am writing with an ease such as I haven't known for a long time. I hope to have some real results by the fall. Am in a state of great inspiration.

I often send books to Natasha although I don't really know whether they are of any use to her. I suppose it's a real Tower of Babel in Plessis [-Robinson]. I don't know whether Raya went there alone or with all her family.

I'll call you on the phone in the very near future. The thought that you're sitting in the city, instead of breathing the air of the fields and woods, depresses me. I beseech Mera to take some knitting and some Russian books, get a cab and drive Mama to the park. Let her feed the little old lady milk and dry bread and spend the money assigned to meat on taxis to take her for drives in the countryside.

Damn Steiner! You'd have had plenty of reading matter if he had been responsible and, above all, it's not so easy to find such a nice edition of Pushkin. I'll call him up today.

Am sending things for the Aunts. Ah, if only I could arrange to live in Odessa! Good-bye for now.

Your I, who sends up prayers for you.

Moscow, June 2, 1936

At last summer is here. It's great. Sometimes I'm even overcome by laziness.

It turns out now that my mouth, i.e., all my teeth, will only be ready by the end of July. Up till now, I have been attended by a Kremlin dentist, and now that the time has come for bridgework, it is being done by another Kremlin dentist, Shapiro, our former neighbor from Obukhovo Lane. I suppose I'll have an indestructible mouth after all this.

And so it doesn't look as if I will be able to move anywhere until [the end of?] July.

No news from Vienna except a word from my publisher informing me that the money will be sent to Fenya in the course of June so that she'll be able to move to some spa on July first.

Am writing to Zhenya today. I am very curious to know how they are making out with Raya staying with them. I'll mention the snapshots and about installing a telephone for her once again.

In the course of June, I will become a landowner and the owner of a house. A comfortable summer settlement has been established about twenty miles from Moscow and now they are building a two-story house with all modern convenience there for me. The house will be ready by June 20th and it will include half a hectare of forest land. It would really be ideal if it wasn't a special settlement for writers, but anyway, we've all agreed to keep to ourselves and to abstain from visiting one another.

Did my friend Tids. . .el come and see you and say hello from me?

I.

Moscow, June 7, 1936

I am very depressed. It doesn't look as if Alexei Maximovich [Gorky] will get away with it this time. Although the doctors sound a bit more hopeful today, I don't believe them.

For the rest, everything's fine. Since I don't suppose any longer that you'll get the books from Vienna, I'll send you another lot which you should get by July first or even around June 15. I suppose you'll spend July out of town. Personally, I'd like it best if you moved as far south as possible, somewhere nearer to the sun.

Haven't had any news from Zhenya for the past two weeks. I'll write again soon. Perhaps, after all, everything will turn out all right.

I.

Moscow, June 17, 1936

This is your own flesh-and-blood son and brother writing and he is now the proud owner of a false tooth that no one would ever notice. So hail to you, Mama dear, and you, my ravishing sister, and you, amiable Grisha! Can it be that you still haven't received word of me through Vienna? I understand that you have and so I must ask you to acknowledge.

Then I must report that yesterday I saw Sima who has gone to Leningrad for a few days. She reckons to be home at the end of the month and is taking a load of presents for her little girls Fenya and Enta. [This is obviously a codified message. Sima must have been taking things for Babel's mother and wife.—Tr.—MacA.] What else is there? I have sent fifty rubles to the Odessa aunts. It's quite hot around here and I don't feel too much like working, but I must. Steiner has promised to come over. I have also been assured that they will send you some money due to me at the end of the month and I hope that this will enable you to go off on your vacation.

Have just sent off an angry letter to Zhenya, angry because of her silence. In the next few days, I reckon to get a more or less accurate idea of when I'll be able to go and see my family and when I know, I'll call you on the phone.

I started with a joke but must end on a grave note. The state of Gorky's health is still rather precarious but he is fighting for life like a lion and we keep swinging from despair to hope. In the past few days, the doctors have sounded a little bit more optimistic. André Gide is flying in today. I am going to meet him.

I wish you sunshine, good health and good cheer,

I.

[A postcard with a view of Moscow.]

Moscow, June 19, 1936

Dear Mamachen,

It is a great loss for our entire country and it is also a personal blow to me. That man was my conscience and my judge, an example to me. I was linked to him by twenty years of unspoiled friendship and affection. The way for me to live up to his memory now is to live and work, and to do both those things well. Gorky's body is lying in state in the Hall of Columns, and endless crowds file past his coffin. It's a hot summer day. I think I'll go out for a bit. I'll write again soon.

I.

Moscow, June 24, 1936

I was supposed to leave with the others for the London writers' congress on July 18th. Now, because of Gorky's death, our trip has been postponed until the fall. I've had to make radical changes in my plans for the summer. Now I am leaving for Odessa in the middle of July and will stay there for at least two months. My dental treatment will be finished at the beginning of the coming month. I'll come back to Moscow from Odessa, to start on my family trip.

Sima left yesterday. She took lots of presents for Fenya and Enta with her. I have sent word that both of them should move to summer quarters. Now that Fenya has finally managed to get herself a pension, I hope she will pay more attention to her health and stop squandering her energy on a lot of nonsense.

There haven't been any letters from you for quite some time now and I am very worried. What do they write to you from Vienna? We are having a very hot summer here and I am very pleased about it. Originally, I intended to spend the second half of the summer in southern France but I am sure that Odessa will be a worthy substitute for any country or climate. I am only sad that my meeting with you will be delayed for three months.

I'll ring you up one of these days. What worries me most is the idea that you might allow the summer to pass without going anywhere. How expensive is life in France this year? Couldn't you manage to go south? Or to Italy? I am expecting a detailed letter from you giving me all the plans for your *villégiature*. And with that, good-bye *de tout mon coeur*. Kisses to all of you,

I.

Moscow, July 12, 1936

My lovely Sister,

Best wishes on your birthday. *Passons*, don't let's dwell on these dates. Please buy yourself a present out of Mama's capital.

I haven't had a letter from Zhenya for two or three weeks either. Have no idea *ce qu'elles deviennent*. I don't know whether you saw Sima. I suppose you did. All these things interest me a great deal.

Am sending you the little Gronfein and would like you to send him back to me. He's of the same species as Natasha but, of course, she's much better looking. . . .

Katya left for Odessa yesterday and we promised each other to meet there at the end of July. We are having an Egyptian heat wave and brilliant sunshine every day. Today the temperature reached 105 degrees in the sun. A southern flower, I feel great. The hotter the better.

Your voice came over the telephone very clearly last time, and so, in a few days, I'll give myself that pleasure once more.

I didn't get it quite straight: did you actually receive the Tolstoi books I sent you or were you simply notified that they had arrived? Answer by airmail. I sent you the first four volumes.

I am very excited thinking of Odessa. I need not so much rest as a change of setting; I have a thirst for a southern landscape, for the sea. I'll let you know by telegram before I go. At first, you'll have to address your letters to me c/o General Delivery, Central Post Office, Odessa.

Don't forget to congratulate Natasha. Today I'll reprimand her mama for not writing.

A very convenient opportunity for seeing Natasha has been lost because of this terrible bereavement and now I can see no other possibility until the fall, although I will do my utmost. I have become so painstaking in my writing that it verges on imbecility. I hope to discover something new. They'll start publishing my things in the fall. I no longer do any writing on order and so my luxurious *train de vie* must be moderated and my numerous dependents scattered throughout the towns of the Soviet Union will also have to content themselves with tighter rations.

Steiner is arriving at last, on the 15th, and so I have a nice prospect of cigars, neckties, razor blades, etc.

I bow low to you,

Your loyal, tireless, prayerful,

I.

P.S. You can have a copy of the picture made and keep it for yourselves.

Moscow, July 22, 1936

A few days ago it turned out that Steiner wasn't coming back to Moscow and so I was forced to attend to the apartment. That delayed my departure for a few days. I am leaving on the 27th now. Before leaving I'll send you a wire and will phone on the chance that you are back in Brussels already. My situation now is as follows: my dental treatment is completed so I have regained complete freedom of movement; my debts are all paid off; all the assignments I took upon myself have been done, and so now I intend to go back to my native soil and devote myself to "pure art" without having to bother about money or other considerations. And speaking of "pure art," it is the only thing that can bring me success in life and thus be helpful to Natasha, Fenya and others.

Once I am "free" in Odessa, I'll write to you at length about my work, about dates and so on.

They are completing construction on a huge summerhouse outside Moscow for me, but I'll just keep it in reserve, as something to exchange. Ah, how I wish it stood on the Odessa seashore!

I am very pleased to be going down to Odessa—I know I'll both rest there and do a lot of serious work.

From you, in the weeks to come, I expect the following: *voyages de plaisir*, cures, a return to nature, and in general, a luxurious life in which the taxi should replace the streetcar.

As I keep shucking off unnecessary business, I'll write to you more often. Tell me—what sort of a time did you have in the Ardennes? What kind of a place is it? From August on we'll be tossing letters back and forth from one sea to another.

Your intercessor,

I.

Moscow, July 30, 1936

Am leaving for Kiev tomorrow. Will stay there for two days. I suppose I'll get to Odessa on the fourth or fifth. My address now is General Delivery, Central Post Office, Odessa, as I informed you by telegram. Will write to you at length from there. I am full of clear-cut, long-range projects and I hope that contact with my native soil will give me the strength to carry them out. We are having African temperatures all the time and I wish I could transfer some of the heat to Brussels. Write to me often from Ostend. I'd like to know what sort of a season you're having there and what sort of people you come across. Did Raya come and see you? What impression did she make on you?

I've received word from Boris that he reckons to see Fenya by the end of August. As to Sima, she's fine; Enta intends to exert great pressure on her and, of course, I can't object to that. On the contrary, I think that everyone, including Annushka and Fenya, should help her in this business.

The only thing that makes me sad about leaving Moscow is that it will take me substantially farther away from you: I won't have a chance to call you on the phone, letters will take longer to reach you and I won't have any opportunities to send you something with people going your way. But I have trusted people in Moscow who will take care of that. That is the only drawback to my trip. For the rest, I am sure it will do me infinite good, and for your sake too, *mes enfants*, I hope I am right. I send you my love. Write as often as you can. Don't be angry with Zhenya. She's probably running around in circles, wherever she is. Please keep in touch with her. Well, I must go and pack.

Je vous embrasse,
I.

Odessa, August 8, 1936

My unforgettable fellow Odessans,

I have wasted a week on moving from hotel to hotel and on suffering from suffocating heat. Yesterday I got myself a place on Yevangelichesky Lane near the Lermontov Sanatorium, where I am going to take my cure. Yesterday the doctors examined me and found that I was simply suffering from overwork and there was nothing else wrong with me. One of them, a physical therapist said to me: "If it weren't for your bronchi, one would envy you your constitution."

I will have my nose treated again by Kalina, since last year it had such a marvelous effect. I'll do the inhalations, sun myself, swim in the sea, take all sorts of baths, and go through physical therapy with all sorts of gadgets too.

Odessa is as charming as ever, but it looks poor and shabby. Yesterday I bumped into Katya and Lyakhetsky near the Lermontov Sanatorium. They are taking all sorts of treatments there and it was they who actually found me my room.

The weather here is truly gorgeous. The heat wave has abated but it was really getting out of hand—temperatures up to 140 degrees were registered in the sun (and even in Moscow a temperature of 120 was registered). Now, for three days, we have been having extremely pleasant, cool, sunny weather.

I haven't yet seen any aunts and uncles, except the Lyakhetskys, but won't fail to visit them.

How are things in Ostend? Has Zhenya written to you? I am so sad that I cannot transfer to you be it only one quarter of our Odessa sun.

I'll keep you posted on all the gossip of my spa and you must pay me back in kind. This is only the second day that I've been resting and, already, a completely different mug glares back at me from the mirror.

My address is still General Delivery, Central Post Office, Odessa.

My best regards to Grisha,

I.

[A postcard: A view of Odessa.]

Odessa, August 10, 1936

The heat has passed. It's cool and windy and a gale blew up during the night. Am starting my nose treatment on the fourteenth—inhalations, Bakh's Lamp and all the trimmings, such as baths and massage. I am feeling infinitely better than I did in Moscow. I live in a villa that, according to Katya, used to belong to Birnbaum.* The Lyakhetskys live nearby on ——sky [illegible] Boulevard. Iosif Lyakhetsky is an extremely cranky man. My landlady feeds me my dinner. A sample menu: blue bullhead fish, wheat gruel, melon and other typical Odessa dishes, but no mackerel, which is very short this year.

Write more often.

I.

* The Birnbaums were cousins of Babel's mother.

Odessa, August 13, 1936

Got your letter—the first letter I've received in Odessa. Here, unlike, alas, Ostend, the weather is superb. So far, except for Katya, I haven't seen anyone. I am relaxing after the Moscow rat race and storing up new energy. I couldn't have done a smarter thing than come to Odessa. I am starting on my treatments on the fifteenth, for the doctors have advised me to give my body the maximum rest and sleep before embarking upon the course of treatment, and I am attending to that as best I can now. I wish you, above all, lots of sun and fine weather. Am writing to Zhenya and Natasha by the same mail.

I.

Odessa, August 25, 1936

Nothing new to report. I'm taking my course of treatment, swimming, walking around and breathing in the Odessa air that is so full of poetry and literature. I place great hopes in that air. Am living in luxurious but temporary quarters. I went to Blizhnie-Melnitsy—that'd be an ideal spot for you if only it was on the sea. I am lackadaisically looking for a cottage for myself. No news from Zhenya. The aunts are fine. The only trouble is that the weather is beginning to deteriorate and it looks like spring. How are things with you? Write to me more often, my precious ones,

I.

Odessa, August 28, 1936

Mes enfants,
I can't understand what you are complaining about. I write to you very regularly and I suppose a whole pile of my letters must have accumulated in Brussels by now. I am very sorry to hear that your vacation is coming to an end.

Alas, the Belgian weather must have migrated here—for the past three days we've had cold weather and a biting wind. Nevertheless I am thriving. I wonder what made you imagine all those frightening things about my ills? I am just repeating the course of inhalations and the Bakh Lamp treatment I underwent last year under the same unfading Kalina.

I am without any news of Zhenya here, or of Sima and Borya. Borya promised he would write to me at the end of August and I don't know whether he has kept his word. As a rule, he is extremely reliable. Katya and her most idiotic husband—who on top of everything else has lost half of one finger of his left hand—left yesterday for Moscow. I am waiting here for fair weather and send you my blessings. Write *par avion.*

I.B.

Odessa, September 1, 1936

Yesterday in the streetcar I had my watch cut off me. It was one of my favorite possessions. Well, since once upon a time I used to make up epics about such thieves, I have no right to complain. This is the major piece of news I have to report.

I've had a guest: on his way to Yalta, Eisenstein stopped over at my place. In a few days they are beginning to shoot my screenplay* and we revised the last few scenes together. Most likely I'll take a little trip to Yalta toward the end of September, eat some grapes there and attend the shooting of the most important scenes. Eisenstein told me that I am hardly recognizable, both physically and mentally, since he saw me last in Moscow. I work ten times better than I did in Moscow.

I.B.

* Eisenstein was working on the film *Bezhin Meadow,* based on the Turgenev story of the same name; the original scenario, by Alexander Rzheshecsky, was revised by Babel. The cameraman was Tissé, and the cast included Yelena Telesheva, Boris Zakava, and Vitya Kartashov.

Odessa, September 5, 1936

I still live near the Lermontov Sanatorium but these are my last days here. There are several apartments available from which I can choose and tomorrow I'll most probably pick one of them. I came here without any specific complaints but badly overworked and exhausted by the Moscow rat race. Now I am feeling better by the hour, rather than by the day. Both body and soul are finding their balance. They won't get me away from here to go anywhere except to Brussels. I think my work here will prove to be of a different quality too.

Thus far I've seen very few people—following my doctors' orders, I've mostly rested and slept.

I find it awfully depressing that letters take so long to get here and that I can't call you on the phone. Moscow nowadays is a real modern capital with all the conveniences, while here things are as they were in the old days and, although it gladdens my heart, I find it rather inconvenient in some ways. For some time the weather has been so-so, but it seems to be getting a little better. "That weather," as they say in Odessa.

I.

Odessa, September 10, 1936

I am sending you a letter written in Natasha's own hand and I want it back without fail. Zhenya writes wonders about her. Their address is Kensington Hotel, La Croix, Var. It is near St. Raphael. So our family is sitting before three different seas.

It was Sima who helped them to take that trip. Natasha, as you might expect, has taken over the whole hotel and charms everyone. Zhenya asks everyone to forgive her for not writing, explaining that it is due to her poor penmanship and a violent aversion to the epistolary art. She is fine. The place where they are staying is a blessed land.

As to me, those who've seen me in Moscow say they don't recognize me here, so hale and hearty have I become. And I feel better every day. I cannot tell you how clever it was of me to leave Moscow. I'll stay here a bit longer, until I've finished a little book dear to my heart. I am waiting for you to send me some pictures of yourselves and will then send you some of me in exchange.

I must admit that I am looking around here for a house in the countryside for permanent occupation. I want to have a place where I could hide and write whenever I feel the need, for otherwise the tempo and the rhythm of our life is such that before I realize it, it will be too late, and I will never find time enough for meditation and the painstaking practice of my trade.

Odessa is full of tourists, mostly Americans who came from Odessa originally and who have returned here under the auspices of Intourist to visit their relatives after thirty or forty years' absence. I wish Rosa would follow their example. In the London Hotel the prices are incredible. Hospital Street, Market Street, and Court House Street are thronged with Jews going to see their American uncles. Shouts, exclamations, hugs—it's all quite easy to imagine. . . .

I too, of course, would like my uncles to pay me a visit.

IB.

Odessa, September 17, 1936

A delightful combination of aromas! Summer is back and so is *la joie de vivre.* Happy [Jewish] New Year. Yesterday I went with that fool Lyakhetsky (he's come back) to the synagogue, the one on Masterskaya Street (behind Kolontai Street). An atmosphere so familiar to me in my childhood—all those faces, the old women so *freilach* (merry), old men with thunderous voices. I am terribly glad I went. Of course, I couldn't do without the usual prayer, the special one, addressed to a different God and mostly about you.

Now, since Zhenya has acknowledged her guilt, you ought to write to her. You have her address. What is the weather like in Brussels?

I've been repeatedly invited to go to Yalta and if I do, I'll wire you.

Salut,
IB.

Odessa, September 22, 1936

Am leaving for Yalta on the twenty-sixth. My address—c/o Eisenstein, Film Studios, Yalta. I suppose there'll be time for me to get one or two letters from you there. The weather here is gorgeous now and in Yalta it must be even better. There is a flat calm and I am keeping my fingers crossed and hoping the sea won't be too rough on the twenty-sixth, for I don't get on too well when there's any pitching. I'll eat some grapes in Yalta, travel along the southern coast of the Crimea a bit and then come back to Odessa. My villa here is ready now. My address remains the same though. Write without fail. When I get back, I'll devote myself to all my relatives, knit woolies for them and pay their membership fees.

I think there is a letter from you for me at the post office. I got there late yesterday and they refused to let me have it. Allow for the fact that I am a very busy man, while you aren't busy at all, and write very often. Mailing expenses will be refunded to you. And on that note, accept the regards of your nephew and first cousin.

I.B.

[A postcard with a view of Chorgun Settlement, Crimea.]

Yalta, September 29, 1936

Have arrived here from Odessa. I feared rough sea but the crossing turned out to be a dream. It's summer weather here and everyone is bathing in the sea. I'll spend ten days or so here. I am staying in the former Hotel Russia. My balcony gives on the sea front and the sea is about ten steps away. They summoned me here to do things that I had already attended to in Odessa, so I can spend my time resting and doing some work for myself. I feel great and am only sorry that I can't share with you all the beauty surrounding me. It's the *haute saison* in the Crimea now, the grape season and so on. I don't know whether there'll be time for me to get a letter from you while I am here.

Thrive, and the best of luck to you,

I.

[A postcard: The sea coast at Massandra, Crimea.]

Yalta, October 4, 1936

I have been here since the 27th. We've had two gray days since then, but on all the others the sun has borne down on the vineyards and palm groves as if it had been hired especially to do so. Eisenstein and I aren't in any hurry to get on with our work, for we don't mind staying here a few days extra. I'll leave here around the 12th or the 14th, so you'd better address your letters to Odessa. I am in complete ignorance of what is going on in the world in general and with you in particular, because my letters are not forwarded to me. I hope you are all right. I write to you very seldom and curse myself for it, but I get so lazy in the sun and with lounging around in all these lovely gardens that letter writing somehow doesn't come off, although my thoughts are with you.

IB.

[Postcard with a view of Simferopol.]

Yalta, October 7, 1936

I live here like in the bosom of Christ. I eat grapes, swim in the sea on sunny days, work for my own pleasure. . . . We have snatched a limousine belonging to the film studios and drive around to places like Miskhor, Turzuf and Alupka. We also intend to go to Massandra and are trying to get a pass to the famous wine cellars, to taste the distinguished wines. Our group is leaving here on the 12th—all the others are going to Moscow, I to Odessa. I beseech the former God our Lord to bestow his blessings upon all of you, and I also wish that some of the Yalta climate could be transferred to Brussels, and some of the Brussels tobacco shops transferred to Yalta.

I.

[Postcard: Another view of Simferopol.]

Yalta, October 10, 1936

Am leaving for Odessa in three days or so. From tomorrow on, I will have finished working and will go driving around here—to Livadya, to Turzuf, to Alupka. Today we're having "that weather," as they say in Odessa. I hope I won't be seasick on my way back. I am feeling fine and, above all, my head is working incomparably better than it did in Moscow. I would also like to go to Tessile which is half way between Yalta and Sebastopol. It was there that I saw Gordy for the last time. My thoughts and my heart return to him constantly. I hope to find a pile of letters from you in Odessa.

I.

[Postcard: A third view of Simferopol.]

[Undated.]

Am still in the Crimea. The weather is bad and we are in no hurry to go anywhere. So both Eisenstein and I lounge around in our palatial rooms and add the last unhurried touches to the scenario. We have only one more day of shooting to do, but we have to wait for the sun. Yesterday I climbed up to Ai-Petri, the mountain grazing grounds. The view of Yalta and the sea from there is famous. I hope we'll move from here in two or three days. Write to Odessa.

I.

Yalta, October 19, 1936

Am catching the boat for Odessa the day after tomorrow in the morning. The weather has been miserable all week but today the sun is shining and the sea is flat, and I hope it will be the same the day after tomorrow. Eisenstein is leaving for Moscow this evening. The climate here is very healthy but I haven't been out too much and haven't seen enough of the countryside either. I mostly sit in my hotel room with its balcony overhanging the sea and watch the ships coming in and leaving. I'll write you a long letter from Odessa where I hope to find many letters from you.

Hugs and kisses, *mes amies,*

I.

Odessa, October 23, 1936

Arrived here last night. We got into a bit of rough weather just after we left Yalta but, from Sebastopol on, the sea was like cold soup in a tureen, which is much more suitable for a sea wolf like me, and I returned to Odessa feeling great. The sky here is overcast but it isn't cold. I've just come back from the post office where a terrifying heap of correspondence was waiting for me. This is only a preliminary note—as soon as I've put my affairs in order here I'll sit down and write you a proper letter. For the time being my policy will be the following—to work as much as possible and not to go back to Moscow before I have finished with what I am doing. I think I will follow Mera's advice and have a course of massage, for otherwise I'll lose my line. I'll also take warm sea baths. About the piece of land and the vegetable patch—I'll write to you after the 25th, for by that time I'll have complete information on the subject. And now, I trust you won't fail to carry out my directive to be in good health.

IB.

Odessa, October 25, 1936

Am writing this at the post office, so don't be too demanding as to the penmanship. Besides, I have been concocting literature from morning to night and now my brain is on leave of absence. As I wrote to you, I came back on the 22nd and here it's only on the evening of the 25th that I've come out of my room, so now I'm feeling completely cockeyed.

I believe I have stumbled on some workable ideas and that's why I am in such a hurry. Now I must earn the trips on assignment for myself, because I no longer have a benefactor to look after me. I don't want to go to Moscow until I've finished my work here and am terribly afraid the movie people will summon me for something. I am quite satisfied with the work I did with Eisenstein in Yalta and only hope the film studios won't find a reason to bother me about the business.*

I am longing to get myself a little house with a garden here in Odessa—which is the only place I can work in—far away from the outside world's hustle and bustle. I know that you are wishing for exactly the same thing, the difference being, alas, that it is infinitely easier for me to realize than for you. And so, before I go off on all sorts of travels and wanderings, I would like to make sure of such a cottage for myself. I think it will be a very useful thing to have, both for my work and my family. I have become convinced that Moscow is a place where one should go to have oneself a good time, to get the money that is coming to him and to sign contracts, while work should be done somewhere in the country, close to nature. And we have been doing just the contrary up till now. I will keep you well posted on my progress in the field. I wish you too would get yourselves a little garden and a car, for that would make your life both much healthier and more fun. In the meantime, aside from the Moscow apartment, I have a place outside Moscow—a huge, newly built villa. However, I dislike the fact that it is located in the writers' settlement and if I can, I will exchange it for something of comparable value elsewhere.

The weather in our native town is quite nippy now but it is clear and sunny. It is really remarkable though, how much I have become regenerated here, both physically and mentally. For my belly, there are uninterrupted symphonies here—flounder, mullet, halvah, bagels with poppy seeds—in brief, food fit for artists.

Well, I see that, despite the fact that I am writing from the post office, I have managed to scribble enough to exhaust the ink in my *stylo*. My love and kisses, until tomorrow or the day after, and, I hope, until our not-too-distant meeting.

I.

It's frightening to reread the rot I have written here.

* But Babel's hopes were frustrated. The film was not authorized and Eisenstein, who had undergone bitter criticism for his "ideologically inadequate" direction, was forced to defend himself in a painful speech of self-criticism before the personnel of *Mosfilm* on April 25, 1937. The responsibility also fell on Eisenstein's collaborators, including Babel.

[A postcard: The *Rischelevskaya* Monument in Odessa.]

Odessa, October 29, 1936

Here is our unfading *duc* who, as before, performs the labors that humans refuse to tackle—"Let's leave that to the *duc*," they say and, besides, he has to listen to all sorts of speeches. They still say, "It's just like talking to the *duc* . . ."

We are having a warm autumn and a warm rain is falling. My work is going along satisfactorily and I am leading a quiet existence: go to bed at eleven, get up at seven, eat "that" food, which is exactly like it was in my childhood at home, only a bit more luxurious maybe. I feel I am growing more intelligent as a result of that food. I'll write a longer letter tomorrow. I am swamped by urgent matters I must attend to now.

[In the MS this letter is datelined from Moscow, with a handwritten note stating it is really from Odessa.]

Moscow, October 30, 1936

Happy [Jewish] New Year. In a hundred years, a thousand well-wishers couldn't wish as many blessings on you as I heap upon your heads today. Looking back, I can say that for the first time in several years I have moved ahead from a literary dead stop and I hope that next year I will have some proof to vindicate that statement. Another virtue I have acquired in the course of 1936 is the habit, or rather the need, for painstaking, uninterrupted work. The drawback in my life is the dispersion of my family that, *entre nous*, causes me much greater pain than I care to show.

Will you go to Paris in January? How are Sima, Marysaia, Borya? And I repeat: *Une bonne et heureuse année* . . .

I.

Odessa, November 1, 1936

I haven't experienced such blissful peace and quiet for a long time, as now that, I dare say, I've taken myself completely out of active life. My room is so silent and tranquil that I want to do nothing else but write. And so, I am trying to catch up with the things I am behind in and to accumulate some reserves for the future, for if I have to go to Moscow, etc. They are already calling for me about some movie business but, for the time being, I am managing to put them off. I believe there's been a real improvement in my writing and I am trying not to lose my rhythm and pace.

Tomorrow, I'll write to Zhenya and will categorically protest against Natasha's trip to Switzerland, because the situation today is very precarious and it is outright dangerous to part with the child. I'm going to the post office tomorrow and am hoping to find a letter from you there. Tonight, I'll pay a visit to Anyuta and will write to you tomorrow giving you my impressions. The weather is overcast but warm. I go out for quiet strolls all alone and feel perfectly happy.

I.

Odessa, November 11, 1936

Got Mama's letter of October 31. I was very surprised at what Mama wrote about the parcels—that you have to pay duty for them in Brussels. Is it really so? Then, of course, my request for the cigars is withdrawn. I was assuming, and still do, that the customs duties only had to be paid once. If that is the case, would you please add to the cigars some insertable toothbrushes, Gibbs (I have the handle), and as many packs of La Croix cigarette paper as you can manage.

I am being summoned to Moscow on movie business but am trying to avoid going there and demanding that the film people come here. I am terribly reluctant to move from here as I have just warmed up in my writing. I think, though, that I'll have to go to Moscow for a couple of weeks anyway toward the end of December.

I am waiting to hear the details of Borya's life from you, how he is getting along in his studies, etc. As to my Odessa headquarters, I am in a dilemma: I have decided not to move too far out of the city—it is quiet enough even on De Ribas Street, God knows. On the other hand, the municipality is offering me any lot I care to pick. It wouldn't make any sense for me to take Kovalevsky's summer place which is far away, since it would have to be my winter quarters too. And so, from all I've seen, I like Near Mills and Gubayevka (near the Seventh Station) best. I hope that, in the next few days, I will be able to make a definite choice.

I share your worry about Natasha and I don't think Zhenya should pack her off to Switzerland—in the times we are living in, it is shockingly irresponsible. In general, the European state of "imbalance" weighs on me, if only for purely family reasons. For the rest, I seem to be having a good streak just now, or what they now call a "production upswing."

And with that—good-bye. I hope that the political storm will spare Brussels. What are your own feelings on the subject? I send you my love, my dear friends, and innumerable kisses.

Yours,

I.

[A postcard: The Pushkin Monument.]

Odessa, November 15, 1936

Yesterday I scribbled you a disconnected postcard at the post office. The wires from the film studios are getting more and more insistent. I must go. I'll do my best not to stay in Moscow longer than a month and to go on with my writing there—I feel I've just got warmed up here. I am very sad to be leaving but it can't be helped. I'll find out lots about what's going on in the world and get some information about the Paris fair. I suppose I'll be in Moscow on the 25th or 26th. For the remaining ten days here I'll only interrupt my work for the intake of food and for brief strolls. The more I work, the better it is.

Odessa, November 21, 1936

Am leaving for Moscow in five days or so. Looking back at my stay in Odessa I feel rather satisfied. Although I haven't reached the final draft of my composition, I've got sufficiently far ahead with it that even Moscow will be unlikely to prevent my going on with it. I feel I have stumbled on a new form and that makes me feel more self-confident and sure of myself than ever before.

Yesterday I went to see my former math teacher Poprushenko. It was very moving. The old man spent the evening playing the piano for me. I dined at Moshe's [illegible] surrounded by spiteful women from the Rakhmilovich clan. Tonya Gershun [illegible] was there and she reminisced about Mera in the most enthusiastic terms. I went to the Food Institute—its director is Lyonya Cherkes —and met Natanson's son there, a young doctor with a rather Levantine face. *Voilà.* . . .

Odessa, November 24, 1936

Winter is here. Yesterday there was a heavy snowfall and today icicles are hanging from the windowsills. In a way, it is quite pleasant, for a change. Am leaving for Moscow on the 27th. Nowadays, the express train takes only twenty-six hours to get there: it leaves at two in the afternoon and gets in on the next day toward evening.

This is the third day now that I haven't worked. I have finished my rough draft and now I must stop for a while, busy myself with something else, catch my breath and, then, get back to it. I reckon to whip it into shape for publication in two or three months.

I have been spending my rest period on reading the newspapers and catching up with the news. Ah, what threatening clouds on the horizon! Even little Belgium is in turmoil. Please write to me more often. How do you feel? How is Grisha's work? Things are not too quiet in France either. It's all very bad. The only hope is that the instinct of self-preservation will triumph in the end.

I.

Moscow, December 7, 1936

I am once again in Moscow's iron grip but this time I am behaving more intelligently. I am not squandering my energy and am trying to stick to my Odessa work schedule. Of course, as soon as I arrived I caught a head cold but I got rid of it thanks to a foreign drug (something like Albin Leo—is there such a thing?). I got rid of it in a single day. It is still fall weather here and on the Constitution Day [the celebration of the November, 1936, adoption of the constitution—Tr.—MacA.] we had fog and drizzle. I have a lot of work to do, too much in fact, because now, on top of my writing, there are the movies. My screenplay for Eisenstein is complete and now I have to do one for Alexandrov* (the director of the films *Gay Children* and *Circus*). Every minute of my time is assigned to some task and I have to act like a Parisian business-man now and invite business acquaintances of mind to dinner every day, for I can't find any other time to see them.

I hope my book will be published next spring. Slowly but surely it is moving toward completion. In my opinion, it is quite interest-ing. I am sending you just a card because I must go out of town on business. But soon I'll get into the Moscow mode of life and then I'll write often. I expect the same of you. Have sent Anyuta's and Sonya's "pensions" to them.

I.

---

* Grigori Vasilevich Alexandrov, film director, was assistant to and later the collaborator of Eisenstein.

Moscow, December 12, 1936

My dear relatives,

I have no time to write, no time even to scribble a postcard. Formerly, I did one thing at a time and it was either for my soul or for profit, and I used to manage, but now I have to do both simultaneously. I must finish one more screenplay for Alexandrov, the director of *Gay Children* and *Circus*; it is difficult work and, I must admit, rather unwelcome. Now that I want to write (which, as we all know, doesn't happen very often) I am forced to busy myself with something else. I am trying to combine both things but then I really have to give up letter-writing, social life and reading, not only books but even newspapers. My most hectic month will be December. After that, things will ease up a bit.

Yesterday I had a free evening and spent it with Gorky's family. We sat in his rooms and recalled the past, feeling both easy and sad at the same time. Late last night my constant and unchanging companion, Lifshit, came back from his vacation which he had spent in Batum.

We're having a wonderful winter in Moscow—moderately cold,

clear, windless days, so I can breathe here just as well as in Odessa. I want to ask Mera for a favor: she must complete her dental treatment whatever it may cost. Although it's true that I had my teeth attended to for free at the Kremlin Hospital, I am very pleased now that I sat it out to the end and I have quite forgotten what it is like to have toothache. I feel fine and, above all, am pleased with the fact that my working capacity is increasing rather than diminishing. My apartment is warm, quiet and spacious, logs crackle in the fireplaces, from my window I can see the carved outlines of the snow-covered trees. Ah, if only my brain keeps working well.

I have spoken to Katya on the telephone many times, although I haven't seen her yet, being so busy. She sounds quite cheerful. I have sent fifty rubles to Sonya and a hundred to Anyuta.

Each day I open my newspaper with apprehension. There are heavy stormclouds on the political horizon and, besides general, civic worries, I have people whose destiny worries me directly.

I'll try to get you on the phone either tomorrow or the day after. I wish you (1) health, (2) quiet, (3) an income double the minimum wage and (4) an automobile.

IB.

Moscow, December 18, 1936

As usual I write you little, in bits and pieces and sporadically, but I have a good excuse: I created a scandal with the movie people. I want to break my contract, even if that will put them in a difficult situation. I got such a taste for "pure art" in Odessa that now I can't concern myself with other things. I must finish the book. I can see that there are going to be tremendous troubles with the movie company in the next few days, but I will stand fast. If I really succeed in getting free of my commitments to the second film (the first with Eisenstein is finished) I'll be a happy man.

May the ex-god help me.

I sign myself your grandpa,

I.

Moscow, December 22, 1936

Just now I received a letter from Mera—yesterday one from Zhenya. My insane Swede (actually he's been cured for a long time) visited her in Paris on his way from Stockholm to Barcelona. He is on his way—as one would expect—to the International Brigade. He is to fight the fascists and I am sure will be a good soldier. I wish him all the best. He writes about Natasha—he's crazy about her. I envy Mera's going to Paris. Are you going to take the trip in January?

Here I've had all sorts of professional bothers. According to my recent contract with the movie company, I was supposed to get busy with scripts immediately after my arrival. I realize now that what before seemed to me a trifling piece of work became impossible as soon as I found myself in something approaching writing form. It was too unbearable to tear myself away from my own work. So I sent over a statement breaking my contract; there was, as Zoshchenko would say, screaming and screeching, but yesterday all ended happily and I am a blessed and fairly free man.

I solemnly reprimand mother for her conduct, and hope she will make amends. As for Mera, by my new teeth, now capable of cracking nuts, I advise her to follow my example.

I.

1 9 3 7

So the telephone call didn't come off too well. The reception was awful—apparently it depends on all sorts of conditions. I hope we'll be luckier next time. I'll ring again very soon.

I am enjoying my freedom from the movies and am doing my own writing. My preliminary work will soon be complete and then I'll put it away for a while in order to write the final draft with a clear head. This all shows that the year that has just begun is an important one for me.

Mera, write to me, please, and tell me what your dental treatment consists of and whether you have really attended seriously to the business. I am sorry you aren't going to Paris, although what you all really need now is not Paris but the South—we all come to life in the sunshine. But where could you go now? I suppose Switzerland would really be the best place. Do you have any possibility of going in that direction, though? For your information, the temperature here was just 32 degrees yesterday and the day before, if it was below freezing, it was only slightly so and the weather was very pleasant. . . .

I.

[A postcard.]

Yesterday the phone rang—Fraenkel. Sender Fraenkel from Estonia, my schoolmate whom I've only seen once since graduation in Saratov. And now we meet. He is a respectable businessman in

what used to be Revel, a very pleasant petit bourgeois with a ro-
tund little belly. His brothers are dispersed throughout the European capitals. His business is quite good. Lifshits and I went to
his hotel and tomorrow we are giving a big dinner party in his
honor. It was a strange meeting after twenty years.

What's new with you? When you get yourself a car you'll see
that it will give you a lot of headaches but you won't have much
time to be bored.

I.

*Moscow, February 27, 1937**

I won't write a long letter now, because I intend to leave for the
villa where Gorky used to live, to stay with his family there. I'll
rest a bit amidst the snows there. It is very cold here but calm and
sunny. Yesterday, Zhenya left for the Alps. She went to some place
near Grenoble. She promises that upon her return she'll have a
telephone installed in her house. She had given me all sorts of
errands to do and I am doing them with great joy—it's mostly
books for Natasha and all sorts of knickknacks.

Iza has stayed in Plessis [Robinson] to keep the old woman
company. A news item: Natasha had a tooth pulled and, according
to Zhenya, behaved heroically. In general, Natasha's triumphal
procession over human hearts continues.

I have sent you Katayev's† Odessa story *Lonely White Sail*. I'm
sure you'll enjoy it. One of these days I'll send you a batch of the
most interesting books available here.

I hope to be talking to you tomorrow.

I.

* This letter is dated May 27 in MS., January 27 in the Italian translation,
Racconti proibiti e lettere intime. February 27 seems more likely than either,
since it is winter, which rules out May, and since he is just leaving for Gorky's
house, which rules out January. See the next letter, from Gorky's house, which
is dated March 5.

† Valentin Petrovich Katayev, born in 1897, is the author of the novels:
Lonely White Sail, the action of which takes place in the Odessa of 1905;
I am the Son of the Working People; and *Time, Forward!* These books were

Uspenskoye, March 5, 1937

I have been living in the late Gorky's house just outside Moscow for five days now. The weather is gorgeous—lots of snow and sun. The house is empty but from time to time I get the impression that the shade of its departed master is lurking around. I intend to go over to Molodenovo. Again and again it is demonstrated to me that I cannot work if I live in Moscow. I have definitely reserved the lot on the seashore near Odessa between the Great Fountain and the Kovalevsky Summer House. Building will start in the spring. I have escaped from the city because I must do some urgent work. I'll call you on the telephone the very first day I get back to Moscow. There is havoc in our apartment still and so, for the time being, write to Katya's address.

Sima came to Moscow for a few hours and then rushed off to Leningrad. She'll be back in Moscow on the 13th or 14th and I'll see her then. A Dutchman with whom I spoke on the phone once when I was in Brussels came to see me; he promised to look you up when he's in Brussels. I'll try to get the books Mera asked me for when I'm in Moscow. According to my calculations, Zhenya must have returned to Paris—with Natasha I hope.

Now, the main thing: how can we get Mama on her feet again after her illness? Dose she need special care and a diet? Perhaps it would be best to send her off somewhere?

I am very worried about the reports of the increasing cost of living in Paris. I wonder how Zhenya is managing there. I hope this sad trend doesn't spread to Belgium as well.

Write more often. My head and heart are only just beginning to recover after Moscow—soon I will be in form and will then write to you more regularly.

I kiss you all delicately,

I.

---

widely read throughout the Soviet Union and films of the same name have been based on them.

Moscow, March 11, 1937

Just returned from the countryside and am going back there again tomorrow. We are having spring weather, the snow is melting and soon the streams will be running. I am up to my neck in business. Am meeting Katya this evening. *L'inénarrable* Iosif was here; he spent the few days of his stay in uninterrupted quarrels with his family and then left for Odessa.

Then, I must see Sima who is coming from Leningrad. That, actually, is what I have come here for.

I have nothing else to report except, perhaps, the fact that I have started making a neat copy of the fruits of my many years of meditation—as usual, I find that instead of weighty volumes I have less than a sparrow's beak to show and that's sure to cause a great outcry.

I am enjoying my life in the country house tremendously: I've grown accustomed to the uncanny atmosphere and to the absence of the master. . . . The mystical aspect of the matter is that twenty years ago I made my start in his house, and now, in another house of his, with the master gone, I must continue. Physically, I feel great but since there's nothing to distract me from my work in the country, I get very tired by evening. I haven't managed to get to Molodenovo yet, but spent a whole day at the stud farm.

Will write again tomorrow before leaving.

Above all, be well,

I.

Moscow, March 28, 1937

Happy holidays! Due to Katya's improvidence, I have no matzos and so would you please eat my share for me.

Our violinists are in Brussels now and, as might be expected, there are four boys and girls from Odessa among them, all of them

Stolyarsky's pupils and outstanding virtuosos. I hope they'll give a concert and you will have an opportunity to hear them.

I have nothing new to report—still plugging on. I would have liked very much to go down to Odessa and to find some reliable man to whom to entrust the construction of my house, but it looks as though I'll have to spend the whole month of April in Moscow, or rather, just outside Moscow.

Good-bye. Have you thought over what I wrote to you about the South? I think that it would help you to rid yourselves of a considerable number of complaints.

Salut,

I.

I sent a small sum to Sonya today.

Moscow, April 13, 1937

My worthy Mendelevich,

I was very surprised at what you said yesterday about letters. I write at least once—or rather twice—a week. So what could have happened to the letters? Ask your concierge—or perhaps you don't have one? Could the letters have got lost while you were in Ostend?

Yesterday I forgot to ask you whether our Odessa boys, Stolyarsky's pupils, performed in public in Brussels and whether you went to hear them. Of the five laureates, four are Pyotr Salomonovich's [Stolyarsky's] pupils. He himself is coming to Moscow with something like forty-six of his pupils—almost a whole orchestra—they are to perform in the Conservatory and I must go without fail.

I am writing to Zhenya at the same time. Haven't had any news from her in the past ten or fifteen days. I am very curious to know whether Sima sent you some of the things or whether she contented herself with a platonic greeting. As to Baya, I believe I told you everything there was to tell yesterday. With respect to diseases, our Mama is in her second childhood and I am keeping my fingers crossed for fear she should catch the measles, mumps or whooping cough now.

I.

Uspenskoye, April 26, 1937

Just got the letter forwarded to me by Lyakhetsky. Am very happy to hear that Borya and Sima are well. I wish you were basking in the warm sunshine instead of being soaked under the rain. We are having a wonderful spring (and today, although there is no sun, it's very warm). Indeed, the spring is so lovely that I lack the strength of will to move to town. I am immersed in strenuous, albeit pleasurable, labors here.

In Moscow now there's a parade of young talent. The day before yesterday Stolyarsky's school performed with great success. He still has many an Oistrakh or Gillels up his sleeve. Did you hear the other three violinists play? Did Mama go to the concert? Why, they are the most genuine chips off the Odessa block.

Have sent a hundred rubles to Anyuta and, by May first, will send some money to Sonya too. It seems that everything's all right now with that old fool Iosif's job and so he is staying in Moscow. I got a letter from Zhenya; it contains much the same as yours. Am addressing a letter to Natasha at her "spa," *sacrebleu*, how the time goes!

I shall insist that Zhenya absolutely must work at the Exhibition. I don't dare to give you advice from a distance concerning your moving to Paris. Do whatever you think is best for you and Mama and just keep in mind what a beneficent effect sunshine has upon us all.

Please keep a sharp lookout for an occasion to send me a few cigars and other blessings of a tobaccoey nature with someone. I am sure somebody must be about to come over here. If you hear of someone, let me know and I will send you an exact order.

I swear and promise to send you the books from Moscow. I am working so hard and am so busy that it seems impossible for me to get out to a bookstore in time, for the good books here sell out immediately and after that they are very hard to get.

I must ask you most insistently to put Mama on her feet and get her into the physical shape of a grenadier guard so that she can stroll without difficulty all over the Paris Exhibition.

And with that, I remain your worshipful nephew,

I.

Moscow, May 1, 1937

Have come to town for the holidays. This day is so bright and pleasant in Moscow that I didn't feel like staying in the country. The lovely spring here has reached its peak. Tomorrow, large and very beautiful diesel boats will arrive in Moscow directly from the Volga by the new canal. I'll go to meet them along with the city's millions.

I still have no set plans and don't know whether I'll go to Odessa or to Enta. I am feeling rather resigned about them—the plans— now; my life has just worked out in such a way that I'm completely swallowed up by my work, and I suppose it's best that way, after all. I'll find out whether Stolyarsky is here and if he hasn't left yet, I'll go and see him. How are things with the sunshine over there? Do you bask in the sun sometimes. I demand of Mama that she regain her normal state and go to Paris for the Exhibition. And so I wish hot weather upon you and fire in your hearts.

I.

Moscow, May 17, 1937

Have spent a few days in town attending the stormy literary meetings, the gravity of which you know from the newspapers. Their beneficent effect upon the future is beyond doubt but in the meantime it keeps breaking one's writing rhythm. Today, I am going back home to the countryside. As I grow older, my thirst for work increases.

Am very sad that there are no letters from you. I would have been so happy if, instead of sitting in your sour, gray Brussels, you were dancing on green lawns or were engaged in a game of water polo with Mama.

Don't be lazy, write more often.

I.

Moscow, July 10, 1937

Am off to Kashira until the 19th. Will write more from there. Haven't heard a thing from you and just hope that everything's *all right* [English in the original.—Tr.—MacA.] with you. I've had a letter from Zhenya. She says she intends to go and spend a month with you. I am delighted about it. She praises Natasha no end and says the girl has never looked so well. I hope you'll have a good month together.

Zhenya worked for a month in our pavilion at the Exhibition but, alas, she got overtired very quickly and went off on a trip. That rather saddens me because she had a good opportunity there to strengthen her position among the Soviet colony and she failed to take full advantage of it.

Her letter came from somewhere in the Alps where, without wasting any time, she went to rest, after which she intends to go to Paris for a short while and from there, will go to join you. I am very sorry she didn't stay and work at the Exhibition.

Please don't congratulate me on my birthdays any more and I'll return you the favor and abstain from congratulating Mera, although deep down in my heart I'll call all the blessings of heaven and earth down upon her.

I sent off Sonya's allowance yesterday.

Your loving,

I.

Moscow, July 30, 1937

My dear, silent relatives,

Just now, when letters should be bouncing off you, you've filled your mouths with water. Is it possible that Zhenya didn't come? She wrote that she would be in Brussels as early as the 17th. I feel as if I'm sitting on hot coals here. Please write to me quickly.

I have no particular news to report and am grateful to the former Creator for that. Katya has left for Odessa, although the doctors insisted that she should go to one of the Caucasian resorts.

A former classmate, Borya Shorman—one of the triad Cherkes-Shorman-Babel—came to stay with me here. He has turned into a very meek, limping, bookkeeping creature.

According to my calculations, Sima should now be either in Leningrad or in Moscow but I haven't heard a word from her.

I am comparatively poor now since I have discarded all extraneous work, reserving myself exclusively for pure literature. I reckon that this period of poverty will come to an end in a couple of months and then there won't be any need for me to take on assignments from outside. I have written a few new stories and I will send them to you one by one as they are published. As before, I'm hoping I'll be able to go to Odessa toward the end of August. Physically, this year, I've been feeling fine, a thing I would like to hear from you too.

And so, where are my progeny and her mother? I don't suppose you'd be too surprised if I told you that I was missing you all an awful lot.

Our weather has one constant element—rain. But today is an exceptional day, my day off, and it isn't raining.

How does the balance sheet of your *villégiature* stand? How many pounds have you gained?

Have nothing else to write and so I send you my love,

I.

Moscow, August 26, 1937

Very worthy and dear three generations, namely, the senior, the intermediary and the young,

Returned today from ancient Kashira where, besides plentiful sour apples and nonstop rain for ten days, I didn't see anything good.

But then, I wrote. Nowadays that unnatural occupation brings me more consolation than it used to because it is drawing nearer to publication, that is, it is becoming a tangible proposition, whereas before I kept losing my way in a forest of three pine trees. I am sending you an issue of the magazine *Krasnaya Nov* [*Red Novelties*] that contains a mediocre little story of mine.* My future contributions will be better.

Natasha's pictures lit up the gray, overcast day for me today. She is now quite a middle-aged girl and looks very sweet. And the way I feel nowadays, it seems that if she aged another tiny bit more, we would soon wind up by being the same age. Then I'd have a pal to play with at last, for as things stand now, wherever I look, I find only people either much smarter or much stupider than me and it is quite impossible to find someone on my own level. Please, have your picture taken more often because those pieces of cardboard give me tremendous joy. I only wish I could have completed our family group personally.

Mama's picture fascinates me too. I think I ought to send it to *Ce Soir* which has a game called *Jeu de ressemblance*, for that would enable some handsome, middle-aged Frenchwoman to win 250 francs because of her resemblance to Mama. The only trouble, *mes enfants*, is that the passport has expired and I don't quite understand where it should be sent to be renewed—to Moscow or to Paris, and whether I can't do something to speed up its extension.

Today I'll try to get through to you on the phone. If I can't, I'll give it another try tomorrow and if I fail again, I'll write.

I have just returned from Kashira and am sort of standing at a crossroads. Still, I think I'll decide it this way: I'll attend to my material business here for some time in advance and then move toward Odessa in pursuit of the sun and inspiration, for that is where my inspiration seems to live. And then I have to see to the building of my house for they sent me notification that they had allotted me the last and also the best lot on the seashore, and all this time I haven't taken advantage of it. I'll write about all these things in a few days when everything is set.

So, perhaps until this evening, when I hope to hear your voices, My love and kisses to every one of you,

I.

* "The Kiss" is Babel's last story to be published in the Soviet Union. It appeared in the July, 1937, issue of *Krasnaya Nov*.

Moscow, September 6, 1937

In the first place, allow me to inform you that today is Rosh Hashanah and also to congratulate you on this new, many-thousand-year-old Jewish year.

On Yom Kippur, I'll go to the synagogue.

In the second place—I still haven't recovered from the excitement that gripped me when I heard Natasha's and Zhenya's voices. I hope that Zhenya will have a phone installed in her house now. Natasha's accent is very amusing and moving. Write to me about her in more detail.

In the third place—I am very pleased with the news about Grisha's happiness. When did the wedding take place? To what tribe and clan does that Belgian wife belong? In brief, I want to know everything.

Now about Mama. I didn't get a very accurate idea about her passport from our phone conversation. Will it be very difficult? Could they refuse? Should I go to the Ministry of Foreign Affairs here? Please write to me about it all.

As to me—nothing new, as before. Still just as eager to work. I ought to be going to Odessa, to the sunshine, for here autumn has arrived and the rain is pouring down. But I am afraid to scare off my eagerness to write. And so I'll decide in a couple of weeks or so.

Did Mera hear Katya's moans on the phone? Looking at it from the side, I felt it was rather funny.

I.

[Date of this letter not very clear in MS.]

Moscow, October 11, 1937

My venerable and nervous Mama,

What's the matter and why all this fuss? I write letters to you like a hired hand and I assume that the interruption in my letters is due to the fact that they have discontinued the airmail, starting October 3, and the letters that were sent had to go by the usual, i.e., slow, channels.

I am fine except for an ever-growing longing for the sun. I am trying to arrange my business so that it will allow me to go South.

In this part of the country, the sky is already breathing autumn and the older I get the more I am convinced that bad weather is not a thing a man ought to get resigned to.

For the rest, my hard-working routine continues without any other interests.

In my last letters, I asked you many questions and I am still waiting for you to answer them. I got a letter from Zhenya—*tout va bien.*

Your postmaster,

I.

Moscow, October 14, 1937

It has tried to snow several times in the last three days. It's cold and the sky is the color of lead. And then, I keep getting insistent invitations from the Kiev Film Studios to go there. If I manage to wind up my business in Moscow in a few days, I may go and bask in the sun there.

I am much saddened by Couturier's death.* I felt very friendly toward that man. I remember the meals he cooked himself, our trips to Villejuif, our cheerful talks over a glass of red wine. My heart feels very heavy—he died too soon.

Everything else is fine and unchanged, and I hope that it is the same with you.

Salut,

I.

* Paul Vaillant Couturier, writer and Communist mayor of Villejuif, a workers' suburb of Paris. On June 30, 1935, Babel, together with other Soviet delegates to the International Congress in Defense of Culture and Peace, attended the inauguration ceremonies of the boulevard named in honor of Maxim Gorky in Villejuif.

Kiev, November 7, 1937

The primeval sun rose near . . . [illegible] and since then, it has only set at night. . . . Life should be one long holiday here —the weather is amazing and one is simply reluctant to go indoors.

I am staying in Lipki, in the excellent apartment of Dovzhenko, the director.* Lipki, which was always a beautiful district, is incomparably more beautiful now with its pretty, new-style houses, amazingly laid-out parks full of statues and, down below, the fragrant valley of the Dnieper. I spent all last evening walking around the illuminated city and greatly enjoyed myself . . .

Write to me c/o General Delivery, Kiev. Since I have more time to myself here, I will write to you more regularly.

Your fan,

I.

* Alexander Petrovich Dovzhenko (1894-1956), born in the Ukraine, was a film scenarist and, from 1926, a film director.

Kiev, November 12, 1937

I have started working for the film studios here. The work isn't too difficult but there's lots of it and so I suppose I'll have to sit in Kiev for quite a while. Write to me, as indicated above, c/o General Delivery.

I am living in unbelievable comfort. The apartment is sparkling clean, the cook is excellent, etc. However, I'm not in top peak mental form just now. I'm rather over-tired and in need of a breather.

The weather is very mild and damp. I do hope I get news of you very soon, for no sooner do I leave Moscow than I feel completely cut off from you.

I'll write more often for there are far fewer things to distract me here.

I.

Kiev, November 16, 1937

There has been a heavy snowfall. Everything is white. In front of my window a tree stands weighed down by the first snow.

I am leading a peaceful existence in a quiet, warm apartment with a good library. The screenplay for the novel *How the Steel Was Tempered,** is progressing satisfactorily, although it is taking me away from my true work. However, if it is successful, it will certainly confer many advantages upon me.

It's not definite yet where I'll go from here, to Moscow or to Odessa. The only thing that bothers me each time I get farther away from Moscow is the feeling that it takes me even farther away from you—your letters don't reach me, I can't call you on the phone and I worry about you even more than usual.

Write to the same address: General Delivery, Central Post Office.

Will that meeting of yours with those from Paris take place? I sure wish it would.

Lots of love and kisses,

I.

---

* *How the Steel Was Tempered* was a novel by Nikolai Alexeyevich Ostrovsky (1904-1936). Ostrovsky joined Budyonny's cavalry in 1920, as did Babel, and was severely wounded during the campaign. The hero of the novel, Pavel Korchagin, remains the prototype of the young Communist of the period. The book went into more than two hundred printings in the Soviet Union and was widely translated abroad.

[A postcard.]

Kiev, November 26, 1937

The work on which I am engaged here is presenting great difficulties. We are making a film script of Ostrovsky's novel *How the Steel Was Tempered*, a chronologically presented, biographical, plotless novel which is not too suitable for the screen. I suppose that in about a week I will know how much time will be allowed for the completion of this work. And so my address will remain the same until then: General Delivery, Central Post Office, Kiev. I am very depressed because there aren't any letters from you.

Luckily, my health and my working capacity are at a fine pitch.

I.

Kiev, November 26, 1937

The blissful times when I could hear your voices in the Moscow phone receiver are gone. . . .

I am living here in something that might sound like a sanatorium, isolated from the rest of the world, in clean, quiet privacy; going out for walks and being fed a well-balanced diet of food and work throughout the whole day and part of the night.

According to my agreement, I must deliver my screenplay by December third and so I must squeeze all I can out of myself, especially since there are so many people waiting for me to deliver my stuff—the directors, the actors, the cameramen, the whole studio . . .

The weather is fine and the people around here talk that half-Russian, half-Ukrainian dialect that is so dear to my heart. Somehow, my usual worries have abated, except for one—my concern for you and for those in [Plessis] Robinson, which never eases up.

I must be off to the post office now. Maybe there'll be something from you for me today.

I.

Kiev, November 27, 1937

When I went to the post office yesterday to mail my letter to you, I found the first letter from you to reach me in Kiev. One piece of news contained in it has got me rather worried, namely, that Natasha is doing well at school. Sinful soul that I am, I have a weakness for the so-called boobies, those who dwell at the bottom of the class. True, of course, things may have changed now and I am quite wrong.

I would be terribly happy if you could all spend your vacations together and I am writing a letter to that effect to Zhenya today (no letters from her for quite some time). How is Sima? I haven't heard a thing about her.

After reading Mera's letter in which she says her health is quite satisfactory, I feel as if I had won two hundred thousand in the National Lottery and am now full of energy and a feeling of security. It would seem good news is good for one. I demand categorically that you should not be sick and should have as pleasant a time as possible.

Here, everything's fine. I am working at full steam but then, I am surrounded by peace and quiet.

I.

Kiev, December 1, 1937

Dear Mater,

Yesterday, I received your letter with your picture. Your eyes have their old luster, a fact that gladdened my heart and, to be even with you, I'll send you a picture of mine in which I look my most handsome. I liked your photo so much that I've given it to be blown up and, as an exception to my rule, I'll exhibit it in my room, in which, up till now, only one single picture has hung: a horse and rider. I suppose it's high time for me to become sentimental.

Now I can tell you definitely that my Kiev work will be completed within ten to fourteen days. I came here in a quite exhausted state but I was able to muster my energy and cope with a difficult assignment quite rapidly.

As soon as my further itinerary—whether to Moscow or Odessa —is determined, I'll let you know. I am really feeling very well indeed now, for comfort, quiet and the fact that there's no one to pester me do count for quite a lot.

Yesterday I went for a walk in Lipki, which overlooks the Dnieper, and was quite reluctant to go back home, the air was so fresh, pure and crystalline. . . .

It would be so nice if our Parisians went to spend the holidays with you.

Your hard-working,

I.

Kiev, December 7, 1937

Today, I've been in Kiev for a month.

In all that time I've had one letter from you and none from Zhenya. Now, since I am fully afflicted with that family trait of "worrying," I cannot stay still in one place. It is true that I haven't been to the post office for two days: the day before yesterday because I was busy until night at the film studios and yesterday because of the sheet-ice which made it quite out of the question to try and crawl down from the Lipki heights.

I have another week or so of work here and then there is a job in Odessa, although it isn't decided yet whether I'll go there or not.

I am still working under very peaceful and favorable conditions and my "customers" seem to be quite satisfied with me.

Since you, on the other hand, have nothing to do with yourselves, why on earth don't you go on a letter-writing binge?

I.

Kiev, December 10, 1937

Got a letter from Zhenya. Not gay. Lyova's business operations are unsuccessful and this seems to be what is preventing Zhenya and Natasha from going to see you in Brussels. It is quite depressing. Zhenya writes about Natasha's studies. No need to wake her up in the morning and no need to prod her—looks as if she has taken after our side of the family. I read that with a feeling of mixed joy and sadness which I am sure you will understand. I sent them a letter in an attempt to cheer them up, but writing it, I felt how helpless I was to do anything for them at this distance. All I can do is hope that Lyova will somehow recover after his disasters whatever they are and, materially, their life will again be what it used to be.

Here, everything is just as before. I suppose I'll be through with my work here by the 15th, except perhaps for some quite insignificant odds and ends. Although I am working terribly hard, I feel fine—I suppose life must require discipline and a certain diet of work.

Remember to write more often,

I.

Kiev, December 14, 1937

I have reached the last phase of my work and have been walking around for three days, as snappy and snarly as a dog—I can't manage the last scenes. (It isn't really any fault of mine but rather the unsuitability of the novel for the screen.) I am so furious, because, if it wasn't for that, instead of boring Kiev, I could perhaps have taken a little trip to Odessa and been by the sea—true, the winter sea, the sea nevertheless.

Received a thank-you letter from Sonya which I found so funny that I decided to send it on to you. Sklyar [Sonya's husband] is past seventy-eight now but, according to Sonya, he keeps grumbling about not having enough work to do when he is so full of energy and zeal. There's a man to emulate.

Write often and don't forget your hard-working,

I.

Kiev, December 27, 1937

It looks as if I'll have to meet the New Year here in Kiev. I send you my most ardent New Year's wishes. I don't suppose I have to spell out what my wishes are—you already know, as it is the cherished longings of my heart.

As to my work here, you may assume that in a week or so it will be completed for all practical purposes, although I still don't know where I am going from here—to Moscow or to Odessa. For the moment it looks as though I'll have to leave urgently for Moscow, but things could change within a week.

For three days now, I have been writing to you "one-sidedly" because, owing to a lack of time, I haven't been to the post office in all that time.

Phoned to Leningrad at nine this morning. I had a message for Lyusya, but she had gone out to work and I spoke to Volodya. He sounded cheerful and told me that he felt fine. I suppose she'll call me up.

I.

1 9 3 8

Kiev, January 3, 1938

The situation is unchanged, if I chose to disregard the fact that my Moscow publishers, the studios and other creditors, furious at my protracted absence, are threatening me with frightful vengeance. However, I have decided, and I believe correctly, not to move from here until I have completed the important assemblage work for which I am responsible. Its completion will enable me to rest for a while and have a bit of time to myself.

So I met the New Year laboring in an austere environment and with a firm resolution to work hard in the coming year and, if possible, with tangible results.

Quite by accident, I have met my best school-friend, Mirosha Berkov, here. He is still the same warm and comforting person he used to be. He has worked in a bank for twenty years, is married to a friend of Mera's—Kadya Fran. We spent a sentimental evening devoted to reminiscences of Odessa and the dispatching of prayers to the former God that he may send you well-being, health, money and all sorts of achievements.

I haven't had any letters from you for a long time. Probably you are under the impression that I have moved away from here already. But I haven't.

Yours,
I.B.

Kiev, January 9, 1938

The mother of Russia's cities must take herself for Vologda at the least—it is not less than five below, the snow is deep, skates cut the ice noisily, people have donned their skis, and all the other winter joys are at hand.

I am trudging along through the drifts of my jigsaw-like assignment and slowly but surely am moving toward its completion. I think I'll be through by the 20th but am not yet sure whether I'll have to take the screenplay to Moscow for approval myself or whether I'll be able to slip off to Odessa for a few days, to that refuge of all sufferers—the London Hotel. I would like to see my racy aunts.

I feel very, very well—knock on wood—and don't even get tired, although I am working like an inmate of a forced labor camp. The only thing that worries me is my Parisians, and their life worries me more than I can say. I don't know how bad Lyova's business is or how the old woman is over there. I would be so happy if you managed to get Zhenya and Natasha over to you, to distract them a little bit, for my heart tells me that they are going through a sad period just now. Please keep writing to the Kiev address. Your letters will be forwarded to me.

Well, see to it that you remain in good health.

I.

Kiev, January 21, 1938

Most worthy Mamachen,

At long last, I have something new for you: during the entire day of the 18th I was on the verge of illness: my throat was sore, I was slightly feverish. But then I took the necessary steps (consisting mostly of the lavish use of lemon), cutting the evil at the root, and the danger was past.

We are having weather here, my good friends, that makes things look like the illustrations to fairy tales with winter settings: snow, mellow light, stars peeking through the pines—"real lovely" as my Moscow landlady would say.

I've received a letter from Zhenya in which she informs me that Noël was celebrated nicely and that, along with a staggering doll, Natasha received an album for her stamp collection, since she's turned out to be an ardent philatelist. Ah, good Lord, what an elderly daughter I have! Well, anyhow, it sounds as if everything's all right with them.

In conclusion, you can see yourselves that my anchor has got stuck solidly in the riverbed of the Dnieper, so that I am afraid to give you a date for my departure, although I know that my stay here is coming to an end.

Keep writing to the same address,

I.B.

Kiev, January 26, 1938

My worthiest ones,

I got a New Year's card from Natasha too and in it she listed all the presents she got for Noël, namely, a doll, an album for her stamp collection and a box of paints. She had presents from everyone except her Papa. According to Zhenya's letters, Natasha is a good and intelligent little girl—but I always try to avoid thinking about these things, because a great deal of bitterness always gets mixed with such thoughts.

Zhenya's recent letters sound more cheerful and lead me to believe that her financial affairs are in a better state.

My work is almost finished and it has met with everyone's approval so far, except for one man's—mine. I have taken back a few scenes to do some additional work on them and will sit over them for another week or so.

I have really had my fill of Kiev, but such a lovely, mild winter could never have been had in Moscow.

You misunderstood what I wrote to you about debts. I had in mind moral creditors who are ranting and raving because, for the sake of a scenario, I have stopped my literary work. That was what I meant by debts. As to money, I am sorry to say it has very low priority with me.

My sore throat has vanished without a trace and all my energy is now directed toward changing my environment and getting down to some other work, for I have been sitting here for too long and am becoming stale.

Well, on that note, good-bye, and look after your health.

I.

Kiev, February 9, 1938

Am still frozen in the same position.

What a hellishly hard job I've got to do! According to people's reactions, everything's fine, but if the directors try to mess with it, everything will collapse. Making a sober appraisal of the situation, I can see that I won't get to Moscow before February 20th. Nevertheless, when you answer this letter, write to Katya's address.

I am feeling fine. The blood of my ancestors is more and more obvious in me and I can easily picture myself standing behind the counter of a shop, selling things for eighteen hours a day.

Please don't indulge in any unnecessary excesses: don't consume too much vodka, don't paint the town red and try to be in the shape of a prize fighter on the eve of a fight.

I.

Kiev, February 15, 1938

There's nothing eternal under the sun. . . .

I've finished that hellish job and I cannot imagine anything more difficult than it was (of course, in that particular field). The fruit of my labors is now being typed, then it will be discussed and then presented for official approval. All these formal procedures should only take a few days and so I reckon to set out for Moscow around the 20th and, when I get there, to find a letter from you at Katya's.

I am simply delighted to be rid of this drag and am looking forward to my own, true writing as if it were a joy ride. And, if I were told that Mera had left for [Plessis] Robinson, my happiness would be doubled.

I am now working out a schedule for myself of rest and walks around Kiev. We've had yet another big snowfall and it has turned colder. The weather is crisp and clear. I hope in my next letter I'll be able to give you the exact date of my departure from here.

Yours,
I.

[A postcard.]

Kiev, February 19, 1938

I turned in my work on the 15th and am still sitting in Kiev because those in command have left for a conference in Moscow and there's no one here to look at my work, discuss it, pay for it. . . . In everyday language this is called a piece of bad luck. They will all be back here tonight and I hope to be able to leave for Moscow on the 22nd or, at the latest, the 23rd. Having thrown this tremendous load off my back, I now feel as light as a feather. Am writing simultaneously to Zhenya and perhaps my letter will find Mera there. And with that, best regards from your son who is now strolling down Kraschatik Avenue.

I.B.

Kiev, February 28, 1938

Am writing this two hours before the train leaves. The scenario has been accepted and highly commended. As soon as I get to Moscow, I'll try to get through to you on the phone.

I feel well. There is a breath of spring in the Kiev air but I suppose it'll still be winter in Moscow. Write at length about everything to Katya's address. I haven't had any letters from you for a long time.

IB.

Moscow, March 3, 1938

This is my third day in Moscow. It's not the same weather here —it's gloomy and there are lots of snowdrifts, although it really isn't too cold. I have masses of things to do that have accumulated during my four-month absence, so much, in fact, that I haven't been able to have a minute to myself until now to write to you. It is true that yesterday I had dinner at the Lyakhetskys. It was a very Jewish dinner with gefilte fish, chopped egg, cherry liqueur, etc. But I didn't see too much of Katya, as she came in late from work. I'll see her again tomorrow and have a long talk with her. I am waiting for my fees now and as soon as I get the money, I'll send some of it to the Sklyars and to Anyuta.

Yesterday I sent you as "printed matter" two issues of *Krasnaya Nov* and two books. When you are through with them, send them on to Zhenya. I will send reading matter to both addresses.

Did Mera go to see Natasha?

What news is there about Grisha's relatives? Not too gay, I'm sure. . . .

Today my scenario was presented to *GUK* [*Glavnoye Upravlenie Kinematografii*—Chief Administration of the Motion Picture Industry] where it must go through all the established stages, to be approved for production. I am sure, however, that I will still have to do more work on it, because in the film business there is always some additional rewriting and correction to do. That's quite inevitable. So I still won't be able to go off on long strolls and have myself a good time. Instead, I find myself sitting at my table once again.

Look after yourselves and be well,

IB.

Moscow, March 20, 1938

I swear and promise that from now on I'll write to you more often. Now, on top of my usual work, I have to see lots of people, something I didn't have to do in Kiev. And so I am hardly able to cope with the stream of work, matters I must attend to, and people. I am busy finishing off old movie commitments, putting some final touches to some scenes (for shooting already) of *How the Steel Was Tempered.*

In ten to fifteen days or so, I'll have to go to Kiev once more, and there I'll find the spring in full bloom. I wish I could manage to get to Odessa too and attend to matters connected with the summerhouse there. However, I am not at all sure I'll be able to manage it. The main thing is to get rid of all current business so that, by the middle of April at least, I can devote myself exclusively to what they call *belles lettres*. I feel I am ready for it.

I got a thank-you letter from Sonya with a complete listing of the things she bought with the money. Those iron oldsters are wearing wonderfully well. At the end of the month I'll send them and Anyuta a bit more cash.

The news of Natasha's loud behavior and moderate achievements give me great joy, a joy that I would be ashamed, of course, to express publicly. I have at last bought postage stamps and sent them to her and I hope they'll adorn her album. I'm working like a beast of burden, feeling incredibly well—knock on wood—and wish the same for you.

IB.

Moscow, March 25, 1938

Blackish, pockmarked snow is piled along the edges of the sidewalks. The torrents of spring are flowing, although the spring itself is only slowly stirring. The sun shines one day and the next it's overcast. Although, to tell the truth, sitting within four walls, my interest in all these things is purely theoretical—I have no time to go out for a walk. My Kiev customers are insisting that I should go there before they begin shooting and I suppose I'll have to go in the beginning of April. So far though, neither the exact date of my departure nor the duration of my stay have been fixed and so, please just keep writing to Katya's address. I am still in a blessed state: all I am interested in is work and there's nothing that can distract me from it.

As to you, the only thing I demand of you is to be well. I have no other claims upon you.

IB.

Moscow, April 6, 1938

I was very worried because of your long silence. But when I finally got a letter from you yesterday, it didn't cheer me up much. I cannot help thinking of Sonya who lives under considerably worse conditions than Mama and who nevertheless is full of pep, who runs her house and is quite capable of dragging home coal all the way from Prokhorovskaya Street and a can of kerosene from Stenovaya Street. I am relying on the Shvekhvel blood and, in the summer, on the sun that is so good for us natives of Odessa. I wish reform for myself and Mama—for myself too, because, as Utesov claims, I give the impression of being an anti-social element mostly because I am a sentimental son. And speaking of Utesov, he is coming to see me this evening and we'll have a good laugh to your health.

Everything's fine with me here. Above all. I am happy when I'm working. As to Zhenya, I wonder whether it is right for you to send her your last pennies, for, after all, she has both a husband and a brother helping her. Your main concern is to see to it that the little old lady goes around turned out as elegantly as a doll.

I.

Moscow, April 16, 1938

(1) From yesterday on, have been eating the finest matzos brought in from somewhere around Minsk. (They were presented to me by some kind-hearted old woman.) I wish you had some of the same. Are you celebrating this best of all Judaic festivals? Have you kosherized your crockery for Passover? Well, in brief, a happy Passover to you.

(2) Have received a message from Natasha, traced magnificently in her own hand, in which she thanks me for the books and the stamps and announces that they are going to the seashore for the Easter holidays, which pleases me no end. Wouldn't it be possible for you to meet them somewhere?

I am trying to check my longing to leave for Odessa and am getting rid of affairs that tie me down in Moscow. In a few days, I am moving to what is supposed to be my private villa. At first I didn't want to live in the so-called writers' settlement, but when I realized that the villas were quite far away from one another and that I wouldn't have to meet my brother authors, I decided to move there. The settlement, about fifteen miles from Moscow, is called Peredelkino. It is located in the middle of a wood (where, by the way, the layer of snow is still quite thick).

And so there you have a picture of my spring. The sun is a rare guest and I think it's high time it came to stay for good.

I.

Moscow, April 29, 1938

The holidays start tomorrow. I am leaving for the Peshkov's [Gorky's family] summerhouse tomorrow and will stay there until May third. As you know already, Ada is staying here with her daughter—a very energetic and cheerful creature, although of a strongly pronounced Semitic type. Ada is a hefty, middle-sized woman besieged by worries, while I picture myself as a youth still. But actually, that's what I am temperamentally. I suppose that literary activities are quite propitious for the maintenance of eternal youth—the dreaminess that goes with that activity and the gift of permanent renewal that goes with the dreaminess.

I got theater tickets for Ada, including some for the Arts Theater. I am very glad if she can have a change from her *vie mesquine* with her kindly, stupid, enthusiastic husband in Odessa.

I am feeling extremely well and am experiencing a tide of what is usually referred to as "creative force." That tide dissolves all other worldly preoccupations and if I am sorry about one thing it is that you do not have such a safety valve. I am longing to hear cheerful news from you about your physical state, for, after all, why shouldn't my continuous, ardent prayers reach their addressee?

I.

Peredelkino, May 13, 1938

I have just traced out a letter to Natasha in my best penmanship and slipped a few packages of stamps into it. I have been living in my villa for more than two days now and am getting accustomed to being a landowner. The house is very comfortable, but the pine wood it stands in is only newly planted and there is precious little furniture. I must organize myself here. But in the meantime, I am already wallowing in bliss, silence and an atmosphere which is propitious for work. I am also elated by the fact that there is no telephone here. There is only running water here in the summer, but there is a well and the water in it is excellent. There is electricity so that my passion, the electric gadgets—kettle, coffee pot and hot plate—function without letup. My estate is about fifteen miles from Moscow along an excellent highway—the Mozhaisk Road; it is thirty-five minutes by train (I live a little over half a mile from the station); in Moscow the train comes into the Kiev (formerly Briansk) Station. I have brought a number of books with me and read them in the evenings, a thing

I could never manage in Moscow where all my evenings are taken up. I have a citizeness answering to the name of Motya to serve me here. Her husband, who works on a nearby state farm, lives here too, as does their five-year-old daughter who has been so frightened by my reputation that she sticks her finger in her mouth and stares at me in petrified silence.

I.

Peredelkino, May 24, 1938

I am living in my summer place and that's why I write less often—I still don't know where the nearest post office is. Living in a summer villa near Moscow means that we have to light the stove every day for otherwise we would risk freezing to death. Ah, what a climate!

All around my house there is hammering, scraping and digging going on. Bricklayers and painters are at work. The electricity has been laid in. The gardener attached to my private lot is digging beds in which radishes, lettuce, cucumbers, etc., will be planted. I'll also get chickens and pigeons and then we'll live like a regular household here.

Tomorrow I'll have to go to Moscow for a couple of days.

I wonder did you go to the pianists' contest? Our press is full of long accounts of it. Gillels, of course, is one of our Odessa townsmen, the older brother of Mira Gillels, the violinist who studied under Stolyarsky. I am sure he won't disgrace our Odessa.

What's new with you? I've been so absorbed in the fuss connected with the villa, that I feel I have neglected you a bit and I feel I haven't heard from you for a very long time. For me, nothing is changed—lots of work for body and soul, living, thinking. . . . Have you had any letters from Zhenya and Natasha?

Above all, be well.

IB.

Peredelkino, June 21, 1938

Among the news worthy of your attention—I have acquired three pairs of pigeons which, at present, are undergoing the process of adjustment and courting. As soon as they are married, we'll start letting them out. We have fixed them up with a beautiful dovecote on top of the cowshed, where a cow is living which the husband of my house help brought here from a hundred and sixty miles away. We are also expecting the arrival of five hens and a rooster, after which both the chicken and dairy farms will start operating at full blast.

I have now been in Peredelkino for nine days without budging; my days are filled with the labor of writing and farming chores. Tonight though, I'm going to Moscow. I'll try to send you some books and also some very nice stamps I have saved for Natasha from there.

I feel wonderful living close to nature. No phone calls here and my work proceeds infinitely better than it did in Moscow. I've heard from Katya that she has some letters for me from you. I'll answer them from Moscow. The weather this year has been cloudy and rainy.

I.

Moscow, July 25, 1938

It is well-nigh impossible to amaze anyone in the Soviet Union with beautiful school buildings, but, nevertheless, the pictures of Natasha's school did make a tremendous impression upon me. If one can judge by the principal's notes, it would seem that the studies are well organized too. In my opinion, the remarks on the student's character are not jotted down in automatic clichés but show great insight. Also, Zhenya has sent me a picture of Natasha in Norman dress—she looks so appealing and pretty in it—simply a lovable lass (in the Gronfein style, which pleases me). And on top of all that, I have received in Natasha's own hand, a listing of presents received, including *Le Jeu des Sept Familles*, a stylo, balls, writing paper *et une vraie montre*. In addition, she mentions the prospect of getting a bicycle and a hundred and fifty francs from Tante Marie, and even gives a report of a film she was taken to—very interesting, *mais un peu triste*. What a grownup person!

I must comment here that the granddaughter in her Norman dress looks better than the grandmother in her Brussels photograph. However, being a layman in medical science I console myself with the thought that thin people are healthier than fat ones—it is easier for their hearts to do their work and they feel better. Am I right?

I.

Moscow, July 26, 1938

My work, my old-fashioned farm life and the remoteness of the post office have caused me to lose touch with you completely—a fact that I unrestrainedly bemoan.

Despite the Egyptian heat wave, I'll stay in Moscow for a couple of days for change and relaxation. My summer villa is my working place and the city is a place of relaxation.

It would be difficult for me to give you even a vague idea of the splendors of my villa—it is a winterized, two-story house with all sorts of annexes, surrounded by several acres of wood and so isolated from the other houses that I have my shower outside and naked, for there is not, nor can there be, anyone around.

The number of my hens has now reached ten—with still just one rooster to cope; the cow is gradually putting on weight; the weather is magnificently sunny, but it is cool in the forest. And when I think of Brussels, erected on a site that breeds fogs and on all sorts of mud—a feeling of pity and rage takes my breath away.

Today I'll attend the Physical Culture Day show (a repetition of the parade of Physical Culturists on Red Square). It is an absolutely magical sight, involving thirty-five thousand participants.

If we could borrow a bit of health from one of them, it would take care of all our troubles.

I.

Moscow, *July 31, 1938*

Have decided to prolong my stay in Moscow for a few more days to get through with all my business and then be able to stay longer at the villa. Besides, I might just as well wait until I get a letter from you here, for otherwise it won't be much of a life anyway.

Here, it's been uniformly terribly hot every day and I have two or three showers a day and drink bottles and bottles of iced Narzan mineral water.

Katya is preparing for her trip. She keeps darting all over town and it seems to be quite impossible to get hold of her.

Yesterday, Katayev and I went to the races, then we drove to a restaurant for dinner and, talking of our young years and Odessa, emptied a bottle of genuine French Bordeaux.

Except for my work, I have nothing new to report, and I suppose I'd better not write about it. And so, I am awaiting some moderately reassuring news from you.

I.

Peredelkino, August 25, 1938

Today's paper notes that Moscow hasn't seen a heat wave comparable to the present one for forty-one years. So there you have it. And to think that you complain in your letter that you have been waiting in vain for the sun in Normandy. The sweat is pouring into my eyes as I read those lines, saying to myself—the world really is a big place.

I went to Moscow to attend to some business on the 22nd. It was so stuffy there that I couldn't sleep at night, so I came back here, spurning all my affairs, which I decided could wait for cooler weather.

For the time being I have postponed my trip to Odessa because

I have decided to prepare my Peredelkino place for the winter. And by the way, a picture of it has already been registered on film and the photograph will be sent to you in due course.

Of the important news, I can inform you that the dovecote population has been enriched by four new specimens. In expectation of very long letters from you,

> Yours,
>
> I.

Moscow, September 11, 1938

Is it possible that the time has passed so quickly and you are already back in Brussels! I have just sent a postcard to Zhenya and am now going to the Kursk Railroad Station: I am going on an outing—to Yasnaya Polyana, to visit Tolstoi's grave.*

I'll be back tomorrow night and will write to you upon my return. Thank the former God—I have nothing new to report, except the fact that the unprecedented heat has abated somewhat, and the wind had begun to blow, driving clouds of dust before it.

I am very anxious to hear all about your vacation and am waiting for the pictures.

> I.

* The 110th anniversary of Leo Tolstoi's birth was being solemnly celebrated throughout the Soviet Union.

Moscow, September 20, 1938

We've had a few fall days but today the sun is shining again. I came up to town from the country this morning.

It was a cold day there and we gave the fires a trial run in the house. The results were good and it felt delightful to be sitting in a warm room and gazing at the forest around me.

I am not really sorry now that I didn't go anywhere this year for the summer turned out to be an exceptional one and, despite everything, I still managed to spend it more sensibly than any pre-ceding one—I spent my time "farming," took many long walks through the countryside and breathed the air of the pine forest.

I don't remember whether I wrote to you about the ecstatic im-pression left upon me by Yasnaya Polyana—I found myself stand-ing in Tolstoi's ascetic rooms and felt that his thought still con-tinued its furious activity there.

When I arrived this morning, I found Mama's letter here. But, *mes enfants*, where are the pictures I asked for? If I claimed that I wasn't envious of Mama when I read her description of Natasha, it would be untrue.

I.

Peredelkino, September 26, 1938

We are having beautiful and sunny although quite cool days. The leaves are falling.

Everything would be so nice and quiet if it weren't for the newspapers that are brought to me from town and that fill me with anxiety. After reading them, I have to do violence to myself to regain my composure and go on with my work.

Am leaving for Moscow for a couple of days. I want to look for books to send to Natasha. I reckon to be back on the 28th, in the evening.

I have a stock of firewood for the winter. In the coming days, the house will undergo an overhauling—the foundation will be strengthened and the rather dried-up floors will be relaid. I hope it'll be nice and warm here in the winter. I have brought all my books from town and, at night, sit by the fire reading Sholom Aleichem in our highly original tongue.

Moscow, October 3, 1938

My glorious and very worthy relatives,

We are having a very nice spell of weather—the sun is shining and it is warm—something I wish for you too.

I am very sad that I am not in Odessa at this moment for all my jockey friends have gone there with their horses and now, under the fairy-tale Odessa sky, are smashing all the existing speed records.

It would be so nice if I could stay with them for a time, say at the Fourth Station, near the race track. . . . Well, I'd be happy to go to paradise while I am at it, but then, with my sins, I'm not entitled to it.

A very skilled photographer has taken a picture of my mug and I'll send it to you as soon as it's ready. Conversely, I am waiting very impatiently for you to send me some family photographs.

But whatever else—be well.

I.

Moscow, October 9, 1938

I came up to town yesterday and will stay here until the 11th. Although the fall has arrived, it is still so infinitely preferable to sit in the villa by a blazing fire, gaze at the forest, which has turned yellow now, walk along the leaf-strewn paths, rather than being on business in Moscow, that I am already longing to go back.

Haven't had any news from you for a long time and without it I feel depressed and sad. I am still waiting impatiently for your pictures. I have already learned Natasha's school report by heart and am in dire need of new spiritual nourishment. I would like very much to know how Grisha is doing, whether he is working and whether he "is making progresses" as a certain Jewish woman in Odessa used to say.

I.

Moscow, October 19, 1938

Have just received Mama's letter. Is it possible that I forgot to mention in my previous letters that Natasha's photographs arrived quite a while ago, has been enlarged and now adorns the walls of my room? And now I am impatiently expecting you to continue sending them. And you, did you get the pictures of my villa? Only now has the place become real bliss—the rain is falling on the forest, the wind is whistling, while in my room, the light on my working table is lit and I am pacing up and down in my warm slippers.

This year I have made an experiment: with the arrival of the cold days I have stopped taking showers in the morning and I haven't had a trace of a cold. Obviously, it was all due to cold water and stepping on the cold tile floor in my bare feet.

I'll send you the books any day now and I suppose I ought also to collect some newspapers and send them to you. My health is still good, although I am working rather too much for a man of my profession—some interruptions and a certain dose of laziness would do me good.

It would be very nice if Mera and Grisha went to see Natasha. Until tomorrow.

I.

Peredelkino, October 25, 1938

Did you get the pictures of my villa? I am expecting you to send me a new set of family pictures. Am leaving for Moscow today or, at the latest, tomorrow, and will then send you a few issues of *Novy Mir* right away. Koltsov's "Spanish Diary" is very interesting. I have four of the issues here and the rest are in town. I'll send everything I have. Among my varied functions, there is the following: "Deputy Chairman of the Editorial Board of the State Literary Publishing House"—so I suppose I can ask them for a few samples of contemporary literature as a reward for my services, and send them to you.

I am enjoying the fall in Peredelkino but the place is soon due for repairs, during which I'll have to sit out two weeks in town. I am feeling fine and wish you felt the same.

I.

Peredelkino, November 9, 1938

Dear Mamachen, Sisterchen and Esculapius,

I have been here, in "my villa" since the third, and at the present moment, in the depths of night, the first big snow is coming down on it in the moonlight. Very beautiful. . . . Although the villa is being repaired and in some places they have taken up the floor, it is still habitable and I am taking advantage of it. Am leaving for town tomorrow and from there, going straight to the Peshkovs. On the November 7th holiday [old style, October 25th—anniversary of the Bolshevik Revolution.—Tr.—Mac A.], I was also at their place.

I am getting along slowly but surely—working and working. I understand that this occupation is supposed to be very hygienic and that all great toilers live for a hundred years. We'll see. Write to me with soup spoons and with teaspoons and more often, whatever else you do. Be well now.

I.

Peredelkino, December 2, 1938

I have spent several fine days in my villa. The weather is unbelievably mild—it's a real spring. A little snow falls which melts instantly. I have walked and worked a great deal—incomparably more effectively than in Moscow. Tomorrow I am going into town. Besides other more pressing matters, I want to see the new Eisenstein film *Alexander Nevsky* and my friend, the astounding Jewish actor Michoels, in the stage version of Sholom Aleichem's *Tevie, the Milkman*. (By the way, I'd like to translate a few chapters of that book.) I intend to come back here in a few days. My dream is to find letters from you on my return, and meanwhile stay in good and thriving health.

I.

1 9 3 9

Moscow, January 2, 1939

Made futile attempts to reach you on the phone on New Year's Eve; there was such a line-up of callers that I would've had to wait till maybe seven in the morning. I couldn't hold out and went to sleep. Anyway, I suppose if I'd reached you at seven I'd have wakened you. Still, it's an awful shame. I hadn't even sent you a telegram since I expected to hear your live voices. And so, a happy New Year to you. If I were God, you'd live better than anyone ever dreamed of living. But since I am not endowed with divine powers, I must content myself with wishes, the scope and content of which you are well aware of. As to me, the year 1939 finds me in great working form. The only trouble is that I haven't enough time for creative writing.

I send you my love from the bottom of my heart.

I.B.

Moscow, January 12, 1939

I am carrying out a plan that I have nurtured in my heart for a long time: I am sitting day and night doing work on order, trying to finish it by February first in order to devote myself unstintingly to my own writing. It's costing me a tremendous effort but I hope the scheme is worth the candle.

Yesterday I saw the sample enlargements of the pictures you sent me—very nice. As soon as they are ready, I'll send some to you. Natasha has a very expressive face in them.

We are having a cold wave again, with temperatures of five below and less, but I am holding up wonderfully—the flu is roaming around somewhere, but has not stepped onto my territory. Owing to the huge amount of work I have, I am leading an isolated life and in both heart and mind am constantly with you. If I were God, you would be both athletes and millionaires, *je vous assure.*

I.

Moscow, January 20, 1939

Fine, clear, sunny weather, spring—can you imagine that? Have come out for a walk this morning and am writing this in a café. I have nothing new to report except that I am trying doggedly to stick to my schedule and get rid of all extraneous business by February first.

The repairs to the villa were held up because they failed to deliver the lumber. But now that obstacle has been removed and I hope to be able to return there to stay by February 15th.

Write more often—your artless compositions are rays of sunlight in my life. When I return home, I'll write to you again.

I.

Moscow, January 25, 1939

Yesterday I turned in the most urgent and difficult part of the work I had on order and felt as if a mountain had fallen off my back. What I still have left to do is much less difficult. I hope I'll be able to think of myself a bit now. During the next few days, I'll try to work while having a rest, or rather have a rest while working. We are having a delightfully mild winter and I try to go out and walk for a couple of hours each day and recommend you to do the same. The repairs to the villa will only be finished on February 15th.

From now on, I'll write to you more often.

I.

Moscow, January 28, 1939

Except for a feeling of sadness left in me in the mornings after I have read the war communiqués* I have nothing new to tell you. I am working hard and dreaming of more poetic and less time-consuming work. We are having a wonderful winter and only recently did we have a real snowfall. I go out for walks and sometimes stand for hours by the fence of the ice-skating rink at Chistyye Prudy, admiring the people and the radiance of the light on the ice and enjoying the pure, icy air. Of the news from everyday life, I ought to report the appearance of bananas in the stores —the first in twenty years—on which we all pounce with greed and joy. I wish I were getting more letters from you, for my filial devotion does need something to feed on.

I.

* Communiqués, that is, of the Spanish Civil War. Franco's troops had entered Barcelona on January 26th, and the conflict was drawing to a close.

Moscow, February 7, 1939

Dear Mamachen, Sisterchen and Grisha,

I get your letters regularly. I don't write to you too often because there is no letup in my work. Of course, I couldn't manage to finish everything by February first, but I did hand in a fair share of it. I am moving relentlessly ahead and I hope that in a few days my life will be devoted to pure sounds and prayers. I am longing to go back to the villa but the capital overhaul has still not been completed. I won't be able to move back there before the end of the month. I have received a lovely letter from Natasha, written in her own hand. She writes about the good time she had during her holidays. I would be awfully glad if Mera went to see them. And if she did, couldn't she take Grandma along too? I don't suppose a trip by car would be too tiring for her. I'll send you the books in the very near future. There is only one thing about which *je vous supplie*—write often.

I.

Moscow, February 24, 1939

It is our equivalent of Sunday today—the day off. I decided to spend it unthinkingly—to give my brains a rest. In the morning I drove out to Peredelkino. The overhaul of the villa is coming to an end and it'll be a real reinforced concrete house. They have built a new brick foundation, relaid all the flooring on the ground floor and are now putting down parquet there. Everything will be ready by the first and then I'll really have a house that will last me for years. And although I have no neighbors too close by, I want, nevertheless, to put up a high wall around my garden. My pigeons are all there. My house help had bought a new cow. Now, having returned from my villa, I am having my lunch (for hors d'oeuvre, I'm having radish with goose dripping). Afterward, I'll go to the hippodrome. I haven't been there for four months. Then I'll go with a friend to a restaurant which specializes in shashlyk. And that's my complete program for the day.

Moscow, March 1, 1939

Nothing new. Although winter has made a re-entry here, I am thinking of spring. In five days or so, I'll move to the villa and, in a few months, perhaps I'll be able to go somewhere south.

Did Mera carry out her plan and go and see Natasha? When I think that you are only three hours away from them, I think I'd be traveling that distance every week. Natasha must be quite a grown-up young lady by now. Am sending you an almanac that came out a few days ago and a small selection of books. How are the members of Borya's household getting on? I would like it so much if Mama decided to stir from her lair and went to pay Natasha a visit.

I am waiting for "pleasant news from you" as they used to write in the old days.

I.

Moscow, March 6, 1939

Today is an important day for sports lovers—the Winter Derby. And so I am going to the enchanted circle. The weather is very mild. There was a light snowfall yesterday. Yesterday, I went to my estate: the laying of the new brick foundation and of the flooring has been completed and now they are laying the parquet. I reckon I'll be able to move in there by the tenth. I am very pleased about it. The rest is fine and unchanged. I can hear hooting downstairs —it is the car that is taking me to the race track. Write more often and don't be put off by a lack of topics to write about—to me you are the most interesting of writers.

I.

Moscow, March, 18, 1939

According to my calculations, in a couple of weeks I'll be a well-off man, well rid of daily drudgery. Then I'll become a model correspondent. In the meantime, however, I feel very guilty because I don't write often enough. I haven't written for so long because I was looking for suitable books for Natasha; yesterday I sent her a letter. It is a great shame Mera couldn't go to see them.

I will go to my Peredelkino villa at the end of this month—the main part of the overhaul has been completed and now I have only to wait for the paint to dry and for the parquet to be planed and polished, and a supply of ice put into the cellar.

The day before yesterday my first pigeon chick came out of its egg and today we are expecting the second one.

I still hope to go to Odessa for the summer. I could rest and mend my health there just as well as in the Caucasus. But, perhaps just to spite everybody, I am feeling well, although my brains are a bit overworked. But that can easily be remedied. Will send you some books today or tomorrow. Iosif and Katya [illegible]. . . .

Moscow, March 31, 1939

Yesterday, I threw a great load off my back by handing in some work. Am leaving today for Leningrad for ten days or so, to get rid of the tail ends. I am very pleased to be going there because they are having a beautiful spring. Besides, I'll remember old times, go and visit places I haven't seen for a long time, visit the Hermitage, take a trip to Peterhof. It will shake me up a bit, for I've been sitting too long in the same place. Keep writing to my Moscow address though, for I suppose the answer to this card will find me in Moscow. As soon as I come back here, I'll rush off to Peredelkino and then to Odessa. I want to get my fill of sea bathing this year. I can now see through to the bottom of the work I have on order and my mood has improved correspondingly. I will write often from Leningrad and will write one letter to you in collaboration with Lyusya. The spring appeared to have started sparkling for good around here, but it hasn't shown itself for two days now.

Leningrad, April 3, 1939

What an amazing city! But I am only seeing it out of the windows of taxicabs and buses, for I don't have time to go out for a walk. And it will go on like that for another five days.

Leningrad met me with a burst of wind and a cold wave. I have a vast program of sightseeing though and intend to visit the museums and the out-of-town spots I came to know when I used to be a correspondent in Petrograd.

I wrote to Zhenya and Natasha the day I left Moscow. Zhenya, of course, has let all her documents expire, a fact that saddens me a great deal. I still haven't been to Lyusya's and won't be able to go there for another three or four days, when the rush of affairs weighing on me will have abated a bit. Otherwise, I have no acquaintances left here. In a few days, I'll be able to tell you exactly how long I will stay here.

Je vous embrasse,

I.

Leningrad, April 7, 1939

Last night, I went out for a walk along the Neva embankments through the Petersburg fog. A fairy-tale town. I have only got the feel of it now. I hope I'll have more time to myself during the last days of my stay here and will be able to roam around on foot a bit.

My work is progressing satisfactorily and by April 15th I'll be able to leave for Moscow. Only today will I be able to call Lyusya on the phone and fix a date for tomorrow. Until now, there hasn't been much point in my calling her since I hadn't a minute to spare anyway. It is the first spring day today, with the wind blowing in from the sea. And although it is not our southern sea but only a cold one, it sets my heart beating anyway.

How is your collective health? Is it possible that even now that it's spring, none of you are going to pay a visit to Natasha? How is Borya? What are your plans for the summer? I wish they were based on Natasha's whereabouts.

I.

Leningrad, April 11, 1939

My work is progressing well and I hope to be through the Leningrad phase of it within a few days. Tomorrow is the day off and I want to spend it like all working people, that is, resting. I'll visit the Hermitage and perhaps will manage to take a trip to Peterhof. I have asked Lyusya to come and see me (I don't expect to get much fun out of the other members of her family, so I have postponed a general meeting till the last day of my stay). Lyusya looks fine despite the fact that she was recently afflicted with an inflammation of the inner ear.

The northern sun is shining here but, alas, it gives off no warmth. And they call this April! I've received a report from the majordomo of my estate that my parquet floors are polished now, that the fires are lit in the rooms in expectation of the master. I reckon to be in Moscow on the 18th. I understand it is warmer there. I miss your letters very much and hope to find a big pile of them when I get back.

I.

Leningrad, April 20, 1939

OOf! . . . A mountain has fallen from my shoulders. I've just completed my job—I wrote a scenario in twenty days! Now, I suppose, I'll be able to lead an "honest life." Am leaving for Moscow on the 22nd, in the evening.

I have already visited the Hermitage and am going to Peterhof tomorrow. The completion of my labors has coincided with the first spring day—the sun is shining. I'll go and have a walk now after my righteous efforts.

I've seen Lyusya twice and must be at their house this evening. She complained to me that she never received an answer to her letters from you. And, by the way, be well whatever else you do.

I.

Astoria Hotel, Leningrad,
April 22, 1939

Am walking around for the second day in a row and spring is here to make it even better. Went to dinner at Zoshchenko's yesterday, after which, until five o'clock in the morning, sat with my 1938 publisher, who goes back to my Gorky period. Then, at dawn, I walked down Kamenostrovsky Parade, across the Troitsky Bridge, past the Winter Palace, in this amazing city, so quiet at that hour. Am leaving tonight. I reckon to find a large pile of letters from you upon my arrival. I intend to move to the villa by tomorrow night. Well, that'll be all for the time being.

I.

[Incomplete]

Moscow, April 25, 1939

As you can see I'm back in my pseudo native city (in fact, I don't consider it that—I remain loyal to Odessa). Today, I sent a more or less respectable amount of money to Sonya. I hope it will help her a bit. Katya wants to have that matriarch from the Shvevel family come to Moscow to distract her. In the next few days I will send something to Anyuta. I hope you write them even if only occasionally.

I am leaving the country as soon as tomorrow. It is a humid season, but it will be beautiful there. The house is now fixed up enough to last for fifty years . . . As for my plans, I only know that during the summer, perhaps at the beginning of it, I will come to Odessa. You don't plan to go to Natasha's? It would be very good if you visited those recluses, and a real consolation for me.

How is Boris? His New Years greetings are really moving, but won't this sudden sentimental effusion be a perfect excuse for then forgetting about the poor old women for the whole year? You wrote to me, quite a while ago, that she was to come to Brussels in January, but I have heard no news of her arrival. Please . . .

Moscow, May 5, 1939

Got in yesterday and am leaving today. Am very happy that Mera has at last gone to see Zhenya and Natasha. Am waiting for a full account. I have already written to you that I've sent a small sum to Sonya in Odessa and that I intend to do the same for Anyuta. They are quite all right. I have reprimanded Katya for her unreliability in letter-writing and she has promised me to mend her ways. I was very glad to hear that you had met Borya. How long is it since he last came to see you? I believe he was about to visit you way back in January, unless I've got it all mixed up and he is on his second visit to Brussels now. I feel very good—knock on wood—and with a summer villa like mine, I don't really need to go south even. Nevertheless, I will go there this year without fail. Will send you some books next time. Now I have a whole trainload of them ready for Natasha.

I.

Peredelkino, May 10, 1939

For your information, it has been snowing for two days now. Talk of a May 10th! I suppose even your Brussels climate would envy this.

I am already installed in my country seat and am feeling wonderful, except that I am bored with having to go on lighting fires. Am going to Moscow for one day tomorrow. Perhaps there will be a letter from Mera there; I wonder how her trip has been. It is such a shame Mama couldn't go with her on that excursion.

I have sent off some books for Natasha and now that the granddaughter has been taken care of, I must think of her grandmother and will try to get some recent literature for her too tomorrow.

Nothing new about me—I'm absorbed in work. I am finishing my last assignment—for the movies (a film about Gorky) and will soon devote myself to the final polishing of my true work. I reckon to hand it in to the publishers by the fall. Write more often because I have no time for reading long books and your messages are the best reading there is for me. How is Grisha? How is Boris? Do you see him often?

I.

[Last letter received from Babel.]

APPENDIX

I

Review by P. Markov of *Sunset* *

Babel's play *Sunset* gives a picture of a way of life which is remarkable for its literary qualities. It was staged by the Moscow Art Theater. Its subject is the bygone mores on which his *Odessa Stories* are also based. In the play these mores are subjected to philosophical examination. Babel makes the Moldavanka's customs the backdrop for a story of the sunset of man's life—of the decline of the mighty Mendel Krik who, toward the end of his days, experiences romantic longings and fruitless desires. Babel handled his subject with epic simplicity, terseness, calm and economy. Without taking the side of any one character in the play, he sums up his own feelings in the concluding words of the rabbi: "Day is day and evening is evening."

It is possible to disagree with Babel's idea, but it is quite impossible to fail to recognize the boldness and polish of the play. Its shortcoming is not in its philosophical nature, but rather in the fact that its philosophy is alien to our epoch.

The long-vanished, shadowy mores do not strike us as amusing and they cannot be brought back to life even by Babel's subtle psychological portrayals. In trying to emphasize the social message in this play, the Art Theater failed to grasp fully the basic nature of Babel's drama. Out of Babel's warm, live characters, the Theater made exaggerated masks. The quiet, calm development of the script was

---

* This review first appeared in *Novy Mir*, no. 4, 1928. See note to Babel's letter of April 28, 1928.

turned into a spasmodic succession of scenes. The clash between the author's and the director's views was so obvious that at times one had the impression that the staged drama had been written by someone else.

Also, the social message of the play would have been understood more clearly if the staging had been based on the general meaning of the drama rather than on its individual characters. This is so because *Sunset,* on the whole, with Mendel's ruin, Benya's triumph and all that random despair, cruelty and debauchery, is a profound condemnation of the old, vanished Moldavanka life, as Babel had seen it and thought about it.

We can expect of artists like Babel and Alexei Tolstoi* that they should show us the mores of a different environment now.

IIa

An Open Letter to Maxim Gorky by Semyon Budyonny†

Dear Alexei Maximovich,

Our national dailies, *Pravda* and *Izvestia,* on September 30 carried an excerpt from your pamphlet "To Rural and War Correspondents—How I Learnt to Write."

In that piece, in discussing the main trends in literature—Romanticism and Realism—you state the following:

"Gogol wrote *How Ivan Ivanovich Quarelled with Ivan Nikiforovich, Old World Landowners* and *Dead Souls,* and he also wrote *Taras Bulba.* In the first three he portrayed people with dead souls—that is, a sinister truth; such people did exist and still exist to this very day and thus, in portraying them, Gogol wrote as a "realist."

"In *Taras Bulba* he showed the Zaporozhe Cossacks as Godfearing knights and strong men who would lift an enemy on a

---

* Tolstoi, Alexei Nikolayevich (1883-1945). Leading Soviet writer, distant relative of Count Leo Nikolayevich Tolstoi (1828-1910).

† This article first appeared in *Krasnaya Gazeta,* October 26, 1928. See note to Babel's letter of October 28, 1928.

spear, although the shaft of a spear could not possibly have supported a load of two hundred pounds without snapping. Anyway, no such Zaporozhe Cossacks existed and Gogol's story is a beautiful untruth. Here, as in all the stories told by Rudny Panko, Gogol is a romantic who has grown tired of watching the dull life of "dead souls."

"Comrade Budyonny has pounced upon Babel's *Red Cavalry* and I don't believe he should have, because Budyonny himself likes to embellish the outside not only of his men, but of his horses too. Babel, on the other hand, embellished his men on the inside, which, in my opinion, is better and more truthful than what Gogol did for his Zaporozhe Cossacks.

"Man is still a beast in many respects and, culturally, he is only an adolescent. It is always useful to embellish and to praise him."

Although it is very difficult for me to argue with you on literary matters, nevertheless, since *Red Cavalry* has come up as a subject of discussion once again, I must say that I cannot agree with you, Alexei Maximovich, despite all my respect for you, and I will try to explain why I criticized *Red Cavalry* and why I think I did so with good reason.

To start with, I believe [a writer] should know his source material and I dare say Babel was never and could never have been a genuine, active combat soldier in the First Cavalry. I know that he hung around with some unit deep in the rear, one of those units that, to our misfortune, were always a drag upon our fighting men. To be precise, Babel was in the backwaters of our First Cavalry. What does Babel write about that gives him the right to use such a broad title as *Red Cavalry?*

Babel indulges in old women's gossip, digs into old women's garbage, and tells with horror about some Red Army man taking a loaf of bread and a chicken somewhere, He invents things that never happened, slings dirt at our best Communist commanders, lets his imagination run wild, simply lies . . .

The subject matter of Babel's stories is distorted by the impressions of an erotomanic author. His topics range from the ravings of a mad Jew to the looting of a Catholic church, to the thrashing the cavalrymen give to their own foot soldiers, to the portrayal of a syphilitic Red Army man and end with a display of the author's scientific curiosity, when he wishes to see what a Jewish woman raped by about ten Makhno men looks like. Just as he looks upon life as a sunny meadow in May with mares and stallions on it, so he also views the operations of the Red Cavalry and he sees them through the prism of eroticism.

I happen to know for certain that while Babel saw women's breasts and bare legs around the army's field kitchens, Pani Eliza's servants' quarters, in the middle of the forest, awake and asleep, in various combinations, there were a few other things the First Cavalry was doing that Babel did not see.

And that's quite natural and understandable. How could Babel possibly have seen from the deep rear the spots where the fate of the workers and peasants was being decided. He just couldn't have.

I believe that if Babel wanted to give a title which would correspond to his genre of writing, he should have called his book *In the Backwaters of the Red Cavalry*. That would have been more accurate.

Now I ask: did the author maintain even the most elementary truthfulness, the least respect for historical perspective that is a must for realistic art? He didn't and it is the more shocking in that he is dealing with men of whom some are still alive and with facts familiar to every Red Army man. Alas, Alexei Maximovich, there is not the least concern for truthfulness in it.

I believe, Alexei Maximovich, that you will agree with me that to describe the heroic class struggle, a struggle unprecedented in the history of mankind, it is necessary before anything else to grasp the nature of those classes, i.e., to at least be partly familiar with Marxist dialectics. And it so happens that Babel doesn't qualify by those standards. And that is why his attempt to depict the life and the traditions of the First Cavalry reads like a lampoon and is permeated by a petty-bourgeois outlook.

Of course, the heroic fighters of the First Cavalry are simple, plain, often almost illiterate, men, but "pieces of art" like this one, appearing at a moment when we are witnessing decisive battles between labor and capital, are not only unwelcome, but, I believe, outright harmful.

That is why I have criticized Babel's *Red Cavalry*. And I am not the only one to do so, for all the revolutionary masses with whom we are building socialism before your eyes are on my side.

How can one say, in view of all this, that Babel depicted his Red Cavalrymen better and more truthfully than Gogol did his Zaporozhe Cossacks? Is it possible that a sensitive person like you, Alexei Maximovich, has failed to feel that, even when he gave us his "beautiful untruth" about the Zaporozhe Cossacks, Gogol, being a great artist, avoided a sordid tone, while Babel, the alleged realist, has so embellished his fighting men from inside that, to this day, I keep receiving letters protesting against his crude, deliberate and arrogant slander of the First Red Cavalry.

For a long time, we have considered Babel's book as a lampoon, and I wouldn't have mentioned it again if it hadn't been mentioned by you, Alexei Maximovich, just when you were telling our new proletarian rural and war correspondents how to write.

I do not think that they should describe the inspiration of our days the way Babel did.

With my deepest respect,

S. Budyonny

IIb

Gorky's Answer to Budyonny's Letter of October 26, 1928 *

Dear Comrade Budyonny,

I cannot agree with your opinion of Babel's *Red Cavalry* and I firmly protest your evaluation of that talented writer.

You say that Babel "hung around with some unit deep in the rear." That cannot take anything away either from Babel or his book. In order to make soup the cook does not have to sit in the pot. The author of *War and Peace* never took part in the fighting against Napoleon, and Gogol was not a Zaporozhe Cossack.

You talk about Babel's erotomania. I have just re-read Babel's book and I found no symptoms of that disease in it, although, of course, I do not wish to deny the presence of certain erotic details in his stories. And this is as it should be. War always awakens an enraged eroticism. And that is something you can learn from any war, from the behavior of the Germans in Belgium, as well as from the behavior of the Russians in East Prussia. I am inclined to consider it a natural although abnormal heightening of the instinct for the

* The following was published in *Pravda*, November 27, 1928. See note to Babel's letter of October 20, 1928.

preservation of the species, an instinct common in people who are facing death.

I am a careful reader but I didn't find in Babel's book anything that suggests a "lampoon." On the contrary, his book awakened love and respect in me for the fighting men of the Red Cavalry by showing them to me as real heroes—they are fearless and they feel deeply the greatness of their cause. I cannot think of another such colorful, lively portrayal of individual fighting men, another such description of the psychology of the mass of the Red Army that would have helped me to understand the strength that enabled it to accomplish that extraordinary campaign; it has no parallel in Russian literature.

The attack of the French cavalry in Zola's *La Débâcle* shows only the mechanical movement of the mass of fighters and their mechanical clash.

Nor can I agree with you that our fighting men are "simple plain men." I wouldn't have thought they were even without Babel, who with such talent has supplemented my understanding of the heroism of an army which is the first in history to know what it is fighting for and what it is going to go on fighting for.

Allow me to tell you, Comrade Budyonny, that the abrupt and unjustified tone of your letter visits an undeserved insult on a young writer.

Our writers live in a moment of transition under the complex conditions of a country in which there are at least 20,000,000 individual owners and only 2,000,000 Marxists, of whom almost half mouth Marxist precepts about as intelligently as parrots repeat human words. It is impossible under these conditions to make very strict demands of ideological consistency upon these writers. Our life is contradictory and it is not at all as didactic as the past, which can easily teach us whom to love and whom to hate. A writer is a man who lives by the truth, using the color of imagination in order to generate in his reader a reaction of active love or active hatred. You must not forget that people have been brought up with religious views on ownership and that all the misfortunes, all the tragedies of life, all its nasty sides, are rooted in the proprietary instinct which from ancient times has been celebrated as the foundation of the state and the main source of private happiness.

It is impossible to re-educate in ten years people who have been brought up for thousands of years to worship gold and money. But we, in our own interest, must make allowances for and treat carefully every man who can help us in our struggle against the decaying but still strong props of the disgraceful past. Babel is a talented man. There are not so many of us that we can afford to spurn talented and useful men. You are not right, Comrade Budyonny! You are mistaken, and you have forgotten that scores of thousands of your fighting men heed your judgments. To be correct and useful a critic must be objective and considerate of our young literary forces.

Most respectfully yours,

M. Gorky

IIIa

Our People on the Riviera by Bruno Yasensky*

An interview with Babel by the Polish poet Alexander Dan has been published in No. 21 (334) of the Polish literary weekly *Wiadomosci Literackie*, which is published in Warsaw and financed by the Ministry of Foreign Affairs and which is the mouthpiece of the loyal "Belvedere" group of pro-Pilsudski writers.

Dan reports a conversation held on a French Riviera beach. We feel that the Soviet reader might like to know about this conversation and so we offer some excerpts here in literal translation.

Dan spoke about Paris, and here is what Babel answered:

". . . You've repeated the words *in vain* several times. It's a good phrase, a frightening one.

"I was in the Red Army. I know what a man is. I observed him, we may say, from every angle. There was plenty of death all around us. I've stopped distinguishing the dead from the living.

"Did you say *in vain?* A frightening phrase and very much on the mark. We pulled man from his sleep and drew buckets of hot blood out of him. We could do nothing else. And then we saw he was giving out on us.

"I rumbled through vast fields strewn with corpses on my Propaganda Train, writing leaflets and sowing them all over dead terri-

* The following was published in *Literaturnaya Gazeta*, no. 28, 1930. See note to Babel's letter of July 22, 1930.

tories. The earth was fattened by blood then and by the leaflets with which we were trying to fertilize it.

"We were squeezed back again into our stifling, dead house. Propaganda had devoured my lungs, sucked my blood—anemia. The doctors said: 'Sure, what do you expect in these conditions?' I told them: 'Injections? Fine, but what I need is injections of faith!' They seem to have understood. They patted me on the shoulder and advised me to go to Europe.

"Europe sounds so beautiful and so proud! But what would I do there? Sun—water—tennis—rest—pills. Well, I guess a bit of azure blue could do no harm.

"The last azure I saw was in 1914. After that the sky became like dirty cotton wool. From 1917 on, it turned into the Red Flag.

"Now both war and revolution are finished. I must sit here on the Riviera. In one hour the sun won't be here any more. Evening will have arrived, and evening which looks like a jug, as that sweet hooligan Yesenin wrote. Probably he sat here thinking of switches from our native Russian woods until one of them became a noose and strangled him, damn it! *

"By the way, do you know Gedali? He is greater than Lenin. Lenin has created the international of oppressed people, while Gedali sticks the good people together. What a crazy idea of genius! 'Good people unite!' 'The Revolution of Kindness!' My blood reeked * when I heard those words, and I laughed,

"Today I smell of sun, of water and of pills, I pound my chest and I cry out:

" 'Greetings to you, Gedali, the creator of the Fourth International, the inspired bard of the new Executive Committee. Come to us,' I shout with my tattered lungs."

Actually, it is quite unnecessary to comment. We aren't interested in the ideas of Babel, who last saw "azure in 1914," for whom the revolution is over and who considers the Soviet Union "a stifling dead house." We don't believe that either pills or injections of faith could help him at this point.

What concerns us is that a Soviet writer who is sunbathing carefree on the Riviera should be so ready to give an open-hearted interview of this sort which later appears in the bourgeois Polish press:

* Babel sometimes tried to produce an effect by the use of unexpected combinations of words, but "my blood reeked" and Yesenin hanging himself on a switch sound more like parodies of Babel than genuine Babel experiments. (Tr.—MacA.)

If we think of the Red-baiting now prevailing in Poland where the population is being prepared for a crusade against the USSR, Babel's verbiage acquires a different coloration.

In the preceding issue, *Wiadomosci Literackie* carries on Page One a report of its own Moscow correspondent to the effect that Mayakovsky killed himself because he was disappointed in the Soviet regime and that he even said so in a letter to Stalin and to his literary colleagues. In such an atmosphere Babel's juicy "revelations" are, from the objective viewpoint, just one more libel of the Soviet Union "from an unimpeachable source."

It is possible that Babel's interviewer has distorted his words, or even that the whole interview is nothing but a fabrication.

In that case, Babel must at once deny the words attributed to him, words that deprive him of the right to call himself a Soviet writer.

Bruno Yasensky

IIIᵇ

The Secretariat of FOSP on the Spurious Interview with I. Babel *

The "interview" with I. Babel which appeared in the Polish press—in the paper *Wiadomosci Literackie* about which Comrade Bruno Yasensky wrote in *Literaturnaya Gazeta*, was discussed at a meeting of the secretariat of FOSP the day before yesterday.

The editor of *Literaturnaya Gazeta*, Comrade B. Olkhovy, declared that it was clear from Comrade Babel's letters to the editor of *Literaturnaya Gazeta* that, in what purports to be an interview published in the Polish press, we are dealing with a blatant forgery. Had the matter concerned Babel alone, then it would be sufficient to print his refutation. But with the long series of hostile articles about Soviet literature and writers which we have seen lately, this incident takes on great significance and cries out for a retort from the entire Soviet community of writers and, in the first place, from FOSP.

* The following was the press release issued after the FOSP meeting. See note to Babel's letter of July 22, 1930.

I. Babel has told the members of the Secretariat of FOSP what he thinks of the article in the Soviet newspaper.

I. Babel does not know Polish. Naturally, he doesn't follow the Polish press. And he only knew about Alexander Dan's piece from Bruno Yasensky's article. Because of this, he could not refute the fabrications of the Polish paper in good time.

It is typical of this sort of thing that the article should appear two years after I. Babel had returned from his trip abroad. While he was abroad, Babel was subjected to baiting. Obviously, the information in the present article by Alexander Dan was not available at that time.

The fact that Babel published *Red Cavalry* and *Odessa Stories* and then fell silent for a little while was enough to inspire this bourgeois scribbler to make a slanderous attack.

"I was looking for a new language," Babel explains, "a new form suitable to the pioneering role Soviet literature is called upon to play. I acted as a most loyal soldier in the Soviet literary army. My particular needs as a writer demanded that I should leave the noisy life of the literary centers in order to pursue this quest. For the last two years I have lived at the roots: in villages, on collective farms and factories. I am trying to study the building of our new society from within. The unique, unprecedented pace and manner of our development should really find its expression in our literature at last. Factory, collective farm, village—these have prompted me to write a new book. During the last year of intensive work I have realized how many of my colleagues have lost their way in a forest of three pine trees, instead of halting their daily rush in order to search out this new road which we need. . . .

"As for the falsehoods which are being spread about us abroad, we must," Babel declares, "combat them without mercy, Otherwise the brickbat that hits me today may hit dozens of other Soviet writers tomorrow."

In conclusion Babel announces that he has requested our embassy in Poland to sue the Polish paper *Wiadomosci Literackie* in his name for printing libellous statements.

The writers T. T. Batrak, Tarasov-Rodionov, Kirillov and Zlinchenko expressed their opinions on the subject.

Babel's silence in recent years indicates not a crisis but a creative reorientation. This turning point in his work deserves our careful attention and so we look forward to the appearance of his new book with great interest.

We strongly protest against the insinuations of the bourgeois press, which takes advantage of the slightest opportunity to make a prominent writer seem to disparage Soviet literature. These foreign provocateurs deserve to have their wrists slapped.

D. Kalm

IV

A Boy by Maxim Gorky*

They'd warned me: I'd have a visitor—a boy poet. Well, what about it? For boys and girls to make up verse is quite a usual occurrence in this country. It is never too easy to handle them, because for the most part they are quite bad at writing poetry. Often it is all too evident that they have no business writing poetry, for they do not have the ear for words and sounds which is a must for a poet just as it is for a musician. It happens that a child may come up with some pretty good stuff, but in such cases his effort usually turns out to be strongly inspired by some important poet, whether of the past or contemporary. Sometimes it can be said that these poems are more copied than inspired. So we find ourselves forced to say rather unpleasant things to these too-youthful poets in whom little vanities have already been awakened and whom their parents, relatives and schoolmates have pronounced "talented."

Nowadays, people are in too much of a hurry "to live and to experience life," and we are in too much of a hurry to encourage them. And premature praise is not a very helpful thing in our time of unrelenting competition. As a matter of fact, it may be extremely harmful.

Our children are wonderful people and they are worthy of being treated with responsibility.

So the poet arrived. A strong, handsome boy of ten and a half who looked perhaps three years older. Even in the way he greeted me I detected something unfamiliar to me, something hard to define.

Neither those who are convinced of their talent nor the shy ones

* The following was published in *Pravda*, August 8, 1934. See note to Babel's letter of June 8, 1934.

greet people that way. There was in him none of the brashness that conveys, "Here I am, start admiring!"

Nor could I detect any of the embarrassment with which many young versifiers come to an established author—the way schoolboys present themselves for an exam. This ten-year-old seemed to be aware of an intellectual parity with adults.

"Which of the old poets do you particularly like?" I asked him.

"Pushkin, of course," he said with assurance.

"And of the prose writers?"

"Turgenev."

He named Turgenev with slightly less assurance and added: "But I haven't read him for a long time."

"How long would that be?"

"About six months."

I could not help thinking that I could hardly read at all at this boy's age, that the only book I read was the Psalter in Church Slavonic and that there was a time when for six months I had never even had a chance to hold a book in my hands.

I then asked the poet:

"You write lyric verse, don't you?"

"No, I write political verse rather. But I have also written some lyric poetry. I believe two or three of them have been preserved among my papers. They were translations from the German: Schiller and Heine."

And at this point he added, perhaps with slight embarrassment:

"A small collection of my poems has even been published."

I felt that I did not know how to speak to this person. I even felt it was embarrassing to look him straight in the face. My visitor was a mystifying sight. Next to him sat his mother and I had the impression that she was just as embarrassed as he was.

And, as if to confirm my impression, she said hurriedly:

"He is terribly interested in politics. When his father comes home from work, the first thing he does is to take his newspapers. He is the Guide of his Pioneer troop. He has taken a great many civic duties upon himself. But imagine, he never seems tired! Yes, in general, our children are amazing nowadays. His sister started to talk before she was seven months old—she's eighteen months old now and speaks perfectly. I am simply at a loss to know what to do with such children."

I suggested the boy read me some of his poems. He remained silent for a few seconds and to encourage him I said:

"There are instances when one must not be embarrassed about one's gifts."

"This is from Potemkin's letter to Rayevsky," the ten-year-old man announced.

"By Potemkin the poet?" I asked.

"No, by Catherine the Second's favorite. Why, is there a poet called Potemkin, too?"

"There was one once."

"I'll read a poem about Hitler and Goebbels," the poet said.

I expected something ridiculous, something that would lay bare the bankruptcy of this extraordinary phenomenon. But nothing of the sort—there was nothing ridiculous in what I heard and the phenomenon looked even more extraordinary.

The boy was a poor reader, however, and went in for those wailings that some grown-up poets try to pass off as poetic quality. But his verses were reminiscent of Mayakovsky's and seemed technically sound to me. Of course, I may be mistaken, for I was struck by the strength of the boy's emotional conviction and his implacable hatred for the human monsters he was describing. The verse might be ugly but how beautiful, surprising and socially new was this youngster's rejection of those evil men and of their evil deeds. The healthy boy read with such intense violence that for a couple of minutes I hesitated to look into his face, afraid of seeing it all twisted and distorted. But his face was simply flushed, his dark eyes were sparkling and they were no longer the eyes of a ten-year-old boy. They were the eyes of an adult who has filled each word with the seething pitch of hatred, a hatred that can only be provoked by the deepest love for the working people who are perishing at the hands of monsters and murderers, those who are persecuting Dimitrov now and trying to murder Thaelmann, as they have killed so many fighters for the freedom of the proletariat.

It is very difficult to convey the revolutionary emotion of the young poet who recited to me, to Babel and to all the others who were there to listen to him about glorious hatred mobilized for the sake of love.

It was frightening to think that this song was being sung by a child and not by a grown-up. When he finished I felt sad to think that adult poets do not possess that amazing strength of expression that had developed in this little boy who, in the course of his brief life, had not yet had the occasion to suffer, but who nevertheless hated suffering so intensely and, at the same time, had that burning loathing for those who brought more and more suffering to the workers who were shackled by the chains of capitalism externally and poisoned by a petty-bourgeois mentality internally.

After he had read his poem and had sat for a couple of minutes amidst a general stunned silence, the poet got up and went out to play with some other children. And he played ball shouting, laughing, absorbed in the game, as is usual for a healthy, normal, ten-year-old boy. In general, he didn't look at all as one would expect a child prodigy to look, quite unlike those child prodigies who, when they are fifty, are still referred to as Mitya, Misha or Yasha.

I am very sorry that I did not write down even a few lines of his poem.

Saying good-by to him, I said I was not going to praise him or give him advice, except that he should study without overstraining himself and that he should remember that he was still only a child.

He thanked me, smiled at me understandingly and said:

"You know, some professors told me not to get swell-headed. But I'm not really such a little fool. I love studying and I want to learn. To know everything and to work well—that is what I think happiness is!"

V

Our Great Enemy—Trite Vulgarity by Isaac Babel *

There has never before been a time in the history of mankind when the ruling class (in our country, the working class and their party) was followed by millions and tens of millions of hard-working people linked together by one single thought, one single idea, one common aspiration. From this viewpoint, our Congress is of incredible and unprecedented interest. We have had congresses of engineers, professors, chemists, and builders, but this time it is a congress of engineers of human souls—people who by their very trade are disunited (and they must be disunited because of the difference in their feelings, tastes, methods of work).

* The following speech by Babel was published in *Pravda*, August 25, 1934. See note to Babel's letter of November 14, 1934.

Despite this, I don't believe that any of the congresses gathered here has ever felt so strongly united as we do.

Like the rest of the working class, we are united by a community of ideas, thought and struggle.

That struggle doesn't need many words, but those words must be good words. As to trite, vulgar, commonplace, contrived clichés—we are very tired of them. Such words, I think, actually help our enemies. Trite vulgarity in print is no longer a weakness today—it is a crime. Even more, trite vulgarity is the counter-revolution—in my opinion, it is the enemy.

I recently witnessed the following incident. An assembly worker had given his wife a bad beating. People gathered round them. I listened to what was being said. One said: "What a lousy man—he's beaten up his wife." Another remarked: "He must've had a fit." A third man disagreed: "The hell it was a fit—he's simply a counter-revolutionary."

I was deeply moved when I heard those words. Since such a concept has penetrated the deep, dark layers of our people, it goes to show the Revolution is definitely triumphant! No words can keep up with that feeling. Our great and noble task is to fire people with noble feelings.

Observe the transformation that has occurred in our newspapers. We were all aware that they were rather dull and colorless and failed to reflect the diversity of our life. But then miracles started happening to us.

With miraculous speed, they were transformed—our press became livelier and the fact that the newspapers' turn came around is a happy turn of events!

The first scaffoldings are coming down from the edifice of socialism and the most shortsighted can already recognize the outlines of that building and its beauty, and all of us here are witnesses to the fact that our entire country with her 170 million inhabitants is penetrated with a sensation of, we may say, its own physical vigor.

But those who are called upon to express that sensation are not always up to the task. And so occasionally some really rather dejected-looking character will suddenly start shouting about how happy he is and start trumpeting and booming all over the place, making a spectacle of himself that is liable to make people sick. (Applause)

But that individual with his government-issued eyes becomes even more frightening when he feels he has to tell people about his love. (Laughter) Love is spoken of in unbearably loud tones in our land nowadays and if I were a woman, I'd be terror-stricken. If it goes on

like this, our women's eardrums will burst; if it goes on like this, declarations of love among us will soon be made through a loudspeaker,
like anouncements in a sports stadium. Things have already reached
a point where the objects of our love have been forced to protest. Gorky has been driven to such a point that yesterday he had to
decline a demonstration of love.

I am joking, but the serious aspect of it is that, in our profession, it
is our duty to help the triumph of the new Bolshevik taste in this country. That will be a political achievement of the first magnitude, because it is our luck that it is impossible for us to have an unpolitical
achievement.

And it will be the birth of the style of our epoch. I do not
see any room for verbiage in our epoch, in the ability to ramble on at
great length while the thought beneath is so brief.

No, the style of our period must be characterized by courage and
restraint, by fire, passion, strength and joy.

Marx once said that the important thing was not to describe the
world but to transform it. In one sixth of the globe great changes have
taken place and now we must attack our themes in a new way. We
must have a new style. And we won't learn that new style from old
books.

We must learn. But where?

Speaking of the use of words, I must mention a man who doesn't
have any special professional dealings with words. Nevertheless, look
how Stalin hammers out his speeches, how his words are wrought of
iron, how terse they are, how muscular, how much respect they show
for the reader. (Applause) I don't suggest here that we should all
write like Stalin, but I do say that we must all work at our words as he
does. (Applause)

I have spoken about the respect due to the reader. Well, the reader,
nowadays, is really giving us plenty of trouble. To borrow Zoshchenko's
expression, he's a regular drainpipe. (Laughter)

Now, foreign authors tell us that they search for their readers with
a flashlight in broad daylight. But in our land it is the readers who
march at us in closed formation. It's a real cavalry attack. They rush
at us with their hands extended and you'd better think twice before
you put a stone in that hand—what they are after is artistic bread.

Of course, we must come to an agreement with our readers. They
demand it, sometimes with touching directness. And so we'd better
warn the reader. Bread—that we'll be able to put into his out-

stretched hand, but when it comes to the shape of the loaf or the quality, that's quite another matter and he'd better take a good look at it himself.

Some readers naively make a demand: "All right, describe me." And the writer thinks: "All right, I'll give him that description and make it true and honest." But that won't do. Into a description of Ivan Ivanovich there must be injected a philosophical view, some lofty ideas. For without ideas, there can be no literature.

Respect for the reader. I am suffering from a hypertrophy of that feeling. I respect the reader so much that it makes me numb and I fall silent. And so so I keep silence. (Laughter)

And when I think of an audience of 500 readers consisting of Party district committee secretaries, people who know ten times more than all the writers put together about bee-keeping, farming and how to build gigantic steel plants, who have been all over the country and who, just like us, are "engineers of human souls," I realize that I cannot get away with empty talk and school-kid stuff. If one says something, it has to be something serious and to the point.

Now, speaking of silence, I cannot avoid talking about myself, the past master of that art. (Laughter) I must admit that if I lived in a capitalist country, I would have long since croaked from starvation and no one would have cared whether, as Ehrenburg puts it, I was a rabbit or a she-elephant. My capitalist publisher would have forced me to be a rabbit and as such he would have forced me to leap around, and if I hadn't leapt, he would have forced me to become a grocer's assistant.

But in our country people take into consideration whether you are a rabbit or a she-elephant. They don't push you in the belly if you have something inside there and they don't insist too much on whether the baby will be a redhead, just light brown, or very dark, on what sort of things he'll have to say.

I am not happy about my silence. Indeed, it saddens me. But perhaps this is one more proof of the attitude toward the writer in this country.

I think that, as Gorky said yesterday, Sobolev's words, "We have everything" should be written on our flag. The Party and the government have given us everything, depriving us only of one privilege—that of writing badly.

It must be said frankly, without false modesty: it is a very important privilege that has been taken away from us and we took full advantage of it. And so, Comrades, we declare at this writers' congress: Let us renounce completely that old privilege.

(Applause)

VI

Self-Discipline in a Writer: I. Babel Concerning D. Furmanov*

Comrades,

I have been unable to gather sufficient material and to prepare myself properly for this occasion. Only a pressing need to contribute my own memories has brought me to this tribune today.

I arrived from the Crimea two days ago. In the company of a French writer, I had been to see Gorky and we were given a glimpse of the extraordinary life of that great man. Old and ailing, Gorky was working heroically, even lying on a table with oxygen tanks. There have been very few such heroic examples in the history of mankind.

And again, as usual, Gorky spoke of our life. He said that we do not write well, that we do not study enough, that having written one book we are satisfied or we follow it up by writing less and less well, because our knowledge is limited, because we do not have proper respect for the best reading audience in the world.

When Gorky said these things, I thought, indeed, they are sinful human ways. And I began to search my memory for the righteous and the sinners. And I'll tell you honestly that I found plenty of sinners but only one righteous man—a man who died ten years ago and in whose honor we are gathered here today.

I had occasion to spend many evenings with the Furmanovs in their house on Nishchekinsky Lane. We spoke of his book. That book, which sold hundreds and thousands of copies, didn't fully satisfy Furmanov. He was growing rapidly. Each month his talent as a writer expanded. I wish you knew how he loved words, how he appreciated the most exquisite combinations of words when he listened to the ancient Greek and Latin poets. At those moments I was greatly

* The following was published in the magazine *Moskva*, no. 4, 1936. See note to Babel's letter of February 18, 1935.

moved watching him. He appeared to me as the embodiment of the proletarian who has mastered the poetic art.

Remember what his life was—he never chose the line of least resistance. Before the Revolution he fought against the Tsarist regime; after the Revolution he went to the front; after the front he picked for himself the most dangerous sector—the sector where the battle over poetry and art was being fought. I have never witnessed any more terrifying, more desperate struggle in my whole life. The speed with which he mastered the arts was amazing. I suppose that, too, led him to his grave.

Two days ago, in this very room, we were remembering Bagritsky. I knew him, too, and I want to say that with each passing year his poetry comes more and more alive. This is so because he brought us the truth.

But think of Furmanov in that connection. Two years ago we witnessed an unprecedented event in the annals of the history of literature and art: the pages of Furmanov's book opened and out of them stepped live people, the true heroes, the true children of our country.

When I saw the film [made from the book], here is what I was thinking—I felt that the directors who had staged it were devoid of genius, that we had other more talented directors, directors endowed with greater virtuosity. Nor can I say that the actors in the picture were particularly remarkable either. We have many good actors. So I asked myself what made the picture so immensely powerful, why there were no arguments about it, how it was that for the first time genuine art had come to our country and been reflected in our hearts, why our hearts were so stirred as we watched Chapayev? The answer to this, I am sure, is that the film wasn't produced by a film studio— it was created by our whole country.

And this is why, Comrades, quite ordinary people succeeded in creating this film of genius. It was created by the whole country, inspired by the very air of our land. It shows what a level we have attained in art, and is based on the understanding, on the feelings of heroism, of kindness, of courage, and the revolutionary spirit that are alive in our country.

What does all this mean, Comrades? It means that the ideals for which the late Chapayev strove are still being pursued by our entire country.

For eight years, our country read Chapayev. And what happened after those eight years? Our country responded to Chapayev by creating this film bearing his name. She conveyed to him thus how well she understood him, how much she appreciated him. You have experienced yourselves, Comrades, the impression made by the film. I believe that every human being in whom there beats a Soviet heart, an honest and incorruptible Soviet heart, every man who passionately, intently and purely, without vanity or pretense, tries to master the summits of the arts and the sciences, every student of our workers' colleges, every member of the Young Communist League, every college student and Red Army man who approaches art and learning with the same self-discipline and passion as did Furmanov—that these are the ones who are pursuing his cause directly. To me, the film *Chapayev* is the best proof that the people of our land are continuing to pursue the same cause.

Comrades, it is certain that a writer whose ideas are pursued by millions and tens of millions of men is both lucky and great when those men belong to the first country in the world to be governed by the workers. There is no doubt that it is a great and invincible work and, therefore, that Furmanov, who started it, is lucky and great.

About the Author

A protégé of Maxim Gorky, Isaac Babel was born in 1894 and rose to fame in the 1920s for such works as *Red Cavalry* and *Odessa Tales*. But as Stalin's regime turned overtly repressive in the 1930s, Babel found it increasingly hard to write or publish. He was finally arrested in 1939, and died on January 27, 1940, in a Russian concentration camp. Only in 1957 was he "rehabilitated" in his native country, where today he is considered—as he is throughout the world—a seminal figure of modern Russian letters.